SPANISH PRACTICES

Richard Townsend

Chiselbury

For Ophelia and Alba

Acknowledgements

I would like to thank all of those who have helped turn 'Spanish Practices' from an idea into reality, in particular the following:

- Prim and James Y for seeding the idea;

- My family, in-laws and friends, both Spanish and British, who inspired much of the content of the novel;

- Jim L, Nicholas B, David F, Hilary J, Hugh B, Rosa, Isabel and William for reading the typescript at various stages, sometimes more than once;

- Valeria V, Nick B, David H, Edward P, Wim and Sarah V, for their help and guidance in navigating the publishing world;

- Stuart Leasor at Chiselbury for placing his confidence in a late starter in the fiction game.

NOTES:

1. Spanish Practices - definition

Extract from en.wikipedia.org (11/10/22):

"The terms **Spanish practices** or **old Spanish customs** are British expressions that refer to irregular or restrictive practices in workers' interests."

For the avoidance of doubt, the term is largely germane to this novel in its wider sense, i.e. "the way Spaniards conduct their lives".

2. Surnames – Spanish practices

Extract from en.wikipedia.org (15/10/22):

"Spanish names comprise... two surnames (the first surname of each parent). Traditionally the first surname is the father's surname, and the second is the mother's... The practice is to use... the first surname generally...; the complete name is reserved for legal, formal and documentary matters. Both surnames are sometimes systematically used when the first surname is very common."

Table of Contents

Chapter I: Heirs and Graces

1

In retrospect, it might seem careless to have allowed a coup d'état to eclipse a very first encounter with my intended "political family". Certainly, it was unfortunate, perhaps ominous, even. And what bad luck to have picked the very day: 23-F, as 23 February 1981 has become known. But how could we have known that any such thing might disturb the deep coma of a Spanish provincial afternoon?

Looking back at the TV footage, though, it doesn't look especially menacing. The colonel in his shiny-black, three-cornered hat seems unsure what to do next as he mounts the podium, waving a pistol at various ministers and firing a few rounds at the ceiling. It looks like comic opera for real, and the moustachioed colonel seems half aware of that himself.

But as soon as news broke that tanks were on the streets, that a state of emergency could be declared at any moment, my future relatives woke up...

These events followed a lunch held in my honour, as son-in-law designate.

It's 3:30 p.m. by the time we sit down at the station restaurant, foggy and pungent with smoke from the emblematic *Ducados* brand of black tobacco blended with *Agua Brava* aftershave. "We" in this case comprises Marina's close family, the Expósitos, that is: Don Cipriano ("*Papi*") – gruff, taciturn, distant; Gloria or Gloriuca ("*Mamí*") his extrovert and voluble wife; and Marina's three siblings – Chus (22), Marta (13) and "baby" Sancho (11). There are several cousins and aunts too, among whom "Aunt Macu", Mamí's sister, seems to enjoy special status. She doesn't stay long, though, for it's she who runs the winery, the family business. It's unclear to me how the rest of them fit together. I suspect they're here to check me out, the new curiosity and mooted interloper.

In this gathering, Mamí holds court (that's "Ma-*MEE*", with the stress on the final syllable). She's clearly in her element here, in full flood with a captive audience hanging on her every word as her anecdotes bubble up one after another. These are drawn from family history, mostly from her golden years in Africa, "*Gui-NE-a*" as she calls it. In the gaps, she delivers withering asides to present and absent alike, which she obviously savours – certainly, she's the one cackling loudest at every punchline. But in my case, the medley of voices, my patchy grasp of context and my ropey Spanish rob me of much agency other than to grin inanely, hoping not to be quizzed too closely.

That keeps me out of trouble until Papí ("Pa-*PEE*") forces me to reveal my hand on the thorny topic of Gibraltar. Fortunately, it's not the first time I've been interrogated on the subject, so I did some homework: handed over, I learned, *in perpetuity* to Great Britain in 1713, under the Treaty of Utrecht. Sham erudition of that sort, I find, usually bails me out; but it's a bit of a blunder here. I might have guessed that Papí's politics would lie well to the right of the late General Franco's; and he, too, has a few dubious facts at the ready. It was a *bogus treaty*, he says, *a French imposition* cooked up with the connivance of *La Gran...* The dysfunctional royal family, the fickle climate, the abysmal food and, for those of a historical bent, Pirate Drake and the theft of Gibraltar: those are the few facts that Spaniards are likely to recall about "Great" Britain, "*La Gran...*" as it's styled by traditional types such as Papí. For the missing word, you're expected to infer "Lady of the Night" or some spicier synonym.

We head home after the meal. Mamí could have walked the short distance several times over while Papí fetched the car, but I can see she expects to be driven. Not that the interval goes to waste: she uses the moment to admire the cut of her skirt and check the state of her hair, reflected in a shop window. There isn't room for all of us in Papí's Fiat, so Marina and I set off home on foot with her siblings.

Bárcena de la Mina is a glorified village that evidently aims higher. It describes itself as a "*villa*", a "country town", which sounds orderly and genteel. But it's misleading. Recently, it has grown at warp speed and it's a mess. There's no planning, no order of any kind; houses stand at sixes and sevens rather than in neat rows; there's no attempt at zoning – a few large dwellings with high stone walls survive right in the centre of town. Ancient houses and farm buildings in various stages of distress stand cheek-by-jowl with four- or five-storey blocks erected on the cheap since the Civil War.

The family seat, at No. 15, Perpetuo Socorro, is also a bit of an eyesore. Marina told me there used to be an old *palacio* (grand townhouse) on the site, but Papí's interests never ran to antiquities and, apart from the old perimeter wall, it made way for a humdrum replacement. In a nod to country life (cattle downstairs, people upstairs) the house, like many others round here, features an overhanging upper storey. Whatever the allusions, it's aesthetically unfortunate, the proportions hardly redeemed by the gaudy red brick, fake roof tiles and dollops of cement wherever inspiration ran short.

The sitting room – gloomy, thanks to the protruding upper floor – showcases a family narrative set over several generations in Africa. The walls, doors and furniture are sculpted from tropical hardwoods; ivory tusks and statuettes adorn the flat spaces; there's an etiolated leopard skin pinned to the panelling over the sofa; and photos of small children in pith helmets – Marina and Chus – chaperoned by black manservants, complete the tableau. Lending a patina of sophistication are rows of identikit classics in leather bindings, which look largely unmolested. In a corner is a miniature garden of shiny pot plants. One of these, a long, thin, spiky excrescence, goes by the name of *lengua de suegra* – mother-in-law's tongue.

Few Spaniards prize tranquility highly and, in any case, football trumps all else. So as soon as we come in, Papí switches on the TV expectantly, while others curl up for a snooze on the sofa. But there's no football on either channel… and Papí starts to rant and curse.

"*¡Hostias!*"[1] he swears, as footage from the Spanish Parliament, where a new government is due to be sworn in, plays on both channels… Then the colonel and his acolytes storm in: "*¿Qué coño…?*"[2]

Moments later, images of tanks trundling through the streets flash across the screen. That's when, without warning, the family bundles me out of the house: no time for farewells, not even to Marina. She blows kisses anxiously from the porch, as Chus, the elder son, frogmarches me to the station: "Sorry about this," he says, "nothing personal, of course. But a curfew is on the cards. And after that, who knows?"

He's in luck: the next train leaves in ten minutes and he waits on the platform until he's quite sure I've gone. Once I'm on my way, clattering and rocking through the black towards the provincial capital, I realise that this fling-turned-fixture with jade-eyed Marina, in the teeth of reflex scepticism from both families, now faces more intractable

---

[1] "Body of Christ!" (the host at Communion)
[2] "what the f***?"

obstacles.

Martial law, did he mean? Civil war, even? Should I bail out altogether, while it's still possible? But what disillusion! What ignominy! For a while, everything was set fair: for me personally as well as for this country and its brittle truce…

Perhaps I shouldn't make too much of a first encounter with my future in-laws in such trying circumstances. However, the instinctive shutdown and summary expulsion of the foreign body from the family's midst does leave a sour aftertaste.

2

The unseemly denouement of my first visit does not, after all, prove terminal. We owe the reprieve, it turns out, to King Juan Carlos, "The Brief", as he's known, who backed the fledgling democracy in its moment of crisis. It has taken everyone by surprise. The new King was judged a playboy, a stooge of the late *Generalísimo*, and was not respected. But it seems he stood the rebels down and defused the situation. In tribute, the young rake earns himself an unlikely epithet in the morning papers: he's extolled as the "Saviour of Democracy".

One month later, therefore, I find myself riding the narrow-gauge railway once more, heading for a more in-depth induction. It's a Saturday, and it's a welcome break from the classes I'm teaching. An Englishman by the name of Benedict has hired me – a risk on his part, given my limited experience. The snag is that lessons start at six in the morning – some man of affairs who can only make it at that hour. Benedict was sceptical, he didn't think it'd work, but agreed to give it a try. In the meanwhile, it helps with the bills.

This bit of Spain defies the clichés. For a start, it's deep green and dripping damp. It's also densely populated. The railway meanders through a lumpy, bosky landscape, juxtaposing stretches of arcadia with formless sprawl. There are a few smokestacks, mostly without the smoke, so probably slated for demolition.

These places must have grown like weeds as the rural hinterland emptied out. The textile factory may sound dreary, but it's more appealing to the young than indenture to the dairy herd. And by all accounts, the once formidable fishing industry isn't what it once was either: they've pillaged the local seas and the few remaining fishermen travel halfway round the globe in search of fresh booty. Meanwhile, the middle generation drifts to the towns, exchanging farms for *pisos*, flats being the summit of sophistication for those who've abandoned their rural roots. A phalanx of brick blocks is Bárcena's welcome to travellers arriving by train.

"You know what? I quite *like* the *pisos*…" That was a remark by my Hispanophile friend Jack that I've puzzled over ever since. It's very much in character for him to make iconoclastic comments of that kind. Who could possibly applaud these grim slabs? But perhaps I'm starting to grasp what he meant. They're quintessential and, above all, they're unpretentious.

Perhaps Jack's take on the flats is akin to mine about the language. This is one of the last redoubts against the inexorable march of English. However painful it is wrestling with the local vernacular, the language is a cache of secrets that keeps this place different.

When I meet Marina in Bárcena she leads me to a ramshackle building in the main square, still defiantly named *Plaza del Generalísimo* in honour of the late *Caudillo*. It's a decrepit, single-storey warehouse pitched visibly to the left, like a vessel shipping water. How apt it is that

Marina refers to it as *"la nave"*, "warehouse" and "ship" sharing the same word in Spanish… She says the subsidence results from the abandoned mines below, the ones that account for the town's foundation centuries ago. The ship looks stricken, as if ready to slip beneath the waves. Emblazoned below the eaves, there's an inscription: *Bodegas Sancho Pinar E Hijos. Casa fundada en 1846.* This is the winery, the family business, founded in 1846, reputedly the oldest in the province.

Right behind the *bodega* runs the main road, part of the main East-West highway, threading a tortuous course along the ragged coastline. Although it's a Saturday, a stream of *"Pegaso"* trucks, badged with a winged horse prancing through a hoop high up on the bonnet, snorts along the main thoroughfare, scrunching through the gears as they slow down for the road junction. That's where a turning heads inland, up the valley towards the arid interior beyond the pass.

Sharing an exterior wall with the *bodega* is a three-storey *casona* (large townhouse) of similar vintage. It's also crooked, if less so than the warehouse. Marina talks about it as if it were still grand, but that's no longer the case. It's dilapidated, derelict, even. The casement windows droop from their hinges, some windowpanes are cracked and the balconies sag like pork bellies. A few of the roof tiles are slipping and others missing altogether.

Here's what Marina says about it: "That's where I was brought up, by my grandmother and my aunt. My mother decided I was too weak for Africa, or so she claims. More like she got bored of me. So, she left me here when I was three. Not that my brother Chus came too. Mamí had a soft spot for the son and heir." It's obviously a sore point. But she doesn't dwell on it: "The house was in bad shape even then; I remember rolling marbles down the sloping floor. They didn't need a push, even."

"And your parents stayed on in Africa?"

"Yes, for at least ten years after that. It wasn't exciting. My aunt worked late every day and my grandmother never went out once she was widowed – other than to Mass, of course, head to toe in black."

"So, what happened to the house?"

"When my parents were thrown out of Africa, they needed their own place and soon after, my grandmother and my aunt decided to move too. They built a new house outside town and forgot all about this one. It slowly fell apart."

Before I could ask why they didn't sell it then, or at least keep it in good shape, she adds: "Anyway, there's often doubt about who really owns what and who pays for the upkeep. There are so many fights about that kind of thing. It's the inheritance laws… everything divided up over and over again. Lots of cousins, all claiming a share, but unwilling to spend a single *duro.*"[3]

Then she takes me round the back, alongside the main road, and points to a window on the top floor.

"My Aunt Macu and I slept in that room. The hours I spent watching the rain from up there! I would have done anything, absolutely *anything* to escape. Imagine the three of us: a spinster, a widow and me. God, I was bored! I read lots of books, I suppose… But I wanted a bomb to go off, anything to make something happen."

"That bad?"

"Yes. That bad… Our only visitor was my mother's brother, Uncle Toño, from Madrid. He thought I was trouble, and took it as his duty, as the man of the house, to tell me off… But his dentures kept slipping whenever he

---

[3] Five *peseta* coin

scolded me. Slightly spoiled the effect..."

Marina now tells me about the *bodega*. According to her, it's the fount of the family fortunes, though it sounds like its apogee lies in the past. The *bodega* has kept several generations in comfort, even during the Civil War, when Marina's grandfather kept the family going by bartering wine for comestibles.

"But it's not quite what it was," she tells me. "Before, they had half the province sewn up. Recently, their only rival – in the next village – woke up. For all my aunt's contempt for *Vinos Aurelio*, they seem to be making headway. A bit more dynamic and go-ahead, I suspect... My aunt's obsessed with them."

The *bodega's* open on Saturday mornings, when the market comes to Bárcena. On entry, our eyes take time to adjust – there's a single window shedding a wan light via a makeshift kiosk on the left-hand side of the main door and a few naked bulbs dangling from the beams among the cobwebs. Several elderly workers in long overalls and outsized leather gloves roll barrels about the floor and a strong vinous odour suffuses everything. In the kiosk, the aunt I met the other day sits behind a Formica desk, counting banknotes and writing up numbers in a ledger by hand.

This is Aunt Macu, Mamí's younger sister. *Macu* is a shortening of *Inmaculada,* one of a family of such old-style Christian names, often heavily disguised: for instance, *Chuchi or Chus* (from *Jesús), Quique (Enrique), Monchi (Ramón), Chencho (Lorenzo)* and – a personal favourite, this one – *Ludi (Luz Divina)*. Aunt Macu is single and has been slaving in this dingy box for over 20 years, first as helper to her late father and latterly running the show.

Initially, she's a little guarded towards the would-be abductor but mellows once she starts showing off the winery, half losing me in the technicalities. I gather that, as well as ageing, blending and bottling table wines, they supply bars with white wine from so-called *soleras*. These are very old casks, some housed on the clients' own premises, some at the *bodega*. They regularly top them up with newer wine, which blends with the old, delivering a prized lunchtime tipple to the locals. They must be well maintained in terms of temperature, humidity etc. Otherwise, the wine spoils.

"We do things properly," Aunt Macu claims, "as you can see. Unlike those upstarts from Tobillo! *Vinos Aurelio*, my foot! It's little more than a bottling plant! They expect to reinvent an age-old trade on the cheap. Everyone'll know what they're up to, soon enough!"

Aunt Macu introduces me to her cousin José Angel. He belongs to the other branch of the family, the Pinar Mogros, the cousins who share the *bodega* with Mamí and her siblings (the Pinar Vázquezs).[4] José Angel pours us a couple of glasses from a special *solera*, one of several huge, dusty barrels up the far end of the winery, explaining as he does so that, as well as the literal meaning, the word *solera* also means something venerable and grounded. *Bodegas Pinar*, he obviously thinks, has "*solera*", just as it has "*soleras*". The wine itself is an acquired taste, I reckon: it's a second cousin of dry sherry, which tastes musty, yeasty and woody. Still, after a couple of glasses, I'm starting to think it's quite palatable.

When we emerge onto the street, still blinking, we bump straight into Marina's brother, Chus, who's heading for the bar, where we join him for more drinks – he certainly downs industrial quantities of alcohol. Chus spouts excitedly about how, after more than ten years, he is

---

[4] See Appendix – Family Tree

planning to return to Africa.

During the "Scramble for Africa", that late colonial spasm, Spain joined the frenzy and carried off a few wooden spoons, including Equatorial Guinea, deep in the armpit of that continent. It comprises an island and a small rectangle of mainland. Papí's family has been there from the start, working for the colonial administration and exploiting tropical produce of various kinds. There was a revolution a few years ago when the colonials, including Marina's family, were ejected; but now there's a rapprochement and the old hands are drifting back. That's where Chus, newly equipped with a degree in topography, will be joining his father shortly after our wedding.

3

As for the wedding ceremony itself, matters of protocol and ritual are best left to Mamí. Otherwise, Marina warns me, all kinds of squabbles will vitiate the event. In the interests of economy, there will be no more than 50 guests and, since close Spanish family attends *ex officio*, this leaves a tiny quota for me: parents, a sibling and a token friend, which will be Jack, a great Hispanophile, Spanish scholar and *de facto* best man. Unsatisfactory perhaps, but I resolve to stay positive and embrace this folkloric or anthropological experience as best I can.

Picture this: a small Romanesque church in the lap of the country; it's raining stair rods and it's unseasonably chilly; Marina's family is overflowing on the bride's side of the aisle, while my contingent looks lonely on the groom's side. Don Poncho, an eminent theologian, will conduct the ceremony. He's a brother of Marina's uncle, Benigno Blasco, who is married to Mamí's elder sister, Aunt Ludi. They and all nine children are on parade today.

As it happens, we owe Don Poncho a debt of gratitude.

It was his influence that enabled us to survive a skirmish with the church authorities, who were threatening to scupper the whole event when apprised of my heretical confession.

"But I'm just as Christian as Marina!" I objected, disingenuously.

"That cannot be. There's only the one true path, and it's through the Roman Catholic faith. Are you prepared to be received into the true religion before your union?"

When I balked at this, Don Poncho intervened, tabling a compromise whereby a solemn promise was made to christen and raise our children in the Catholic faith; that alone saved the church wedding, without which doubts about legitimacy would have pursued us to the grave.

Don Poncho expounds the sacrament in front of us before it's my duty, as protagonist, to recite a few lines in Spanish. I acquit myself respectably, save for one obvious stumble (my first brush with the word *bendición* – blessing). I could claim to have been distracted by the luxuriant tufts sprouting from Don Poncho's ears and nose; but the truth is I assumed it was a misprint, one syllable short. Fortunately, though, the crucial formula trips off my tongue without mishap: "I, Richard, take you, Marina…" Meanwhile, Uncle Benigno, our photographer, stalks about the church with a cine camera. The whole affair's mercifully brief and, once it's over, we decamp to a *Parador* in nearby Villafranca del Conde for the reception, where a timely ray of sunshine allows us to congregate outside for more snaps.

And how's my welcome in this family? On the surface, it's courteous and friendly. Spanish society evidently prizes dignity and decorum highly. No doubt that accounts for the ubiquity of *revistas del corazón* – "magazines of the heart" – their magic residing in sympathetic narratives featuring minor royalty, politicians, bullfighters and so forth. Nothing's allowed to spoil the lovingly curated tableaux. And I think that informs the family's reaction to me: by instinct, they present an elegant and sanitised face to the exterior – the exterior being my assigned habitat, at least for the time being.

The background, however, causes me to wonder how pleased they really are. Before my arrival, Marina looked to have landed a young man by the name of Quique, a cousin and an *ingeniero de caminos* – highways engineer – no less. In any circumstances, it would be a blunder to lose such a catch, every Spanish parent's dream son-in-law. But to have stalked, hooked, played and finally beached so enviable a specimen, only to throw him back in exchange for a harmless, but nonetheless invasive creature with few compelling qualities… It's an error of epic proportions. No matter that Marina ditched her *ingeniero* well before my arrival – reacting, she says, to his old school *machismo*. Her deed will be viewed not just as foolish and impudent, but as an infringement of the natural order, a betrayal of her duty as a daughter and a stain on her record. My presence reminds them of that act of insurrection.

And, according to Marina, her mother grilled her several times about my station in life. It placed Marina in a quandary. Pitch it too low and I'd be cast among the *"muertos de hambre"*, as they put it, one of "the starving", with attendant lowly status in the family. Embellish it too much, on the other hand, and I'd be deemed a *"potentado"*, a big fish (my ghastly and misleading nickname, 'Rico', possibly contributing to the confusion, in this event). If so, Mamí could easily jump to undesirable conclusions. For Marina claims her mother is perpetually penurious and quite shameless about taking her chances with anyone remotely promising. Marina therefore plumped for the nebulous and anodyne *"profesor"*, which indeed has a chance of coming true when I return home. Mamí was duly disappointed, but at least it freed me from pressure to chip into the family budget for the time being.

Be that as it may, two days after the ceremony, we have an administrative matter to wrap up at the registry office in Pueblo de la Vega, where the marriage will be recorded. Leafing through the form, I see I'm expected to enter a "First Surname" and a "Second Surname".

"How can I do that?" I ask Marina. "I've only got one surname as far as I know."

"Everyone has two surnames over here," she explains: "Their father's first surname, followed by their mother's first surname. That's why I'm 'Expósito Pinar' – Papí's first surname, 'Expósito', followed by Mamí's, 'Pinar'. Confusing for you, I know, but in your case, it shouldn't be a problem. Luckily, your parents seem to have given you plenty of names, for some reason… just put the second last one as your 'First Surname' and your very last one as 'Second Surname'. It won't be quite right, but as long as it says exactly the same as your passport, I don't suppose it'll matter…"

That seems to work; after the formalities we're presented with a neat little booklet in blue, with the national crest on the cover. This is the "Family Book", the *Libro de Familia* issued to all newlyweds. With each new child, it has to be updated. I notice it has one page each for up to ten children, a large and random number, as far as I can tell. Then I recall that several of Marina's friends claim to be "one of ten". Is it coincidence? Or were the parents' reproductive endeavours influenced by available space in the Family Book? A flaw in this theory is Aunt Ludi and her nine. I can only assume they, too, aspired to fill up the Family Book, but ran out of steam on the home straight.

4

Back in London, we have a few groceries and some wedding presents to remind us of the Spanish connection; among them is the A-Z of cookery, the *Manual de Cocina*, that helps us work out what to do in the kitchen. We have a few trophies including ornamental plates from Talavera and a nice set of linen and monogrammed towels. There are two tickets for the Christmas lottery – Uncle Toño's present – offering a glimmer of hope in our straitened circumstances.

Between us, we need to find a means of sustenance, pronto. In my case, it's bound to be teaching or academia of some kind: at least I know what it involves; I have a scintilla of credibility; and the holidays are alluring. Then one day, a serendipitous encounter with a former research fellow at my *alma mater* gives me just the break I need... I land a lowly position in the History Faculty. It won't make us rich, but it'll keep us out of the Marshalsea; and it'll allow us to spend the lengthy vacations in Bárcena.

Meanwhile, Marina's periodic calls keep us in touch with family developments... Papí left for Africa straight after the wedding; from Mamí, there's no evident pining for him, as far as I can make out; but Chus is another matter altogether. He followed his father not long after, leaving Mamí bereft.

"What will she do?" I ask Marina. "I mean, you always said he was the favourite."

"Don't remind me. He used to steal my stuff when I was at boarding school. Mamí refused to believe it."

"But your mother won't enjoy looking after your brother and sister, I would have thought. Won't she go crazy?"

"Yes, probably, especially now, with Sancho's tantrums. He's so volatile! I suppose there's always Julio Iglesias for solace."

"Of course. How could I forget?"

We're alluding to Mamí's penchant for that crooner, one of whose more saccharine numbers, played time and again on the gramophone in the weeks before we left, reliably brought a tear to her eye and once or twice required a second application of mascara.

Benigno's wedding photos duly surface. I agree with Marina that they're truly horrible, *impresentables*, as she terms it. The whole event looks funereal, amplified by my mother's granite expression (she's as sceptical about the alliance as anyone – *"it won't last"*) and by the sepia palette that for Spanish photographers denotes subtlety and class. However, a few days later I decide to take another look… Gone! Under pressure, Marina comes clean: she binned the whole album, which means that the photos will be in landfill by now… I'm starting to learn (*pace* Julio Iglesias) that sentimentality seldom counts for much in my new family.

On one of Marina's calls a few weeks after our departure, Mamí enquires if there's *"any news?"* Just in case Marina's in any doubt about her meaning, she says: "I mean *happy* news, of course!"

Marina has no option but to disappoint. Mamí's clearly upset about it, adding, à propos of myself: "I take it there's nothing wrong with him? Have you had him checked over yet? If not, you must make an appointment right away. Or I can arrange it here if that makes it easier? These things can't be left to chance, you know. I hope he hasn't he misled you. I'm sure you'd have one well on the way by now if only you'd married Quique! By the way, you do realise that Lupita's expecting?"

Apart from the allusion to Marina's "ex", it's strange that Mamí should resort to Lupita, her neighbour's daughter, as an example, because in Bárcena, Lupita's pregnancy is tainted with scandal. She was unmarried at conception, and even a shotgun ceremony failed to dispel the odour (happily evoked by Mamí herself, to the right audience), especially as nobody much likes the husband. The family lives right opposite; Lupita and Marina were once friends at their convent school – "*Las Jesusas*" as it's named, "The (female) Jesuses".

Indeed, paying our respects to Lupita's family becomes a fixture of most visits to Bárcena. By all accounts, her mother, Anunciación – Nunci as she's known – issues from highly respectable stock. Moreover, her sister married into the powerful Ruiz-Toledo family, owners of the textile factory – the other major enterprise in Bárcena, to which the *bodega* bravely considers itself a peer. Perhaps this accounts for Nunci's mildly condescending manner, despite her diminutive stature. The downside for Nunci of her exalted connections, though, is the need to fend off supplicants for introductions (*"enchufes"*) to propitiate employment. *Enchufes*, literally "plugs" as in *"connectors for electrical devices"*, are a way of life over there. As far as I can see, few jobs, right down to roadsweep, are secured without them.

Nunci's husband, Curro, is more down to earth. Despite his dapper exterior (as a town councillor, he must keep up standards), from sightings in his garden or allotment it looks as if he'd feel just as comfortable husbanding livestock on a *finca* on the Castilian tableland. Indeed, he's a vet, but one of the old school; he makes a living from sows and heifers rather than *mascotas* (pets). They're a kind and hospitable couple, albeit troubled by the disintegration of their world and smarting from their

17

daughter's indiscretion. They miss the Old Regime, as does their sole son, Paco, who belongs to a diminishing core of young fogeys sporting unmistakable trademarks: oiled-back hair; burgundy loafers; Lacoste T-shirt and a red and yellow watch strap with the national crest: *Una, Grande, Libre* – United, Great and Free.

Our visits reflect the esteem in which Lupita's family is held, especially by Mamí, whose manner morphs subtly in Nunci's presence. It's not that she's any less outspoken or theatrical than usual; maybe the reverse is true – singing for her supper, as it were. But I can't be alone in sensing a slight deference to the lady of the house, a sort of exaggerated delicacy in her deportment. It's as if the intimacy she enjoys with Nunci must be nurtured with utmost care, securing as it does Mamí's own position, close to the pinnacle of the local hierarchy.

That status is further enhanced by the proximity of the church and Mamí's role in it. Here she takes classes for village children, reads the lesson on Sundays and, along with her sisters and Nunci, occupies a front-row pew – any would-be usurpers are summarily moved on.

The bells regularly clang over the rooftops. Sometimes, it's a death-knell, prompting Mamí to comment, as she works it out: "That must be Toñín! Or perhaps Anselmo, at last? It would be a release after his suffering. Or even Dolores. She was in terrible shape at Mass."

After a quick change of outfit and fresh lipstick, she leaves for church to identify the deceased. She can then share the news among friends and neighbours with authority, thereby pre-empting suspense ahead of tomorrow's *esquela* (death announcement).

The church itself may no longer be the largest building in the village (nowadays, that's the Ruiz-Toledo's textile factory on the main road outside, and even the *bodega* may be larger too) but it's still the most distinguished, despite the indignities it has endured over the years. At some point, a condom-shaped cap was added to the square tower, ostensibly to pin it together. More recently, in the name of progress, the young new priest Don Pedro removed the old flagstones that were its chief internal glory, causing upset among some parishioners, including Aunt Macu, who generally hates change.

"Our Church must reform from the ground up," Don Pedro told her, when challenged. "We're not here to gratify antiquarians! The Church's mission is to offer worship to our Lord and to seek salvation for us sinners through his son Jesus Christ."

There's a view he must be a *progre,* one of the new-style clergy, often left wing, undermining the last bastions of the old faith. Paradoxically, Aunt Macu is relaxed about that aspect of Don Pedro, if not about the flagstones – a spirit of contradiction nourishing her liberal side.

Mamí is also forgiving, but for different reasons: "I do miss Don Ricardo, but there's no denying that Don Pedro confesses *so much better!*"

On our visits I find few diversions in Bárcena. However, we have a few rituals to discharge. These include trips to the beach, a few miles distant with Mamí in toe; perhaps one excursion to the interior, to reconnect with "classic" Spain; and, before leaving for home, a visit to the grocer's, *Tienda de Ultramarinos Rubén*, to stock up with local victuals, palliatives for the British winter. We also call on the *bodega,* not just to collect two litres of their special white wine vinegar; we also hope that Aunt Macu, custodian of the family piggybank, might be moved to a little largesse. This seldom fails, though she keeps us guessing until the last moment and, even then, the exact quantum fluctuates wildly, depending on her inscrutable assessment of our behaviour. A disappointing *propina* could result from forgetting Abuela's Saint's Day or failing to pay our respects the moment we arrive. We can only guess – the factors placing us in or out of favour are deliberately opaque.

Our outings are punctuated by chance encounters with family friends, relations and wider acquaintances. I dread them, because they're asymmetric. If time allows, as we are approaching, I ask Marina whether I already met whoever it is, and if so, try to pin down key co-ordinates: "school friend; loves bars and sunbathing; baby just started talking"; "Benigno's cousin, the one who knows all about Liverpool FC in the 1970s; wife Daniela a one-time squeeze of Papí's"; "part of the African contingent with a drink problem". On the other hand, nobody's in any doubt about who I am, because Mamí's vicissitudes are followed across the village and foreigners in Bárcena are so rare that it's all too obvious who I must be.

Then there's the whole question of greetings. Is kissing sanctioned for the women and, if so, which ones? Just the young and/or relatives only? Up to what age, roughly? One kiss or more? Left to right or the other way round?

If that's a minefield, the male-on-male greetings are trickier still, especially for uptight Anglo-Saxons wary of physical contact and emotional incontinence. The hearty embraces, cheek and neck tweaking, and slaps on the back simply do not come naturally; they are embarrassing ordeals to be endured. And where do you park your face while all this is going on?

The hidden advantages of English provenance shouldn't be overlooked, though: we are rightly celebrated for our skills when it comes to discussing the weather and we would doubtless take the title in any open contest. But Spaniards must be close runners-up. The subject is an icebreaker in any encounter and it always comes to the rescue. For a start, they have an expression that works whatever the weather – sun, rain, wind, snow, no matter: "*Vaya día*", they say – "what a lovely / filthy / bitter / boiling / windy / gloomy day" (adjective supplied by implication alone). I have made the formula my own and find it invaluable, buying me precious time while I try to work out who it is I'm talking to.

Papí returns once a year, usually coinciding with the boar hunt that starts in autumn. Any vestiges of the romance that originally catalysed Mamí's escape from her mother's clutches, and her elopement with Cipriano to Africa, are well buried. Instead, almost all dialogue between Papí and Mamí has degraded into tetchy bickering. It starts the moment he arrives bearing an unwelcome gift, typically something live – a parrot, a monkey, a dog.

"What did you bring that for? You know I hate dogs! It's an *autorregalo*, isn't it? You just leave it here for me to look after and clean up its mess until next time you come."

"I shan't bother in future."

"Please don't! You don't even care for them yourself, never take them with you, not even hunting. What are they for? Guard dogs? Or are they meant to keep me captive in your absence?"

Papí doesn't answer, he just leaves for the wooded valleys towards the pass – without the dog, though sometimes dragging a reluctant Sancho, whom he wants to initiate into the *macho* mysteries of the chase. There he joins a group of hard-bitten country types for the annual cull.

The fate of the assorted *mascotas* is generally a harsh one, for Mamí's resentment finds an outlet in studious neglect. The monkey turns out to be a troublesome companion, leaping around the sitting room, defecating uncontrollably

21

and sending the ornaments flying. Next time we come, there's no sign of it and we learn that it succumbed to illness – which I interpret as homesickness and depression. Or perhaps Curro the vet obliged, by putting it out of its misery. There's a special term for this: *"sacrificar"*, as in *"they sacrificed the monkey"*.

The dogs and parrots last a bit longer but fare little better in the end. A wire enclosure in one corner of the garden hosts a succession of snappy terriers, generally named *Flecha*. Their life expectancy is measured in months. Usually, it's one of the neighbours, tiring of the perpetual yapping, who pitches a venomous chop over the wall to speed them on their way. The parrots live in a cage in the kitchen where they mimic the comings and goings and the chuntering of Mamí's gadgets, the fridge or washing machine. Mamí persuades her sister Ludi to relieve her of the first of these. Unfortunately, Papí takes this as a vote of confidence and before long, supplies a second.

But there's another bone of contention between them: it centres on Sancho. Now in his mid-teens, Sancho shows little academic aptitude (he rudely spurns my offer of English lessons), and the question of his future is looming. Alone at a lunch with her parents one day, Marina having abandoned me for a reunion (alumnae of The Female Jesuses) they suspend the usual decorum generally afforded to me in favour of an ill-tempered row. Papí, it appears, is grooming Sancho to join the returning African diaspora; as a first step, he's planning to take him to Guinea over the summer.

"You're doing *what*?" Mamí explodes, evidently in the dark about the plan.

"Yes, I'm taking him with me. He'll love it: it's in the blood. And what's the alternative? Rolling barrels for your sister at *Bodegas Pinar?* Can't you see that's got no future?

Pinar's been asleep for years. It's a stagnant trade and these days, there's competition. No, no, there's nothing there for Sancho. Africa's the future."

"I'm not losing another son."

"Have you forgotten?" Papí says.

"Forgotten what?"

"Your own escape… From your mother."

"I think it's you that's forgotten. Getting thrown out, I mean! Everything stuffed in one suitcase, nothing to show for all those years! Africa isn't what it was. It'll happen all over again… And he'll pick up your bad habits."

Perhaps she's alluding to his roving eye. I've already heard about Daniela from Marina, and there have been others, many others according to her. Papí doesn't rise to the bait, not in my earshot, anyway.

But Mamí evidently loses the argument; for shortly after, we learn that Sancho will indeed spend a month in the African jungle with his father and brother.

The rest of Papí's visits comprise daily excursions to *Casa Polín* in neighbouring Ontaneda for preprandials with friends. That means we're kept waiting even longer than usual. Lunch cannot commence without him, so half past three or four o'clock becomes the norm whenever he's home.

There's one member of the family who knows all about England, thanks to a stint as an *au pair*, and an unexpected bonus of our residence in London is the annual visit from the fourth of Aunt Ludi's nine, Cousin Paloma. The name means "dove", alias the Holy Ghost, and indeed, there's something diaphanous about her (though more prosaically, the name also means "pigeon"). She's studying to become a teacher. Paloma's very bright, sweet and charming, although she's also stubborn and feisty, despite the demure exterior. She's especially dogmatic about

English fiction, about which she's uncommonly well informed.

On the recommendation of my Hispanophile friend Jack, I read Graham Greene's recent novel, *Monsignor Quixote*. It would "*help me understand my new family*", apparently. It's a skit based on the quixotic exploits of a Catholic priest (the Monsignor) and his communist companion, Mayor Sancho. When I tell Paloma about it, I'm taken aback by her reaction: "Frankly, I don't see how you could like any such thing. Greene has a totally outdated, folkloric idea of Spain that has *nothing* to do with the present day. You don't really buy into that kind of nonsense, do you?"

I hazard the view that yes, maybe I do *buy into* it, in the sense that much of what I've experienced suggests the quixotic spirit is far from dead, in Bárcena at least – the air of make-believe seems all too consistent with it. Innocuous enough, in my view, but I have the impression of wading deep into half intimated culture wars. And probably my biggest error is to concede that this admittedly clichéd view of the country appeals to me rather more than the rationalist-technocratic paradigm which Paloma and, as far as I can see, much of her cohort espouse.

In any event, that mild disagreement marks the last of the annual visits from Cousin Paloma.

5

Dear Jack,
Thanks for your news… Well done cutting the cord at last. I know how much you hated the Ministry, but taking the plunge is hard. I'm sure the venture will do well, the timing's good and there should be lots of interest – you're on the right side of history (English devouring the world, I

mean). In the end, other tongues will be quaint survivals, like Basque today. But I'll write about that another time: meanwhile, allow me to transport you somewhere else…

Remember when my mother-in-law cornered you at the wedding for half an hour of African reminiscences? Well, finally we made it and, right now, here we are, stuck in the capital of Equatorial Guinea, Malabo ("Santa Isabel" as my ex-colonial relatives stubbornly call it), waiting for a flight home. It won't have escaped you that the antics of my in-laws are generally unpredictable and sometimes borderline farcical. This trip has been true to form.

Anyhow, thanks to a tropical storm, our plane circled overhead, took fright and retreated to a safe haven, leaving us stranded. But this morning, five days on, they told us our flight was on its way at last. As I write, we're at the air strip, waiting; but until I see the plane on the apron, I won't believe it. I assure you that yet another night at the Panáfrica with its leaky pipes and cockroaches ogling from the shower drain has scant appeal.

We have nobody to blame but ourselves, since the trip was our idea. Marina's brother Sancho, who visited his father here last year, warned us against it – "don't expect much, especially from Papí or Chus" – but curiosity got the better of us. Marina had memories of her infancy she wanted to revisit; and I was keen to probe the family legend for myself.

As Sancho predicted, it's been a let-down. For a start, the airline lost our bags, muddling up "Malabo" with "Málaga". Once we located them, we spent a day telexing Madrid to stop them from forwarding the bags, as we couldn't pick them up and they'd get lost altogether. But it left us without a book, a camera or a change of clothes and we soon learned it's hard to replace such things out here. We scrounged a few basics from a Spanish doctor and the nuns in Bata, the main continental town, but that's all. Bata's a short hop on a light plane from Malabo (I got soaked by the leaky aircraft door).

It's all far removed from the palmy, ocean-lapped idyll that Mamí evokes. Papí and his cronies come down to Bata from time to time for supplies; however, they live in a so-called patio or compound in the interior, which is where they took us. It's a red mud clearing a couple of hundred metres wide, with half a dozen raised wooden huts and a collection of steel storage containers. There's also a barracks for the locals. Heavy trucks and equipment are parked round the perimeter, which is fenced off with barbed wire and large mesh gates. Dense jungle looms on all sides.

As well as Papí, "Masa Cipri" and Chus, "Masa Chus", as the locals call them ("Masa" being a corruption of "Master"), Papí's youngest brother, Sote, recently joined the desperadoes, about 15 in all, mostly Spaniards plus a few French and Belgians, probably on the run – either from their wives or something worse. There aren't any women, at least, no European women, except for Marina. There are about 30 Guineanos *working as cooks, general hands or lumberjacks: timber's the whole point of the affair these days (they're no longer the genteel "coffee planters" or officials that my mother-in-law evokes). Every night the Europeans sit in the porch of one of the larger huts. Hunks of bushmeat and yucca are served with lashings of liquor – a thin local beer,* Whisky DYC *(Spanish version of Scotch) and the racily named* Focking Gin, *in a bottle nearly identical to* Gordon's, *which warns the drinker to "bewear (sic) of imitations".*

We witnessed the logging business in action after a long drive by Land Rover deep into the forest, sliding in and out of troughs scored in the mud by the heavy lifters. After an hour or so we arrived at the scene. Sote, Chus and others were issuing orders to the African workers lashing ropes round a huge hardwood tree trunk. In seconds, the chainsaws sliced through a hundred years of timber and the tree crashed to the ground, ripping surrounding vegetation with it. Then the mastodon was stripped to the spine and torn out of the undergrowth, where it was lifted and lashed between two sets of wheels. Shortly after, it set off on the long grind down to the coast.

One night we lived through a small drama. After an even boozier evening than usual we retired to our own hut and managed to cheat the mosquitos long enough to get to sleep. But it didn't last: we were roused suddenly by shouts and commotion − though it was unclear what was afoot. Next, we heard gunshots, then more shouting; the action seemed to be receding and we heard vehicles racing out of the gates in hot pursuit. A while later, we emerged onto the now floodlit scene to hear the story. It turned out the cook had let in the gang, which headed for the safe while the night watchman slept… But, at that moment, Papí staggered across the veranda for midnight bladder relief. He spied three shadowy figures heading for the admin block, home of the safe. He grabbed his gun and started firing… Fortunately, there were no casualties, but it transpired the police were part of the hit squad. So there were no arrests on either side.

Here's a bit of Papí's history I've patched together. After ejection from Guinea at independence, he and others tried to conjure up the magic elsewhere. That's how, without Mamí or Chus, he came to live in a sweaty province in Colombia, close to the Panamanian border. Neither that venture, nor its predecessor in Guatemala, seem to have prospered, but by then, a decade later, the coast was clear to return to Guinea, although colonial days were by now a fading memory…

But hang on, what's that? A plane just landed… It's got to be ours, at last. Maybe we'll get out after all… And now what's that I see? Those look like our bags! The lost ones! Out of the plane straight onto the tarmac… I must run…

6

Safely back in Bárcena, reunited with our personal effects, the remaining fixture of the summer is the annual lunch with the cousins, hosted by Aunt Macu. There are 13 first cousins between the Pinar siblings: Mamí's four (the Expósito Pinars) plus Aunt Ludi's nine (the Blasco Pinars). Ludi's clutch comprises three girls and six boys, born every two or three years in a sequence akin to the black keys on a piano, right to the very last, when a whole octave separates the afterthought, still an infant, from the pack. Until the *Caudillo's* death a decade ago, any self-respecting household was duty-bound to raise a brood at least as large as Aunt Ludi's – indeed, that was the message of our Family Book. But now the tide is turning, small families are the norm, in sympathy, perhaps, with the country's new European friends. Joining "Europe" is feted as a mark of acceptance, graduation to the club of serious nations. "*Now*

28

we're Europeans…" prefaces many a remark.

The party will take place in the house Aunt Macu and her mother built when they abandoned the *casona* in town. Originally, it stood alone in the flat countryside, *la mies*, as it's called, between Bárcena and the river; but it's starting to fill up with the kind of semi-agricultural detritus that litters the outskirts of most towns round here: jerry-built stables and chicken coops; vegetable plots; garages and lean-tos; and most recently, a few showy mansions, mostly home to politicians. The grandest of these belongs to Juanma, the mayor, one of Papí's best friends, with whom he spends many hours at *Casa Polín* during his visits.

We're the first to arrive and, unusually for her, Aunt Macu is decidedly animated, eager to show off the strip of land she recently acquired, doubling the size of her already generous plot. In fact, I haven't seen her quite so enraptured since the time she extolled some bucolic *pueblo* near Bárcena as the *"most beautiful in the world."* It was an accolade that invited challenge: I'm not aware of her venturing far beyond provincial confines, other than on occasional wine-buying expeditions to desiccated parts of the country. So who's she to judge?

"My idea," she explains, gesticulating from the balustrade above the new plot, "is for a series of small, intimate gardens either side of the central avenue leading down to the pond. A rockery, a rose garden, a bower blooming with wildflowers and so on. There'll be a summer house for you and the family down at the bottom there when the time comes."

At the moment, it doesn't look promising and that's before we enter the annex itself. On the steps between old and new, a dozen terracotta pots lie in pieces, spilling earth and geraniums onto the path. Aunt Macu catches my frown: "A mess, isn't it? But I'm leaving it like that because

I want to show the rascal's mother what he did to my plants. Nothing but trouble, the Ortega family; the youngster's the worst: out of control... Over there, in the flats, that's where they live," she says, pointing to one of the untidy blocks with a bird's eye view of her garden.

We pick our way between the shattered pots down to the lower level.

The sleepers for the avenue have been laid in a straight line with gaps in between, as if rebuilding the railway itself. The ground is swampy, so a network of trenches shaped like a fish skeleton provides drainage into the pond at the bottom – with luck they'll mellow once overgrown a bit. But the only trees in the boggy terrain are alder and willow, sprouting like weeds. At the moment, the summerhouse is no more than a foundation slab. A wall is under construction round the perimeter but, in the interests of economy, Aunt Macu has opted for yellowish breeze blocks rather than local stone. Moreover, the Ortegas' block is far from the only one gawping brazenly over the wall. Apart from the frogs croaking and leaping into the pond, it's a rather dank and charmless piece of ground so it's hard to echo her excitement.

"It should be nice once the plants grow a bit... But who's going to look after all this?" Marina asks.

"Oh that'll be me. At least, for the most part. You know how much I love gardening. That's how I plan to spend my retirement."

It sounds unlikely. Aunt Macu's idea of gardening is pottering among the roses, dead-heading for half an hour. Obviously, she has hired hands for the structural piece, but once that's done, maintaining it will be a full-time job.

"It's a *chapuza*," Marina says once we're out of earshot. Loosely translated, *chapuza* ("cha-POO-tha") means a botched job, a Heath Robinson affair, a shoddy solution, a short-cut, something unfinished or untidy. It's a national institution. There's a saying that "*Spaniards hate trouble more than they dislike a shoddy job*," not forgetting the reluctance to incur expense, which also plays a part. A *chapuza* is that pile of assorted rubble and rock-hard cement (some still in bags) in the grass outside a new house long after the workmen left; it's the bedsprings used in place of field gates, the old tyres covering the silage, or the bathtubs in place of cattle troughs that pepper this dairy country.

Stretching the concept a little, a *chapuza* is corner-cutting in order to avoid, postpone or mitigate any brush with officialdom, *Las Autoridades*, including payment for a stamp or other irksome paperwork. Marina, for example, enjoys "real" and "official" birthdays (one day apart) owing to just one such sleight of hand – the lure of the bar having caused Papí to miss the deadline for registering her birth. (Dare I add that Marina herself bears a few scars from the *chapuza* affliction: I'm thinking, for example, of the seeming order of our home, so often belied the moment you open a cupboard door, when the entire stacked-up contents debouch onto the floor…)

Abuela, like a ball of black wool in her widow's weeds, sits by the fireplace in the penumbra. She starts to unravel when we enter but Marina signals her to stay put. Abuela says little these days, but mutters and nods agreement with everyone. Otherwise, she's mesmerised by the click of her rosary beads. The housekeeper, Nuria, hovers in the background, collecting nuggets to share with her friends.

Soon, we hear Uncle Toño, elder brother to Mamí and Aunts Ludi and Macu, emerging from his holiday digs down the passage, padding towards us in his bedroom slippers; but to palpable relief, he branches off towards the kitchen. In the mornings, Uncle Toño's a bit of a fright, a scarecrow in string vest and pyjama bottoms, bleary eyed, comb-over as wild as the Medusa's head, dentures missing. However, once he's swallowed a *carajillo* or two (coffee with a shot of brandy), pulled on a shirt, glued down his locks and reattached his teeth, he's ready for battle, and he joins us in the sitting room.

A while ago, I travelled to Madrid on an errand and Marina fixed me up for the couple of nights with Uncle Toño, whom I hadn't met before. I looked forward to that trip, picturing a penthouse above the turrets of the *Plaza Mayor*, somewhere suitable for the savvy lawyer of my imaginings. Had I known that Toño in fact worked as a scribe for the *Official State Bulletin*, my expectations might have been better aligned with reality. We met at Chamartín Station, whence he led me down a succession of dreary streets to his abode.

A penthouse it was not, nor an apartment, nor even a flat. Nor did it enjoy a view over the rooftops of the old town. It was a bedsit, with one small window onto a blind lightwell, sweltering in the August evening. I had no choice but to share the only bed with him. There I passed two sleepless nights, sweating on a lumpy mattress with springs that groaned and pinged at the slightest twitch. I struggled to avoid inhaling his garlic-scented breath, while trying to discourage snoring with sharp clicks of the tongue; and in the morning, my first encounter was with Toño's teeth, refracted to a grimace in a glass of water by the sink.

Joining us in Aunt Macu's sitting room, Uncle Toño heads straight over to me with a conspiratorial grin – I'm the only other male for the time being and, despite the trials of the Madrid visit, we've become friends. He embarks on his usual routine, rasping rare dissent from the sell-out to "*our European friends, hahaha,*" or "*jajaja*" as it's rendered in Spanish, in tribute to those guttural "h"s that sound like the "ch" in "loch". He chortles at the sheer absurdity of it all, especially that "*clown of a Presidente*", a socialist and a favourite bugbear. By all accounts, Uncle Toño was once a lawyer of promise. However, neither his cossetted upbringing as only son, nor his first job in the African graveyard in his brother-in-law's slipstream helped him find his niche; in the end, Guinean independence involved a brutal ejection. The sole option remaining was a role in public administration. Far from a cushy sinecure, it's a role for a *chupatintas*, an "ink-sucker".

Uncle Toño once vied for the title of Family Intellectual with Aunt Macu and, since Aunt Ludi's marriage, with his new brother-in-law Benigno, a claim he had to renounce following years of self-abuse and tropical maladies. However, he retains supremacy in one field: philology; and both Aunt Macu and Benigno defer to him on the subject. Uncle Toño's delighted to have found an empty vessel (me), a willing receptacle for his wisdom on Spanish syntax, etymology and orthography that he decants whenever we meet.

Aunt Macu believes in high culture too, at least in theory. That explains the sagging bookshelves of semi-learned tomes, probably unread and doubtless unreadable, lining the airless room. Every day, she buys a whole bundle of newspapers, national and local, right wing and left, to keep abreast of debate; for her politics is an idiosyncratic mix of bleeding-heart liberalism and "*hang 'em, flog 'em*" authoritarianism. It depends on the day. Whatever, Aunt Macu's the family's moral compass and guardian of high standards, always ready to censure the degenerate ways of Spanish youth and this new-fangled "*democracy, as they call it*". Unlike flaky Uncle Toño or outsider Uncle Benigno, she enjoys unchallenged authority over the family, of which she has become *de facto* matriarch, thanks to her tight grip on the purse-strings.

Marina tells me that, when their father died, Aunt Macu persuaded her siblings to entrust her with their voting rights at the winery. Her argument was that they, the Pinar Vázquez cousins, had to speak with a single voice in order to control the Pinar Mogro cousins, who between them own the other half of the *bodega*. The Pinar Mogro interest is split three ways between one brother and two sisters (who aren't always in agreement) and Aunt Macu was confident that, provided she could count on her side's interests, she could divide and rule the opposition. Uncle Toño, still wrestling with his alcohol habit, felt unable to exercise male precedence and quietly acquiesced in the arrangement "*so long as I get my dividend*". Indeed, dividends continue to flow, but Aunt Macu enjoys *de facto* control, voting for the whole Pinar Vázquez clan, including Abuela. All of this was officially documented at the notary, as a result of which Macu's natural authority is backed by real clout.

She's also a stern gatekeeper of authentic Spanish taste. In the first instance, this relates to her belief in Spanish wines as the pinnacle of viticultural achievement. She swills and quaffs the *bodega's* own blend, *Tinto del Abuelo*, "Grandfather's Red", sourced from the broiling plains of La Mancha, as if it were a Rioja *Gran Reserva*. But it's not confined to wine. Macu has no doubt that Spanish taste and style, across the spectrum, is far superior to anything else. And in the guise of an offer we can't refuse, Macu has decided to place a sample of these timeless values right into our lair.

"I'm making you gift," she declares, using the time before the cousins arrive. (She's not inclined to repeat the gesture for the whole family; not yet, anyway). "It's for your new house. Magín's making you some chairs. I'm having them shipped over."

It's tantamount to surrogate parenthood, enabling spinster Macu to seed the gene pool beyond local shores. As intimated, it will take the form of eight traditional dining chairs from her preferred cabinet maker, the one who made Papí's furniture from tropical hardwoods. I fear they'll be just as ungainly and won't fit in. The acme of elegance they will not be, for sure. But it's a fait accompli, to be borne stoically, in the interests of peaceful coexistence.

Today, all but one of the nine Blasco cousins from their Bárcena holiday *dacha*, are expected, the absentee being the eldest, Puri (Purificación). She's a nun: not a "cloistered" nun, but seldom sighted in Bárcena. In fact, I understand she lost her faith a while ago and now dedicates her life to good works in Latin America.

In our demographic, that leaves: Beni, an austere, aspiring physicist; Domingo, a recent graduate; Paloma, the doe-eyed but independent-minded teacher trainee; and Julito, the family wordsmith. Nacho, Rosita and Rodrigo, are still of school age. The toddler, Pepe, will, with luck, stay asleep, at least some of the time. In our generation, only Sancho joins Marina from the Expósito clan – but Mamí should compensate for that, in volume, at least. She enjoys a close bond with Julito; today she arrives side-saddle on the back of his scooter, grasping the seat with one hand and holding her hair in place with the other. Julito, as usual, is in mid-story. Mamí adores her nephew Julito. He's such an amusing raconteur, almost in her class! She rather wishes one of her own offspring shared his talent.

Everyone enjoys this bit of theatre except Sancho. He must resent his cousin's usurpation of a role rightfully his own; and he doesn't appreciate his cousin's storytelling. Mamí's his mother, not Julito's. And anyway, Sancho's old enough to ride a scooter, though funding for a machine remains out of his reach. In any case, he shares little with Julito and it's not merely the result of age difference.

We're still awaiting the rest of the Blascos from the *dacha* a few hundred metres away. Why the delay? Even this family starts developing an appetite by four in the afternoon.

At that moment the front gate squeals and Rosita comes in. She's wheeling Pepe's pushchair and runs up to the house, anxiously exclaiming: "They're trapped! All of them!"

"*¡Ave María purísima!*[5]" Mamí exclaims, histrionically, while Aunt Macu steps in, demonstrating the leadership she's admired for: "Rosita! Calm down! What do you mean, trapped?"

"It was Vasca… her chain broke. She turned on us – Nacho tried to catch her, and she bit him. Then she chased them inside. Now they can't leave. I escaped because I was by the gate with Pepe."

"Benigno! Of course. I knew it!" Mamí says, combative once more. "What did he expect? Didn't I warn him about that animal? '*Guard dog*', *jajaja*. Now it turns on his own family! That mongrel should be sacrificed straight away. As if last time wasn't enough! I'll never forgive Ramón… Always chasing the easy sales, no questions asked… to think we shared the school bench! *¡Dios mío, Dios mío, Dios mío!*"

She's alluding to the time, just weeks ago, when burglars ransacked the *dacha* and Aunt Ludi lost most of her jewellery, while the dog was suborned with a string of sausages. Mamí is particularly upset that her butcher, Ramón, supplied the bait, as betrayed by scraps of

---

[5] "Hail Mary, most pure"

monogrammed wrapper at the scene.

Short of calling the *Guardia Civil*, which would be terminal for Vasca, Uncle Benigno's the only one who can sort this out, the only person who controls the she-wolf. Benigno will have to catch her and liberate the family. The hitch is that, right now, he's at work, many leagues away. Even if he can drop everything, it'll take hours to arrive over the mountains in the "*Peh-oo-seh-OTT*", as Mamí calls his shooting brake.

So the annual *fiesta* starts off on a subdued note. However, before long, Mamí and Julito fall into their familiar blend of banter and gossip and, in due course, we all forget about stranded Aunt Ludi and the cousins. Only Sancho, looking a bit morose, stays aloof.

7

After early hopes were dashed, Mamí concluded that Marina would never bring her grandchildren. It's a lament long adopted into her core repertoire, shared in plangent tones with any more or less willing audience: "No, no, she's not a mother yet, of course she's not a mother. Far from it: she *can't* become a mother. And even if she could, she doesn't *want* to become a mother! *¡Virgen María! So* selfish! *So* cruel!"

Nor does elder son Chus show any sign of settling down. Judging by the scraps we're fed, he's more than fully supplied with female company, while avoiding needless entrapment. According to him, he's a magnet for all the beautiful girls in Guinea: that's what he propounds to his Fan Club – a club that grows every year as he showers disbelieving Bárcena with the fruits of his endeavours, hiring the *Politena* for evenings at a stretch for Bacchanalian reunions, all at his expense.

Mamí, however, has other plans for him that she shares

in strictest confidence with chosen listeners: "My poor Chus! These wicked stories! Of course, it's jealousy. That's how they thank him! But how happy he'll be with Maite! It's the perfect match."

Maite is neighbour Nunci's second daughter. After Lupita's unfortunate liaison and emergency wedding, followed by the birth of her son, hopes are now vested in the virginal Maite, among the most eligible matches Bárcena can offer. At one time, Mamí aimed even higher, hoping her son might yet scoop the lovely heiress, Cayetana Ruiz-Toledo... But even she reluctantly conceded that Cayetana was way out of Chus' league, destined for some *triunfador*, likely a *Marqués* or a *Conde*, from among the so-called *pijos*, the swells from Madrid.

However, days before our summer visit, we are the ones who confound Mamí's expectations. There was no trickery. Marina was not misled. For we can confirm beyond reasonable doubt that the equipment, his and hers, is fully functional, after all. That's to say that Marina's expecting later in the year.

By the time we arrive, Mamí has spread the news far and wide. We realise this before we've even set foot inside No. 15 because we're intercepted at the gate by Maite and her brother Paco.

"I gather congratulations are called for!" shouts Paco, a wag and man of the world, signalling Marina's now visible bump. "It won't surprise you your mother shared the happy news... and all the effort that's gone into bringing it about, *jajaja*. Nothing spared, no suffering too great, to spawn the blue-eyed son and heir, by all accounts!"

Mamí greets Marina with the warmest hug she's earned since infancy. It transpires that she's found time for several visits to Pueblo de la Vega, our nearest big town, in search of outfits for the new arrival. (All are sky blue: as Paco intimated, she knows it's a boy.) She has also excavated the garage and the cupboards in the search for hand-me-downs: the contents are strewn about the *mirador*[6] by her bedroom. Alas, an infestation of moths seems to have taken care of much of it.

But during the same visit, our own news is trumped. One day at lunch Chus announces to a stunned family that he plans to marry. Yes: Chus to marry! But his *novia* is not the coveted Maite, let alone Cayetana Ruiz-Toledo. Instead, it's Conchi Palacio, daughter of yet another of Mamí's schoolday contemporaries, Remedios. It's not quite the glittering match Mamí aspired to – neither Remedios nor her husband José belong to Bárcena's élite – but at least they're respectable folk. José runs a thriving hardware store on the main thoroughfare in nearby Tobillo, the kind of establishment that spreads assorted wicker chairs, pitchforks, earthenware cooking pots, scythes and clogs across the pavement. Remedios, too, is inoffensive, if no soulmate for her opposite number. Conchi has a reputation as a Good Time Girl, a stalwart of the discotheque and a beach bunny, but she's well-liked by everyone, and at least nobody's stepping out of line.

Before long, Mamí has decided to make a virtue of necessity: "I'm so happy for Chus! I never thought he'd settle down. Of course, I would have loved him to marry Maite," she says wistfully, "but Conchi's so pretty – much prettier than Maite, for certain. Such lovely hair, such lovely skin! And doesn't she dress beautifully? They make such a happy couple! She's such fun, too – really enjoys life. I always thought Maite was a bit full of her studies and all that. Not very feminine, don't you agree? And she could lose a bit of weight, too!"

---

[6] glass gallery

39

Chus and Conchi won't be wasting time. There will be a simple church blessing with the family, courtesy of Don Pedro, followed by a party with the Fan Club at the Gran Hotel de la Vega, a few miles outside Bárcena. Chus will pay for everything. Then the happy couple will depart for Africa. In Conchi's case, it will be her first visit. She's full of anticipation for her new life.

Chapter II: Heir Raising

1

Unfortunately, Conchi Palacio doesn't take to Guinea quite as well as expected. Arguably, she should have sampled it first; perhaps she should have listened to the Cassandras; maybe she should have discounted the blandishments of Chus and his parents. Conchi evidently pictured herself under the coconut palms like a matador's wife on a spread out of *¡Hola!* magazine.

The reality falls woefully short and she's quite unprepared for such isolation, the sole white female other than the Bata nuns, as far as she's aware; she's miserable, confined to this rancid compound, alone all day long, the only compensation being temporary respite from the rebarbative menfolk, those hairy misfits that return to the *patio* of an evening and turn on the horseplay at her expense, a toxic blend of banter and innuendo. Nor had she predicted her new husband's open dalliance with several local girls – there's one he particularly fancies who's only about 15 years old! And he's in a near perpetual state of inebriation. Conchi's complaints are scarcely heeded, and she becomes morose – so much so that even Chus realises something's amiss and dispatches her to the Bata nuns for a few days to recover.

But by this stage she's had enough and decides to escape. In a reverse elopement, she scrounges a seat for the hop back to Malabo. Then, before Chus realises she's left the mainland, she's safely aboard the flight from Malabo back home.

Back in Bárcena, her return causes a stir. Mamí seethes with fury: that her Chus should thus be spurned!

"She's a common whore," she says, "telling stories like

that. Not even six months! I might have guessed: just as useless as her mother; useless at school; useless now. *¡Madre mía!* Just as well there aren't any children…"

The rest of the family suddenly remembers Conchi's shortcomings too. Aunt Macu, for one, always knew she wasn't up to it, "*…socially, I mean*".

"And I've always known," she adds, "that no good ever came out of Tobillo."

For Tobillo, a short distance along the main road from Bárcena, has long been blemished in the family's eyes by the presence of the *bodega's* unscrupulous competitor, *Vinos Aurelio.* Along with the *Ferretería Palacio,* it's among the few signs of life in that now stagnant backwater.

The Palacio family rarely ventures to the Bárcena lights; otherwise, every foray to the shops would be blighted by the risk of an encounter with Remedios, José, Conchi herself or her brother Fernando, who's particularly incensed by his sister's ill-treatment.

However, it soon blows over, the main reason being that at last, Mamí has become a grandmother. Once the new-born is old enough to fly, Marina and baby Clara head to Bárcena for official review.

Ever since the pregnancy was confirmed, Mamí has been acutely frustrated, because her efforts to micro-manage the process from afar have come to nought. Two or three days past the due date, for instance, she started agitating for emergency intervention, to no avail. Then, *post partum*, she vainly lobbied for Marina to stay housebound for at least two weeks. Now, at last united with her new granddaughter, she intends to compensate, playing the adoring grandmother, smothering the infant with affection and parading her through the streets of Bárcena in a pram at every opportunity.

The cultural rift over baby-rearing is unexpected, by me

at least. Mamí and I are at opposite extremes, while Marina takes up the middle ground, torn between Spanish indulgence and British denial. In my case, it's not underpinned by much theory, experience or learning; instead, it reflects a sense of despair that if this doesn't stop soon ("this" being the imperious infant's demands), life as we knew it will be *over*. That reaction, combined with a half-forgotten legacy of fierce nannies and disapproving aunts, encourages me to persuade Marina that she should "*just let the infant cry*" instead of picking Clara up every time she squeals in her cot. "*Otherwise, she'll never settle.*"

"You see? What did it take? Not even five minutes," I say, after Clara quickly stops wailing when Marina road-tests the new strategy. "If only you'd listen once in a while. Not everything I say is wrong on principle, you know."

But then Mamí comes down, cradling Clara, who has a pink dummy stuffed in her mouth.

"You can't leave the baby howling like that! It's inhuman! If she's hungry, you must feed her. If she has a dirty nappy, you must change her. If she's unhappy, you must comfort her. Marina, you should know better!"

It's a clear signal for me to step back and leave it to the experts.

Then there's the whole issue of baby clothes. All the utilitarian garments contributed by British well-wishers make way for hand-embroidered outfits. Mamí's outraged we haven't had the baby's ears pierced – it's the top priority for new-born baby girls. How will people know what it is otherwise? That's all the more pressing after Marina, in a show of defiance, starts using the baby blue kit her mother acquired when her instincts wrongly predicted a boy.

Consistent with her suspicion of gratuitous learning, Mamí takes the view that use of both languages is a form of child-abuse. As she rocks the baby, she regularly hums her reservations to Clara about *"how many things have to fit into this poor little baby's head…"*

Aunt Macu will be godmother and, in the interests of equity, Uncle Toño will be godfather. Aunt Macu's delighted: "I'll go straight to the bank and set up an account for baby Clara. Every birthday I'll put money in the account, so by the time she comes of age, she'll have a nice little nest egg." The following day she proudly shows Marina the savings book, already boasting a tidy sum by way of down payment.

Not to be outdone, Uncle Toño strikes back with a rare gift of his own. It's the two hefty tomes of the *Diccionario de la Lengua Española*, the official dictionary published by the *Real Academia Española*. The message is clear: he may not be rich, he may not have fulfilled his promise, but he's just as cultivated as his sister. While he's extolling this peerless publication, there's room for a touch of chauvinism, too:

"You do realise that Spanish is the most logical language in the world?" he asks me. "For a start, each letter can be pronounced only one way, one sound per symbol. Didn't you say the letter 'a' alone can be pronounced five or six different ways in English? That wouldn't do in Spanish! One sound only per vowel – 'a-e-i-o-u'. Same applies to the consonants: that's why 'ñ', 'll' and 'ch' are all separate letters in the Spanish alphabet – they correspond to distinct sounds: here, let me show you…"

He opens the dictionary at the letter "*ch*", which does indeed command a discrete entry, falling after the letter "*c*" by itself. I nod in acknowledgement and admiration.

"One day I'll explain the accents too – properly called irregular stress indicators, in fact, because they don't change the phonetics. With those rules and the letters, it's almost impossible to mispronounce anything!"

While this is afoot in Bárcena, Aunt Macu's chairs arrive in the UK. On our return, I receive a call from the Port Authority telling me I've 48 hours to settle with HM Customs & Excise and remove the four crates from the dockside, as they are blocking the traffic. Otherwise, they will be treated as unclaimed and they "*cannot guarantee their future*".

When I get to the port, a morning's drive from home, I find the offending crates stacked up on the quayside. They look gigantic. Magín has boxed them up in pairs, taking no chances with Atlantic storms. Even if I could shift them, I certainly wouldn't be able to fit a single box in the back of the car. The Port Authority informs me there's a charge for moving the crates off the boat to their current position and for occupying premium space on the quayside.

Then I tackle Customs. Theoretically, there's no duty (we're all in the EEC these days) but the paperwork has been prepared wrongly (a fine is due) and the merchandise can't be inspected (another fine). I'll therefore have to arrange payment of the fees and fines (banker's draft only) as well as a Customs assessment (crowbar not supplied), the earliest time for which is tomorrow morning (overnight stay). After that, I'll need a freight company to load them up and take them home.

Suffice to say that the crates eventually arrive home, are barely squeezed through the narrow front door and deposited into the back of the small sitting room. There they sit, vast and reproachful, until I summon the energy to break them up, liberate the chairs and transport the detritus to the local dump.

The bill for the whole exercise including fines, fees and fares probably exceeds the cost of the chairs themselves. And my instincts were right. They really do not fit in physically (too big), aesthetically (too rustic) or functionally…

In this last respect, is it unreasonable to expect a chair to fulfil its basic purpose efficiently – namely, to facilitate the act of sitting in a modicum of comfort? When we try them out, Aunt Macu's chairs fail dismally on this count. The design may be time-honoured, but unless the human frame has evolved radically over the intervening centuries, its merits are elusive. The backposts rise perpendicular from the floor to their very apex (they do not splay out either at the bottom or at the top, unlike most designs); hence, without sitting bolt upright, the only contact between backrest and upper body occurs right at the top crossbar, not far below the shoulders. This means the whole human spine runs like a lonely hypotenuse down to the junction point between the pelvis and the hard seat board. Backache is a given.

That's why we decide to stow them away in the loft. However, that also poses a challenge. So large are the chairs that the only way is to enter the loft, dismantle the access ladder; extract other junk; pass the chairs through the narrow hatch one by-one; then reassemble the ladder. Once in the loft, there's not much room left for anything else. Nor is it likely they will re-emerge any time soon. Aunt Macu's surrogate gene pool has been dammed.

2

Happily, we're now expecting a more important arrival than the chairs, which once more dominates our thoughts and preoccupations – a sibling for Clara. Mamí refrains from predictions, so maybe that's why this time, it really is a boy: James. Mamí decides to greet the new grandson on our turf, discovering she can catch a bus all the way from Pueblo de la Vega to London in 48 hours. It's her very first trip to England.

"No luck this time, then!" she says after cursory inspection of the infant, whom we've brought to meet her. She's right that new-born James is rather wrinkly with a matted mop of jet-black hair (baby Clara was more *"presentable"*, in Mamí's idiom).

"Perhaps he'll be the ugly duckling that turns into the graceful swan," she adds in a conciliatory moment.

Her inspection of Britain is cursory too. She doesn't take to it well, there are simply too many foreigners, precious few of them proficient in what she calls *"Cristiano"*.

When we finally make it to Bárcena for the christening, Sancho and Marta become godparents. That means there are no big gifts this time but Sancho, who's just started rolling barrels at the *bodega*, claims he'll teach James the trade one day and Marta will make up for it with babysitting.

A more significant challenge is an unexpected hitch over the name. It's not simply that Mamí and Aunt Macu find "James" unpalatably British (on their lips, it comes out as *"Yams"*). When we take the Family Book to be updated in Pueblo de la Vega, it turns out The Authorities also take a dim view.

"I'm sorry, but you can't choose that name, it's not recognised," the official tells us, extracting a book from a shelf behind him. "It's a foreign name. Let me see: *'Yams'*, you said? Spelt with a *'jota'*? You've got three, perhaps four, choices. You can call him Jaime, Jaume, Iago or maybe Santiago. You need to decide which of those it's to be."

Marina and I are both ruffled. This hurdle did not apply in Clara's case. Finally (though it won't be popular in Bárcena) we decide on the Catalan version, Jaume, on the grounds that Shakespeare blighted the name Iago several centuries ago, Santiago sounds too holy, and Jaime starts with a guttural CH as in 'loch' – not an easy one for my compatriots. But in practice, of course, we carry on calling him James or Yams. What happens, we wonder, if your names include "Fitzjames" like the Dukes of Alba? *Fitzjaume*? *Fitzsantiago*?

Papí, who loves small children, is relaxed about the name and generally quite enthusiastic about his grandson: boys in particular give him an excuse to indulge the fantasies he never quite outgrew. He's no longer up to crafting catapults, shooting pigeons and squirrels with an airgun, or building huts in the garden but, when the time comes, he'll be good at bellowing instructions from the side-lines, just as he does in the African *bosque*. In a rare gesture of homage, he and Juanma create a cot and a highchair from one of the blocks of mahogany Papí brought home from Africa. (They're objects of surprising elegance – in a different league from Magín's ergonomically challenged chairs.)

But, on past form, Papí's enthusiasm will wane soon enough. Once the young start answering back or disappoint in other ways, he loses interest. For instance, we watched Sancho, Marina's younger brother, fall from grace, having failed to share his father's passion for the boar hunt at an age when Papí felt he should be showing manly traits. Worse, he showed little interest in Africa on his introductory trip to the *bosque*, which Papí took as a personal slight.

In any event, Papí spends more time at home these days. He hasn't abandoned Africa for good, but his utility to Chus and his acolytes at the compound is waning fast. Decades of unhealthy living in the forest have exacted a price; he now wheezes and struggles for breath, not that he plans to mend his ways too drastically.

After one severe attack, Mamí arranges a check-up. He submits sheepishly to the usual tests; then a few days later they return to the doctor for the results and attendant inquisition: "How much are you smoking these days?"

"Oh, it's under control… I'm giving up. Rather late, I suppose."

"Alcohol?"

"Yes, the odd drink, but I've cut right back too."

The doctor sends him behind a curtain to undress for examination. Mamí, who's anticipated this exchange, seizes the moment to unfold a note she's prepared for the doctor.

"*Bebe y fuma muchísimo,*" it reads, "*he drinks and smokes a great deal.*"

The doctor nods and taps the side of his nose knowingly.

After the investigation the doctor emerges, looking grave. Papí's lungs are treacle and his liver's shot; he must quit tobacco and alcohol forthwith. If not, he can measure his time in months. And in future, he'll need oxygen on standby, round the clock.

Thereafter, the sight of Papí, watching football from his reclining armchair, harnessed to his oxygen bottle by a tubular snaffle bit, becomes a familiar one. He still manages his preprandial visits to *Casa Polín*, though, where the code of *omertà* keeps his consumption of intoxicants and tobacco under wraps.

3

Mamí has developed a foolproof strategy for managing her grandchildren as they grow. It comprises a compelling roster of TV-on-demand, rides at the *feria*, midnight bedtimes and trips to *Golosinas*, the sweet shop. Not surprisingly, she's their favourite person; but it's our lot to suffer the collateral damage: they're becoming spoilt, bolshy even.

That's why the time has come to find a small place of

our own – not in Bárcena itself, but in the countryside nearby; a buffer of a few kilometres should suffice. I can't help thinking of the freedom it'll bring, the escape from stifling Bárcena and the in-laws. With perfect timing, an unexpected legacy and tenure at the University after almost a decade of toil have brought this within reach.

Though Mamí passed her test, Papí never allowed her to drive and now she relies on charity or even the toytown railway for any sallies from the village. That's why she objects so strongly to our plan. A nice little *piso* in Bárcena: now that would make sense. But whose idea is this? (She's looking fiercely at me at this point, the closest she comes to rebuke, in my case. I have weird ideas about so many things.) Isn't it enough to be dumped by a wayward husband, then by a favourite son? Don't we live in exile already? Now she won't see her grandchildren even when they're here! Anyway, what will we do in the middle of nowhere? Nothing of any interest ever happens in the countryside, it's the epitome of tedium and a one-way ticket to social oblivion.

I've noticed this before: on such subjects, the gulf separating me not just from Mamí but from Spaniards at large is nigh on unbridgeable. The statement "*estaba ASÍ*" ("it was like THIS" – i.e. "*rammed*") is almost always delivered in approving tones in Spain. The words earn a special gesture: index and middle fingers raised tapping the thumb three or four times in quick succession. Sometimes, a third and even a fourth finger are enlisted, depending on just *how* rammed it really was. Any advocacy of lonely beaches, quiet bars and remote countryside provokes incredulity, disapproval, even (anti-social, snobbish, elitist…).

When we share our idea with Aunt Macu, however, her reaction is closer to our own than to Mamí's. Hers is an idealised, mawkish, idea of the countryside – at least of the Spanish countryside, and especially the countryside of this sliver of the northern seaboard. As we already know, it's reliably held to be *"the most beautiful place on earth"*, so of course it's right to bring up the family there. She asks José Angel, her cousin at the *bodega* who supplies the local bars, to help us find a place. He's in touch with all the local gossip and always knows what's on sale.

The moment arrives after a few reconnaissance trips with José Angel. Papí joins us, watching and grunting advice from the passenger seat. After turning down a plane-lined backroad that meanders by a stream through the trees, it rises onto fields above, until the sea appears to the right and hazy peaks to the left. At the top is a settlement and beyond that, down a narrow road without issue, we find a secluded village of a few dozen houses. It lies about one kilometre from the beach as the crow flies, though by road it's more like three. It's just close enough to hear the murmur of the surf breaking on the shore. José Angel says the whole area was declared a Natural Park a few years back, when some big cheese from Madrid fell for it.

Even Papí signals his approval by staggering out of the car for a closer look, dragging his oxygen bottle around in his left hand. From the ridges, both the ocean and the mountain peaks are visible at once. It's almost untouched, a proper survival, with cows on the ground floor of every farmhouse and, as we later discover, bats racing round at dusk and owls shrieking into the pitch night sky. It's called Valledal – "little valley". Our bit is the "lower quarter" – the *barrio bajo* – while the "upper quarter", the *barrio alto*, is the settlement we came through at the summit.

Certainly, the house itself leaves much to be desired. It's at least 200 or 300 years old, built of porous sandstone with undulating Roman roof tiles. There's a single cold tap for the whole building and not even an outside privy; it's risky to venture upstairs because the floorboards are rotten, and the roof has partially collapsed; two barns that join the house to a neighbouring property also look ripe for demolition. There's half an acre or so around the house but, like most of these old farms, it's bisected by a track running right past the main front door. However, it loops back to the road – evidently, it serves only for access to the house and barns, and leads nowhere else. There's also a concrete lamp post right outside the front door.

Once word escapes that *forasteros* are interested, half a dozen villagers appear out of nowhere like fruit flies, just as unpredictable and not a lot more welcome. All are curious and eager to show willing.

Monchi's the first one to introduce himself with hearty slaps on the back, saying "*We're going to be great friends*". He tells us he owns the dwelling right behind, the one with a majestic walnut tree in the garden. "*My pension,*" he says, grinning, as I admire the magnificent specimen – it must be one of the biggest in the entire province… He and his wife Fátima also run a guest house just beyond.

Monchi ensures I know just where the boundaries run. Quadrangular stumps mark the corners, and, in a trice, he starts banging posts into the ground and stringing them together to outline the plot. When he reaches the front, he follows the edge of the track, rather than crossing it. Papí sees I'm bothered by that: "Don't worry about the track," he says, "you'll get that fixed soon enough. Just move it round the edge of your land and you won't hear another word. And even if you do, you can always…" (he rubs forefinger and thumb together in the air, suggestively) "…that never fails."

Another neighbour, a small, leather-skinned man called

Tomás with a burnt-out *Ducado* stub glued to his lower lip, shows the party round proprietorially. He's enjoying himself hugely, rushing round busily, leading me up the uneven stairs and emitting wheezy laughs at every cue.

I can't help noticing an ugly crack between the outside wall and the balcony. It looks bad, to my unskilled eye. I'm reassured by the agent, Benencio, though:

"*¡Eso no es na'!*" he says. "*That's nothin'!*"

Papí, the polymath, also claims it'll be easy to fix.

Also, there's that brutalist lamp post. Papí assumes it's the light I object to, saying that "*Yams'll fix it in no time with a catapult and a couple of stones*".

We plan to meet at the agent's office in an hour's time. But beforehand, José Angel suggests we visit the chapel at Santa Rita, down a track leading off the road just behind the house. "You'll love it!" he says, though he doesn't offer to join us. It would be a challenge even in his Nissan "*PAT-rol*", and his vital statistics could pose problems on foot. Papí, of course, is in no fit state for physical exertion of that kind.

Marina and I therefore make our way down alone. It's a steep, stony track into another bowl-shaped valley, backed by high hills and still heavily wooded. At the bottom, there's a large stone house, a *casona*, in poor shape. Nearby is the *capilla*, the lone chapel that José Angel was alluding to. It's a simple rectangle, probably seventeenth century, with a tower typical of the area, a stone arch above the façade with a crowning pediment, at the base of which a tree has seeded itself in the mortar. It looks precarious, roots wedged between the stones, contorted trunk and canopy cantilevered above. There's no discernible source of nourishment. Yet it has grown to a bushy seven or eight metres. It sways gently in the breeze like some idiosyncratic ensign.

The agent's office is in Villafranca del Conde, the small town by the coast 15 minutes away. Here, following a short council of war in a café, we decide to make an offer; later on, we learn that it's been accepted.

4

Everything's falling into place with indecent haste – a week ago, it was a vague project but now it looks as if, half intended, it might actually happen. Marina and I go to *El Politena* to take stock and, tentatively, to celebrate our impending purchase.

From our perch by the bar we hear English voices, a rare sound in these parts. When I swivel round to establish their source, I see a tall man who looks somehow familiar. He's obviously trying to place me, too. After overcoming our mutual reticence, it turns out this is Benedict, the owner of the English language school where I taught about a decade earlier. I haven't seen him since I let him down by oversleeping the 6 a.m. class – an ignominious debut to a nascent teaching career. Still, Benedict and his wife Jane don't seem to bear any ill will; instead, they enjoy teasing me about it.

"Blow me down if it's not my reliable old pedagogue friend!" Benedict exclaims. "Ten years, is it? Not still teaching, are we? If so, God help the pupils, dare I say!"

It seems he's still running the same school, plus a few new ones in other locations. I steer the subject from the history towards our current plans.

"Nice part of the country, that!" he declares about Valledal. "Right on the pilgrim route if I'm not mistaken. Nowadays everyone's forgotten the original route followed the coast… stands to reason when you remember the rest of Spain was in Moorish hands at the time. I'm talking about the eleventh century, by the way. I expect you even have a Pilgrims' Room in the house, if others round there are anything to go by."

"That area seems to have been spared most of the eucalyptus – the worst of it, anyway." It's Jane speaking now, not to be outdone by her loquacious husband. "You know about them, I take it?"

She tells the story, probably apocryphal, of how much of the coast came to be colonised by this antipodean species. According to her, during World War I, the Spaniards, neutral in that conflict, spotted the chance to sell their timber to the allies for trench props. Chestnut and oak were sent north by the trainload. Eucalyptus was the preferred replacement, thriving in the warm, humid climate, a bit of a visual blight, but quick-growing and fibrous, ideal for high quality paper. Luckily, it only grows in the immediate coastal area because, a short way inland, the terrain rises steeply, and the climate becomes too harsh.

"But if you really want to know about that area," Benedict interrupts, "you need to talk to Guillermo. Let me see if he's still here..." He disappears into the penumbra and presently returns with his friend, a stocky character with strawberry-blond hair.

"I hear you're buying in Valledal?" Guillermo asks. "Tell me more! Where, exactly?" When we describe it, he nods and adds: "Ah yes, I know the very spot. Delightful! I'll tell you all about it. I'm very familiar with the area. But sorry, I can't stop now. How'd you like to come to my house for a drink? Lunchtime tomorrow?"

Guillermo's house is reached via one of the valleys perpendicular to the coast, away from the busy eucalyptus strip. It dominates a small village about 15 kilometres from Bárcena. It's a memorable place: a proper seventeenth century *palacio* with arcades on the ground floor, a *mirador* above and a library inside.

Guillermo peppers us with questions about our deal but says little about Valledal. He does, however, expound on the famous 'Conde' whose title affixed itself to the historic name of 'Villafranca', our nearest town. This was the Conde de Maestegui, who played a key role in its transformation from humble fishing village to celebrated watering-hole. His masterstroke was to ensure the railway was routed inland, thereby preserving some of the *Belle Epoque* magic that might otherwise have vanished. It boasts a collection of mansions, of which the finest, a rare survival, enjoys a commanding view all round: it's a so-called *Casa de Indianos*, built by Maestegui himself in the 1890s, at the height of his fame as a tobacco baron. These days, however, the house belongs to the fabled dynasty of the moment, the Ruiz-Toledos, which they bring into service for the "*veraneo*", the brief summer season, when Villafranca's population swells from a handful to several thousand.

"Who's the agent?" Guillermo asks as he leads us to the car. When I say it's Benencio Bayona, he adds: "Pity! Had you said Casas Muguillo, I could perhaps have been helpful… I mean with the price you're paying. Muguillo's an old friend, you see, and he owes me!"

Next day our agent, Benencio, tracks us down by phone. He wants to know if we're really serious.

"Yes of course! Nothing's changed our end. Why?"

"Just that I took a call from someone saying he really wanted that house. When I told him it was under offer, he said he would pay more. He said he met you and claimed you wouldn't have the funds. I just wanted to know you're quite sure about it before I turn him down."

It takes a few seconds to realise the gazumper must be Guillermo.

When I explain this to José Angel, he's taken aback: "If it had been with Muguillo, I wouldn't have taken you near the place. Muguillo lost his job at one of the banks in Pueblo for embezzlement... After that, he became an estate agent. God knows what he's up to. But he's doing well, by all accounts."

5

A few months later, Mamí calls with news of Abuela's death. It's no surprise: she was well into her nineties; latterly, she spent her life dozing in her armchair, no longer even clicking her rosary.

There's little grief in evidence from Mamí: on the contrary, she seems quite pleased about it. According to Marina, the mother-daughter relationship was fraught all along and Mamí never ceased plotting her escape, even as a girl. That's why she married so young, seizing the first acceptable proposal (Papí) who, in addition to a comely profile, brought a one-way ticket to Africa.

But for all Abuela's quirks, Marina was devoted to her after all those years in her orbit, albeit under Aunt Macu's watchful eye. The following evening, therefore, she boards a plane home for the funeral.

On arrival, a scene of chaos greets her. But it's nothing to do with Abuela's death: the cause is brother Chus's imminent arrival. He just rang from Madrid saying he was on his way. He was in Bárcena only six months ago and generally, at least two years pass at a stretch without an appearance.

"But he shouldn't be here at all!" Mamí says. "What'll everyone think? No job or what? I don't believe he came for the funeral – I only sent the telegram yesterday... Crafty as ever, your brother! He made that up on the spot! Once he realised what happened... He can't have known.

Anyway, they never liked one another. No, no, there's something else going on and I don't like it!"

It does seem unlikely that Chus would rush home for his grandmother's funeral, even without the logistical challenge involved.

Whatever, Chus brings his usual high spirits, regaling his audience with implausible anecdotes of the jungle. mostly involving guns, alcohol and women in varying permutations. He bills himself as a seasoned habitué of the African jungle, fearless action man and irresistible lothario. The family half-listens, bored and incredulous. How often have they swallowed this kind of hogwash?

On the eve of the funeral, Chus disappears on one his legendary binges. These are all-night affairs with the Fan Club and, though it's mandatory for such occasions to run until first light (anything less would be embarrassing), Chus would normally appear for a restorative preprandial at the bar the next day. But there's no sign of him this time. In a moment of panic, Mamí decides to send out his younger siblings to track him down.

As they leave, she says: "Now listen! You must be very careful, understand what I mean? I don't want you saying Chus has gone missing or may have drunk too much, or anything like that. Just say we need his help with the preparations. I don't want questions, not at a time like this, not at a time of such trial..." she adds, with a timely tear in her eye.

Sancho and Marta trawl Chus's haunts to no avail – he was spotted at several favourites early in the morning but after that, the trail runs cold. There's no sign of him when the time comes for the funeral.

The funeral's a first-class affair, starting in the church and afterwards at Bárcena's cemetery on a knoll outside town. The crowd is huge. The Pinar cousins, Blascos and

Expósitos are almost all on parade – even the elusive Cousin Puri, the nun – with the notable absence of Chus, whose presence in Bárcena is now well known. Then the mourners decamp to the cemetery, a rectangular, whitewashed construction ringed by cypresses and bougainvillea. Inside, there is a little garden with slots for coffins on all sides, some empty, some sealed. Only once Abuela is safely stowed in her drawer does Chus reappear. He is awaiting the returning family on the doorstep at home, dishevelled and minus one shoe.

The backstory gradually emerges. Chus, it transpires, is no longer in Guinea. He moved on to neighbouring Gabon. Despite his sorry appearance, he's puffed up with his habitual optimism. The conditions are so much better, the trees so much taller and the opportunities so much greater! He has signed up with *Concessionnaires Africaines, S.A., "CASA"*, a top, top, top firm, where his experience will be properly valued, and the money is extraordinary. Then, as an afterthought, with a laugh and a half-wink for my benefit he adds: "And my new girlfriend? She's truly *despanpanante*"![7]

It's a step too far even for Mamí: "Is that all you think about? Can't you keep your pants on for five minutes? Not even sober for your grandmother's funeral? What are they going to say? Make yourself scarce right now!"

The 30-year-old Chus retires meekly to his bedroom upstairs.

Then suddenly Mamí wheels round to Marina: she deserves her share of the blame, despite her neutrality, or perhaps because of it. It's unforgivable for her not to have leapt to her brother's defence.

"And what have you ever done for your brother? You

---

[7] A knockout

and your tall stories, ever since I can remember. And what have you ever done for me? With your foreign airs, your studies, your know-it-all husband. You've no idea what your brother's been through…"

No, Marina has no idea what he's been through, unless Mamí means his African upbringing, during which Chus, the only white boy, was made to play the clown for the adults' amusement and was plied with drink by the rabble in the *patio* well before his tenth birthday. That's Marina's contention, at least. On return from Africa, the favoured son joined his parents at the new house in Bárcena, while his sister was despatched to convent school as a boarder. While she was away, Chus allegedly rifled through her belongings seeking funds for his many habits – an accusation roundly dismissed as "*impossible*" by his mother.

The following day, a telegram arrives from Bata, signed off by Papí's youngest brother, *Masa* Sote. In a few short lines it offers sympathy to Abuela's family; states that nobody knows where Chus has gone; and reveals he was "let go" by the company (but, tantalisingly, with no details).

6

Dear Jack,

That was a good idea of yours to meet half-way, though I must say, I'd expected more from Alcázar de los Caballeros. Such a sonorous name for that fly-blown joint! But the Templar church, the lechazo[8] and your company made it all worthwhile. All in all, a great occasion and I'm glad the news on the venture is good. There's no question that you've tapped into a craze for the English language. Good timing!

---

[8] Suckling lamb

As expected, soon after I got back here from Alcázar, the moment arrived to sign the escrituras[9] *for the house we're buying. That part went broadly to plan, though we hadn't reckoned on a swingeing property tax nobody had mentioned before. Then, when the time came to sign the deeds, the official demanded my* carnet.[10] *When I confessed I didn't own any such thing, he snapped: "What do you mean, you don't have an identity card? Without an ID card, how do you know who you are?"*

Fortunately, it turned out my passport would suffice, but I needed an official translation, which, happily, we secured in short order. However, there were other shocks in store.

To set the ball rolling with the works, we fixed a date in Valledal with the builders (my father-in-law's friends). Up until now, we've been wary of the neighbours: they're a bit over-eager and intrusive. But this time we made a more promising acquaintance: Socorro, alias "Soco", who lives with her husband and son on the other side of the field in front of the house, across the "Valledal" that lends its name to the village. It's at least a hundred metres across, but we hear everything, whether it's donkeys a-braying, scythes a-sharpening or radios a-blaring. I expect we could eavesdrop from the garden on still days. Sound travels both ways, so presumably the commotion prompted her visit.

Soco fits the archetype of a rotund, rubicund farmer's wife. We watched her stately progress down the hill towards us. She's friendly and talkative and it took no time to break the ice. Since the builders hadn't arrived, we went indoors to show her round – though it turned out she already

---

[9] Property Deeds
[10] Identity Card

knew the house better than we do.

"But why do you want to come here of all places?"

"Well, partly because this is where I come from," Marina said, hoping to turn her provenance to advantage.

"You, from here? How so?"

"Bodegas Pinar – that's my family."

"Aha! Bodegas Pinar if you please! That may be, but then you certainly are not from here, as I thought," Soco replied. *"Not even I am from here. I'm from Río Escondido. Yes, it's only two kilometres over the hill but as far as Valledal's concerned, I'm* forastera*! I'm certainly not from here. And you know what? I think they're right. Totally different mentality up here. I won't say which is better, but here's a clue: there used to be a path down to the beach. Then the villagers cut it off – didn't want an 'invasion', that's the story, especially by these so-called 'pilgrims' that pass this way nowadays. So expect a certain caution towards outsiders. But don't let me influence you. You can tell me what you think in a few years' time."*

There was nowhere to sit inside, so Soco asked us to come for a drink at her place once we'd dispatched the builders. We could hear them slamming the van doors outside.

The meeting with the builders revealed a chasm that starts with basic terminology. We plan to "restore" the place; they intend to "rebuild" it, with major ramifications in terms of cost. In the interests of character, we hope to salvage wonky windows and doors, leave bulges and imperfections in the walls and retain the so-called lumbre, *the hooded fireplace in the kitchen used for smoking hams and sausages, which, the builders tell us "has to go": "es* un trasto",[11] *as they phrase it. They want to expunge all signs of the past, which, for most people round here, remind them of the drudgery and poverty they've hardly left behind.*

Suddenly, one of the builders had a brainwave.

"Aha!" he said, "I know what you mean... Estilo rústico:[12] *Got it!" At which he rushed off to the van and returned, clutching a brochure from a builders' merchant and a handful of photos of a job they had completed a while before.*

Estilo rústico, *however, was not what we had in mind. Imagine the aesthetics of Fred Flintstone crossed with Asterix the Gaul – a cartoonish fusion of Stone Age and Celtic – and you'll understand why it wasn't right. They looked a bit crestfallen.*

We were back to the drawing board. The only thing we could agree on was demolition of the two barns linking us to the neighbours and rebuilding the roof, to staunch the leaks. We can lay new flooring from another block of tropical timber contributed by Papí. The stone from the barns can be reused for a wall round the back, thereby separating us more cleanly from Monchi and co.

Once they'd gone, we made our way up to Soco's place. It's a classic pocket-sized farmhouse that makes few concessions to comfort: half the ground floor hosts a dozen cows and milking equipment. Next door is a dark sitting room, almost no natural light, with a couple of sofas, shiny from use, a few shelves bedecked with garish ornaments, and a gaping TV set in pride of place (always on, loud). Worst of all is the kitchen, where, from a glimpse through

---

[11] Piece of crap
[12] Rustic style

the doorway, cooking takes place on a cast iron range. Whenever Soco opened the door, steam billowed into the sitting room, carrying the aroma of whatever she was preparing for supper.

The rest of the family appeared briefly – milking doesn't wait, so we earned no more than cursory grunts. Soco's son is called Miguel and, confusingly, her husband is known by the diminutive "Miguelín". While that's consistent with their stature (young Miguel takes after his mother) it's mildly disconcerting for the father to be the "little" one. That's why they address their son Miguel as "Chato", a kind of generic sobriquet meaning "flat-nose", I gather.

Soon, we were talking about our purchase again. We still hadn't satisfied her basic question: why here of all places? Soco thought everyone wanted to get out of here, as fast as possible. There's no school, no shop, no bar (except in summer) and above all, no future for the young. And is it really worth rebuilding one of these old farms? Wouldn't it be better to build anew? That's what she's doing! That is, if her sale goes through – she's received an offer for one of her fields.

Then, unwittingly, she rolled a depth charge overboard.

"You've heard of Santa Rita? They're the ones buying my field. That's the project just down the hill. You could have reserved one of the nice new villas down there! They'll be amazing."

The local searches, such as they were, revealed the boundaries, the water supply, the electricity connection, and the absence of a sewage system. There were no rights of way other than the track in front and nothing much else to worry about. But nobody mentioned a giant development on the doorstep! What about José Angel? What about Papí? Weren't our advisers, our guardians of local lore, supposed to know everything about the area? José Angel even sent us down to look at the chapel! Moreover, the area is supposed to be a "Natural Park", whatever that means.

Soco, though, is delighted about Santa Rita. It'll turn this moribund backwater into "a new Miami", quite apart from bringing buyers for her fields, some of which lie just where the golf course will be. We didn't contradict her: with luck, she'll be an ally in the village and she'd think we were completely deranged, subversive even, if we showed signs of opposing the development. It promises to make her rich. I know just how sensitive such subjects are, having flirted rupture with Mamí's neighbour Curro (married to her great friend, the illustrious Nunci), by deploring free-for-all development along the coast. Curro tarred me as both elitist and lefty for such views… In his book, the land's theirs, why shouldn't they do as they please?

Next day, we had an appointment at the town hall in Tobillo, capital of the comarca to which Valledal belongs, to progress our bid to move the track by the house. As it happens, Monchi's father, Alberto, is president of the Junta Vecinal (parish council) for the village, one of half a dozen wards. When we discussed it with Alberto, he made encouraging noises and Tomás also agreed that there "shouldn't be any trouble".

About the only inside intelligence we have (our enchufe) is from Rosuca, who happens to be a cousin of Marina's and holds the post of assistant to the mayor in Tobillo. That's how we were able to fix up an audience at such short notice.

When we met the mayor, we tabled our idea of diverting the track round the edge. Everything will be sited on our land, and it will mean a small detour for the few people who use it.

The mayor sucked his teeth ominously as we explained.

"Difficult," he said at last, "these things always are difficult. You say you've got support from Don Alberto? That's a start; but expect opposition. It really doesn't matter if anyone's inconvenienced or not. They just won't like it. They won't like it because they don't like change; they won't like it because there's nothing in it for them. But I'll bring it up at the next meeting. I'll need proper drawings, though... prepared to professional standards, by an aparejador.*"*[13]

Then we asked him what he could tell us about Santa Rita.

"Want to see the plans?" he said, lighting up the room with a sudden beam. I suspect it's his favourite topic, you can be sure there's lucre for him somewhere. Perhaps the promoters issued a few shares to him, or promised him a cut-price villa, to keep him sweet, or possibly he has deals with the building firms. He called Rosuca and told her to bring out the plans, which she fetched from a filing cabinet and spread out on a table in the next room.

It took a few moments to find our house. The planned development is truly ambitious – on a totally different scale from anything else round here. There will be scores of "chalés"*, some detached, some terraced, laid out round a new golf course. Right in the centre, the old casona we visited a few months ago is the nexus of the whole enterprise.*

---

[13] Surveyor

66

It's destined to be the clubhouse. The chapel with the little tree seeded in the tower masonry, where it waves in the breeze, has been hijacked as a logo. According to the mayor, the golf course will meet "championship standards" and he expects the first bulldozers to get to work "within a year to 18 months" smoothing out the ground and getting rid of much despised maleza *– undergrowth, fallen leaves, scrub… or more simply, plain, bothersome, nature.*

Even Papí looked a bit sheepish when we brought him up to date. There's no hiding from his and José Angel's ignorance about the Santa Rita project. After all, it must have been in the papers. But he's more sanguine about the track. In his view, the mayor's "difficult" is simply his way of pitching for a backhander to push it through: "Of course he doesn't want it to sound easy! Otherwise, why would you pay him?" The thought restored his mettle.

"Anyway, I've always said we should just get on and do it! Nobody can possibly object. Let's just cut the mayor's cut!" he says, rather pleased with the turn of phrase.

Since then, we unearthed a bit more about Santa Rita. It's backed by some big beasts, including the illustrious Ruiz-Toledos, owners of Bárcena's textile factory and related by marriage to Mamí's best friend Nunci next door. We also discover that one of the promoters is that strange fellow I told you about, the redhead who tried to gazump us…

Assuming we get all this sorted out I hope I'll persuade you to come and inspect the damage in the not-too-distant future.

Abrazos, Rico.

7

One thing that surprised Marina on her trip for Abuela's funeral was her brother Chus's eager pursuit of a divorce from Conchi Palacio. In the past, whenever the shadow of bureaucracy loomed, Chus had showed himself a true disciple of the *Chapuza* School of Filing & Administration. It was a given he would ignore any trouble of this sort until the bailiffs or the *Guardia Civil* turned up on the doorstep. On this occasion, though, he took the *Talgo* sleeper to Madrid to sort it out in person.

Now we know why: Chus has remarried. The lucky bride is Titi, that Gabonese girlfriend, the one he described as *"despanpanante"* at an ill-judged moment. We're promised a first meeting with Titi later in the year.

It's Christmas, and Marina's sister Marta (in charge of logistics nowadays) reminds us to bring the *"meenth-eh-PEE-ess"* (mince pies), which caused such a stir a couple of years back. Now we need a special suitcase for them, along with a growing list of favourites including brandy butter, smoked salmon, Christmas pudding and so on, all of which seem to be popular, despite the dire reputation of British cuisine. Mamí makes sure we remember neighbour Nunci (a compulsory visit, not to be made empty-handed); and we're about to set a further precedent by extending the bounty to Soco and family.

On arrival, Papí gives us a taste of progress on our project: "You won't recognise the place! The bulldozers have done their work and the new track's built. Not a squeak out of anyone, as expected…"

That includes us, as it happens. Papí was as good as his word, for once, to *"get on and do it"*. We had no idea. But our inspection will have to follow the Bárcena round, a duty for the first morning of every visit.

There are two mandatory stops on the tour, the *bodega* and the bank; it should be over within an hour if we start early. But it's seldom that simple and we're out of sync with Bárcena rhythms, where nothing starts early, nothing happens quickly, and the unforeseen always intervenes. We're hijacked by encounters on the street (the standard greeting already *"when are you leaving?"*) and there's not much I can do to thwart Marina's dives into her favourite emporia. For she subscribes to that controversial theorem that a bargain is tantamount to a saving.

Thus, by the time we reach the bank at Plaza Ruiz-Toledo No. 1, the queue snakes right back to the door, meaning that, when we reach our new friend, the trainee teller Asun at the counter, we can't avoid airing our affairs in public. There's always suspense as Asun prints off a copy of our statement, because payments are outsourced to Aunt Macu, and, increasingly, she's remiss about keeping us informed.

Today, we're horrified to see our balance only a whisker clear of negative territory. Our account needs an urgent transfusion before the cheques start bouncing.

"But why didn't anyone tell us we were running this low?"

"I advised your aunt about it. She said the pound sterling wasn't what it used to be. But yes, I would advise you to make a transfer in the next day or two."

Unless I'm imagining things, there are a few knowing smirks, 'tut-tuts' even, among the waiting customers as we steer our way back past the queue onto the street and from there to the *bodega* for an explanation.

"Oh, I meant to tell you about that," Aunt Macu says. "Your father sent the diggers in, which had to be paid for and it's a costly business: I made sure there was enough in the account to cover it. Always best to pay one's bills on time!"

"But…" Marina starts, then drops it. There's no doubt she's taken aback, though, as she tells me on the way to Valledal. Aunt Macu would never have been so dilatory, so casual, in the past. She may be difficult, but she's supposed to be the incarnation of dependability and economy!

As we come down the hill into the village, we're greeted by an inflatable Santa shinning up one of the balconies with a sack over his back. The parish has looped together several speakers, which hang from the lampposts. These rehearse a menu of children's carols, *"Campanas de Belén"*, *"Los Peces en el Río"* and other classics, on a perpetual loop.

The first sign of activity at the house at Valledal takes the form of a huge orange digger, its steel paw arched over the garden in suspended animation. It has already clawed a path through the mud for the new track, but the work looks far from finished. Meanwhile, the original track remains intact. Between them, a tuft of greenery survives, an island in a sea of mud; next to it is the concrete lamp post, a solitary exclamation mark. The two collapsing barns joining us to our immediate neighbour have gone. Papí was certainly right that we'd barely recognise the place.

The interior, on the other hand, seems broadly unchanged. That's the problem. Not much progress has been made since the summer, despite the financial haemorrhage.

Up at Soco's house our new friend folds us into her bosom one by one. The house and barn are winking with Christmas lights and decorations. Even the cows have tinsel round their horns, to six-year-old Clara's delight – she has a special love for them, which she gratifies by helping with the milking. Dotted about the house are baskets of sweets of the Spanish variety: tooth-extracting *turrón*, croup-inducing *polvorones*, and diabetes-triggering *yemas*. Soco serves *calimochos*, a blend of Coke and red wine, for which she proudly uses top-of-the-range *Tinto del Abuelo* from *Bodegas Pinar*. Everything takes place to the accompaniment of a TV show. It's the lottery results, sung by choirboys, prize-by-prize. The men of the house follow raptly from the sofa, checking the numbers against their chits, cursing in disappointment at any near miss.

Soco tells us that our work on the track has caused quite a stir here in Valledal. She can't hide a mischievous grin when she tells us this.

"Two of your neighbours came out to protest... I could hear them from up here yelling "*¿Qué coño hacéis?*"[14] and such like. The digger kept on working for a bit until I thought it would get nasty."

"Who was complaining?" I ask.

"One of them was certainly Tomás, and Monchi was there, too, letting Tomás do the talking. I think your immediate neighbours, the old couple Gusti and Dolores, might have been watching, but I couldn't hear them. Monchi's father, Alberto, came after a bit, trying to calm things down. That was about a week ago, since when the digger hasn't budged."

"It's the first we heard of it."

"Didn't you receive a letter?"

"Not that we know of. We thought the work was done."

"Well, check inside the house," Soco suggests.

It's now dark, there's no light in the house and we can barely see by the orange glow from the lamp post outside the front door. There's a lot of rubbish in the entrance all scrambled up with leaves, but no letters. However, we do

---

[14] "What the f*** are you doing?"

discover a letterbox outside. It's a rusty green affair screwed to the back of the lamp post. We don't have a key, but we manage to prise several waterlogged missives from inside, one of which bears the official crest of the *Ayuntamiento de Tobillo*, the town hall. It's a fiercely worded instruction to desist from all work on the track forthwith unless otherwise notified and on no account to disturb any existing rights of way.

That rather dampens our spirits. But meeting Titi back in Bárcena takes our minds off it. She's tall and willowy, statuesque even, but not exactly *despanpanante*. Not at all Chus's busty type, we think, but perhaps he's changing? Settling down at last? Titi speaks next to nothing but French, which makes for stilted communication. But we can all see she's well on the way to producing an heir to the eldest son and a cousin for Clara and James.

"*¡Bueno, bueno, bueno!*"[15] Mamí remarks, as if the implications have only just sunk in. "I already have two English grandchildren. Now I'll have an African one too! *¡Madre mía!*"

8

Shortly before our arrival later in the New Year the family suffers another bereavement. It's Uncle Toño this time, long since a spectre and clearly struggling with the job at the *Bulletin.* He drops dead in the street in Madrid, outside that bedsit I once stayed at. Mamí transmits the news, telling Marina not to come – the funeral will be a "*third class affair*," she says. We do, however, make the trip for what is indeed a pitiful event, with scarcely two rows of mourners in the cavernous church.

---

[15] well, well, well

"*¡Bah! ¡Cuatro gatos!*"[16] Mamí opines, "as expected. That's why I told you not to come…"

But I, for one, will miss Uncle Toño. I enjoyed our escapades to *El Politena*, where he would buy me a *caña* (draught beer) or a *carajillo* and continue my education on the niceties of the Spanish language. It's only a few months since he was railing against the pollution of the language by the creeping adoption of foreign orthography – the letters "*k*" and "*w*" being targets for special excoriation.

"We always got on well without them," he said. "Take the word *güisqui*, for example. It's orthographically and phonetically perfect like that. Why do we now meddle with a whole system by writing it as '*whisky*'? Just to please Europe? And what's wrong with '*quiosco*'? Or, for that matter, '*quilómetro*'? And I realise our upside-down punctuation make you foreigners laugh, but that's logical, too: it lets you know what to expect…" Those were among the last words he said to me, so very much in character.

Apart from that unsatisfactory bed and a stash of still valid lottery tickets, Uncle Toño's sole asset of value is his stake in the *bodega*. That prompts Aunt Macu to take further steps to secure its future. She argues that it's vital to consolidate family interests, and to that end, proposes that her sisters now transfer their shares to her outright, including their share of Uncle Toño's inheritance. The argument is the same as before – about keeping control, not leaving anything to chance. Another visit to the *notario* ensures that the transfers are executed, leaving Aunt Macu undisputed Queen of the Pinar Vázquez interests. Her sisters are paid a lump sum and promised a monthly stipend by way of compensation.

"Of course, you'll still get a dividend; only it'll come

---

[16] "Four cats", i.e., pitiful turnout

from me, not directly from the *bodega*."

By now there are a few signs of progress in the house. The dismissal of Papí's builders caused a minor stir (belonging as they do to Bárcena's élite) but the new ones seem less dogmatic: they scratch their heads in puzzlement at some of our notions, but consent to leave most of the fixtures untouched, including the *lumbre*, the traditional fireplace, a rare survivor in the village.

It's clear that damp in various guises, rising, condensing, penetrating, poses a perennial challenge in old houses like this. One corner of the house is tucked into the higher ground to the rear; the entire stonework rests on clay, seemingly without foundations; and the porous sandstone sucks up water like blotting paper. Soco tells us that everyone round here "*just lives with it*"; it's true that our inquiries about damp courses and similar techniques are greeted with bafflement. They must know it's insoluble, short of rebuilding from scratch.

A scar still testifies to Papí's new track, gradually vanishing beneath a carpet of nettles and thistles sprouting from the rutted ground. The few saplings planted over the winter – orange and lemon trees as well as the more obvious fig, chestnut and walnut – look spindly and vulnerable, but still viable. We add two holm oaks at the far end of the garden where it meets the road into the village. In time, these should help clothe the denuded landscape. We also plant an evergreen magnolia where the barns used to be, but this prompts a rare encounter with our immediate neighbours, the elusive couple, Gusti and Dolores, who must be 70 plus.

Dolores pops up from behind the wall, wagging an index finger at me, her way of telling me the plant must be moved further back.

She doesn't articulate – she just knows I'm a *forastero*,

who won't understand. I often find the locals refuse to try *on principle*. But it's not just me. Even Marina's affected by this phenomenon. She sometimes faces quizzical looks when speaking to her compatriots, accompanied by questions along the lines of: "*Where are you from? Your Spanish really isn't bad, you know? Almost no accent at all! Congratulations!*" Another time, having lent the house key to a workman, we return to find he'd attached a tag to it, labelled '*Marina la Inglesa*'. I've infected her; she's becoming an outsider just like me.

Down at Santa Rita there's activity too. Apart from bulldozers flattening the ground in various directions, surveyors dot the land, wielding tripods and theodolites. The bosky, unkempt valley with its thick undergrowth and reminders of an unforgiving past gradually yields to the type of sanitised, curated landscape everyone prefers. Scaffolding surrounds the future clubhouse. Only the chapel, still flagging its solitary sapling, remains untouched. Its stylised image adorns many a sign dotted about the site: "*Próxima construcción de chalés y campo de golf*".

It's early days; but a quiet stoicism has taken root. In the evening light, with Soco's son Chato prodding the cattle, bells clanging, down to fresh grass with a switch, it all still looks pastoral. The swifts swoop and screech in the dusk; then the first bats appear, and the fireflies start to wink as the light drains away.

Chapter III: Heir Conditioning

1

The family business, *Bodegas Sancho Pinar*, is a lodestar in the Bárcena firmament. Aunt Macu keeps reminding us about that, recapping the unique history of this, the oldest business in the province. A favourite refrain is how *"we kept half the village going during the War"* (the *Civil* War, she means) and another how *"we were selling wine soon after we drove out Napoleon, for heaven's sake!"* While both are exaggerations, they underline the point that this is a venerable institution, in a class of its own with a reputation as such in the whole province.

To make sure the message is not lost on me, to make quite sure I realise the good fortune that brought me into its orbit, Aunt Macu takes advantage of a short interlude one morning when I find myself alone with her in the kiosk while Marina's out bargain-hunting.

"I hope you realise just how lucky you are to have married my niece? Perhaps you don't know: the Ruiz-Toledos approached us a few years ago… They wanted to buy a stake!"

Call it unappreciative on my part, but I'd never really thought of Marina as a *"braguetazo"*, to borrow the local vernacular – "a large knickersful" being the literal translation or, more idiomatically, a "big catch".

"No, I had no idea about that."

"But you do know who I mean, I suppose? The family that owns Bárcena's largest business, the textile factory. There's even a square named after them. Perhaps it's a coincidence, but that's where you'll find the bank."

"So what became of the approach?"

"Couldn't agree terms, for better or worse. They didn't

fully value our *solera* trade. So we agreed to disagree. Perhaps it's for the best. Not easy, the Ruiz-Toledos."

But it's not only Aunt Macu who believes in the business. Outsiders also extol its virtues. In our dealings with local tradesmen, the simple words "*send the account to Bodegas Pinar*" ensure that any qualms about our creditworthiness evaporate. And even Soco, a barometer in such matters, may have questioned Marina's local credentials, but never the prestige of *Bodegas Pinar*.

At a time of mass unemployment, the prospect of a job with the family firm has strong appeal for the young, once they've shaken off any lingering idealism. To Papí's disappointment (he had him earmarked for Africa), Marina's younger brother Sancho was first to tread this path, aged just 16. The role was a lowly one. Sancho, for all his charm and quiet erudition, failed to shine at school and in Aunt Macu's book, that's a big handicap. For almost a decade, Sancho has been loading up the lorries, sending them on their way panting and belching up the cloudy valleys every morning with supplies for the smallest and most remote bars in the province. It's heavy, physical work, and consequently, Sancho's now "*built like a wardrobe*" as his sister puts it.

Recently, however, Aunt Macu made a significant concession. In future, Sancho would accompany the lorries in person. In so doing, he would learn the art of *solera* management, the process whereby the barrels are topped-up *in situ* and, by dint of graft and craft, prevented from spoiling. Aunt Macu thus transformed her nephew's prospects: not only will he master the trade; but he'll also meet the clients, the proprietors of bars not just in Bárcena and immediate environs, but in countless villages across the countryside. Together, these comprise the bedrock of the affair.

Sancho is taking his role-change as a promotion and eagerly awaiting the moment his aunt will divulge the long-promised pay rise. But nothing happens. The weeks go by, until he can no longer contain himself and summons the courage to broach the subject: "Aunt, I wondered… can you let me know about my pay sometime soon?"

"What is there to say on the subject? I never said anything about a pay rise, did I? No, no, I don't think that would be right, not right at all. Far too soon! This is a vocation, not a mere job or a money-grubbing scheme. And don't forget: you're extremely privileged already. Which of your friends has your prospects, I'd like to know? Least of all after flunking their exams! Maybe in three, four years, once you've shown you can do the job properly, we'll think about it."

Sancho's disillusion is palpable. But Aunt Macu's right: he has few choices, and in any case, the new role is a big upgrade on the previous one.

Marina often warns me not to be fooled by Aunt Macu's studied mildness in my presence. According to Marina, it's a front. Even so, it's a surprise to catch Aunt Macu in mid-rant one day, the butt of her anger once again being Sancho: "But I've told you before! Countless times! Didn't you see it coming? No clues? No revealing body language? You tell me now, now, when it's too late to do anything about it. Had I known, of course I wouldn't have let them steal a client under our very noses like that! Fast asleep, are you? No business sense at all? To think I do all this for you! And you expect a pay rise? Those fools at Polín will regret it! *Aurelio's* wines may be cheap, but it's for a reason… They're up to here!"

She squeezes her own throat in her right hand to signify asphyxiation, presumably implying financial stress.

"So it might save Polín a few *duros* in the short term, but not for long! Don't they know the wine comes from Morocco? Third rate only because there's no fourth! Their customers will desert them in droves, make no mistake! They don't even have *soleras* anymore!"

Sancho's just the messenger, reporting the loss of a valued client to a rival. The fact that it's Casa Polín, Papí's favourite bar, and the offending competitor is the ancestral rival, *Vinos Aurelio*, makes it extra painful.

As soon as she sees me in the background, Aunt Macu changes tack – these demonstrations of rage are reserved for nephews and nieces. Instead, she resorts to repetition of bromides, how "*we've never borrowed anything, always paid on time…*" and that those like *Aurelio* who live beyond their means will "*pay the price*". Not forgetting that they trade out of Tobillo, of all the boondocks.

Apparently, there's a history with *Aurelio* that makes their recent success doubly galling… a split in the family a few generations back. A younger branch of the Pinars, a grandson of Pinar's founder via the distaff line, one Aurelio Caudal, set up the rival. Whatever Aunt Macu claims or hopes, *Aurelio* seems to be prospering – boasting a swish new fleet of trucks and an up-to-date facility that makes *Pinar* look antiquated. Annoyingly, it doesn't seem to matter that it's a relative upstart, doesn't enjoy the Pinar name, turned its back on the traditional *solera* trade, and bears the stigma of cheerless Tobillo.

Moreover, there have been a few run-ins over the last few years, some of them public. There was the time *Aurelio* stole the contract from Pinar to supply the wine for the *fiestas,* breaking decades of tradition. (Aunt Macu's verdict: "*Of course, they bribed the mayor*").

Another time, she suffered personal humiliation at the bank, of all places, where she's generally feted as an esteemed customer. Standing at the guichet as Asun counted her wodge of thousand peseta notes, Aunt Macu watched as Don Emilio, the bank manager, approached, arms outstretched to greet his honoured client. She beamed; but at the last moment Don Emilio cruised straight past, his gaze locked on bigger fry at the other counter behind her. Had the favoured client been a Ruiz-Toledo, she might have endured the slight; but she watched with indignation as the greeting was instead offered to none other than Gonzalo Caudal, owner of *Vinos Aurelio*, who the manager wrapped in an effusive *abrazo*. Deep down, Aunt Macu's jealous that Caudal owns the entire *Aurelio* enterprise. None of this haggling with awkward family members for him!

Aunt Macu's probably feeling vulnerable following another sudden death in the family – this time José Angel, her cousin from the Pinar Mogro side, the one who found the house in Valledal for us, who collapsed one day on one of his client visits, right in the middle of the bar, among so many people he knew and loved. All those years in the wine trade, with his responsibility for clients, exacted a toll, especially on his liver. Attending the funeral for this popular Bárcena figure is one of our first duties on arrival in Bárcena this year. Sancho's *de facto* promotion surely has something to do with it.

José Angel's share of the *bodega* falls to his two spinster sisters, Chábeli and Adelina. Since childhood, neither has ventured inside the *bodega*, but they've always derived a good living from it. Though born in Bárcena, they long since took refuge in the provincial capital and, consciously or not, have developed a patronising air towards their birthplace. In particular, the anachronistic *bodega* and its eccentricities provide a fund of stories for their parties, in which a caricature of Aunt Macu plays a key part. Echoes of their mockery found a way back to her via José Angel.

That's why Aunt Macu not only misses José Angel's support and contacts but worries over her flighty and entitled cousins, who may now loom larger in the *bodega's* affairs. She barely hides her disdain when they appear unannounced one morning, catching her in her booth, surrounded by the paraphernalia of office life, as she painstakingly writes up the ledger by hand.

"We thought we should take a fresh look now we're involved," Chábeli says, causing her cousin to start involuntarily.

"Of course... I'll ask Sancho to show you round…" she responds. "It's been a while, hasn't it? But let's keep the arrangement we had with your brother, shall we? I see no reason to change the annual get-together. Then I can bring you properly up to speed and we'll agree the dividend as usual." Then, sensing the incipient frowns forming across their smooth brows, she reluctantly adds: "Of course, any ideas are more than welcome."

For a few months, a stream of helpful suggestions issues from the two sisters, evidently discovering their business acumen for the first time. These range from the mundane "*need for a thorough clean-up*" at the *bodega* to the pharaonic "*chain of bars across the province*" which they think would "*make the most of our reputation.*" But there's no discussion of cost or who'll meet it. They even question whether there's a better way of keeping the books "*instead of writing them up by hand*".

"And how would I know whose fault it is if there's a mistake?" responds a now needled Aunt Macu to this last suggestion. It sounds plausible enough, except that she's the only person allowed to touch the ledgers in the first place (her own rule). That's how it's been for over 20 years and she's the one with the sole silver key to the glass cabinet behind her desk, where the ledgers, running back almost to 1846, are stowed whenever she's out. Her question is therefore moot.

Of course, she's under no illusion that her ways aren't outdated. Typewriters are hardly new and she's aware there are even better tools nowadays. The real motive is that she enjoys forming the elegant cursive that flows from one page to the next. Each ledger is a work of art, like a medieval manuscript. It's also one of her links to the past, heightening her sense of belonging to a tradition that reaches back to a time when wine was brought over the *cordillera* by mule in pigskins. Today's leather-bound ledger looks little different from the early ones, except it is not yet twisted out of shape or discoloured by damp.

Aunt Macu deals with each suggestion scrupulously and correctly: "*Good idea. We'll look into it.*" She knows the novelty will fade and their interest will wane; and before long, she's proved right. Their interest is superficial; just so long as the dividend arrives on time.

2

Meanwhile, another member of the clan, Aunt Ludi's third eldest, Domingo, who looks like an El Greco apostle, with his triangular skull, sallow complexion and watery eyes, has also joined the firm. He had long been angling to do so and, unlike his cousin Sancho, Domingo's a gifted student, excelling effortlessly and boasting *sobresaliente* (outstanding) in almost every subject. Moreover, he has a degree in food science and a season's experience at one of the top winemakers in Argentina. These credentials impress even Aunt Macu. She decides he'd make an ideal apprentice and, who knows? In ten, or – on second thoughts – 20 years' time he might be ready to assume some of her own duties.

However, Aunt Macu seems unaware of the whole story of Domingo's apprenticeship. Had he stuck with his original tale that, after the harvest (March to April in the southern hemisphere) there was little for him to do, everyone would have accepted his early return without demur. But Domingo rashly confided in his gossipy brother, Julito, that his departure had not been altogether amicable. Julito then decanted the secret into another leaky vessel, his aunt Gloriuca, and from there, it soon became common knowledge among all the close family, including housekeeper Nuria, but excluding, apparently, Aunt Macu herself – the one person who might have benefited from it.

According to the Argentines, not only was Domingo "*by no means a team player*", but his wilful interference in the wine-making process had "*caused the company material loss*". For Domingo may look seraphic thanks to his pallor, his big, mournful, eyes and long-suffering frown, but his behaviour is sometimes far from saintly. He's a tortured soul, short on emotional intelligence, unrealistic, and at the same time, fiercely ambitious and sure of his intellectual prowess. Despite his somewhat gauche and gawky demeanour, he's ambitious and pushy.

Before he joined the *bodega*, Domingo shared all sorts of notions – Sancho his preferred audience – about how *Bodegas Pinar* should "*turn into a proper business*". He, too, had ideas for new products, going upmarket, going down market, moving the warehouse, turning it into a bar, reducing the workforce, expanding it... Once on the payroll, however, Domingo soon realised his aunt wasn't interested.

"Yes, yes, that may be but what we need now is to concentrate on the task in hand. Have you found those invoices yet? I need them right now. They're long overdue."

The armchair strategist shrivelled back into diffidence

in her company.

A few months into the job Domingo confides in Sancho what torture it is sharing that claustrophobic little box with his aunt. Not only is the work tedious, but worse, he finds himself co-opted into her routine, unable to escape scrutiny day in, day out. If she notices him gazing vacantly at the wall, she snaps him out of his reverie. If he requests time off, even when ill, it generally earns short shrift. Macu refuses to take holidays (*"never have in 30 years and I'm not starting now"*) and never misses a day for illness, however infectious (*"usually malingering, in my experience. Best cure is nearly always an honest day's work"*). Such statements brook no discussion.

"That's the way we've always done it; it's always worked that way; and that's the way we mean to carry on."

Much of her day is spent writing up the ledger and counting notes and coins, interrupted by calls from suppliers and clients. Occasionally, elderly ladies clutching empty bottles come in off the street to request a refill of wine, *vermut,* or the *bodega's* aromatic vinegar, for which they hand over a clutch of coins. It's another of Aunt Macu's principles that nobody should be turned away, however humble – that's what Pinar's about: a company with deep roots in the local community, not like *"most firms nowadays"* that *"simply don't care".*

A highlight of her week is the sortie to the bank, where she generally wallows in the deference afforded to her as a woman of means, hence her outrage at Gonzalo Caudal's usurpation that time. She's especially revered now her interests have outgrown the simple needs of the *bodega;* for she has quietly amassed a property portfolio across the province. As well as the house she shared with her mother and now owns outright, she boasts half a dozen garages and two flats in Bárcena, and a luxurious second-floor apartment overlooking the sea on the corniche in the capital.

She breaks her day at two thirty for the short drive back home in her *arrastra pozas* or "puddle-scooper", an antiquated SEAT Ritmo. Travelling the few hundred metres between home and the *bodega* is, in fact, the sole use she makes of the vehicle. It's the only time she feels safe at the wheel, especially as there's no need to change gear (she's worked out a route that starts and ends facing forwards and she can manage in second gear throughout). Even then, there are risks. On one occasion, she ran out of fuel on the level crossing that bisects her route, just by the station. Fortunately, the Ritmo came to rest athwart the tracks, right in front of a stationary locomotive. When the sirens sounded and the barriers came down, the train driver jumped from his cabin and helped push Macu and her car to safety. It gave her a nasty turn. In fairness, filling the tank is such a rare event for her, it's hardly surprising it slips her mind.

Once safely home with housekeeper, Nuria, her break is as closely choreographed as the rest of her day. First, there's 15 minutes for the press, half for the local *Voz del Golfo*, half for the nationals, split between *ABC* and *El País* (because Aunt Macu transcends politics, considering herself both conservative *and* liberal. In fact, she doesn't like to be pigeonholed at all, her politics being an eclectic mix across the spectrum). Then 45 minutes are dedicated to lunch, followed by a quick *siesta*. Afterwards, she returns to her desk at the *bodega* until eight or nine in the evening, when at last she calls time by noisily fixing up the shutters.

This last hour of the day, alone in her pool of yellow light, is the most satisfying. After a few final entries including intra-day totals, she shuts the leather tome with a heavy *whump*. Then she extracts a bunch of keys from the folds of her serge skirt and jangles through them until she finds the little silver one that unlocks the glass-fronted metal cabinet behind her desk. That's where the ledger resides, alongside the dozens of earlier volumes. Then she patrols the *bodega* to ensure everything has been tidied away properly. Finally, she takes a *copa* from the office and fills it from one or another hallowed *solera*. The pale, mellow nectar reassures her all is right with the world, and she can finally retire home to bed with a clear conscience.

Domingo's arrival, though, has upset her. On one hand, she expects him to learn the trade from the bottom up, putting in hours of low-paid work, just as she did when her father held sway. Once he has served a proper apprenticeship, he should be in line for promotion, but until then, his main responsibilities are to cover basic bookkeeping functions: reconciliations, accounts payable, collections. Logically, she should welcome his refusal to leave before she does. Why, then does she find his presence so irritating? He's an intrusion on her space. She's not looking for a business partner and she would prefer him to leave along with the rest of the workforce so she can enjoy the quiet hours of the evening unmolested.

3

For his part, Domingo's torn between his usual impatience and the need to hold down the job. The affront to his dignity of these footling tasks rankles deeply; but he cannot afford to give them up until he's worked out an alternative and, right now, he's far from sure what that might be. He therefore concludes that, mundane though his duties are, he should at least execute them diligently and, within the limited scope of his responsibilities, try to make a mark.

Reconciliations, of course, are an insult to the intelligence of a fellow of his gifts. All he has to do is to check that money in minus money out equals cash, physical and at bank; and it usually does, except when his mind strays and he makes a slip. On those occasions, a second count generally clears up the error. But once, after a recount of takings from one of the older drivers, Domingo is still short by one thousand *pesetas*. Instead of waiting for his aunt to return from the bank, he immediately strides out of the kiosk to collar the driver Chencho and demand an explanation. Fortunately, Sancho defuses the situation, appearing at the crucial moment, waving the errant one thousand *peseta* note. It materialised when he was clearing the truck, between the front seats, where it had evidently slipped undetected.

As for accounts payable, even Aunt Macu agrees it won't be demanding.

"Since we always pay our debts on time," she assures her nephew, "it's a very simple matter." Then, in apparent contradiction, she adds: "Just check how much we have in the bank before you pay the bigger bills."

The most challenging part of his role, however, is collections. This requires him to keep tabs on who owes what to the firm and how up to date they are with their payments. Aunt Macu impresses on him the heavy burden it entails: cajoling debtors is a role that demands both firmness and tact. Yes, debts must of course be collected, but without unravelling the delicate web that binds local commerce. That's especially vital for *Bodegas Pinar*, with its reputation at the hub of a close and financially fragile community: *noblesse oblige*.

Once Domingo settles to the task, he realises that rather more juggling will be needed than intimated. The statement shows regular outflows to the owner families, that is to Chábeli and Adelina as well as to Aunt Macu herself, leaving little left to meet "*those bigger bills*", some of which will soon be overdue. At the same time, there seems to have been little effort made to chase debtors who, as far as he can tell, habitually spin out payment for months. Some of them date right back to the Franco era, for goodness' sake! Surely those outstandings will never be recovered? It crosses his mind that, maybe, the accounts are a bit of a fiction, or at the least, self-delusion?

There's one entry that features prominently among the debtors, with large sums overdue by six months or more. But while the other debtors have names as well as numbers, for some reason this one (or is it more than one?) has no name. In this case, the only identification is the number: 54330-7. When he asks his aunt about it she tells him *"not to worry about that one"*. But as time goes by, it arouses his curiosity, especially as it's so large. Moreover, he starts to see it as an opportunity.

If he can establish the identity of the debtor, he should be able to work out a way of collecting the debt. His aunt should take notice of that – banking the largest outstanding debt! That way, perhaps she'll pay him more attention and – who knows? – even start treating him as he deserves: as part of the management.

4

Dear Jack,

Thank you for your letter. Your thoughts on how this country's changing struck a chord with me and in that context, I thought you'd be interested in my recent experience.

As you know, it's almost 15 years since I became an honorary member of this clan. "Honorary" describes it well, I think, because right from the start, it's been a detached, vicarious, experience. I've always felt like a spectator in the front row of a show: not any show, mind, but one of those performances in which, every so often, one of the actors jumps off the stage and collars a member of the audience – me – for an impromptu walk-on part.

Other than an occasional "how's your mother?" I struggle to recall a single instance of curiosity about whatever else might fill up my time when I'm not here. Should I fail to come for a year or two, I suppose my mother-in-law might eventually remark that "he must be very busy" or, caustically, quiz her daughter about whether "your husband deserted you too"; and to be fair, should Marina arrive on the doorstep with bruises and a black eye one day, I'm sure searching inquiries into my behaviour would follow. But in the meantime, the Pinar family dances to its own tune; it is resolutely unfazed by off-stage cacophony, imagined or real.

I'm not complaining: it suits me well that way. And perhaps it's mutual, anyway, because do I properly grasp the dynamics of this strange family? My perceptions are mediated through frosted glass. I'm not even sure what they think about me, let alone anything else. But I'm telling you this because something unexpected happened last week. That paragon of discretion and inscrutability, Doña Inmaculada, "Aunt Macu", took me aside on one of our periodic visits to the bodega to ask if she could see me, by myself, in private. Since our intercourse usually sticks unwaveringly to platitudes, with occasional digressions into such things as the lamentable state of public mores, you can imagine my astonishment at such a rare departure. In fact, when I set off to join her at home on Sunday I was pretty *anxious: not only, for once, about the terrifying Blondi I'd have to negotiate on my way to the front door, but about what on earth might have prompted this initiative.*

Once we're seated in the dim light of her sitting room, Aunt Macu spreads out a newspaper article on the table; then she invites me to read it undisturbed, while she helps Nuria boil up some coffee in the kitchen. It's a double page spread from Voz del Golfo, *one of the main organs of the regional press, entitled* Caída a pico del Consumo del Vino, *reporting on a sharp drop in wine consumption across the region and indeed, the whole country. It makes for depressing reading, even for me; for Aunt Macu it must be much more alarming. The gist of it is that the wine business is in headlong decline, thanks to an unholy trinity of anti-alcohol policies, aggressive promotion of sweet, fizzy drinks, and sharply rising grape prices. Of course, they really are a Holy Trinity, indivisible because they're intrinsic to that "now we're Europeans" meme we hear so often.*

But I suspect Aunt Macu was especially rattled by the remark, allegedly from "one senior industry source", quoted towards the end of the article: "Not all of us are suffering… but it will be the nimble, the brave, the innovative who will survive. We ourselves paved the way by pulling out of the dying solera *business. It was brutal, it was sad, but it paid off". For Aunt Macu, that would be sacrilege from anyone; but though unattributed, it's a safe guess those words came from the lips of Pinar's implacable rival, Gonzalo Caudal, owner of nearby Vinos Aurelio.*

While I was waiting for Macu to reappear with the coffee I was wondering what had prompted her to ask my opinion about this. As you can imagine, my knowledge of such things is vanishingly slight. I suspect that the sudden death of her cousin José Angel means she's looking for a new confidant of some kind. She knows not to expect much from her new associates, José Angel's heirs, Chábeli and Adelina. Her nephew Domingo now works with her, but he's erratic and moody – I'm not sure she's fully at ease with him. And her other nephew, Sancho? As far as she's concerned, he's no more than a blue-collar hand.

Aunt Macu provided an explanation as soon as she returned: "I wanted your views about it because you're family," she said, upsetting all my notions about where I stand, "and you're Anglo-Saxon. You people know all about these things. A 'nation of shopkeepers', isn't that so?"

She then told me that even Bodegas Pinar was starting to feel the chill. It's not quite as harsh as the article states, "at least not for the leaders such as us", she claimed. But even Pinar has experienced steady attrition, especially in the far-flung villages and bars.

"But isn't that because so many villages are emptying out?" I asked her.

From what I've heard the exodus isn't quite as dire as further inland, where there are scores of ghost villages – no doubt there are many in your part of Castile; but it's not far behind. It's bound to affect us. She agreed it could be a factor. But she's also worried about having lost clients to the competition, even some of the untouchables, such as my father-in-law's favourite haunt, Casa Polín. Worse still, in that case, the beneficiaries were rivals Vinos Aurelio. By chance, we happened to witness the moment she learned about it – it really shook her up.

But then she made a statement I never expected to cross her lips: "We need to think about how to change! I'm thinking you'd be able to help me work out what to do. God forbid, but we might even have to move… somewhere modern, with better access and what do they call it? Temperature control? Air conditioning? At least we need to consider the options and come to a view… And once we've done that, we can try to persuade the others."

By "the others" she meant the other cousins, Chábeli and Adelina, who receive a steady stipend from the bodega. Thanks to inheritance laws, there have been repeated splits in ownership, occasionally offset by consolidations, such as when Macu convinced her siblings to transfer everything to herself. I said I thought it would be better to call in the professionals, but she wasn't hearing of that.

"We can't trust anyone round here, not a soul, believe me. As soon as I told them anything, you can be sure it would find its way onto the agenda at Vinos Aurelio! Can you imagine? All our sensitive information in the hands of those bandits! Not just every client, how much we sell of what, but even the secrets of our soleras – the very heart of Bodegas Pinar since our foundation! 'Pulling out of the dying solera business', my foot! Whatever will they claim next? Aurelio pulled out of the solera business because they made such a mess of it – it was way beyond them! They'd be back in a trice if they knew how."

She pauses, then adds: "You know the other meaning of solera, I suppose? I take it Marina enlightened you? The phrase "tiene solera" means that something's 'venerable', and that's our birthright. Nobody else comes close, least of all those scoundrels at *Vinos Aurelio*, who in fact covet nothing more than our soleras. *They gave up not out of foresight, but because their* soleras *always spoiled! They lacked our know-how! Our ancient* soleras, *from which we've nourished a whole province for over a century and a half, underpin our prestige and make us what we are. Can you imagine if that expertise fell into the hands of that unscrupulous gang? Into the hands of those dangerous and unworthy people, who seek nothing but our demise? No, no, we have to work this out for ourselves."*

I refrained from observing that losing control of the solera *business might indeed be a blessing in disguise. Since Aurelio doesn't compete in that field it frees them from all these traditional, probably unprofitable, lines that tie Pinar to a dwindling, impoverished clientele, much of it up in those remote villages. I can't help wondering if they really do "covet nothing more than our soleras". But I judged that any such comment might be impolitic, so I kept quiet.*

"Well, I'd like you to think about it. Then we can take a proper look."

Afterwards, when I told Marina about the conversation, she was sceptical: "That article got her in a panic, but the papers are unreliable and always overstate everything. Voz del Golfo's *one of the worst…" Then, with a smile, she added: "They say the name* Voz del Golfo *is ambiguous for a reason…" When I looked blank, she added: "You do realise 'golfo' doesn't just mean 'gulf' as in 'Gulf of Biscay', or 'Gulf of Cadiz'? It's also slang for 'idle good-for-nothing'. So* Voz del Golfo *can just as well mean the voice of one of those old lags you find perched on barstools round here, leafing through the day's* Voz *over a* carajillo *and pontificating to anyone rash enough to strike up a conversation."*

That may or may not be the case and I'm quite prepared to question the reliability of the local papers. But it doesn't explain why Aunt Macu herself is worried to the point of sharing these secrets with me, a virtual stranger. She must be suffering from attrition at the bodega, perhaps quite serious, whatever the cause.

I really wasn't too keen to get involved, but I didn't refuse either. It seemed to be a family duty to help out as well as I could. With luck, Marina will be proved right: Macu's in a panic and it will all be forgotten soon enough. But if not, I'll see if I can apply a bit of common sense to the situation and try my best.

It's symptomatic of the very changes we were talking about last time. As I see it: in 1986, Spain joins the EEC (or "The European Community", as we're now enjoined to call it). For a while, not much seems to change except that everyone starts boasting about how "we're Europeans now". Gradually, a few of the old roads are "improved", which only helps to speed up the flight from those villages. But it's all very popular.

Then, once a decade or so has elapsed, the pressures have built up so much that, suddenly, the plates slip, and everything else starts to change, fast. That emblematic blend of black tobacco smoke and Agua Brava no longer haunts public buildings the way it used to. Old household brands yield to foreign ones and, with the marketing men in charge, everything must be in English, though nobody much understands a word (no doubt you'll change that).

Spaniards, the vast majority of whom, until recently,

lived out their lives in their villages or towns, start to travel. This time, we found Mamí planning for her nephew Julito to drive her to Rome "to meet the Pope" with her sister and a couple of other elderly ladies. Most surprising of all was our friend Soco from the village, the one who claims she's "not local" because her home village lies a couple of kilometres from Valledal, telling us she and husband Miguelín plan to drive south this summer. They've never even left the province before, as far as I know.

On a separate subject, the time has at last arrived for us to move into the house in Valledal. Perhaps the next time we meet, it'll be there…

Meantime, all the best,

Rico.

5

The day of the move to Valledal is indeed upon us, but it augurs less well than hoped. As we come down the hill into the *barrio bajo* in driving sleet with two stroppy children and a few essentials, it still looks pretty ramshackle. Thanks to budgetary constraints, the original plan has shrunk. Only the original part of the house, about half the footprint, is habitable. But at least it should be watertight, reasonably rodent-resistant and the woodworm should cease munching for a while. The damp, now disguised with new plaster, will stay out of mind for the time being. Sorting these things out properly and completing the second half will have to await fresh funds.

Irksome as ever, though, is that track, still slicing brazenly through the middle, a physical as well as psychological scar. Every so often, a villager makes a gratuitous detour to exercise the right to cut right past our front door – to peer into the house and to assess what other mischief the *forasteros* might be hatching.

There's been visible retaliation for our effrontery as well. The two holm oaks we planted up in the far corner of the garden, where it touches the road into the village, have earned the patent treatment, *la corbata,* or "necktie". It's a simple incision round the bark, close to the base of a tree; and it reliably kills it.

While I'm examining the damage, I notice a figure, arms folded, leaning on the wall, no more than a few metres distant. It's our neighbour Monchi, our self-declared "great friend" from the first day we saw the house.

"I didn't do that!" he says unprompted as I look up. His features revert to an unseemly rictus.

"I wasn't suggesting…"

"*Es que…*" Monchi resumes (they often use the formula "*es que…*", usually in a wheedling tone of voice, before delivering an unpalatable message – "*the thing is that…*" being the approximate equivalent), "*es que*, those trees, they get very large!"

"Yes, that's right: they were oaks – holm oaks."

Monchi waggles his index at me in that time-honoured gesture, as if to say that planting those trees there was an unpardonable transgression, a gross presumption for a newcomer. It's true, I'd forgotten just how much the locals dislike trees of all descriptions and the tedious work generated by any kind of *maleza* (scrub) or leaves.

Then, as an afterthought, Monchi adds:

"You see, we lived in Valledal all our lives… and your house, well, by rights it should be mine, you know…"

My heart plummets. I feel dizzy. Don't tell me there's some bureaucratic screw-up akin to the disputed ownership of Marina's childhood home, the type of ancestral quarrel that so often blights property rights round here?

Fortunately, Monchi lets me off:

"I mean, I was born in your house – in the barn you knocked down, to be exact."

Before the day is out, we walk up the hill to Soco's house for an antidote and an update.

But first, Marina asks her to tell us about that holiday she and Miguelín were planning. Soco looks momentarily sheepish, before conceding that it was "short, very short indeed, in fact". Then the whole story comes out. Once they crossed the pass, they were shocked how dry and empty everything looked on the other side. Used as they are to the clammy, intimate north coast, they felt strangely adrift in this semi-wilderness – endless desiccated steppe rolling away to the horizon. Then Miguelín started fretting about the temperature gauge, creeping ominously above normal. They found a bar in a small town a short distance onto the *meseta* to take stock. Out of the roughly 1,000 kilometres to the south they'd covered only about 100, despite driving for hours. Miguelín looked particularly miserable; he wasn't sure the car would make it. He also started asking why exactly they were doing this, how precisely they would occupy themselves for a whole fortnight down there. But Soco agreed: "I mean, we couldn't really see ourselves sunbathing or anything like that. What else is there to do? Bars? Discotheques? That's when a plan started taking shape in both our minds, only neither of us wanted to admit it." Finally, Miguelín plucked up courage to ask why they didn't just turn round and go home? "I said I couldn't help thinking the same. He was so pleased."

The only downside was the ridicule they'd face, especially after the fanfare with which their neighbours wished them on their way. In preparation, Soco started dreaming up excuses – she couldn't remember if she'd turned off the gas cylinder or perhaps Chato wouldn't cope with the milking for two weeks by himself. But then she thought better of it.

"I decided I'd simply tell everyone how much better life was at home. Anyway, it was true the car was playing up." Then she starts chuckling. No sound comes out, but her whole torso shakes and her cheeks flush more than usual. Soco has a lively sense of the absurd, at her own expense as much as anyone else's.

"There've been some changes down here," she says, when the mirth abates. "Not sure if you know about it but Don Alberto, Monchi's father, has been ill and he's decided to stand down as president". President of the *Junta Vecinal*, the parish council that blocked our rerouted track, she means. "Perhaps you'll have better luck now!"

Soco says the elections haven't happened yet.

"But there seem to be two main factions: Tomás says he wants to stand; and there's the new man from the bar who's been making a stir ever since he took over. Adolfo Posadas Posadas, that is."

We have no illusions about Tomás. Monchi clung to him like ivy in opposition to our track: so what help could we expect from that quarter? For what it's worth, our preferred candidate has to be this fellow Adolfo from the bar, whoever he may be – though as a newcomer, his prospects can't be strong.

"He may be better placed than you think," Soco observes. "He's dynamic and that's why some of the top Santa Rita people wouldn't mind putting him in charge. With them on side, his chances must be good. Everyone wants to sell their fields, after all! Who else is going to buy them? Not Tomás, for certain, or anyone else from round here, for that matter. There's no money!" she says with a wink as she holds up her right hand and rubs forefinger and thumb together.

Soco's prediction proves right. Adolfo's slick campaign leaves Tomás trailing. Quite apart from his links to the Santa Rita syndicate, Adolfo treats village stalwarts, Miguelín among them, to drinks at the bar and to a meal at one of his *chiringuitos*, his new breed of beach bars. It pays off and Don Adolfo Posadas Posadas cruises to an easy victory, becoming *Presidente* of our *Junta Vecinal* with immediate effect.

With so much to-and-fro between Bárcena and Valledal the children develop a strange ritual. "Sign!" they shout periodically, from the back of the car, often in unison. What it means is closely guarded. (For once, it's nothing to do with the *bona fide* signpost in Tobillo to a village called 'Poo', which reliably reduces the children to abject hysteria.) Then one day, James lets slip that the "signs" are harbingers of Christmas: there's an illuminated tree on a hillside, for instance, and a string of green and red bulbs draped across the façade of the Palacios' *ferretería* in Tobillo. Even *Vinos Aurelio*, also on the main drag through Tobillo, qualifies by virtue of a barrel decked out as Santa on the winery forecourt, as does our own "badly sloping" *bodega*, as James describes it, which runs to a few mangy paperchains outside the main door.

But this innocent fun turns out to be polluted by more than just our commercial rivals: one of the children's "signs", a rotating beam in lurid colours that sweeps the countryside for miles around, belongs in fact to one disreputable dive, a *puticlub*, frequented by truckers on the main road.

6

After his aunt's rebuff, Domingo has been looking everywhere for clues to the identity of the mysterious debtor(s) 54330-7, but so far to no avail. The best chance of unlocking the secret must lie among the tomes behind Macu's desk.

His aunt looks puzzled when he tells her he'll stay behind because he needs "to catch up on the backlog."

"I thought the work was too easy for you," she says sarcastically. She has few illusions about Domingo's dedication or diligence.

"Easy, yes, but there's lots of it."

"Well, make sure you lock up – inside and out. Don't forget *Aurelio* would stop at nothing for that client list, not to mention everything else. They're quite capable of dirty tricks – and I'm thinking adulteration here. It's been done before: a bottle of bleach or two… You must be old enough to remember the fake olive oil scandal?"

As soon as the revving, straining Ritmo, wheezing off in second gear, has merged into the hubbub, Domingo sets to work. He doesn't have the key, but the glass-fronted cupboard looks anything but secure. It certainly wouldn't present much of an obstacle should *Aurelio* resort to industrial espionage.

Sure enough, with the help of a screwdriver he's able to dislodge one of the sliding glass doors from its groove. Then it's a question of shuffling the older volumes out of the way before reaching the current ledger. But once open, page upon page of hieroglyphics greet him: even if he could read Macu's handwriting, it would take days of forensics to work out what it all means. However, there are also several binders on the upper shelf; by the looks of it, they contain official correspondence. And it's here that Domingo finds, not a letter or an invoice, but a handwritten memo, bearing the code 54330-7. At a glance, the dates and numbers jotted there tally with the outstanding invoices in the file he's working from. On the back, scrawled in pencil, are the initials "OdN/APP".

There's one way to establish who that may be that doesn't involve Macu herself or the official Register of Companies. Domingo's cousin, Marina's brother Sancho, is fast becoming a fount of wisdom about all matters concerning the *bodega*. He travels all over the province, supplies the wines, collects the empties, services the *soleras* and issues the invoices. Above all, he meets and shares drinks with the clients. Indeed, he has a growing reputation as the best person to call if there's a problem: cloudy *solera*? Stocks low for the *romería*?[17] Sancho's the person for a speedy and reliable solution. Domingo knows that if anyone can establish the identity of OdN/APP, it'll be Sancho. He returns the ledgers to the cupboard, coaxes the glass door back into place and retires for the evening.

The conversation with Sancho yields the information: the initials can of course only mean the big client they won a couple of years back, *Ocios del Norte S.A.* That makes sense, because the owner is Adolfo Posadas Posadas, APP (that bafflingly duplicated name implying, I understand, that mother and father shared a surname before they married, so were probably first cousins).

"What can you tell me about him?"

"He's a pushy local entrepreneur who's bought up a string of *chiringuitos* along the coast. Aunt Macu's delighted, of course. Her big new catch – we seem to have stolen a march on *Aurelio* for once... These *chiringuitos* could be a promising avenue for us, with more to follow, for sure...

---

[17] Village fiesta

All that *tinto de verano*[18] everyone orders these days. Oh, and he owns the bar in Valledal."

7

Piecing this together from Sancho's account after the event, I realise our first meeting with Adolfo must have taken place days after Domingo's raid on Macu's cabinet.

Our point of departure is the Valledal bar, at the top of the hill in the *barrio alto*. A young blonde woman greets us – that'll be Adolfo's girlfriend, Lucía, if Soco's briefing is to be credited. There's no sign of Adolfo himself, but Lucía says he usually drops by in the afternoon.

The scruffy bar itself displays a few dried-up *canapés* under glass – egg mayonnaise on *Pan Bimbo*, the local factory bread, stuffed olives speared onto squares of cheese, that sort of thing. The detritus at the foot of the bar, including cigarette butts, paper napkins, clam shells, toothpicks and excavated prawns scrunches underfoot whenever we step down from our high stools. Still, we have time to kill, so decide to order drinks and brave a few *raciones* (dishes) from the menu to occupy us while we wait.

The sustenance on offer belongs firmly to the genre Marina describes as "*sota, caballo y rey*" – cards in a Spanish deck, the rough equivalent of "Knave, Queen and King" – implying "predictable", "bog standard" or "run of the mill". In establishments of this type, the written menu fulfils a purely symbolic function: under imaginative headings, "*Grupo I*" (starters), "*Grupo II*" (main courses), "*Postres*" (desserts), they present a complete roster of everything that *might conceivably* be available, rather than what's actually in the kitchen, let alone what's bubbling on the hob, ready to serve. Usually, the gulf between ideal and

---

[18] Summer drink made of red wine and *gaseosa*

real is wide. Hence, it's generally simpler to ignore the menu altogether and plump for a few perennials, in the knowledge that no restaurant round here can afford to be without the likes of *croquetas de la casa, morcilla, rabas* or *ensalada mixta*.[19] In any case, that's how we end up choosing several dishes *para picar,* to share. Meanwhile, I commit a small act of treason by ordering *cañas,* beer in place of house red – supplied here by *Bodegas Pinar* – and thereby conniving in that decline I read about in Macu's article from *Voz del Golfo.*

As Lucía rehearses the choices for dessert, comprising a predictable roster of *flan de la casa, tarta al güisqui, tarta helada* and *cuajada,*[20] a burly figure darkens the door. From Lucía's raised eyebrows we infer this is Adolfo.

His domineering presence is palpable, the air of someone used to ordering others around and getting his way. No wonder he was backed for *Presidente* by the Santa Rita syndicate. But he's not otherwise unpleasant, and when he understands our wish to talk in confidence, he ushers us to a smoky office behind the bar.

"You, too, are part of the Pinar dynasty, then?" he says after Marina has played her trump card. "Well, let me say I had a visit from one of your relatives this very morning. Not what I expected, at all! You see, we stock your products right across our restaurants – that's no small commitment on our part, you understand. So I wasn't prepared, so early in our relationship, to be sent some underling to try to extract *cuatro perras*[21] from me. Don't your people realise we have choices? Ever heard of *Vinos*

---

[19] Homemade croquettes, black pudding, squid rings in batter and mixed salad

[20] Homemade custard tart, whisky tart, frozen tart and yoghurt

[21] A few pence

Aurelio? They'd kill for our custom! Needless to say, I sent him packing."

All this leads our discussion into undesirable terrain.

"But let's leave that aside for the time being. I don't suppose that's what you wanted to talk about?"

The moment could scarcely be less propitious to broach the matter of the track. Instead of garnering support we've walked straight into some contretemps with the family business. But now we have little choice but to carry on. We explain the background and the rebuff we received from the *Junta Vecinal* when his predecessor Alberto was in charge.

"So you were simply relying on the goodwill of your neighbours if I'm hearing you right? Not a sensible approach, in my view. These things seldom work out unless there's gain on all sides... Common sense, really. When has anyone given anything away for free round here? Why would your neighbours do that? Anyway, let me think about it. It's not impossible. But there's bound to be a cost. In fact, I have an idea. But first, I need to sort things out with your family."

8

A scene of pandemonium awaits us on arrival at the *bodega* later that afternoon: there's no trace of Domingo, but Aunt Macu is haranguing her other nephew, Sancho, who must just have returned from one of his daily trips into the remoter recesses of the province – this time in the company of his young godson James, now a regular fixture.

"So why did you give him the details?" she asks, indignantly.

"I didn't. He just asked who it could be... and I guessed, which wasn't hard from those letters. He didn't explain why or where they came from. I just thought he

104

was doing his job."

"To think I do all of this for you… and this is my reward! Why do you meddle so? You don't understand these things. I suppose it's my fault! Giving you so much rope… I never thought you were bright, but your cousin? I had hopes for him! What a blow…! A cheat, too… What are you doing here, Marina? Can't you see I'm speaking to your brother in private?"

A couple of hours later, at Mamí's, Sancho fills out the story to the accompaniment of successive whoops, groans and curses from Papí's recumbent armchair: nothing to do with Sancho's narrative, just the big fixture on TV this evening. (Marina often claims that the *futbol* tyranny was her main reason for emigrating…)

It seems that Domingo, armed with details of Adolfo's debts, set off for Villafranca, where his "flagship" *chiringuito* is located. There was of course a risk Aunt Macu would return (he wasn't sure where she'd gone) but should he be missed, he could easily fabricate an alibi – an urgent dental appointment in Pueblo de la Vega, whatever. In any event, he expected his initiative to be applauded. He naively pictured himself delivering a few stern words to the delinquent debtor, bringing in the much-needed funds or at least part thereof, and immediately raising his stock with his aunt. He hadn't expected this adversary, intimidating both in stature and self-assurance.

As soon as Adolfo grasped the tenor of his message, without raising his voice, he queried: "And you are?"

Domingo's confidence evaporated instantly. He could only muster a few words to say he was an emissary for his aunt, Doña Inmaculada, from *Bodegas Pinar*, and that he was looking to settle up.

Adolfo beckoned and, in the patronising tones that seem to be a signature: "Let's speak to your aunt right now, then, shall we?" and he marched Domingo to the telephone in his office. Adolfo sat behind the desk and signalled to Domingo to take a seat opposite. Aunt Macu picked up straight away.

"I believe I have the pleasure of meeting your nephew – Domingo? Yes, yes, that's exactly where he is: right in front of me... He's just shared views about our relationship... Says he's here on your authority – with an instruction to collect certain sums? But I thought we had an agreement about that?"

Domingo couldn't hear what his aunt was saying, but it was obvious she was struggling to salvage the situation. Adolfo didn't seem unduly perturbed. While she spoke, he took the opportunity of suspending the receiver from a great height and allowing the tangled cord to spin until it unravelled completely. When he recovered it, Macu was still talking. He held it away from his ear, rolling his eyes at Domingo. Finally, he said: "Uh-huh, right, I'll tell him to head straight back to Bárcena. You and I will proceed as agreed. But I have another idea about that I'd like to share with you."

When Domingo met his aunt at the *bodega* the conversation was short. She simply told him he'd let down the whole family through this reckless behaviour. What's more, as far as she could see, he didn't even seem to understand what he'd done wrong, let alone show any contrition.

"You can clear your desk right away. Your services are no longer required."

Just as he left, she added: "And next time you stoop to common larceny, take a bit more care! What makes you think I'd file the records in reverse order?"

Marina asked her brother what he thought Domingo would do now.

"I expect he'll pursue that other dream of his. You know he's learning Chinese? In his view it's the future. He's made friends with the Chinese at the takeaway and they're teaching him."

9

A couple of days later, Adolfo appears at the house, unannounced. He asks to inspect the track. He says he needs to understand exactly what's at stake and how it'll affect the neighbours. Part of me is rather anxious at this: we know enough about Valledal to realise that no visit, let alone by the *Presidente de la Junta Vecinal*, will remain secret for long. In all likelihood Monchi, Tomás or, even more likely, Soco, are watching right now, as we pace out the proposed trajectory of the replacement track, following the overgrown traces of Papí's original, ill-fated attempt.

"Well, I can see why you want to move it," Adolfo says once we're indoors. "I agree there's no rational objection to it. But as I think I said before, you need to understand the mentality. *Nobody* wants a neighbour to steal an advantage, however trivial. There must be something in it for them. Question is, what should that be? I've been thinking about that and I reckon that a contribution to the village *romería* might change a few hearts – we run a fund for general expenses. Once you have some support, I'm confident your immediate neighbours would fall into line. Admittedly, they're a tricky bunch – dare I say, well known for that... But what are we talking about? Perhaps fifty, perhaps one hundred thousand *pelas*. Then I'll be seeing your aunt this afternoon about another interesting idea that should help wrap this up... I suggest you discuss that with her once we've spoken."

The "interesting idea" Adolfo wanted to discuss with Macu apparently involves untangling their convoluted financial arrangements. Macu explains it as best she can: it seems that, in return for sorting out our track, we will write off what he owes to the *bodega*. Macu looks embarrassed by the figure, which is certainly egregious; over half a million *pesetas* is the sum at issue – the sum we will have to make good, assuming he's able to push it through at the *Junta*. Despite the expense, I feel proud – imbecilic this, really, but proud nonetheless - to be a principal in my very own *chanchullo*, my own bespoke scam. It feels quite grown-up. It's a rite of passage, a badge of acceptance.

"Until last year he always paid on time – always cash, of course," Aunt Macu continues, "that's why he insisted on keeping it off the books. He doesn't want any record of sums owing or repaid, for reasons I can only guess at. Money laundering, I take it. Or tax evasion. Probably both. It wasn't for me to ask why he had so much cash or where it was coming from; and I couldn't ask why it stopped, either. You understand: this wasn't an opportunity we could let go. Times are hard, as you know," she says, looking at me. "And on that subject: would you be able to join me and my cousins in a few weeks' time? We need to make some decisions."

Macu knows from Sancho that his sister Marta is unhappy in her current role with the tourist board, mostly because she has to live away from home during the week. So now she has another plan. Marta can help out with the books. And there's one great advantage: Marta won't play games. She's not the type to subvert time-honoured practices or to meddle in matters she doesn't comprehend.

These are testing times for the *bodega* in other ways too. The traditionally passive workforce recently turned militant. The instigator is the diminutive but wily Rosana, the cleaner – in Macu's words "she's a troublemaker". In Rosana's view, Macu's "in breach of contract" because since time immemorial, workers at the *bodega* were never held to their contractual hours once their work was done. Ironically, in Britain such informal agreements, based wholly on custom, are known as "Spanish Practices", but they carry overtones of bloody-mindedness on the part of the workforce. In reality, Spanish Practices means the workers hurry to finish their tasks so they can leave early, leading to shoddy work. The term Spanish Practices is, however, unknown in Spain itself, Marina included. (She takes a dim view when I explain: "You mean the Brits blame us for this kind of bad behaviour? Typical!")

Reflecting today's more challenging environment, Macu now insists the workers fulfil their official hours precisely, with any surplus devoted to other ad hoc tasks as required. If not, they can expect their pay to be docked. Workers will be required to clock in and out on a device she plans to fix up. It's a direct affront to hallowed Spanish Practices and, in response, Rosana now sweeps extra slowly. That way, she fills her contractual hours exactly and cannot be fingered for other tasks. Her attitude has infected some of the others. Sancho, for example, finds himself conflicted between loyalty to his aunt and to his co-driver, Chencho, who's toying with the call for a general go-slow, which means grinding up the valleys at 20 instead of 30 kph.

Aunt Macu decides to act. It will be expensive, but she has decided that Rosana is a dangerous radical who must go, before she foments further trouble. Somehow, that result is achieved. The fallout will, however, spread beyond the financial settlement, whatever that was, since she's Mamí's cleaner and also happens to be married to our odd-job man in Valledal, Angel.

10

The meeting with Aunt Macu's cousins cannot be arranged as quickly as expected. Instead, about six months after Domingo's defenestration, we make a special trip by road, hiring a van to fill with furniture for the new house. As part of the removals, some old friends reappear – the six chairs sculpted by Aunt Macu's *ebanistería*, her cabinet maker Magín, that have gathered dust in our attic for the better part of a decade. At last, we've found a use for them; they'll look so much happier in their natural habitat. What's more, by commissioning some cushions from Mari-Ca, Mamí's seamstress, we might also be able to sit on them without undue hardship.

On arrival, we bypass Bárcena, driving straight to Valledal to assess our recent handiwork. Of course, I know roughly what to expect as I come down the hill, as I've played a part in the whole endeavour, if mostly at one remove. But it's remarkable to see the house, at last surrounded by its own garden which, in turn, is enclosed by a nearly complete stone wall. The track down the centre has been grassed over and substituted by its exterior counterpart, following the route prematurely promoted by Papí.

It doesn't take long, as I revel in the novelty, for a few villagers to appear, albeit not the usual ones. In any case, this time they pass along the new route outside the wall. Everyone's keen to inspect the damage.

Some of these are rare sightings indeed. First comes that rather sedate, reclusive lady they call *La Larga*, the "Long One", from the very last house in the village, just where it gives way to pasture that undulates for a few hundred metres before sloping downwards on three sides towards a ring of eucalyptus which severs the direct route down to the beach (at the behest of the locals, to prevent incursions by undesirable types from the campsite). Apparently, La Larga was widowed 30 years ago and has always worn black since then. She seldom emerges from her bunker except to feed the chickens.

Then there is the hippy calling herself Josie, who inhabits a caravan parked in a squalid patch of land close by La Larga, who also decides to cruise past; but as soon as she sees I'm outside she takes fright and, instead of rounding the garden on the new track, decides to beat a retreat.

The farmer, Midas, also materialises. He's the exception round here who made a success of dairy farming, benefitting from the distress of many of the smaller dairymen to acquire their land and livestock cheaply. In this way, he's built up a herd several hundred strong that, apart from one smelly, bat-infested barn right in the middle of the village, are lodged in huge, corrugated sheds dotted about the countryside. The pretext for his visit is our perimeter wall: will his tractors have enough space to negotiate the bends on the track? He looks unhappy. In his view, the track isn't wide enough – we should have left a wider gap… we should realign it now, before there's an "*accident*".

Finally, I perceive a grey head coming into sight from behind the wall as its owner walks up the slope behind it. This is a much more welcome sight, because the head belongs to Pepita, grandmother to three of the few young children left in the village, and a close friend to Soco – in short, another rare ally. I leave the thistles I'm digging out of the turf and cross the garden for a chat. After the usual banter, Pepita suggests I join her up the hill at Soco's.

Soco, however, has sad news: after years of struggle, Miguelín has finally decided to abandon the farm. He intends to sell everything to Midas. It's unclear whether this stems from a simple change of heart on his part or from pressure from his brother, who owns the house and may have realised by now that Valledal is starting to change. After decades, centuries even, during which almost nothing changed except for a gradual exodus of young people as subsistence farming declined, this has started to reverse.

In addition to our own, one or two houses in the village have been sold to *forasteros*. Moreover, the developments at Santa Rita have altered perspectives radically. If there's interest in owning properties down there, a mere few hundred metres away, why shouldn't there be up here too? Miguelín's brother doubtless realises this site has desirable qualities. The house may be squalid and face the wrong way; but it could be rebuilt with a view of the mountains, and that seems to be what the outsiders like best. His brother can retain the plot opposite, which currently hosts a second, smaller, cowshed. This they will demolish, and a tiny dwelling will take its place, which should just about fit on a footprint that, until now, barely housed eight cows – cows that Clara will no longer be able to milk when she's here.

"You can't imagine how much dust you raised with your track," Soco tells me. "What have you done to upset everyone? Miguelín went to some of the meetings, and it sounds like there was real hostility – 'they think they can just come here and start ordering us about'. Monchi claimed you'd 'moved the Pilgrimage Route itself'. Adolfo wasn't having that, though – he said the Route was made up in the first place and hadn't the village done all it could to close it? You were very lucky with Adolfo – if it hadn't been for him… he brought a few extra bodies from Tobillo to help the numbers, too. Of course, they all assumed you'd bribed him," she says with a smirk, "and they thought the contribution to the *romería* was an insult. Anyway, I'm glad you got it done in the end. Looks great, doesn't it? You must be pleased."

11

The gathering for Aunt Macu to present her *visión* as she calls it to cousins Chábeli and Adelina has been set for the following day, at her house. I've been invited and, exceptionally, Macu has also asked her nephew Sancho to attend on the grounds that she's "doing all this for him", a formula she long since added to her go-to repertoire.

Sancho's recently hired sister Marta, on the other hand, will not be attending the meeting. During Aunt Macu's debut foreign trip to Lourdes (seeking a cure for her bunions, apparently, for which the nuns have crafted a special prayer) she failed to open a letter from Social Security, and the scolding she received as a result is still ringing in her ears. That came after express instructions that she should *not* touch the post during her aunt's absence.

"But couldn't you see that letter was urgent? Can't I rely on you for anything, however simple? Whatever happened to common sense? Now there's a fine to pay!"

I've not met the two sisters before, but they can't hide their condescension towards the left-behinds of Bárcena. Chábeli, in particular, cuts a dash in her finery – knee-length mink coat, ivory bangles jangling on wrists, designer handbag. A waft of scent accompanies her theatrical entry, competing with the fug of Macu's sitting room. Adelina is more understated but makes up for it with her smoker's croak, which grates through the house as soon as Macu opens the door for her. Macu would like us all to sit at the round table, but the two cousins lay claim to the armchairs by the fire.

113

There's time for a few pleasantries while Adelina lights up and Nuria brings coffee and biscuits. Of course, these include a sprinkling of the "*¡Vaya día!*" variety, the mercury having dropped below 10 degrees for the first time this year, almost justifying the cousins' choice of outer garments.

But before long, we turn to the main agenda.

"I hope we all had time to read the documents?" Macu asks. She's referring to a folder containing the accounts, with a short note outlining the *bodega*'s current predicament. Also included is a copy of that article from *Voz del Golfo*. Her cousins look puzzled and claim not to have received anything. That's no big surprise: Macu warned me to lower my expectations: she said that, even if they received it, they almost certainly wouldn't read it. However, today's conversation will be a real challenge if they have no inkling of the background.

In any case, I don't suppose the accounts would have helped very much. They take a form that must have been dreamed up by someone whose guiding principle was to preserve the mystique of the accountancy profession. They follow an inflexible format, most of which is wholly irrelevant to any individual case. The simple question: "does this company spend more than it brings in?" (let alone the admittedly trickier: "does it make a profit?") is so expertly camouflaged in the categories that their message surely escapes most people. It certainly escapes me.

"Let me explain," Macu resumes, aping the practised politician with her purring tones, "the three of us are lucky enough to share this wonderful enterprise which has given us all such a good living for many years… But sorry to say, we now face a difficult position at the *bodega*. That's what we need to discuss and agree the action to be taken. Sadly, people just aren't drinking as much wine these days: there's competition everywhere – beer, Kas, Coca Cola. We're starting to notice it. And the big problem is our building. Yes, wonderful though it is in its own way, it's just not flexible and it's a struggle to make it work harder. You know: trucks delivering in the town centre, poor access. No proper temperature control. What I'm saying is we may have to move…"

The cousins look at each other in shock. The idea that the famous *bodega* should abandon its historic site is anathema. All of a sudden, the building they so often mocked has become a priceless asset – the very mention of abandoning it is treason on Macu's part. It has occupied the same premises for over 150 years, its sloping profile so familiar that it's tantamount to Bárcena's unofficial emblem – its very own *Giralda*, its *Sagrada Familia*. Without that, what will they talk about at their dinner parties?

"Of course, I'm not saying this lightly," Macu continues, sensing their agitation. "I'm the very last person… I'm sure you can imagine."

But she has worse news: "In the circumstances we'll have to suspend the dividend, at least for a time. And we'll need to invest…"

The cousins begin dimly to grasp what Macu is saying. It's Adelina who speaks out first: "What are you suggesting, Macu? Tell us exactly what you mean by '*suspend the dividend*'."

"What it means, Ade, is that we won't be able to pay ourselves for a while… What's more, if we do what I suggest, we'll all have to dig deep into our pockets to take our wonderful business into the next generation!"

Chábeli is the one who responds: "But why? It's not our fault it's doing badly! It's you who's running it, Macu, is it not? You must've got it all badly wrong!"

"Steady on!" Macu says, realising the meeting is drifting

badly off course. She turns to Sancho and, finding a pretext to eject him from this embarrassing altercation, sends him to the *bodega* to retrieve her notebook. Nobody speaks until he's left the room.

"Didn't you say last time we saw you everything was going well," Chábeli continues, "and you had a new client who was going to improve prospects? The one with the *chiringuitos*? Now you want us to pay for it because that failed? I don't think so!"

"That's not the way it works," Macu objects. "We can only pay ourselves out of what's left over once we've paid for everything else – employees, suppliers and so on. If there's nothing after that, there's no surplus for us to share. As we own equal stakes, we have to contribute equally to the future…"

Adelina rises from her chair. She suffers a minor coughing fit, spoiling the effect of her righteous indignation: "Macu, quite clearly you've mismanaged our affairs! Now you're asking us to rescue you. If there's anyone who's got to fix it, it's you. Why don't you just cut the wages? How much are you paying the young lad, for instance?"

She means 30-year-old Sancho. Had Macu answered, perhaps they would have been shocked by the paltry sum it actually was.

"Or yourself, for that matter? There's no question of losing our income! It's all we have, and it's not much! What are we going to live off without it? And we certainly won't pour good money after bad… Even if we had it," she adds after a short pause, just in case Macu gets the wrong idea.

For almost 40 years, the cousins have led lives of ease, funded entirely from their inheritance. This increased on their brother José Angel's death so that now each of them owns a quarter of the *bodega*. They have never grasped that there may be risks as well as rewards and that this precious endowment might one day cease giving. For them, their monthly draw is a birthright.

It looks like the meeting will come to a premature close, before Macu has explained the position properly, let alone made the case for new investment. The cousins start flailing around wildly with threats about lawyers, sacking Macu herself, or selling the whole enterprise to the highest bidder. Macu, who's regained some composure, reminds them that, yes, together they may own one half of *Bodegas Pinar*, but that she speaks for the other half. In other words, everything must happen by agreement, or not at all. But that's unlikely to help because it spells paralysis in the absence of engagement at any level.

The cousins declare there's nothing more to discuss until Macu has told them how she plans to fix it. And they expect to be paid as usual, including the Christmas bonus. With that, they gather up their possessions, mink coats and handbags; to a rustle of silk, a whiff of scent and with bangles a-jangling, they head for the door.

Macu and I stay behind for a debrief. She has found a candidate by the name of Iñaki Ybasta, to help with the books. In her view, it'll be transformational. She's already met him once; he's explained how he can bring it back to profit, in his view a matter of mobilising the formidable networks throughout the province to sell other products, especially the ones that are replacing wine – Coke, Kas and other drinks aimed at the next generation.

Soon after, Sancho reappears with Macu's notebook. She asks him to stay behind; but this time it's clear I'm no longer wanted.

A few days pass before I see Sancho again and hear what transpired. Aunt Macu has asked him to run the small offshoot, a distribution hub that the *bodega* runs in

Pueblo de la Vega.

"Congratulations! You must be pleased about that. Long overdue, in my view, though James'll miss your trips. I hope at last you're going to be paid properly."

"Well, not exactly. Yes, a small increase… I'm not going to get rich on it. But she did promise to transfer some shares to me. She's going to meet Perky about it," he says, referring to the family lawyer by that name. (Perky surely can't be his real name, but history's silent on how he came by this eccentric appellation.)

"Haven't we heard that story before?"

"Yes. But it sounded as if it might actually happen this time."

Chapter IV: Heirs Apparent

1

Over the winter, Uncle Benigno retires from his practice and he and Aunt Ludi leave the flat in Madrid to the next generation. They return to their roots, to their rickety but homely *dacha*, as they call it, just outside Bárcena's town limits.

A few years back, the *dacha* stood alone in the meadows studded with poplars and tumbledown farm buildings between Bárcena and the river. But recently, urban outcrops have filled the gaps, especially in their immediate environs. Benigno resisted the temptation to sell up, leaving his lone surviving property, a squat white oblong in its own rustic patch, surrounded by a hedge with villas beyond of the kind favoured by Bárcena's elite, the politicians, contractors, dentists and lawyers who have colonised the nascent suburb.

Benigno, permanently radiating disapproval towards wife and children, has never been easy. Hopes were that retirement might lift his mood, but it seems he exchanged one source of irritation – those entitled clients and their trivial demands – for another: a lack of purpose and structure. When the younger generation is in Bárcena, it bears the brunt of his temper.

For Mamí, her sister's arrival has been a timely boon, a new source of anecdote just when others were running dry. She's now a regular guest at the Blasco table on Sundays, giving her first-hand insight into the antics of her nephews and nieces. That's how, for example, the detail around Domingo's indiscretions finds its way into our circle.

A regular butt of Benigno's outbursts is his son-in-law, Carlos, married to Paloma, the teacher. Carlos is an intelligent, metropolitan, type – a '*progre*' – but he can be tactless, confrontational even, airing political views that reliably needle his father-in-law. Mamí tells us, for instance, of Benigno's tantrum when Carlos claimed Picasso was a Catalan: "Oh, interesting… I thought Picasso was Andaluz. Who else takes the fancy of your Catalan friends? Who else belongs in their Pantheon? Christopher Columbus, perhaps?"

"Funny, that, because Columbus's name was in fact Colom, which is Catalan. But really, do you think the Catalans would lay claim to that flagrant imperialist?"

According to Mamí, this triggered a ten-minute diatribe, during which Carlos kept ice cool, arms folded, immune to criticism, unwilling to budge from either heresy.

Raising tensions further are Carlos' eating habits. He constantly trials new diets and peddles them evangelically to his in-laws. Mamí has a story on the subject she loves to repeat, embellishing it over time as inspiration occurs. Apparently, when Carlos spurned Aunt Ludi's green beans, Benigno issued a fatwa: "In this household, if green beans are on offer, it's green beans that will be eaten. Those who refuse can get their own lunch at Casa Polín." In the later iterations of the story, Carlos rose from the table and set off for the bar.

It's Ludi's third son, Julito, though, who causes greatest upset. He's the gossipy, arty one, Mamí's soulmate, with several songs and a novel to his name as well as a coveted job with the administration in Madrid, drafting speeches for The Authorities. Apart from prestige and near-unsackable tenure, his hours conform to a *jornada intensiva*, leaving afternoons free for other pursuits, in Julito's case, for his creative endeavours. It sounds like a dream job.

But appearances deceive.

"I've given my notice!" Julito announces abruptly to the table one Sunday.

The shocked silence greeting his remark is broken only by the screech of Benigno's chair on the terracotta tiles as he slaps his napkin on the table and storms off. Most likely, he already had an inkling of this.

Once he's left, it's Beni who speaks up for the family:

"Let me get this straight, Julito. The most talented of us all, the family wordsmith, the family poet, wants to turn his back on a stellar career? Why on earth?"

"Because I hate my job! It's not what I want to do with my life. They're crooks, these people, all of them! Twisting words for the unscrupulous, that's what I do for a living! Quite apart from the stress."

"But it's up to you to raise the tone! And I never heard of a job without stress! Not a good one, anyway. What are you going to do instead?"

"I put in an offer on the haberdashers."

"What? Here? *Blanca y Merce*? Are you mad? Purveyor of bras and knickers to the matrons of Bárcena? You'll be bored silly! And you'll struggle, for certain – how'll you support the family? That'll be stressful all right! If you want that kind of life, why not the *bodega*? At least it's a proper business and you'd have prospects."

"Prospects? Me? At Pinar? You're joking! Nothing worse! Sharing a cell with Aunt all day long, watching things crumble? I intend to run my own life, not hers... Look at Domingo! Look at Sancho! In any case, she doesn't want me. She's hiring an accountant to fix her problems..."

"Julito, you're crazy! Think again!"

Paloma, the only other fully-fledged sibling present, also has her say. It hardens Julito's resolve still more. He's adamant; and soon, he's taken over the village haberdashery, *Blanca y Merce.*

It's a lively shop, where footfall is heavy. Single buttons, needles or kirby grips are dispensed in scraps of brown paper, folded and sealed with a patch of tape, and, though that doesn't bring in much revenue, it ensures the doorbell pings without remission and contributes to the sense that this is one of Bárcena's hubs, where customers come for the chat as well as the merchandise.

Julito engages his customers in conversation and settles into a coveted role, managing a clearing house for the town's business, personal as much as commercial. It's a role that comes easily to a member of the Pinar tribe since he's already well-known and liked in town. Moreover, Julito is engaging, witty and, occasionally, indiscreet. That's how more than one wife comes to suspect her husband's infidelities; and it accounts for the troublesome echoes Aunt Macu hears of her own worries about the *bodega*, which she wrongly ascribes to her cousins Chábeli and Adelina.

Julito imagines the numbers will look after themselves, but in practice, costs stubbornly exceed income. There are good reasons for this: he charges all sorts of extras to the haberdashers that the former owners never had to bear, including a car. But for Julito, it's essential – not any old delivery van, but a new Jeep, a proper ambassador for the firm. Moreover, the old ladies still own the building and charge rent. Julito also insists on "freshening things up", coats of paint here, new floors and window dressings there: he wants everyone to notice the ambitious new management. He's not troubled by the losses, arguing that these investments will take time to show a return and he still has funds to fall back on from his years as a civil servant. In any case, this is a slack time of year and business is bound to pick up as the festive season approaches.

When that doesn't materialise, Julito loses some of his chutzpah. He notices that footfall has slackened and wonders what he might be doing wrong. Could it be a reluctance to discuss intimate co-ordinates with him, especially when it comes to underwear? Maybe he did cross a boundary with his remark to one client that her problem bra might be pinching her nipple. It's not he who's embarrassed, but who's to say the Barcena ladies are equally forward? It's noticeable how much better these lines perform when his wife, Tere, takes over on Saturdays. But that hardly accounts for the attrition that gradually amplifies over a few seasons, to the extent that it even calls the business's viability into question.

Julito concludes the problem lies in the low value of items on sale. But he has a solution. By annexing the premises next door, which has been empty for several years, he could turn the enlarged area into a proper emporium under a "leisure" umbrella. He'll close the underwear section and replace it with beach items, crafts and games. In the annex, he will indulge his own passion by opening a bookshop. That way, he'll cover most of Bárcena's leisure pursuits – sunbathing, sewing, and the hot new field of video games, while the bookshop, though a niche taste, will rekindle his own enthusiasm for the whole endeavour.

The launch of the new store, rebranded *Julito & Tere*, is set for a Saturday in August, just before the *fiestas*, the time when much of the province gravitates to Bárcena. To mark the relaunch, Julito plans *canapés* and *Cava*, to which he has invited friends and regulars; he's also fixed posters in several bars and public spots round town to draw a wider audience. It attracts quite a crowd – not just the female customers but some spouses too, lured by the free booze. Most of the men are well known to Julito and enjoy a bit of innuendo at his expense: "Glad you're closing the underwear section! Not before time, in my view!"

As so often, we rely on Mamí – guest of honour at the party – for such snippets. She's not always the most reliable narrator; but her stories are generally true in spirit, if not always to the letter.

She has another one about the event that she's aching to share. According to her, a ping of the doorbell greeted the arrival of Gabi, daughter-in-law of Mamí's neighbour Nunci: that's the rather grand lady boasting kinship with the Ruiz-Toledos, no less. It was no surprise to see Gabi, but what was unexpected was to see her accompanied by her husband, Paco. There's a type of traditional Spaniard – Papí or Benigno, say – who wouldn't normally be seen dead in a shop such as *Julito & Tere*. Paco undoubtedly belongs among them, albeit from a younger demographic.

It's clear he's making a statement; there's a rumour, which Julito may have stoked, that the couple are estranged.

According to Mamí, Paco approaches the counter where Julito's serving the drinks.

"Paco! Good to see you! *Cava*? Or something stronger?"

"I'm not here for drinks, thank you," Paco says within earshot of several customers, "and you won't be surprised that I never drink *Cava*," he adds, enjoying a swipe at Julito's Catalan fizz. Just recently, many have joined a boycott of such products in protest at Catalonia's laundry-list of grievances and demands.

Julito looks at him quizzically, unsure where this is heading.

"I thought I'd clarify something else, for your benefit," Paco says. He beckons to Gabi, who joins him at the counter. He takes her by the waist and draws her close; then he administers a chaste peck to her forehead. "For the avoidance of doubt, that's all," he says.

Then he turns and heads for the exit, leaving Gabi at the counter facing a blushing Julito.

On the way back to Valledal, Marina voices her scepticism about Mamí's narrative.

"You don't really believe that, do you? Wildly embellished, in my opinion. My mother never allowed the truth to interfere with a good story. She has her reputation to think about. That's what keeps her going: she craves attention. Anyway, so what if Julito's indiscreet? He's hardly alone in that, certainly no more so than his aunt, and somebody has to uphold the family tradition!"

2

It's around this time that we coincide with a rare visit to Bárcena by Chus and Titi. They're on official business, presenting their new son, Antoine, to the family.

As expected, Mamí stifles the infant with affection, obsessing to her friends that "you'd never guess he even went on holiday to Africa". Just to be sure, she insists he wear a sun hat and smears him with factor 60, even on cloudy days.

Why the foreign name? It sounds like a deliberate provocation, though Chus insists he's named after Mamí's late brother, Toño.

"It's not written the same way and it sounds quite different!" she counters, "but if you say it's all the same, that's what I'll call him: Toño."

The name sticks, Toño he may now be, but he only understands French. Mamí's convinced that, too, is for show; but in practice, Chus barely addresses his son at all: after a couple of minutes, he loses interest and defers to the females. He'll make up for it when the boy's older, so he says.

That's all we hear from the couple and their son for a while, other than reports of occasional telephone calls. We learn that Titi has given birth once more, this time to a girl, Marga, completing a tidy 2+2 family. They've leased a house in Gabon and Chus even transferred a sum into his Bárcena account, by way of down-payment on a flat. It all seems unexpectedly humdrum.

But one day, Mamí springs a surprise: she tells us that Toño will be leaving Africa and will be coming to live with her. She never quite explains why, nor for how long. Malaria is mooted, but that's a default explanation – it's the reason Mamí gave for Marina's own dispatch from Africa years ago, controversial though that has always been.

Marina has her own theory about the adoption: "My mother's obsessed with Chus, so Toño's a kind of surrogate; when Chus was a boy, my mother kept him all to herself and sent me home to my aunt and grandmother – neither she nor Papí had much time for girls. Now it's the same story with the next generation. She'll mollycoddle Toño and expect love in return – probably in vain. Marga's birth makes it easier. A consolation prize for Titi."

By the time of our next trip to Bárcena, this has become the new reality. Our own children are a bit miffed by their relegation in Mamí's hierarchy, casualties of her passion for her newer grandson, the firstborn male, after all, of her own favourite, elder son.

Toño's a sickly child. Various afflictions come to mind, including the change in diet and climate; it could even be malaria, after all. He's clearly discombobulated. Like his father, he spent his first few years as a would-be Mowgli, wandering free in a way unimaginable in Europe. Suddenly, he's dropped into an alien environment, different from everyone else, addressed in a strange tongue, freedom curtailed. There's little sign of remorse from his parents, who soon head back to Africa. Contact with them becomes as sporadic as before.

Mamí's plan for Toño involves several understudies, who participate whether they like it or not. In the absence of servants, the focus falls on her daughters. That's what they're for, after all.

While Marina's drawn into the show, hers is but a cameo role, reflecting her sporadic presence in Bárcena, her "desertion" as Mamí calls it, glossing over any parallels with her own history. Still, whenever we come, Toño joins our family *de facto*.

But the main burden falls on Marta, still working at the *bodega*, hence handy for childcare duties. Fortunately, Marta adores children and is single herself, though her ideas about upbringing diverge sharply from her mother's. She blames Chus's failings on indulgence; she intends to avoid that error. Where Mamí is capricious, Marta will be consistent; where her mother is soft, she will be firm. She intends to tame Toño.

Rashly, she opens the campaign over the supper table, where everything will take place under her mother's critical gaze. Ever since Toño arrived, his eating habits have been a barometer of Mamí's success: according to her, "the boy eats everything". Marta's experience differs, since Mamí often allows Toño to skip the preliminaries, without which he does indeed eat "everything". So far, Marta has held back, but now she's cooking supper, she's determined to forge a new path.

She chooses that humble perennial of the Spanish table, the *tortilla de patatas*, potato omelette, for the battle. That, too, is a bad choice, because no two cooks agree on the right way to make a *tortilla*. As a reward for good conduct, Marta also prepares a dessert of *tocino del cielo*, "bacon from heaven", a gelatinous, egg yolk concoction suspended in a super-saturated sugar solution, which she knows to be irresistible to her nephew. It remains in sight but out of reach until justice is done to the *tortilla*.

As soon as Toño smells the *tortilla* he knows it's inedible. He pushes away the plate with its neat, glistening yellow slice and hunk of bread. Marta pushes it straight back, telling him that's all there is until he finishes it. Tears start to well up in Toño's eyes.

"It's the onions, isn't it? Thought so! How could you?" Mamí exclaims, outraged at her daughter's stupidity. She takes her grandson protectively round the shoulders. He buries his head in her sleeve and starts whimpering.

"Whoever taught you to use onions? Not me, for certain."

"Of course I use onions, I always do, like everyone else. If you said it had peppers in it or I burnt it, I'd agree. But how do you make a *tortilla* without onions?"

"It's quite simple: *you leave them out*. As they always should be – left out."

"I'm quite sure *you* always used onions until Toño arrived! I remember chopping them up for you… to spare your eyes…"

"Nonsense, I never have, and I never knew a proper cook who made *tortilla* with onions, it's a new-fangled idea. Anyway, what do you know about it? The last time you made it your father refused to eat it – the only time that ever happened. You know perfectly well that's the one thing your nephew won't eat because he's allergic…"

"Allergic?" Marta groans audibly and prepares to escalate in response to this change of tack. But she decides to fight another day on a more even pitch. "Allergies" are a handy prop that Mamí has recently discovered and is learning to wield to devastating effect.

"I can see I'd better leave this to you," Marta says, handing Mamí an unmissable chance for a spiteful retort: "Yes, you're right... leave it to me... as you always do! If you were married like any normal girl, you might make a better job of it! What do you think you're doing hanging out with that *maricón*[22] for a boyfriend? No chance of settling down with him! You know nothing about children; how could you? But until then, stop trying out your ideas on Toño!"

Marta storms out, leaving her parents to manage Toño alone.

Papí of course plays no part in the proceedings, though he's sitting by the TV connected to the oxygen bottle as usual, frowning at the commotion. He contributed little to his own children's upbringing and he's not planning to change that now. The whole thing's an infuriating imposition. Can't he be left in peace for one minute? He hisses an irritated "*sshhh!*"; how's he supposed to follow the match with that racket in the background?

"Thanks for your help, as ever!" Mamí snaps at him. "What a charming, sensitive, supportive, *useful* gentleman I had the good luck to marry!"

For Marta, the dispute triggers other decisions. Living like this in Bárcena, under her aunt's vigil by day and her mother's the rest of the time has become quite intolerable. Between their alternating outbursts, her only company for hours at a time is the scratch and squeak of Aunt Macu's fountain pen.

Marta persuades her former employer to re-engage her at a branch of the tourist board two hours from Bárcena and she resigns from her position at the *bodega*.

"It was never going to work," Sancho concludes. "My

---

[22] Gay boy.

sister idealised it – family business, close to home and friends. It's easy to get the wrong idea – a bit like Cousin Julito at the haberdashers. Fantasy meets reality! She never knew Aunt Macu up close before. Not many survive that… Now Aunt Macu has hired an accountant, a proper one. She was shocked how bad the numbers really were. I don't think she had much idea until the Domingo episode."

3

One Saturday afternoon Papí and Sancho are watching TV in the penumbra when the doorbell rings. Sancho squeezes past the spiky plants in the lobby and opens the front door. It's bright outside and it takes a few moments to register two young men of around 20 standing in the sun. Sancho can't place them: at a guess, they're immigrants seeking help, but they look vaguely familiar and hardly destitute. Strangely, they resemble one another but one is milk white and the other ebony black. After a few awkward seconds sizing each other up, Sancho asks them what they want.

"We'd like to speak to Don Cipriano," the white boy says, ceremoniously. "Your father, I assume? Tell him it's Juan-Pablo and Mateo. We've come to visit him. Is he home?"

"I'll see," says Sancho as he retreats indoors, leaving the two on the doorstep.

His explanation and the mention of their names provokes a fierce retort from Papí: "I don't want to see them, whoever they are! What am I supposed to do for them? Money, I expect? Tell them they've come to the wrong place."

"But they seem to know you… they asked for you by name."

"Nonsense. It's a scam! Send them away this instant.

Street urchins!"

Confused as he is by his father's vehemence, Sancho returns to the two boys and, in hostile tones, tells them to leave the premises forthwith. If not, he says he'll have to call the *Guardia Civil*.

"Don't think you've heard the last from us!" Juan-Pablo says from the safety of the street. "We'll be back. Your father owes us, and he knows it!"

Any attempt to engage Papí about the identity of the two is rebuffed. He refuses to talk about it, claiming he doesn't know who they are.

"And I don't want you saying anything to your mother, either!"

That piques Sancho's curiosity further. He has no intention of obeying his father's instructions. But he'll have to find the right moment to catch Mamí by herself. If Papí becomes agitated, who knows where it might end, what with that tenuous life-support contraption. Though Sancho sometimes describes his father as a *waste of space*, he doesn't want to be held responsible for the *coup de grâce*.

In any case, it occurs to him that Juan-Pablo and Mateo must be relatives – relatives of his own, that is. Could they be half-brothers? The more he thinks about it, the more plausible it becomes. Otherwise, why would two youths come looking for Papí, uttering veiled threats about "owing" them in that way? It explains Papí's evasiveness. In any case, in the infidelity stakes, Papí has form: everyone knows about his fling with schoolmistress Daniela, though it cooled long ago. Moreover, could it account for the familiar look? A family resemblance, perhaps? Finally, it squares with Papí's peregrinations. Twenty years ago or so… that would have been after Papí's ejection from Guinea but before his return, first in Guatemala, then Colombia. If Sancho's right about their ages, it's likely

131

they're offspring of Papí's, sired during his Colombian years. On that occasion, Mamí stayed home in Bárcena with the young siblings (himself and sister Marta) and Chus, while Marina attended convent school in some sandy pine grove on the Castilian tableland. The prospect of managing a teenage girl had been alarming and the chance of mending the long estrangement between mother and daughter had been squandered.

The thought makes Sancho dizzy and confused; he feels guilty even. Really? Two unknown brothers? And he spurned them, turfing them off the premises like that? He acted on instinct, his tendency to intemperance and overreaction, often without reliable evidence. The realisation only came once they'd gone; there's some kind of excuse in that…

He's far from sure how Mamí will react: it could cause a big shock, resulting in major histrionics. Or equally, she could be totally indifferent. Relations with Papí long since reached a state of armed neutrality, punctuated by low-level skirmishes. But they're bound together by economic necessity and, above all, propriety and fear of losing face. Then a third possibility occurs to him – likelihood, come to think of it: Mamí already knows about it and has kept it quiet for years. If so, her deceit is not much better than Papí's.

There's no good moment to speak to her that night. After he's gone to bed, perhaps he's imagining it, but the echoes of his parents' nightly slanging match sound louder than ever. Is that the crockery taking wing, too?

It really is time he moved out. But what options does he have on that derisory wage?

Next morning, Sancho heads for the kitchen while Papí's in bed upstairs. Minutes into his narrative, he circles the crucial point: "… I couldn't help asking myself whether…"

"Where did you get that idea from?" Mamí asks, "Always jumping to conclusions…"

"What conclusions?"

"I can see where you're heading. You're going to claim your father has a second family, aren't you?"

"It crossed my mind."

Quite clearly, his instincts served him well: she's known about this for a while, possibly for decades. Furthermore, she has clearly already discussed yesterday's visit with Papí. He must have divulged the news and she would have grasped the possible fallout immediately, now these two have tracked their father back home. No doubt that was the trigger for last night's fracas.

"I'm sure all sorts of foolish ideas cross your mind. Well, this one's absurd! How could you accuse your father of any such thing? And don't you dare start spreading rumours! Imagine! What am I going to say if this comes out? This is a small town, you know. Anyway, I've seen the photos. Not even good-looking, neither of them! You men, letting me down time after time… If it's not my husband, it's my son – if not one son, then the other. You'll send me to an early grave, the lot of you, mark my words!"

Sancho makes no further comment. But he immediately starts investigating how to drop the Expósito name altogether. He wants nothing further to do with it. If possible, he'll change to just plain "Sancho Pinar", and, if The Authorities insist on two names, it'll have to be "Sancho Pinar y Pinar".

4

Arriving in Valledal after any absence, however short, a priority is the garden tour. This small patch of green may not yet rival the gardens of the Generalife or Aranjuez, but the remarkable transformation of the original bare slab into a small oasis is gratifying. A covering of grass quickly hid the earth and gradually, with added hedges, shrubs and trees (mostly staples such as fig, walnut and chestnut, plus a Mediterranean touch from a few citrus trees that thrive here), the challenge soon switched to controlling the vegetation as it started to take over. Much of the time is therefore spent mowing, extracting nettles and thistles, chopping back ivy and pruning trees.

Bored villagers wander round the exterior to see what exactly this fellow's up to half-way up a tree, and to indulge in a bit of banter: *"¡Jolín! ¿Cómo trabajas, eh?"* ("Jesus! At work again, are you?") *"No paras ¿verdad?"* ("Never stop, do you?"); or the inevitable *"Vaya día de verano/otoño/primavera ¿no es cierto?"* ("What an amazing summer/autumn/spring day, don't you think?") A broad grin follows, accompanied by two or three shakes of the hand (= *"blimey"*).

Mamí pokes fun at my efforts too, though both she and Aunt Macu claim their lunches under our fig tree as of right. Last year, though, Aunt Macu spotted a sinister excrescence on one of the ramblers, whose leaves were contorted and flecked with patches of red and brown. Once we let slip that we brought the plants from England, she defaulted to her semaphore of folded arms and headshaking to imply that, of course, whatever else could be expected from Perfidious Albion? Mutant plants for pirates and fireships these days, right?

This time, a surprise awaits me on my tour. Shockingly, the huge walnut tree in Monchi's garden has vanished. I walk up to the wall to take a closer look – not so easy, now that so much prickly vegetation has taken root. But from one of the clear spots I can see that, apart from the felled walnut tree, nothing separates me from his ugly dwelling on the far side; moreover, a digger has started work on something else. Monchi himself is up a ladder hacking beneath the eaves with a hoe. He catches sight of me from the corner of his eye and raises a finger to signal he's coming over. I watch him descend, then head towards me with a calculated swagger.

"Clearing away the vermin," he says without prompting. "Filthy little creatures that they are."

For me, about the sole redeeming feature of his dwelling were the nesting martins and swallows. But I don't want to be side-tracked.

"What's going on here, though?" I say, pointing at the tree. "Wasn't that your pension?"

"Yes, you're right, it's my pension and I'm retiring. Time to fell the tree and sell the timber."

Retiring from what, exactly, I ask myself. His wife Fátima runs the *posada*, the inn, and Monchi is only ever seen skulking around the village, poking his nose into everyone else's affairs, looking for easy pickings or other trouble. He's the reason everyone clears away tools at night and leaves nothing unlocked. According to Soco, Monchi's a well-known flasher – he tried it out on her and Pepita once, extracting his tackle and relieving his bladder right in front of them by the roadside. She claims they walked on straight past him without flinching, as Soco remarked that she "didn't realise they came that small".

"What a pity – about the only mature tree in the village!"

"You're right, it's a shame. Planted by my grandfather, that was. But needs must."

"And what's going on here?" I ask, pointing to the trench running no more than about one metre from our wall.

"That's where the house is going."

"What house is that?"

"The house I'm building for my son, the one I told you about."

I have no recollection of his telling me any such thing. My Spanish isn't perfect, but I'm pretty sure I wouldn't have missed that. I need to find out exactly what's afoot and the best way of so doing won't be from him: better to consult the plans at the Town Hall in Tobillo. That the structure will be a *pegote* – an eyesore – is a given: Monchi can be relied on to deck it out with orange tiles, glue-on quoins and cornices, or erect a cement staircase to an upper entrance outside: there's no way of controlling such things. But I'm mostly concerned by its proximity to the wall – and there are rules about that, theoretically, at least.

Marina rings her cousin Rosuca at the Town Hall to fix a date for a visit.

"You say it's in the *Barrio Bajo* in Valledal?" Rosuca asks. "Next to you? Strange, because we only have six applications down there and none fits the description. So you won't find any plans here. The foundations must be three metres or more from the boundary. And in any case, the owner can't start without a licence. I'll ask the *aparejador* to take a look next time he's that way."

All this will take weeks, if it happens at all. In the current climate, almost any land classified *urbano*, including most of our immediate surroundings, is fair game and any that's still *rústico* isn't a lot safer, assuming adequate lubrication in the right spots. Indeed, our neighbour Tomás sold the plot below to a doctor from Castile and the adjacent one is also on sale. The only sure way to stop it is to buy out all the neighbours – unthinkable given the extortionate sums sought for any plot, however humble and mangy.

Marina and I decide to stroll down to Santa Rita, ostensibly to calm down but fully expecting another unpleasant surprise down the hill. On the way, there's a redundant silo, hitherto untouched. There are signs of activity here, too – nothing's off limits. However, when we reach the bend in the stony descent with the panoramic view of the project, all seems unexpectedly tranquil. That's partly because the golf course is finished, its lurid fairways diving in and out of the sanitised stands of trees. The clubhouse is also ready, and we can just discern the chapel with its iconic tree beyond, partially obscured by a raised "*pooting*" green, as they call it. The first of two arms that will embrace the course with villas and condos has also been laid out. But so far, there's little more than the street outline, peppered with faux-antique streetlamps and plastic housing for the utilities. There's no sign of activity at the moment, bar a single tractor sluicing weedkiller over the fairways.

Soco will surely know the story, so she's the next port of call back in the village. She's still in the old house but their new home over the road is advancing fast.

"So you haven't heard? *¡Los Ecologistas!*" she remarks scathingly when we explain. "It's gone to court. Look," she says, handing me a recent edition of *Voz del Golfo*.

At the best of times, this kind of article, in dense officialese laced with arcane references to statute, local and national, is impenetrable. It's quite possible to read an account of this kind without grasping the basic message, namely whether such-and-such a development has received the go-ahead or the reverse. Perhaps that's intentional, to keep everyone guessing.

But Miguelín, now a councillor for the regional party, provides more colour: "Yes, those clowns put a stop to the work, claiming the developers didn't have the permits, if you please. Because "it's a *Parque Natural*", they say. But that doesn't mean a thing! The whole point of a *Parque Natural* is to attract the tourists and support property prices!

It's quite simple! What's it got to do with Nature? Still, not to worry, the project's backed by some big names including the Ruiz-Toledos, so it's just a pause, nothing more. It'll be a while – the hearing won't happen until next year… Lucky we sold already! You might as well come and see how our own little project's getting on!"

Miguelín's project is nearing completion and it's only now evident just how tiny the house will be, squeezed onto a plot the size of a couple of garages, with other dwellings fore and aft and the road to one side. There's little to see inside but Miguelín lets on that there are already quarrels with Lorena, the neighbour, about access and parking. Miguelín proposed a plot-swap that would have benefitted both, but according to him, she refused point blank.

Marina inquires about the silos: what's going on there, exactly? That's Monchi, too, we're told; he's turning them into a *lavandería*, a "laundry", the place where, traditionally, housewives soap and scrub the linen on a sloping stone slab. Even round here, it's anachronistic. When we first came to Valledal, children used to collect water from the fountain and our own house had a single cold tap and no privy; but since then, most people have acquired cold and hot water, lavatories, then washing machines. In any case, there aren't any children these days. So what exactly is Monchi's game?

5

Dear Jack,

Glad to get your email. I suppose it'll force me to follow suit: but I know I'm going to miss pen and paper…

*   I thought of you the other day when I fell into rare conversation with our elusive neighbour, Dolores: nothing*

special, because for her, the only topic she trusts me with is the weather. But even that challenged her preconceptions, because when Marina joined in, she suddenly asked her: "Does he [it] understand?"

Even when I cross this hurdle, I'm faced with disbelief I might have acquired even the most rudimentary ideas about this country – basic geography, history, politics… Should I pretend otherwise, they object on principle.

It reminds me what you said about your in-laws. Don't stray onto their turf, whatever you do: they don't like it. Above all, keep your opinions about this country, especially its politics, to yourself…

But don't you agree that it's a blessing for expectations to be so low? It makes for a charmed life, free from entanglements, above the strife.

What, I therefore ask myself, drove me to jeopardise it all the other day? I broke my own rule by taking sides. I convinced nobody and by the end, it became near acrimonious. All I achieved was to notch up a few black marks with the extended family.

A bit of background: once a year Marina's maiden Aunt Inmaculada ("Aunt Macu" as she's known) takes her nephews and nieces out to a restaurant. In the family Aunt Macu still acts as de facto matriarch, though, as I've mentioned, it's emerging that family affairs have been mismanaged during her regime.

This year, about 15 of us plus a clutch of small children decamped to a new venue in an unpromising suburb of Pueblo de la Vega, just off the bypass in the shadow of mushrooming big-box retailers and fast-food joints. But where restaurants are concerned, there seems to be an inverse correlation between dismal environs and fine dining. Focus where it matters, perhaps? To signal its aspirations, the restaurant boasts one of those portholes favoured by Spanish restaurateurs, showcasing their produce to passers-by – a hunk of meat, an octopus, a couple of large fish. But they sometimes forget to freshen up the display. The side of beef and the pasty-eyed red-snapper looked far from happy.

Papí and Benigno view these events as Pinar affairs, which they're entitled to skip. Papí slopes off to Casa Polín with his cronies and Benigno enjoys his garden alone in peace. But this time, Benigno had another reason for non-attendance. He'd just had a row with his son-in-law, Carlos. Unusually, politics weren't the trigger this time, or only obliquely. Benigno, who had arrived that morning, found the garden untouched since he had left, and Carlos bore the brunt of his ire: "Don't you lift a finger? Can't you see it needs work? We do it all so you can lounge in the porch reading The Communist Manifesto or whatever that is?"

As the party set off for Pueblo de la Vega, Benigno, by way of rebuke, positioned the stepladder at the foot of the hedge. If the intent was to prompt Carlos to self-sacrifice, it failed dismally: his son-in-law stayed sprawled in his deckchair with the pamphlet, hairy leg dangling over one side. Instead, Benigno himself climbed the steps and began to tackle the several hundred metres of tangled vegetation, the "hedge", which mostly comprises brambles and other maleza.

Other than those two, most of the family you met all those years ago attended, including seven of the nine cousins. The exceptions were Puri, the secular nun, (we hardly ever see her) and Domingo, the number three cousin recently fired from the bodega. He claimed a "conversation class" at the Chinese takeaway (his way of dodging his aunt, no doubt). On this occasion, even my brother-in-law Chus (minus his Nefertiti) happened to coincide (his return is shrouded in mystery), along with the younger two, Sancho and Marta. A sprinkling from the next generation, in full party finery, spent most of the evening tearing round the restaurant – all of which the other customers tolerated with exemplary stoicism.

Rivalry between cousins is a commonplace, but in this case the split between the sub-clans surpasses mere jealousy. Politically, Aunt Ludi's brood, raised in the metropolis, veer to the left, especially Paloma and her husband Carlos, with Julito on the periphery and even Beni too, so far as his enigmatic persona allows. Conversely, Mamí's four span the right of the spectrum: that blend of provincial and colonial heritage plays a role. Its most vociferous advocates are Chus and, mood allowing, Sancho. It's the New Spain – liberal, internationalist, progressive – pitted against the Old Spain – nationalist, traditionalist, authoritarian.

That's a shade trite: some are more militant than others and it's obvious that, as the Madrid cousins prosper, they struggle to reconcile their left-wingery with their growing material ease. Conversely, the Old School curses modernity but seems quite at home with its comforts and diversions. Whatever, it accounts for a slight frisson on these occasions. Either politics are politely circumvented, or they take over and the event becomes animated, confrontational even.

This time, the three aunts huddled together at one end of the table, freeing centre stage for the older cousins. It ended *in a proper set-to between them, the first I've witnessed in a while. It was Sancho who set the ball rolling. He's the one who spent his youth slaving for a pittance at the winery. He wavers between diffidence and truculence, sometimes losing his temper completely.*

On this occasion the cue to challenge his cousins' nostrums must have become compelling when talk turned to that totem of the progre *value-system, the new status symbol, the Euro… Less vilification would have greeted him had he impugned the Immaculate Conception, though several of the cousins are unfashionably devout (excluding, paradoxically, Puri the "nun").*

"It'll end badly," Sancho said in answer to some comment from his neighbour, Julito's wife, Tere. She specialises in provocative statements. "We love the idea Europe'll bail us out, however much we mess up. Everyone lets rip, thinking somebody else will pick up the tab. It applies to the government too. But one day, that'll be put to the test and then we'll see."

The rebuttal came across the table, from Carlos, ostentatiously waving a can of Coca Cola "Lie" as he did so: "You can't be serious, Sancho, that's gibberish, as well you know… The whole point of the European project is solidarity. Otherwise, we'd be eaten for lunch."

"That's what I mean… the belief in solidarity's the heart of the problem. It encourages speculation and corruption."

That was the moment I broke my rule.

"Couldn't agree more! The world's bought into this idea, the Spanish renaissance, via the euro. Just yesterday, Voz del Golfo *was boasting how Spain is pouring more*

concrete than the rest of Europe combined. And the other day a minister claimed that Spain was "la octava potencia mundial".[23] When you get that far down the list, are you really a potencia at all?"

My intervention was too much for Paloma. I can't help recalling that she visited us on home turf several times. Unlike the rest of the family, she's conducted an in-depth survey of our domestic arrangements and, though we were dirt poor at the time, I suspect we didn't pass muster – politically, I mean. Now I'd given her the proof she'd sought ever since. I was rumbled; she'd raised the mask, as if my words justified the hunch she'd had all along: I had confirmed I was just the sort of bigot, the archetypal, anti-European, "Anglo-Saxon" she had always suspected me to be. Life's so refreshingly straightforward when everyone lives up to the clichés!

Wagging her index finger next to her face she, triumphantly delivered an insult she obviously considered withering: "Aha!" she said. "Just what I expected. I've been thinking about this for a while. I know exactly what you are, Rico… You're an Euroescéptico! Eh-oo-ro-es-THEP-ti-co", she repeated slowly, each of seven syllables a hammer blow to my standing on the Blasco side of the Pinar clan.

In an unguarded moment I'd blown all those years of equivocation, sitting on the fence – probably coming across as a somewhat doltish, but otherwise harmless bystander, invariably on the periphery. That's really the way I hoped it would stay, because now I'll be tarred with the Euroescéptico epithet till death us do part; and I won't

---

[23] The eighth world power

just be remembered for a few words of caution about the euro. In their book, I've probably transformed into a puce-faced neo-liberal, a self-declared facha.[24]

Chus took this as his cue to join in and, stoking the flames, embarked on a still more contentious rant. He wasn't even drunk — after a recent episode, the doctors prescribed a drug that makes him vomit if he so much as sniffs alcohol... Instead, alongside the tall stories, he lets off steam by venting his prejudices. Being Chus, that means Catalonia, when it's not the Basques. Chus launched into a spiel about how the Catalans are the opposite of most secessionist movements because, in this case, the supposedly "oppressed" are, as he put it: "The most prosperous people in the whole country by far, and what they don't like is having to share it with anyone else. The Catalans want independence because they want to keep it for themselves! How does that work as oppression? How does that fit in with the brotherhood of man?"

Paloma has a word for this kind of garbage, too. What we are (you see how I'm swept up in it now) is "espanyolistes" *(she uses the Catalan term), the small-minded Spanish nationalists, the heirs of Franco's* Movimiento, *the type that wears the flag on a watchstrap, or cufflinks and socks in patriotic red and yellow.*

Chus let his brother take over — Sancho was on fire by this stage.

"So, I suppose once they've left Spain, they'll want to rejoin Europe, will they? I thought Catalonia wanted out? One oppressor for another. Instead of Madrid calling the

---

[24] Fascist

shots, it'll be Brussels! For some reason, that's OK…"

Had I license to voice an opinion of my own rather than have them foisted on me, I might have said that a far greater threat than "identikit" Europe, bumbling Brussels, was the march of the multinationals, the Carrefours, the Burger Kings, the Decathlons of this world, all that tat surrounding this restaurant, come to think of it, with their advertising, their Coca Cola "Lie" and other paraphernalia, smuggled in via the Trojan Horse, the English language… That seems to me a far greater challenge to identity, whether Spanish or Catalan.

Beni sensed this; here's another person quick to jump to conclusions. He's the second oldest of the cousins, a promising scientist, steeped in his world of research and currently based with a highly regarded institute abroad. He's a man of few words, but he's fiercely intelligent – so much so that he predicts exactly what I'm thinking long before I work it out myself. On these occasions, he basks quietly, blinking and grinning like an alligator in the shallows, sizing me up, deciding on his moment to strike to maximum effect.

"When you came to Spain, Rico," he said in a soft tenor that commanded instant hush round the table, "I know what you wanted… what you were looking for was 'algo exótico' – something exotic," the last phrase he adds slowly, in English, with a Hispano-Californian twang – "egg-ZAD-ig".

On the face of it, it was a harmless remark; but from the glee among siblings and partners I could see that, as far as they were concerned, he'd delivered a terminal put-down.

I should simply have agreed with Beni; that might have

calmed the situation down. Truth be told, his comment wasn't entirely inaccurate: perhaps I really was "looking for something exotic". A big part of the appeal was how different it was here, that it hadn't sold out to Anglo-Saxon hegemony, multiculturalism, consumerism, along with the usual laundry list of tropes and grievances. And it still retained pockets of a rural culture that have almost vanished elsewhere. Recently, though, I've felt this to be under threat, and much of what I prized about it – the "eggzadig", if you will – is at risk.

Arguably I'm a symptom myself, as Paloma suggested – gentrifying local real estate, for example. Whatever I realise in these moments of lucidity, however, it doesn't prevent those stabs in the stomach every time I see bulldozers tearing out an avenue of planes or ripping down an ancient farmstead. And when I'm under pressure, as I was right then, it plays no role at all. So instead, I said: "Exotic, maybe. But isn't that better than monoculture? By the time there's nothing left but shopping malls and parking lots, and the lesser languages including your own have become quaint curiosities, maybe you'll wake up! But for now, you don't see where this is heading… or if you do, you don't seem to care!"

Carlos stepped in: "Lingua franca, lingua franca!" he said, as if that lapidary phrase crushed all else with its sheer weight. Which maybe it does… from a utilitarian standpoint, in any event.

"But it's not an equal relationship," I responded. "The English language isn't neutral… It brings a view about what civilisation ought to be like… A business arrangement, a profit and loss account – that's the baggage *it brings!"*

And Sancho adds, loudly: "Yes, it takes its superiority for granted and that's why it's a subtle instrument of imperialism, of capitalism, of cultural genocide, even!"

I could feel his rush of euphoria as he spat out those words. There's a kernel of truth in what he says. But the whole discussion was becoming rancorous. Even Chus thought we were taking leave of our senses – it's one thing slamming the Catalans, quite another signing up for this kind of subversive stuff, especially that "cultural genocide" claptrap. We were sounding like Catalans ourselves!

We were surrounded by hostile faces. Paloma seemed upset. The whole table, including the three aunts, took notice – the discussion was obviously getting out of hand. With a couple of flips of the hand, Aunt Macu gestured to Sancho to pipe down.

"That's total nonsense…" Carlos said, intending to have the last word, "'instrument of imperialism', if you please. More like a path to equality, sweeping away all those petty nationalisms. I realise it's disappointing for you, Rico. All that trouble learning our language: bit of a waste of time, right? Why bother, when we all speak perfect English?"

"And Spanish is sweeping away those annoying little curiosities, Catalan, Basque and so on," I replied, reluctant to let this one go, even now. "Rather similar, don't you think? In one breath you're their champions. In the next, you're advocating everything that'll speed their demise."

"Get used to it," Carlos responded, now parading his "perfect English", "Everyone knows English is actually the

global idiom".

"*I think you mean that* nowadays, *English is the global* language," *I said, relishing the gift of two elementary "false friends" in one pithy sentence.*

But Beni retaliated with another put-down, the first time I've heard this one: "The trouble with you, Rico, is you're just so irredeemably, how can I put it…? Analogue!"

At the time, I didn't quite know what to make of that – an up-to-date version of "you're a dinosaur", I assume. But it earns a laugh all round and it more or less seals the discussion.

On a lighter note, even my mother-in-law Gloriuca is starting to pick up the odd English phrase. But she invariably corrupts it slightly. So the phrase "¡eso es crack!" *that's now in fashion, which I suppose means "that's cool" in Spanglish, becomes "¡eso es* crap!" *on her lips…*

By the end of the meal, conversation reverted to safer topics as far as I was concerned. But there was something phony about this truce. For whatever reason, both old and young were becoming bored by the interminable post-prandial chat – the sobremesa *– and it was time to leave.*

But the evening held one further surprise.

When Aunt Ludi and the cousins arrived home at the dacha, there was no sign of Benigno. On seeing Inca's empty kennel, they reckoned he must have taken the mutt for a walk. Then they heard a whimper from the far side of the house. And that's where Paloma, rounding the shed to look for Inca, stumbled upon her father's body… He was lying at the foot of the stepladder, and he was dead…

Perhaps that last shock will displace the memory of our tetchy quarrel over lunch. I hope so, because I expect to be seeing rather more of the cousins in the coming months. That's because I'm eligible for a sabbatical. I'm not sure whether to take it later this year or next, but my thoughts are turning to an extended stay in Valledal. I can tackle the stalled magnum opus. It's about Spanish-German relations before and during the Civil War, this time... Perhaps we can arrange that walk, and I'll tell you more...

Abrazos for now,

Rico.

6

Uncle Benigno's funeral dominates the next few weeks. But Mamí's distracted: as so often, she's fretting about Chus. Why hasn't he left yet? When will he rejoin Titi and the new baby Marga? On inquiry, Chus claims he's not heading back just yet as he has "a lot of things to sort out" – unspecified "things" that don't seem too urgent. Soon it's obvious something's amiss because, one month on, he still shows no sign of leaving. Mamí probes further.

"Well, if you must know, I'm not going back because if I do, I'll be arrested," Chus eventually snaps in irritation.

"*¡Ay! ¡Virgen María!* What is it this time? *¡Vaya disgusto!*"[25]

"I was framed," he answers laconically.

How's she expected to believe that, Mamí protests, with the serial untruths he's told? And his job? What's he to do now? And his wife and baby? More to the point, what's *she* going to do now – now that everyone will be mocking her

---

[25] "How upsetting!"

behind her back and gloating over her misfortune…?

"Other mothers have such wonderful sons who do everything for them and they're the ones that get killed in car accidents!" she says to me, enigmatically. "But what about my son Chus?"

In time, some sort of a story emerges. It's "a" story, not necessarily "the" story. Still, after several iterations plus denials and corrections, some input from Titi and a process of triangulation, a reasonably plausible narrative takes shape.

It runs roughly thus:

The pills, the ones that keep him sober, ran out or – more plausibly – he lost them. Chus has no illusions about his weakness for the bottle and from now on, he intends to take them religiously. He feared the next binge wouldn't be forgiven – it's a miracle he didn't lose his job when he and his friend Sébastien, "Seb", both marinated in alcohol, crashed a truck and smashed company property in the compound where they were lodging. Seb was fired, but Chus survived because, despite his aberrations, he's a canny operator and remains valuable to his employer, *Concessionnaires Africaines S.A. – "CASA"*. In particular, he's well known for keeping the often lazy and unreliable locals in line. That's why he clung onto his job, last warning…

So, one weekend he decided to drop down to Libreville, the better part of a day's drive away, to see if he could replace the medicine – he couldn't afford another episode. Libreville is a much more serious city than Bata or Malabo, with proper hospitals and pharmacies, so this wasn't a ridiculous conceit and he set off at dawn to leave time to seek out the drug.

He toured all three main hospitals in Libreville, but none stocked the vital fix. Traffic was heavy, leaving time for one final effort – he decided to try the *Pharmacie des*

Forestiers which, apart from the reassuring name, was recommended as his best chance at one of the hospitals. But here, too, he drew a blank. The pharmacist had never heard of such a strange, self-abnegating potion that makes the user vomit at any sniff of alcohol.

Hot and morose, Chus needed a boost, so chose to overnight at the Okumé Palace, one of the luxurious hotels in Libreville, renowned for its ocean terrace and, a big plus in Chus's book, pliant women. But he had no time to sample their company because, minutes after dropping his luggage in his room, he happened upon an unexpected and not altogether welcome figure: sitting at the bar sipping beer, he found his erstwhile drinking companion and partner-in-crime from *CASA*, Sébastien.

Seb was already several drinks into the evening and growing restive. Chus's appearance reminded him of his dismissal, about which he was still resentful. Why was *he* singled out for such harsh treatment? That new Ops head, Pierre – the bastard… What did Chus have on him, then? Photographs? Or did Pierre have something on the side with Titi?

It was a joke, of course, but one with an edge of menace. Chus was lucid enough to grasp the danger and, applauding his self-restraint, refrained from taking a swipe at Seb's buck teeth. He would have to summon more of the resolve that had saved him with *CASA*.

Above all, demon drink couldn't be allowed to corrupt him this time, so he decided to pre-empt it by buying a round, promising himself he would make an early getaway. He dutifully ordered another draft *Leffe* for Seb and a Virgin Mary for himself, hoping the spice would mitigate his craving. Nonetheless, it required self-control, watching Seb, right by him, quaffing the corn-yellow nectar from his stoup.

"Did I hear you order a *Virgin* Mary? What have we here? Off the liquor again, my friend, are we? What's become of you? My old drinking mate! We can't have that, can we, surely? No, really not, otherwise how can we have fun like the old times?" Seb turned to the barman and requested a second *Leffe Pression*, "Large one, please, for my friend. And bring us the vodka bottle, too, while you're about it."

And after a few half-hearted attempts, at that point, Chus's resolve began to give. As soon as he placed his lips to the glass, it was full surrender. He jumped aboard that familiar conveyor belt to perdition, as reliable a fixture as the crimson sunset now spanning the ocean in front of the hotel.

Four or five rounds later, Seb floated the idea of a prank on his nemesis, Pierre, whose address in a smart suburb of Libreville was known to him. By now, Chus had entered the spirit and before long was proposing various schemes himself. Daub with insults? Deflate the tyres? Poison the dogs? It all depended on security, so they would have to work it out on the spot. Before leaving, Seb dropped into the hotel kitchen, returning triumphantly with a big bag of sugar.

"Sweetener?" Chus asked, with a grin.

"Sure. Pierre likes his cars, as you know... they soak it up."

Off they went, borrowing Seb's limping pickup, since Chus's vehicle was badged with the *CASA* logo. As they drove through the dimly lit streets Seb instructed Chus to grab the other props – a box of tacks, paint, matches, a crowbar – from beneath the passenger seat and put them in a bag he kicked across the floor from below the driving seat.

"This is it," Seb said after half an hour's drive.

From outside, it was forbidding, a bastion for the elite, with glass shards and coils of razor wire on top of the whitewashed palisade, with multiple cameras on stalks rotating and winking in the dark. There was a barrier and a sentry box at the entrance. Despite the alcohol coursing through his system, Chus still had the presence of mind for a quizzical look at Seb… How are we going to…?

It helped that they were both white. A grin at the sentry, a remark that they've got a couple of things to drop at Number 12 – ten minutes, no more – all expedited with a fistful of lucre – that did the trick; and the barrier rose.

"Forget Number 12," Seb said once they were through, "just a decoy, in case. We want Number 31."

Inside the compound, the headlights revealed a landscape of lush grass dotted with purple and scarlet bougainvillea. The houses were hidden behind wrought-iron gates, each invigilated by CCTV. Number 31 was a good way from the barrier, by the turning circle at the end of one of the crooked arms leading off the main avenue.

"Right," said Seb, "you get out and find the best way in while I deal with the car. Here, don't forget the tools," he added, seeing that Chus had left them by the passenger seat. "Oh, and the sweetener too…"

Chus raised his hood and, peering through the gates, discerned a clutch of f***-you 4x4s – chrome tailpipes, bloated tyres and tinted windows. Sitting ducks! That had to be the target. But how to get in? Round the side, perhaps?

Then, suddenly, he froze. Without warning, the whole place lit up with floodlights, picking him out *chiaroscuro* like a baroque marble; the next moment, dogs began to howl and seconds after that, a siren started blaring.

Chus turned on his heels to make a dash for the car. But where *was* the car? Then he saw the taillights, disappearing over a hump in the road, already too far off for him to catch up.

7

Waking up next morning on a straw mattress, badly bruised, with a sandpaper throat and throbbing skull, Chus soon pieced together the events of the night before. The security men had arrived first, finding him with the bag of props. They beat and kicked him blue before handing him to the police, who added their own insignia before bringing him to this cell at the *Prison Centrale*. He couldn't have managed a statement even if they'd asked for one.

The cell housed bugs of all kinds and Chus spent hours exterminating them, adding to the tally of squashed fauna that had evidently occupied previous inmates. Mercifully alone, he also had time to reflect, wondering if he really had been "framed"... Obviously, Seb couldn't have arranged it all in advance, because their meeting had been chance – he had only chosen the Okumé half an hour beforehand. But once in his clutches, Seb must have seized his opportunity for revenge – revenge on this worm, whose escape from CASA's justice had been at his expense. How gullible Chus had been... what a humiliation for one who prided himself on cunning and worldly wisdom!

One detail bothered him: with all the alarms blaring, how had Seb exited the compound himself, even *with* the car? Surely, the barrier would have been down? Seb was reckless, but not brazen enough, he thought, to smash through the barrier. But of course, very few things round here couldn't be fixed with a wad of banknotes.

Not that he had any of those left now and no cigarettes either – all gone in fees for bringing him here, it would seem. He would have killed for a smoke but couldn't think what currency to use for that or anything else, either inside

154

or outside jail. With next to nothing in the bank, his only resources were his native wit, his white skin, and… his wife Titi… possibly one of the most desirable women in Gabon, truly *despanpanante*, by his own reckoning. As a start, he needed to reach her.

The hatch in the cell door snapped open to reveal two bulging eyes. When the door opened, two warders entered, one with a bowl of gruel, the other standing guard by the door. Attempts to engage them in conversation yielded nothing until Chus tried a few words of Fang – one of several local languages he claims to speak fluently, though perhaps mostly for yelling orders. That earned a few laughs but no favours. Instead, they handed him a bucket to wash in and a mop to clean up the cell, had him empty slops down a drain, and then locked him up again.

So it continued for several weeks, as the solitude, the boredom, the filth, the heat, the absence of comforts took a toll on Chus's habitual optimism.

One day, however, the guards – different ones, this time – told him he had a visitor. He would be granted 15 minutes, no more.

Titi was awaiting him in another room where a few ceiling fans languorously swiped the air. There were other prisoners speaking to visitors through barred guichets and Chus took his place between two ruffians twice his size.

CASA had dropped him, Titi told him, as soon as they found out where he was and that had meant she had to leave the compound too. Back in Libreville, she had played her ace: she had an admirer, now a minister in the national government.

Three weeks later, Chus could leave the country. But there was a condition: he could not return to Gabon at any time, for any reason, unless expressly summoned by the Gabonese authorities. If he breaches the condition, he can expect to return to prison and to be kept there, next time with no prospect of release. Then they drove him to the border – Congo this time, because Guinea's also off-limits for him.

That's the point where pure conjecture takes over. What, exactly, transpired between Titi and the minister, or between Chus and Titi? For sure, Chus confirms that Titi's now living with the minister. Minister of Justice? And is his marriage at an end? None of this is clarified. What's certain is that, this time, Chus has no plans to change his marital status, his residency or anything else. Quite apart from taking a decision, in his view needlessly, there's the paperwork to think about.

He soon returns to normal, albeit a bit bored and penniless. Entertaining his old Fan Club is no longer feasible, at least not at his own expense. But now he has a new seam of stories, which, suitably embroidered, will delight many audiences over the coming months.

In Mamí's view, they're laughing at him – and at her; when she's not making excuses for him she chides him for spinning his shame as a badge of honour. Worse, her new cleaner Luisa picks up the talk about Chus's prison experience, meaning it'll soon be public knowledge. A month ago, Luisa herself was locked up on suspicion of arson and murder after her mother-in-law perished in a fire that burnt her house to the ground. Fortunately, Mamí supported Luisa's alibi that she was looking after Toño on the evening of the fire. But her husband's still inside – apparently, there was a dispute over a piece of land, so there's a motive. Since her release, Luisa's become an expert on prisons.

"*Ay, Señora,*" she says, when they're alone, "I can't believe what Señor Chus says about prison! They looked after me so well! Excellent food, breakfast, lunch, supper, lots to do, nice people, nothing to pay… the only bad thing was, they wouldn't let me go home in the evenings to sleep in my own bed! And in the end, I was so sorry to leave!"

8

One cold winter's evening Mamí and Papí are sitting at home in their funereal sitting room. Chus, Sancho and Marta are out, the TV blathers loudly as usual – no football today, just recycled Mexican soaps – and there's no fire in the hearth. Ironically for a lifelong smoker, a mere hint of smoke can prompt one of Papí's biblical coughing fits these days. They therefore rely on the radiation of a single bar from an electric heater.

Though she lost interest in cooking long ago, Mamí reckons it'll be warmer in the kitchen once she starts making the *sopa de mejillones* – mussel soup – which she plans for supper. Soup is about all Papí eats nowadays, provided he's given free rein with the spice bottle. Mamí long since abandoned that battle. In the days when she took pride in her cooking, Papí adulterated her offerings on the sly from his own supply of *picante*, one of many causes of strife.

She heats the oil in the pan, chops the onions, and starts to fry them, taking care they don't burn – that alone could seep into the sitting room and provoke an attack. But something else sparks an outburst, for soon she hears a guttural hacking and barking from next door, the gruesome preliminaries to a full-on crisis. Papí's coughing and wheezing, spluttering and retching becomes more alarming by the second until unexpectedly, it subsides. Mamí drops everything, more concerned than usual – it's different this time – and finds her husband clinging to the armrests, gasping for breath. Yes, it looks worse than usual, far worse, and she rushes to phone for an ambulance, returning to sit beside him.

Papí continues to struggle for several minutes, then his body slackens – she can see he's fading now, the moment of crisis seems to have passed. She takes him by the hand, her mind dwelling on the point-scoring and resentments that have blighted the last 50 years. She thinks of her youth in Guinea; of her abandonment; of the poverty and scrounging; and of Papí's serial infidelity. But it's too late for all that, too late to decontaminate a terminally sullied relationship. By the time the ambulancemen arrive and start wiring him up to their apparatus, Papí's unconscious… and shortly after, he rattles his last.

Then she remembers the onions on the hob. Mamí returns to a smoke-filled kitchen and a pan of cinders.

By the time we learn about Papí's death a few hours later the body has been removed to the mortuary and the rest of the family has congregated. Marina is booked on a flight for tomorrow morning. Papí died intestate, and Mamí decides on a cremation. She'll deal with the ashes later.

It was unlikely Marina would greet her father's death with outpourings of grief, given the history. But her description of Papí's wake and funeral as "merry" occasions defied expectations. As she phrased it, "I'd forgotten we Spaniards turn almost everything into a fiesta." I expect it reminded her just how dour her adopted countrymen are by comparison.

For as long as I knew Papí, he was choleric and curmudgeonly, but the funeral reminds us that, as propagated by family myth, he was once dashing and popular. There seem to be just enough witnesses alive to lend that credence. And despite everything, despite the sense everyone wanted him gone, Papí is missed. Enthroned in his reclining armchair, he belonged with the mahogany dressers and panelling, a fixture so permanent it's only noticed once it's gone.

Papí, however, never earned much and quickly squandered whatever came his way. Once Mamí returned to Bárcena from Africa, she was forever chasing some promised transfer or cheque, and little has changed since. Aside from his share of the house and a small pension, the sum to credit at Papí's bank stands at €55 on the date of his death.

"Well, it was the end of the month!" is Mamí's retort to Marina's outrage at so pitiful a legacy.

The family could just about enjoy the *Menú del Día* at Casa Polín for that sum but wouldn't get much change. The car, a Toyota 4x4, is rusting fast. In any case, it's not for sale; Chus needs it. It is just as well that Mamí receives a top-up from her sister Macu, supposedly to compensate for her lost dividends from the *bodega*. Even that doesn't come easily. Extracting funds *("mi cheque")* from her sister becomes a monthly ordeal for Mamí. It reminds Marina of the mind games Aunt Macu used to play years ago before finally disgorging the coveted *propina* at the end of our visits.

Several months on, the Blasco cousins arrange a memorial Mass for their father Benigno at San Telmo, a hangar-like church near his beloved *dacha*. Generously, they extend the honour to Papí, too. It's well-meant, but arguably eccentric, since neither Papí nor, as far as I know, Benigno, had faith in anything much, least of all in an afterlife.

Benigno's brother, Don Poncho, the Jesuit who married us, conducts the rites, striking a more sombre note than at Papí's recent funeral. Mamí is sandwiched between Marina and me, clearly unhappy about the event. She strongly resisted coming in the first place and now intends to show her displeasure. Her lips are zipped during the dirge-like responses; she groans audibly at a couple of Poncho's highfalutin platitudes; and she scarcely smothers a grimace when a fellow congregant wheels round for the mandatory handshake. Nor, even, does she rise to join the queue of communicants to partake of the actual body and blood of Our Lord.

"What were we celebrating exactly, I'd like to know?" she asks Marina after the Mass. "What did your father do to deserve that, I wonder? Other than leave us in the lurch, of course." Then, brightening suddenly, she adds: "Aha! That's it! Makes sense. We're celebrating his departure. It's been a long wait. A very long wait. At long last!"

Her fresh indignation was, apparently, sparked by an overdue *carta de pésame*[26] from Daniela, a former mistress of Papí's. At a stroke, all the rancour over his repeated betrayals returned with redoubled fury.

Her mind moves to his ashes, still held in a biodegradable urn at the crematorium, pending a decision on their destiny. To her chagrin, she discovers she cannot dispose of them at will: between the Church and other Authorities, it's all strictly regulated these days.

Marina hazards the view that, in her current mood, her mother would gladly flush Papí's remains down the lavatory or, better still, sprinkle them where they really belong: on the compost heap, along with the rest of the domestic garbage.

---

[26] Letter of condolence

Chapter V: Heir Intake

1

I'm on sabbatical this year and, in that context, what could be more appealing than months at a stretch in off-season Valledal? The primordial soup of a London January lends it special allure. With luck I'll hit a patch of *"viento sur"*, when a south wind clears the Atlantic mists for balmy stretches, sometimes lasting for weeks at a time. I'll enjoy productive mornings writing, followed by a few energetic hours in the garden, pruning or planting. Hence, once Marina's pacified (she'll join for half-term and will return for a longer spell from Easter), I set off full of anticipation for my solitary but promising sojourn in Valledal.

But maybe I allowed my imagination to run ahead a little too fast. I soon realise it won't be quite as expected: the locals see to that. It's not just the clamour of village life that upsets the tranquillity; it's their irrepressible curiosity about what on earth I can be up to here, in the middle of winter, *all by myself*.

First to broach it is Soco, from whom I receive a call within five minutes of the cab dropping me.

"*¡Te vi!*" she declares, triumphantly ("Gotcha!"). Then, after a pause: "And what happened to Marina? Where's *she*?"

When I explain she's coming later, Soco can't resist falling into her patent blend of banter and innuendo: "Oh! Marital tiff, I take it? Well, I wonder what plans you have. I'll be checking up on you and reporting back. Just making sure there's no mischief while she's away!"

Soco's far from alone. I face interrogations from several neighbours (Tomás's wife, Lorena the cleaner, Pepita, Midas and so on – but conspicuously, not from Monchi) usually delivered across the wall. It confirms how weird I really am – corroborating all their prejudices.

The sentiment is shared by the family, with Mamí in pole position. Apart from suspicion of my motives, she had only one day's warning of my unexpected visit – not enough to prime Bárcena with a suitable cover story. It follows that I must lie low for a while so she can prepare her circle and ward against unwelcome gossip.

But aside from that, I find myself dragged into the family's affairs rather more than bargained for. Above all comes renewed engagement with Aunt Macu, who wants my help with her continuing travails at the *bodega*. Over the several years since the fruitless discussions with cousins Chábeli and Adelina, she has mortgaged her properties one by one to keep it afloat. It's exacting a toll – she's lost some of her verve as the obsession with Pinar's future has become ever more consuming.

She tells me that her enthusiasm for Iñaki, the much-vaunted accountant hired as a panacea for her problems, waned long since: he spouts all sorts of businessy nostrums about "*turning the* bodega *round*", "*leveraging the distribution*", "*delivering the product the customer wants*" and so on. But the result? Next to nothing, so far; instead, the *bodega* has teetered ever closer to the abyss. No: Iñaki, she fears, is yet another mountebank, a chancer, not to be trusted, not to be trusted *at all*.

One day, Aunt Macu asks me to join her at the town hall in Bárcena. She's responding to a summons from Oscar Ortega, the victor in the recent mayoral elections, who declared his intention to "*shake things up after the stagnation*", implicating his predecessors Juanma (Papí's friend) and Juanma's son Jorge. In the absence of a formal agenda, Aunt Macu fears some nefarious plan to oust the *bodega* from its iconic warehouse in the centre of town. Yes, the thought crossed her own mind some time back; but now there's a chance her hand might be forced, it's frightening; and she frets about its likely manner of execution, the cost and the loss of face.

On a cold February morning I therefore find myself accompanying her to this assignation.

"What a pleasure! This is *so* long overdue!" Oscar says, bouncing to his feet from his squeaky black chair, beaming, as soon as we're ushered into his ample office with its three casement windows above the square and its crossed flags, one for the region, one for the nation and one for Europe. A solemn portrait of King Juan Carlos I, the Saviour of Democracy, is the only other adornment.

"Yes, last time you were just so high… it's certainly overdue! Don't tell me you're going to replace my geraniums at last? Is that what this is about?"

Aunt Macu thus reminds him of his humble origins; she's not inclined to allow this whippersnapper to patronise her. As a boy, he was a local terror, when he inhabited the flats opposite with those slovenly parents of his; I remember as well as she does the time a stray football from his boot toppled an entire row of potted geraniums in her garden. Since then, she's observed, with growing astonishment, Oscar prospering as owner of a building firm, *Obras y Servicios de Construcción, Acondicionamiento y Rehabilitación – OSCAR*; Oscar building himself a gin palace close to her sister's *dacha*; then, all of a sudden, Oscar standing for mayor and winning the contest outright. It all happened in a trice and the whole trajectory is deeply subversive of the natural order.

"*Jajaja*, sorry about that… But I hung up the boots, you'll be pleased to hear – too busy with the day job! In any case, very good of you to come! Delighted to meet your nephew, too. I thought we should have a chat. You see,

163

I'm planning to publish the *Blueprint for Development*, as promised in the manifesto. It should be ready in two or three months. But I need to take you through how it'll affect *Bodegas Pinar*."

Ortega has indeed decided it's time for the *bodega* to move out of town. How can he propel this aspiring *villa* to distinction with an antiquated warehouse at its very heart, with trucks shunting about and dropping barrels and pallets in the main square? What kind of image does it convey, when the most prominent building in town is so decrepit and visibly sloping? Above all, it's a deterrent for developers who would otherwise revamp the area and "*help enrich us all*". The council will contribute to the costs of moving, of course and, by the way, he knows the perfect location, a *polígono industrial* five minutes away, where he can fix us up with a choice corner spot.

"Anyway, let's make a date for a visit and we can take our discussions forward. I'll send you the *Blueprint* as soon as it's ready. And I promise to replace the geraniums… Better late than never, *jajaja*!"

On our way back to the *bodega* I expect Macu to share her misgivings now that the mayor is indeed forcing her into action. But her reaction is more nuanced than I expected. She has no illusions that Ortega himself stands to profit more than anyone else from it. No doubt the *polígono* belongs to him; or, if not, he has a deal with the owners, and *OSCAR* will surely win the lion's share of any spin-off construction work in Bárcena too. It remains to be seen how much of the cost will fall on her own shoulders.

But Aunt Macu reasons that she herself might also benefit. Apart from the need to move that strikes her in moments of lucidity, it could help force her cousins' hands; it could allow her to draw a line under those lingering Spanish Practices that, amid court actions, she never quite laid to rest; and it could catalyse a clear-out of some of the old lags at the *bodega*, which is chronically overmanned. Thanks to labour laws, the chances of a proper cull of this kind are minimal in the absence of an Act of God or similar: and Aunt Macu calculates that forced relocation might just about count as such.

Just before we part company, Aunt Macu springs an unexpected question on me. In fact, it's so far wide of our normal repertoire that it astonishes me: "Forgive me for asking something personal…" she says, "but I was wondering about your views of my nephew, Sancho?"

Instinctively, I take refuge in banalities, saying, "we get on well" and think he has "a lot to offer". She doesn't respond directly, but after a pause, she says: "I didn't realise he had so much fire in his belly. He's usually so passive with me. But that row at the restaurant last year… it set me thinking…"

A few days later, she arranges the visit to the *polígono* with Ortega but this time, asks Sancho to join in my place. She wants his views about how the operation might work out there. Doubtless, she's testing him afresh.

I take it from this that Aunt Macu is slowly dropping her reservations about her nephew Sancho. She's starting to value his abilities – a suitable bearer for the mantle of late cousin José-Angel, the brother of Chábeli and Adelina, so adored by the clients.

Over the past few years, he's made a reasonable stab at the outpost in Pueblo; at least he's honest and well-liked; sales are steady and, unlike everything else, it just about breaks even. With a bit of support from a decent bookkeeper and herself in the background… Who knows? Maybe Sancho's up to the challenge after all? After he repudiated his father's surname, he even bears the names of the founder himself, verbatim!

With Aunt Macu's car hardly roadworthy (she knows it's unfit for the main highway) and Sancho still too poor to run a car of his own, they make the short trip in one of the trucks, with Sancho taking the wheel.

"So glad you're coming along, Sancho… Never let it be said I'm not doing everything I can for you! And I can't think of a bigger decision for our future – your future, should I say – than this one. Anyway, we must have a serious talk about that."

"But Aunt, I can't be waiting for ever! I can't exist on this salary anymore! And the shares you promised, years ago! What happened about that? You realise I'll soon be 40? No more *serious talks*, please. We've had the same talks dozens of times already – about the role, about the shares, about the pay."

"But what on earth do you need so much money for? Or shares? All family, aren't we? I thought you'd broken off with Ana? You're not getting married or anything! Or is it back on again?"

Sancho shakes his head. That relationship was doomed the moment Ana began (as he put it to Mamí) "*shaping my destiny in terms of matching 'his 'n' hers' dressing gowns*".

But he's not ready to discuss his latest liaison. For, quite recently, Sancho has fallen for Rocío, a nubile creature who, better still, is surely a *braguetazo*,[27] as the only daughter of prosperous Tobillo merchant Gonzalo Caudal and his wife Lucía. Sancho frets about the wisdom of this coupling, though; because for all her charms, Rocío bears a stigma – one that the Pinars will certainly feel acutely, and one he can barely ignore himself. And that's why he hasn't had the nerve to break the news even to Mamí so far, let alone to his aunt.

---

[27] A big catch

As it happens, there's no need to elaborate because, with the truck straining up the hill towards the roundabout just short of the *polígono*, there's a toot from behind as an *Aurelio* truck cruises past, bottles and crates a-jingling at the rear on its way back to base in Tobillo. The mood sinks into despondence as Aunt Macu and Sancho reach the *polígono*. The symbolism's all too poignant.

Superficially, the *polígono* confirms everything Aunt Macu already knows: that the whole operation would be far more efficient out here. Without it, the future looks bleak. But as Ortega waves his arms around enthusiastically, explaining where a second *polígono* will be sited and where he's hoping to persuade a big supermarket chain to locate, her mind drifts elsewhere. How could she ever work out here, in this hangar in a random stretch of country with no link with her beloved Bárcena, other than an ugly stretch of ill-kempt thoroughfare? It's not just the drive itself – a challenge enough, even with a vehicle upgrade – but the sheer magnitude of the dislocation, beyond the territory she's inhabited for 50 years. She'd pine away! Even Tobillo looks attractive by comparison. Then she thinks of the *Aurelio* van, picturing their reaction to the move, how they'd gloat at the comeuppance of snooty *Bodegas Pinar*.

That's what convinces her the time has come for her retirement. The moment really must have arrived, and perhaps Sancho should after all be the chosen one. But she's still not quite ready; she doesn't want to make an error she'll regret to the end of her days. No, she must think it over just one final time.

And that's what she does. Not days or weeks, but several months transpire while she struggles once more with her remaining scruples.

It's an error. Sancho concludes it's yet another aria in

the same interminable Ring Cycle.

Meanwhile, the liaison with Rocío reaches a critical juncture. In a flash of enthusiasm, on a hike with Rocío, half in jest, Sancho proposes. But for Rocío, it's no joke: she turns her pale-blue eyes towards him and asks softly, without demur: "Do you really mean that?"

A week or two later, Aunt Macu finally summons Sancho to the kiosk. There he finds his aunt hunched over the ledgers, a tableau unchanged for as long as he can remember.

"Sancho, I wanted to tell you: it's all decided. I realise I've taken far too long about this, but I just had to get it right! I have an appointment with Perky next Wednesday. We're going to arrange the transfer of a 20% stake into your name, and your salary will be doubled from the beginning of next year, when you will take over as director of *Bodegas Pinar*… I'll retire but will be on hand for support, if need be… I'm so glad it's worked out at long last!"

There's an interval, while she waits for his response and examines his face, wondering why he's so short on enthusiasm. Then it comes: "But Aunt, I'm afraid I can't accept the offer… It's too late for that! I'm engaged to be married!"

"Yes, and? I'm surprised and delighted to hear that you are, it's about time! But I can't see what it's got to do with it. Your grandfather was a married man, and he ran the *bodega* for 40 years! Nobody gives up work just because they marry, do they? Quite the contrary, in fact! It usually gives them a reason not to, especially when new mouths to feed come along!"

"But it's going to be difficult, once I'm married, I'm afraid…"

"Why? What's the problem?"

"The problem, Aunt, is that my *novia* is Rocío

Caudal…"

Aunt Macu brings her hand to her mouth, as if to stifle an exclamation of horror and shock. A stunned silence settles between them, lasting an eternity.

Then Aunt Macu breaks the spell: "Did I really hear that right? You, Sancho Pinar, the one who bears the family name, my very own nephew, the one I singled out to run our venerable business, intends to marry none other than the daughter of our family's ancestral rivals, the Caudals, the owners of *Vinos Aurelio*? I can't believe it! It's devastating and it changes everything! Of course, it means you can't work here, not for one moment longer!"

It's one of the worst moments of disillusion Aunt Macu has experienced in all her years at the *bodega*. Now that she'd decided at last! Now that she was comfortable with her decision! And the grim humiliation of this development will be evident to everyone!

As soon as Sancho's gone, she picks up the phone to Mamí. To her disgust, her sister doesn't share her outrage. Yes, Mamí's initially shocked and indignant, but that's because of her sister's pre-emptive discovery of the match. But she doesn't share her sister's visceral hatred for the Caudals, never having shared her passion for *Bodegas Pinar* or believed in its superiority in the first place. For her, the *bodega* is inseparable from the tedium and drudgery of her youth, before her flight to Guinea. Moreover, the fact that Rocío merits the epithet "*guapísima*" (those pale blue eyes, the lustrous chestnut mane) comfortably trumps any issues of family history; and her mooted bank balance comes an honourable second: who knows? Some of the latter might even find its way in her direction!

Reeling from her sister's indifference to, or even approval of the match, Aunt Macu rehearses the succession options for the *bodega* yet again. Who can she trust? Obviously, it can't be that bounder Iñaki… a real mischief maker, full of talk and hopelessly gauche on the shop floor, pushy and arrogant towards his underlings… Anyway, it's got to be family. Once again, she screens all her nephews and nieces in desperation. Mamí's four are all compromised; and among Aunt Ludi's nine, Domingo left in disgrace; Beni and Nacho have joined the exodus abroad; and while Puri, the godless nun, is wedded to her good works, Paloma is positively welded to the faculty by virtue of her permanent tenure, the gold standard of Spanish teaching jobs. The youngest three are still studying, still unknowns.

That leaves a single hope as candidate for the role: her nephew Julito. Given the history at the haberdashers, she has reservations, but there's no obvious alternative. At least he can't marry the daughter of her worst competitor, not least because he's already locked up with the rather grating and, in her view, featherheaded, Tere. Yes, she herself will have to help out with the *soleras*, for sure: what does Julito know about them? But maybe she'll appreciate a proper role for herself. It'll keep her busy and give her an excuse to keep tabs on everything.

She perceives the enormity of the error she came so near to committing. Because she's not thinking of the consequences for Sancho, now cruelly ostracised, robbed of his prospects. She's thinking how close she came to relinquishing those shares… A straight gift to her lifelong rival! Imagine! She offers a quiet prayer to her maker, realising that her instinctive procrastination, her delivery from that fateful error, could only have been inspired by the Most High.

Julito's attempts to transform the haberdashers into a "leisure" store came to naught; in retrospect, he might have guessed that Bárcena and books would make improbable bedfellows. With savings from his years as a speechwriter running low, Julito cut his losses by closing the shop and taking up a position in public relations for a shopping complex near Madrid.

Here too, he fell into the kind of trap that's dogged him all along. Julito insinuates himself skilfully into almost any social web; that's his strength. But he doesn't always segregate corporate from personal, or fact from hearsay; nor does he always know where to draw the line in his efforts to make friends, to curry favour and be liked.

Once inside, he quickly formed bonds with everyone important, especially the women, including Sarito, PA to the boss. Almost as quickly, he invited confidences, some of which were simply too juicy to stay private.

The circumstances leading to his downfall echoed his public outing at Paco's instigation at the haberdashers. Stories about the boss's love life leaked into the public domain. That led to an inquisition in which Sarito, herself under suspicion, fingered Julito. Less than a year after a promising start, Julito found himself cast adrift with the frightening prospect of supporting Tere and the children without an income.

At this point of existential crisis, Aunt Macu's call arrives, two days after his dismissal. Julito can sense desperation in her voice as she entreats him: "I *need* you, Julito, I *really need* you! How can I convince you to come home? And to come soon?"

Her words imply she knows nothing yet of his dismissal… perhaps his mother Aunt Ludi's shame zipped her lips, which, if true, is a godsend indeed! For it opens a precious window of opportunity that may slam shut at any moment, as soon as his sacking becomes known to his aunt. His scruples about a role at the *bodega*, his scepticism about the setup and the outlook evaporate instantly given his own

171

urgent needs.

That's how Julito lands a package including free use of the five-bedroom flat on the corniche in the local capital; school fees underwritten; an off-the-scale salary; and a meaningful equity stake: in short, a prodigious haul by local standards. They further agree that she'll dismiss Iñaki Ybasta at the earliest opportunity, before Julito takes over, which (she's surprised to hear) he will be able to do within days. *("What? Don't you have to give notice?")* He'll become General Director with full power to bind the company. The only sticking point is the new car. Having managed for decades with the puddle-scooper, and with her lingering contempt for flashy status symbols, it's a step too far for Aunt Macu…. With that exception (Julito will fix it when the time is right) he has landed an extraordinary deal, quite beyond sense and wholly out of character with its instigator, the wary, conservative, frugal Aunt Macu.

Iñaki's dismissal takes place the very next day, Aunt Macu reposing the session with family lawyer Perky from Pueblo de la Vega. The meeting might turn nasty and, to pre-empt that, they plan to offer Iñaki a payoff he can't refuse – €12,000, a generous multiple of his monthly salary, times years of service. A letter setting out terms and conditions is at hand to expedite the deed.

After listening carefully, Iñaki takes the letter, which he quickly scans before derailing them with his reaction: "I'm sorry to say that's completely out of order. This is summary dismissal without cause. And what's this about *'no competition'*? No right to take a new job, even? For twelve months? It's outrageous and totally illegal, of course. I'll…"

"Not so fast! Without cause? Well, if you're looking for reasons," says Aunt Macu, ignoring Perky's stern advice to avoid argument, "let's start with those promises when you joined. Most important, you said you'd *turn the bodega round…*"

"And you said you'd fund it, let's remember. I said it couldn't be done for nothing… All I see is money going out, much of it to the owners, with no investment whatever coming in! No funding, no turnaround! This isn't a negotiation. All I want is a fair settlement, nothing more… I've got all day to work something out…"

With all the money she's poured in to staunch the losses, Aunt Macu finds these remarks particularly egregious.

"But it's a very generous offer… Money isn't everything, you know!"

Sometimes, that's what she really does think, whenever she remembers it's her role to champion old-fashioned frugality.

"I agree: money isn't everything. That's why you won't mind paying me my due. And don't think I'll agree to those restrictions. Unlike some people, I have a family to worry about! Why don't you think it over? I'll be back in an hour," Iñaki says, grabbing his coat from the back of the seat and heading for the door.

He uses the time to drop in at the bank to check the *bodega's* balance – €30,050 as of this morning. He instructs Asun, the bank teller, to freeze the account until further notice, such notice to be given on instruction by *both* signatories only, he stresses. He then kills the rest of the time at the *Politena*, where he calls a friend to check a point of employment law. Then he returns to the *bodega* to settle up.

"We've decided, as a special gesture," Aunt Macu states as soon as they're seated again, "to make an exception. I'm willing to bring your severance up to €15,000 plus holidays. And the competitive restrictions will be reduced to three months. That's an extremely generous offer, I'm sure you'll agree. It's also final…"

"No, I disagree, generous it is not, not at all. I'm afraid it doesn't come close, as you well know. Your lawyer *Señor Letrado* Perky most certainly does! You need to double it. I'm not accepting the employment restrictions and I demand a favourable reference. Failing that, our next meeting will be in court," he replies.

Aunt Macu and Perky request a short interlude to discuss this privately. In Perky's view, Iñaki holds all the cards – *"that's another thing we have to thank socialism for, I'm afraid, Doña Inmaculada!"*

"I should never have trusted a Basque – against my better instincts. Iñaki Ybasta, if you please! Seldom was a name more fitting."

One hour later, Iñaki's back at the bank, clutching a hand-written letter drafted by Perky and signed by Aunt Macu. The account is unfrozen and Asun disburses thirty thousand euros to him in cash. He will desist from seeking alternative employment for one month, but he has agreed the wording for the all-important reference that's promised in one week's time.

Before leaving, Perky helps draft a second letter, the formal offer to Julito, which Aunt Macu signs and dispatches at the post office. Then, bruised and humiliated by the morning's drama, she makes a rare exception to her routine, because she needs to talk; and in moments of stress, it's to her sisters that she turns, for all their shortcomings.

Only Mamí answers the call, and they agree to meet at *El Politena* in half an hour. Aunt Macu may be unaware (she inhabits a universe of her own) but, despite her pleasure at the betrothal, Mamí feels deeply slighted by the outcome at the *bodega*, which will see Julito leapfrog Sancho. Why didn't her sister act earlier? Sancho, who devoted half a working lifetime to the *bodega* and, by common consent, has been the bedrock of the whole affair for at least a decade. Had Aunt Macu sent the right signals at the right time, Mamí would likely not be facing this awkward situation with her second son. Yes, it's a good match, but he can't sponge off Rocío, not on a permanent basis, in any case. What kind of a husband would that make him?

Nor does Aunt Macu know that Mamí already spoke to her sister Ludi who told her the history of Julito's dismissal and Aunt Macu's serendipitous offer.

Aunt Macu goes to the bar directly and orders a *cortado* and a *pincho.* At last, she starts to relax, watching the world pass by, smiling at various friends – Asun from the bank, on a coffee break; Nunci's youngest, the podgy Campitos, returning from school. The familiar sights help her regain a little perspective and composure.

Some time after, she sees Mamí crossing the street to join her, wheeling a shopping trolley.

"Just heard the news," Mamí says, minutes into their tête-à-tête. She's not giving her sister a free pass, not after Sancho's iniquitous treatment. "I must say, I sometimes wonder about our nephew…"

"About Julito? What do you mean, '*wonder about*' him? There's nothing whatever to wonder about, as far as I know – nothing bad, at least. On the contrary, I'm delighted with him! He's just agreed to join us, join the *bodega*, I mean: he answered my prayers."

"Well that works well – for him, anyway. And *you* may be pleased to have him. I gather *they* were *not* pleased to have him and asked him to leave!"

"Asked him to leave?" Aunt Macu asks, remembering her nephew's instant release from his employer and glimpsing the blunder she might just have committed.

"Yes, according to Ludi, he left two days ago, under a cloud… a problem with the boss, she said."

2

Apart from the family duties, there's another interference with my writing agenda, namely my intention to progress some of the building projects here in Valledal. Last year, it was enclosing the attic bedroom; this year, it's the kitchen. And I have several more of these *caprichos*, as Mamí disapprovingly calls them, up my sleeve. What we *really* need (for example) is a *socarrena*, a covered outdoor space tailor-made for the changeable climate…

Perhaps we're infected by the construction virus, along with everyone else round here. For instance, Monchi is busy building just behind us – he's upset with us following our complaint to the council, which resulted in a fine and downsizing of his plans. Then there's the doctor just below, easing an outsized villa into a tiny plot, blocking the seaview. And there are the silos, just over the road, billed as a *lavandería*, which turned out to be another ploy (Monchi again) to avoid restrictions. It's an arms race. But there's one big exception: it's the development down the hill, which lost on appeal. It's quite unprecedented: all the local moguls, including the powerful Ruiz-Toledos, blocked by the court. It surely can't be the last word on the matter, though. That's not the way things work round here in my experience.

Our odd-job-man, Angel, comes for an update about the kitchen project and to take instructions on various tasks. We tour the house and garden, making a list of what needs fixing – a leak here, a rotten beam there, replastering, pruning, transplanting and so on. To an extent, the exercise is academic because, ever since Aunt Macu dismissed his wife Rosana from the *bodega*, Angel has become awkward. He now decides what to do himself. Anything else, anything he doesn't fancy or disagrees with on principle, he ignores – his version of Spanish Practices. For instance, after the bedroom conversion he refused to enclose the top floor staircase without removing the banisters. He has a special term for ideas he doesn't like: "*eso no dice*" ("that won't look right"). It took months before he acquiesced. In my view, the finished job does "*dice*" quite well after all.

All this takes time and, before I've managed even 5,000 words of the writing project, it's time for Marina and the children to join me for half term. Moreover, word of our stay has spread back home, and the next few months promise to be punctuated by visitors.

One of these is our Scottish friend, Hamish, who's been before. Hamish's principal focus on these trips is gastronomic. Just in case we fall short, he brings rare whiskies and keeps track of the preparations, dropping into the kitchen at intervals, lifting lids to sniff whatever's on the stove. If the fridge looks bare, he suggests a remedial shopping expedition. On those outings, he helps craft the menu for the coming few days and deploys his few phrases of schoolboy Italian ("*It's exactly the same as Spanish with a few tweaks*", i.e., an impressionistic sprinkling of lisps, grunts and guttural noises) to acquire the wines (noble, old, pricey). The success of his visit depends on happy congress between himself and his favourite dishes, including *garbanzos*, *migas* and *morcilla*,[28] washed down with copious libations.

These visits, which typically last about a week, conform to a pattern. The first few days are single-mindedly sybaritic. By mid-week, this starts to exact a toll, and

---

[28] Chick peas, breadcrumb hotpot, blood sausage.

Hamish, by now cream-faced, wonders testily why he's feeling "liverish". But instead of abstinence, he prefers alternative remedies – raw garlic and lemon infusions, reminders of which are dotted about the house at convenient staging posts. By the end of the week, still unaccountably queasy, Hamish's thoughts turn to this year's choice of restaurant, where he treats us all to a magnificent farewell feast.

This time, he expects me to join him in "some serious walking". I've tried explaining the locals don't understand the concept – try a stroll down any inviting track round here and see if you emerge without entanglement in impenetrable brambles or eucalyptus thickets. Alternatively, an intimidating mastiff will force a retreat.

Still, to meet his expectations I planned a walk following the crest of the *Sierra de Bárcena*, the first range parallel to the coast, running from Bárcena to San Onofrio de la Sierra for about 25km. But was there a viable path that way? None showed on the map, except for a zig-zag path down to San Onofrio at the far end.

Marina, revealing justifiable mistrust of local cartography and considering me accident-prone, insists I consult Angel on the subject: "He's much the best person to ask. He lives right at the foot of the *Sierra* and he worked in forestry for years. He knows that stretch of country like the back of his hand."

So next time Angel comes, I quiz him about my intended route: "You want to go up there? What, all the way? On foot? *¿A qué Santo?*[29] There's a perfectly good track to San Onofrio along the bottom, passable in any vehicle! I can run you along there if you want. Just let me know when."

---

[29] By what Saint / why on earth?

I try to explain that no, I really do want to go along the top, on foot. That's the whole point. But he looks at the ground and shakes his head, torn between sorrow and disbelief. Then he adds: "Well, there used to be a path. But I haven't been up there for years, nor has anyone else, as far as I know. I'm not sure if it's still there. Even then, it was a *camino, camino!*" which, I take it, signified "a rough and ready affair".

Hamish disregards all such discouragements. Nor is the foul weather any deterrent (*"there's no such thing as bad conditions, just wrong attire,"* he says, claiming a Scottish saying by way of authority). Still, I choose a less challenging walk, down the small road to Rio Escondido, our neighbour Soco's home village.

Even Hamish's enthusiasm wanes as the weather turns and water starts seeping through the *Gore-Tex*. Fortunately, a saviour appears in the guise of Soco, with husband Miguelín at the wheel, heading back to Valledal from her birthplace. As they approach through the mist, they grasp at once that the bedraggled figures could only be us two: who else could be unhinged enough to venture out on foot in a deluge? As we sit on the back seat on the way back to Valledal, steaming up the windows in our soaked clothes, Soco refrains from laughing out loud, but her shaking shoulders betray just how much she is enjoying the encounter with these *forasteros*.

"Well I never expected to owe my life to so lardy a lady," Hamish says once we're safely back home.

At the very end of the sabbatical, we leave the house to one particularly accident-prone couple, Charlie and Priscilla, with their two young sons. They score a hat-trick in a matter of days, starting with drainage malfunction; then the lights trip and they can't find the fusebox; and finally, the gas, the *butano*, runs out. Charlie himself goes missing on an exploratory walk through the eucalyptus, just as dusk falls.

Thereafter, we try letting the house, to recoup some of the outlay. But most prospective tenants are timewasters. The few who follow through either get lost or expect to be met in person at midnight, often both. They moan about the flies, the country aromas, the jangling cowbells and the boisterous *fiestas* – dancing and firecrackers – running into the small hours. And lettings regularly trigger other issues, too. On one occasion, the tenants couldn't work out why their baby kept crying until they discovered a leak, coursing down the inside slope of the roof and dripping straight onto the infant in her cot.

3

Throughout my sabbatical, Chus has been marooned in Bárcena following his ejection from Gabon. He's growing restive. As well as boredom and penury, he feels unwell, complaining of perpetual fatigue, aches and pains.

"Must be Spanish flu," he jokes.

He makes even less effort than usual with his son Toño; he seldom mentions Titi or Marga either, and days pass when he scarcely emerges from his den at all. Eventually, he becomes so sickly and withdrawn that Mamí decides there's no choice but to take him to the doctor.

Both she and Chus are evasive about the verdict. Mamí says Chus has an infection, but luckily, they caught it early and he's taking the medicine. It's no great leap to guess that it must be some kind of VD, perhaps even HIV. Mamí would have been less coy about anything else and to be fair, Chus never made a virtue of abstinence or monogamy. By all accounts, these maladies are rife in equatorial Africa.

However, after a few weeks Chus seems to have

banished the symptoms for now, and the cloud has lifted. The catalyst is a new job he claims to have landed, not in Africa this time, but in Romania, a new supply to sate the bottomless appetite for timber. Chus will join a group in the vanguard, as the country is now "opening up" for its admission to the European Union.

Next time we see him, freshly back from the new job and basking in sunshine by Mamí's kitchen door, Chus has become an expert on Romania and claims to have mastered the language too. Marina, Sancho and I are cornered while he expounds on the landscape, the forests, and the way of life: "Up in the mountains, round the fire, roast bear off the spit – what more could I ask for? That's what I call bliss!"

To seduce Marina (an art history buff), he dials up the tourist guff about medieval monasteries in the mountains. Sancho meanwhile looks annoyed: the times he's been force-fed this garbage!

In my case, Chus wants to sound me out about "*buying one of the…*"

In mid flow he bolts into the kitchen leaving everyone momentarily nonplussed. But it's just the coffee pot bubbling furiously on the hob, threatening to spoil a favourite fix (second only to tobacco, among legal ones), hence the unwonted dynamism.

"…buying one of the villages," he resumes as he returns, cradling an espresso. "Do you realise you can buy an entire village for a few thousand euros?"

I disabuse him of the idea I'm looking for a new project, let alone a duel with another dysfunctional and crooked bureaucracy in a country even more baffling than his own. But he warms to the theme.

"It's an amazing opportunity," he assures me. "But it won't last. This is *hot, hot, hot*! You should really think about it. How about a visit? Come and spend a few days with me – you'd enjoy it. I know all the right people."

Sancho is rolling his eyes at me and I'm thinking of the types he'll fix me up with, ready to strip me down to my underwear; and the cut he'll take, for sure. Still, just to humour him, I research it online; luckily, it transpires that it's currently illegal for foreigners to buy property in Romania…

Finally, of course, he likes the women, rates them highly in one special case: she's called Daria, he's very fond of her and he digs out some photos from his wallet for us to admire. She's attractive, but it's obvious she's several months pregnant. Mamí doesn't appear to have noticed so far, or maybe affects not to do so. Chus plans to introduce her to the family this summer.

That, however, brings an instant backlash from Mamí: "Don't you think I've had enough of that yet? You're still married to the last one, aren't you? No, I don't want to meet her. No, she's not coming to stay. Absolutely not. Don't you dare! Do you honestly believe a 20-year-old fancies you for your pretty face? Next thing, I'll be looking after her too, as well as Toño! Don't let me hear another word about it. Keep a mistress if you must, but not another wife! And whatever you do, don't bring her here. You think I don't know how your mind works… *Vaya cara que tienes, hijo mío.*"[30]

These tirades multiply, each more virulent than the last. Seldom has she sounded more resolute or consistent. Maybe she'll take a stand and follow through, for once.

A few months later, though, we're invited to meet Daria; and Daria is staying at Mamí's after all. Not only that, but she's brought the new baby too. Daria seems

---

[30] What a cheek you've got, my son

bright and kind, but the family sages concur with Mamí that this is all about medium-term budgetary planning on her part. Daria must have miscalculated, imagining she's hooked a wealthy man, treading the path of previous dupes, both of Chus and his father. But it's spark enough to rekindle Mamí's resentment towards her favourite son: "I knew it! That woman cheated you! She's a common whore. Just like the others. You say she loves you? How naïve can you be? And how many children does that make? I mean including the unofficial ones… assuming you haven't lost count, or even know about them… And if you don't, I suggest you keep it that way."

Marina suggests, à propos of "common whores", that babies generally require two parents; but it only raises the temperature further and Mamí turns her anger on her daughter.

And once again, Chus is unwell, prompting Mamí to speculate that he won't be able to return to Romania, and, that in addition to Toño, she'll be landed with an ailing son, plus Daria and the baby.

The sight of his brother languishing at home, sponging off a minimal family budget, stirs Sancho beyond endurance, too. There's one ugly occasion when Sancho, the "wardrobe" almost twice the size of his older brother, flips completely. He grabs his brother by the lapels, lifting him off the ground. He carries him to the wall and bangs him against the mahogany panelling, spelling out his message with each successive thump: "Don't – think – we'll – put – up – with – you – and – your – lot – one – more – second…"

It's an aggression that registers in Chus's skull for the time being.

Next day, he, Daria and the baby head back to Romania, "for good" he tells his mother.

4

After his initial approach, Oscar Ortega mixes threats with inducements to speed the departure of *Bodegas Pinar* from its ancestral landmark in the town centre. Loading and unloading in the renamed *Plaza Nelson Mandela* is restricted to narrow windows, mornings and afternoons; a raised kerb down the centre makes reversing trucks tricky. It's becoming impossible to run and the move cannot be postponed any longer.

Aunt Macu plays next to no role in the move – she's hardly set foot in the new *nave* since the first visit with Sancho – but she does stress about the *soleras*. Four of the largest and oldest barrels still lie in stacks with their valuable cargo at the back of the old building. According to the movers, they're too fragile to be shifted intact without a risky operation involving a crane, for which part of the roof will have to be removed. It causes friction between old and new managements. Aunt Macu concludes there's no alternative to the movers' plan; but Julito insists they syphon off the barrels and transfer the contents to new ones on site at the *polígono*. He's taken advice on the matter and shows his Aunt a short report, which its authors are ready to implement.

"The *soleras* will take a while to settle, I'm sure. But they'll be fine," Julito assures her as she leafs through the report.

"Why should we believe the snake-oil salesmen? It's a huge risk. The *soleras* haven't moved in decades, let alone released their precious essence like that. New barrels? It worries me sick! Don't forget: that's what makes us special, it's the core of our inheritance!"

Julito, however, has already taken steps and Aunt Macu feels she cannot interfere any further. After all, he just adopted his new title, *Director General, Bodegas Pinar e Hijos,* accompanied by an announcement to that effect in the pages of *Voz del Golfo*. She simply cannot overrule his first major decision.

The old building, cavernous but cheerless without the hubbub and hum of machinery, is boarded up, Aunt Macu herself hammers the last nail into the main door alongside the workmen in her own valedictory ceremony. Her final act is to pin a notice to it advising customers of the new premises and management.

The *bodega's* now up for sale. A survey concludes the site is viable, though piles will have to be sunk to stabilise the ground for any fresh development. A sale will therefore be challenging, but, fortunately, the queue of prospectors, many mediated by Ortega, is promising. Meanwhile, the change of management takes place. Aunt Macu finally retires and, from then on, never once darkens the doors of the new facility.

Late that summer, Sancho and Rocío opt for a discreet wedding at the *Gran Hotel de la Vega*, to which surviving parents, Sancho's siblings plus me and a handful of friends on both sides are invited. Rocío herself is an only child and her mother died suddenly, several years ago. Of course, there's no question of Aunt Macu joining the celebration; the same applies to the Blasco cousins.

Days before the lunch, Sancho confides that his father-in-law has offered him a position at *Vinos Aurelio*. For the next few years, he'll work on the commercial side, getting to know the clients; the promise is implicit that, come the old man's retirement, Sancho will take over day-to-day operations. The news reawakens Mamí's spirit and, seated next to Don Gonzalo, she holds court, just as she used to in her heyday.

"Such a charmer, Sancho's father-in-law," she tells us afterwards, glowing from her triumph. "I can't understand why my sisters are so snooty about him. It all seems rather ridiculous."

"Maybe ridiculous, but understandable," Marina responds. "They're in direct competition! Sancho'll be taking clients from *Pinar* or trying to. Imagine: Sancho Pinar, with *Vinos Aurelio*! It looks terrible, quite apart from the confusion it'll cause! What's more, Sancho's a pushy salesman, so don't expect a peaceful co-existence."

Catching up with Sancho after the proceedings, we share this exchange.

"Yes, it'll be awkward," Sancho says, "and between us, I'll be taking on rather more than originally intended. Don Gonzalo has been diagnosed with Parkinson's. I'm thinking of hiring Iñaki to help with the numbers. Not my forte, as you know."

"Iñaki?" I ask. "Didn't Aunt Macu let him go?"

"Only because he couldn't deliver on her unrealistic expectations. I got on well with him. He's very able. We complement one another."

"You really are burning your boats," Marina says.

"I don't have much choice…"

We, too, sample the new set-up when we collect our ration of the prized white wine vinegar from the *bodega*. It's a by-product of the *solera* process that regularly features among the trophies ferried home end-of-season; but because it's unstable, it has never been widely sold, reserved instead for a few special clients on a complimentary basis (mainly, to those with their own *solera*). But an addiction to this potion has developed in our household and we're responsible for spawning a following abroad that begs for supplies. Marina duly rings to pre-order six litres and later in the morning we set off, this year's expedition having the extra lure of a first visit to the *bodega* in its new incarnation.

The new warehouse is quiet, but there are a few trucks badged *BSP* parked on the forecourt and Julito's Jeep, a legacy from the haberdashers, is drawn up alongside. It must rankle, not just its age, but because it still bears the *Julito y Tere* logo. How jokey that sounds, now he's running a serious enterprise!

The bull's hide visage of Chencho, an old hand and survivor of the cull, peers round the back of one of the trucks; as soon as he sees us, he comes over, slapping me on the back extra heartily. Then he takes us into the hangar, pointing out the few points of interest before escorting us into the office.

Julito's transition from poet to entrepreneur, from supplicant to Bárcena mogul, has taken a big leap. He looks much older, fogeyish even, with his blazer and silk cravat, pressed trousers and burgundy loafers; he has gained weight round the midriff and carries his reflecting shades slipped over his oiled-back coif.

"Aha! Cousin Marina! What brings you to our fine new premises?" Julito peers round the side of his screen as he speaks.

"We ordered a few bottles of your famous vinegar…"

"Ah, yes, Lourdes will help you with that."

"Give me five minutes," Lourdes says from the only other desk in the office. "Remind me, how many was it?"

In the past, Lourdes would have rinsed the bottles, filled them with vinegar and handed them over without further ado. But now she puts her head round the door of the office and bawls across the *bodega* for Chencho to take charge.

When we finally land the vinegar in Valledal, instead of the usual elixir, it has the acrid aroma of an antiseptic tincture. We return it; but as a replacement, we're presented with an indifferent red wine substitute which bears no relationship to the real thing. When Marina rings to register her disappointment, Julito hands her back to Lourdes: "You see, we're not doing the white wine vinegar anymore. It takes time and costs money and we can't charge for it."

When we speak to Sancho about it, he immediately concludes: "Chencho told me they're having trouble with the *soleras* since the move. The vinegar must be a symptom of that. They'd be mad to drop it otherwise. The costs are small and it's a unique part of the offer. The clients love it!"

His near daily calls with Chencho give Sancho insight into the fortunes of the new management. For a start, for Julito it feels like banishment out in the *Polígono*, just as Aunt Macu expected; he finds his co-workers uncouth and there are few soulmates among the clients either, mostly small-town bar owners or diehards from the rural hinterland. The exception is Lourdes, the girl in the office who replaced Marta several years back. By dint of craven servility, Lourdes survived several years under Aunt Macu's aegis unscathed.

As a boss, Julito stands out from the throng. He seeks not to dominate; nor does he try to exploit the intimacy with a nubile subordinate in the time-honoured way. Instead, what he seeks is an amenable companion with whom to share the vicissitudes of the *bodega* – with whom to dissect the characters that people his new life. He's gathering material for his next book, for sure. Lourdes adapts slowly, testing the boundaries warily until she's sure it's safe to join in.

Sancho's taken aback by her transformation. What happened to the meek and industrious gofer who spared no efforts to oblige? She's changed into entitled *confidante* and *de facto* deputy to the director. Amongst her responsibilities, she now tends to the public – not that there are so many widows asking for refills as there used to be in Aunt Macu's day. Such as they are, Lourdes seems reluctant to oblige. It's beneath her dignity now.

According to Mamí, complaints multiply about much more than tainted vinegar and Lourdes' surly service. Some say the whole management has gone badly awry, with the MD and his "deputy" spending almost as much time surfing the internet and chatting in the office as out on the road. But much of this reflects ill-will from former staff, laid off in the restructuring. And Mamí, too, is far from impartial: Sancho, the soul of the affair, the absolute epitome of Bárcena life, forced out! Though only a few kilometres distant, Sancho's banishment to Tobillo feels almost as much of an exile as Chus's and Marina's. Mamí holds her sister Macu directly responsible.

But Mamí's sisters are inviolable – they're never the object of her tirades. It belongs to their unwritten code. Instead, Mamí must console herself by sharing – often with Marina and me – anything that supports the view that Julito's appointment is an injustice and a fatal error.

5

One day, Perky, the lawyer winding up Papí's estate, requests a meeting with Mamí. A couple of things have arisen in that context, including a *delicate matter* he'd like to discuss with her, and he suggests they meet at his office in Pueblo de la Vega. Chus is abroad, Sancho's touring suppliers in the south and Marta's at work in the mountains; but we're still enjoying the sabbatical in Valledal.

This places Mamí in a fix. The idea of an interview alone with Perky fills her with dread. Perky enjoys arcane technicalities and jargon which are always obscure, but there's also a twinkle that suggests he's teasing. In short,

189

she needs someone to deconstruct what it all means and, she hopes, to lend gravitas. But she must balance that against the risk this *delicate matter* might involve a revelation she'd rather not share with anyone, including friends, offspring or even her sisters – or rather, *especially* with her sisters.

Perhaps that's why she concludes that I'm the least bad option. Rightly or wrongly, after a long apprenticeship, she now considers me "honorary family", but she knows I'm still reassuringly semi-detached. Added to that, she has internalised all the clichés about British reserve and discretion: hence, in her book, I'm less likely to leak than most. It reminds me of the time she took me to Toño's school in Pueblo de la Vega to discuss his prospects, making the most of my teaching background, though it never had any relevance to Spanish secondary schooling or anything else close.

Marina has another idea. She has vague memories that the *casona* she lived in as a child next to the old *bodega* boasted solid oak fittings, mostly windows, doors and panelling. As far as she knows, they should still be there, and what use are they if the place is crumbling before our eyes? For all she knows, they disappeared long ago, but on inquiry, Aunt Macu tells her: "See what you can find… as far as I know it's all still there. But be careful where you tread! Nobody's been up there for a while and I'm not sure about the floorboards. Also, do keep it to yourselves. Otherwise, the rest of the family will want their share. I'll see if I can find the keys."

A small salvage operation is therefore the other priority and Mamí arranges the meeting with Perky. I find her agitated on the short drive to Pueblo de la Vega and even more so as we climb the stairs to Perky's *despacho* on the third-floor landing, where the diminutive lawyer meets us and steers us to his room. He takes his seat behind an old-style partner's desk backed by legal reference works. Once we've dispensed with the pleasantries about the family, he gets down to business.

"Let's get the easy bit out of the way first, shall we? As you know, there are a couple of matters pending from your husband's estate. You'll remember we discovered the house in Bárcena was never inscribed in the Property Register… This kind of thing's quite common – there would have been tax to pay, you see, and I dare say Don Cipriano felt he'd paid quite enough by then. Well, first the good news: I've managed to sort it out and, once you sign, we can file the papers." He then dazzles us with his account of the legal reefs he navigated to sort it out.

"The bad news is there's a cost. Quite a high one, in fact, because there's the tax itself, plus a fine for non-payment, plus compound interest on both of those since, I believe, 1973, plus administrative charges… and finally, my own small fee…"

He hands over a slip of paper itemising the cost of correcting Papí's historic tax-dodge. It amounts to several thousand euros, and I know all too well who will be expected to meet it. I have walked straight into Mamí's ambush.

Perky then turns to the main agenda.

"I received a letter from a colleague in Barcelona," he starts. "And this is the *delicate matter* I wanted to discuss with you."

Then he glances in my direction, as if to gauge whether to proceed with me in the room. Mamí pronounces me "*de confianza*" – to be trusted – so Perky continues.

"Other than the registration, the inheritance was settled a while ago now and I didn't expect to hear any more about it. But my colleague represents two young men who claim to be… your late husband's sons."

"*¡Virgen María!*" Mamí exclaims, crossing herself and instinctively affecting shock – though of course I know it's nothing of the sort. She gives me an uneasy glance. She's not so sure about my presence now; perhaps she expected Perky's summons to relate solely to settling the property tax, as just discussed; but she's not keen to rehearse this humiliation.

After a short interval she concludes there's no way back, for she jumps straight to the bottom line: "What do they want?"

"I'll come to that in a minute."

"But they'd have to prove it, wouldn't they? I mean, prove paternity?"

"That's what I wrote back," Perky responds. "But according to their lawyer your husband recognised them both, so there's no need. He registered the births at the Spanish Consulate – I have a copy of the certificate. That's why they're living here – they have Spanish citizenship."

That really is news to Mamí. Papí never breathed a word. He probably thought Mamí would forgive a few unofficial offspring, but recognise them? Why would he do that? It's folly, priming a fuse: guaranteed trouble. The first thing they must have done on coming of age was catch a plane over here, armed with Spanish passports. That must have been the time Sancho dismissed them so curtly.

Besides, Mamí asks, confirming she knows more about the claimants than she let on: "How can they be his sons if one's white, the other black and the mother *mestiza*? Their mother was obviously lying when she claimed they were his sons!"

"Well, I'm no expert on genetics but if you want absolute proof, Don Cipriano will have to be exhumed."

"*¡Ni hablar!*[31] she responds, picturing the macabre scene at the cemetery and the drama it would create in Bárcena. "Totally out of the question!"

"Then there's no way of stopping them from contesting the will," Perky goes on. "And though I said the only assets your husband left were his share of the house and the pension, which go to you automatically for the rest of your life *en usufructo*, they just won't accept there's nothing more than the €55 cash at the bank… He must have hidden money away somewhere, they think. They want an investigation…"

Mamí uses the trip home to lecture me about my responsibilities and impress on me the need for discretion. That's unexpected, because, as an unrelated male I fall into a category usually spared such pep talks... Perhaps I really am joining the family after all. She underlines her points with the familiar gesture, wagging her right index finger in admonishment; but in her case, it comes with a twist, as it were. As a young girl, she broke that finger and medical care during the Civil War was patchy. Ever since, her right index finger has sheared off to the left at a 45-degree angle from the top joint. Hence the gesture which, from my vantage point as driver, resembles a question mark, loses much of its menace.

"That means everyone!" she adds, as we arrive, just in case I'm tempted to talk to Marina about it.

But share it with Marina of course I do (she knows most of it already), and she comments that the attitude of the Colombian boys, Juan-Pablo and Mateo, is hardly surprising. In his Colombian days, especially to the young boys, Papí must have cut a dash and come across as a big shot amid the poverty of the Colombian *bosque*. So, what

---

[31] "No way!"

happened to the loot?

And indeed, they're right: it's a mystery to the rest of us too. Where did it go? What's to show for 40 years' toil in the tropics, with the toll it took on his health and his family? If Papí hid any money, its whereabouts is a secret he took with him to the grave. For the time being, there's nothing more we can do but await the "investigation". It's unlikely, but maybe there's an outside chance that some phantom stash will materialise to the advantage of *both* sides.

The salvage operation at the *casona* takes place that afternoon. Armed with keys, a torch and heavy gloves we succeed in dragging open the main door, which has slipped on its hinges and rests directly on the flags. We climb the murky staircase behind, leading up to the apartment above what once was an overflow from the *bodega*. Marina hasn't been up here since childhood and can't hide her shock at the state of the place: full of grit, cobwebs and rodent droppings. The fittings are still there, but most are damp-stained and pockmarked with woodworm. Out of perhaps 30, only one set of double doors and one other single door with glass panels are worthy of rescue.

After arranging for the doors to be fumigated by our friends at *Norteña de Desinfección* we drop in at Mamí's house before heading home. It's dark, but the back door's open; sitting alone on the sofa we find a bored Toño, 'Toni' as he now calls himself, thereby adding a third identity to the mix: "Antoine"; "Toño"; and now "Toni". His face is lit by the screen of his Gameboy, a blob of resentment and reproach.

Mamí tried to interest Toni in a course in machinery maintenance in Pueblo. It'll start when he reaches 18; afterwards, Mamí plans to play her ace with neighbour Nunci to place him at the textile factory. With Toni's majority, at least the threats to send him "back home" will cease for good. Mamí used it countless times over the years; Toni feared that his mother Titi planned to marry him off. It's pure supposition since he and his mother exchanged words only three times over about 12 years, and, since Toni lost his French, they don't even share a language.

In different guises, communication problems also apply to Toni's sister, Marga, whom Chus brought to Bárcena last year to meet the family. Even if she spoke Spanish, it would be hard work: she's moody and monosyllabic, as I discovered on driving her back to the airport at the end of her stay. Conversation was stilted on that long trip. Yes, I'm out of practice with her age group. I tried Harry Potter: hadn't heard of it; school? "*Ennuyeux*" – *boring*; Bárcena? "*Je préfère Monthenault*", Monthenault being the village outside Grenoble where she now lives with her mother Titi, the Gabonese ex-minister, and a medley of half- and stepsiblings. I treated myself to a celebratory *caña* and a *pincho* as soon as she'd checked in and passed security.

In Bárcena, the main topic of interest around Marga, though, is just how *white* she is. In Mamí's rendering, shared with all-comers, it comes out as: "*la nena es blanca, blanca, blanca, blanca, blanca*",[32] by which she means not just *any* white, but white as an egret, or whatever those handkerchief-white birds are, flocks of which are to be seen feasting off bugs on and around local cattle. The first "*blanca*" she utters at a high pitch and each successive "*blanca*" follows at accelerating speed, one semi-tone lower than the preceding one.

---

[32] The girl's white, white, white, white, white.

6

Jack,

Glad we managed to fit in the walk during my sabbatical, but we should try something more challenging next time. Our local pilgrimage route really isn't up to much, is it? I'm inclined to agree with the locals that the whole thing's a make-up for the tourists. What evidence is there that genuine pilgrims passed that way? For a start, I doubt those tracks stringing one abandoned development to another even existed 20 years ago, let alone in the Middle Ages.

Talking of developments, that brings me to the topic of the moment: as you said, this meltdown shows no sign of abating: on the contrary, I'd say it's only just started. Round here, nobody's capitulating yet, not the property-owners at least; they all still think it'll bounce back.

After you left, Marina's dear friend Jo came to stay. Jo's good company, but she can be hard work, especially when she brings her hungry offspring plus friend(s), meaning shopping and cooking for the duration (Jo claims she can't boil an egg – false modesty of course, but that's another story). But this time she came alone. She was looking forward to her trip, asking Marina: "What's on the social calendar for my visit this year?" and "Are we going to invite that nice family you introduced me to last time?"

Anyway, we enjoyed a bit of "disaster tourism" with Jo, who finds the abandoned housing estates and malls almost as poignant as we do. Sic transit gloria mundi *and all that… Since you left, we heard that the Supreme Court finally and definitively quashed the development down the hill, Santa Rita. The site itself is already becoming an archaeological curiosity: it doesn't take long for vegetation to smother a grid of streets and lampposts. It must be unique – one lonely battle fought by the despised* Ecologistas *wins in open court against all the provincial heavies, including the Ruiz-Toledos themselves. Ironically, the courts probably did the developers a favour. If it hadn't stalled, they would be in much deeper by now and all those* chalés *would join the other half-finished, unsaleable, developments all around.*

I should stress that Jo makes up for her deficiencies in the kitchen with her skills in the garden. In fact, she manages to galvanise my own dilatory efforts. As soon as she arrives, she's worked out a plan of action, for instance: "Don't you think the nettles need tackling?" or "Shall we prune the roses during my stay?" She's unfailingly generous, escorting me to the local nursery to treat me to a couple of cypresses or a climbing rose. However idle I'm feeling, I can't let these opportunities go to waste because, apart from the plan itself, she's extraordinarily energetic. This time, she suggested the ivy, which not only smothers much of the perimeter wall, but stands at least four or five feet thick in some places. By the time Jo left, we'd spent four afternoons attacking the worst of it, leaving only the final stretch for me to finish.

About the only items we inherited from the previous owners are two traditional hoes of a kind that, as far as I know, died out in Britain a century ago or more. They consist of a weighty, concave iron blade mounted perpendicular to a long wooden shaft and, for a job like this, they're ideal, slicing as they do deep under the roots of the ivy and making it simple to rip them out by hand. The day after Jo's departure, I got to work. With my very first blow I do indeed swipe deep under the roots of a stubborn hedera helix, *but momentum carries the implement further, making a sharp 'clang' as it hits an unforeseen obstacle beneath. Immediately, a jet of water shoots twenty metres into the air like an oil gusher. I've ruptured a water main I was completely unaware of!*

Within minutes the water saturates that part of the garden. Thanks to the contours, the gathering tsunami misses our house;

instead, it skirts round it, then courses down the drive towards the lower part of the perimeter wall. That proves a temporary obstacle but, in no time, water finds a way through, crosses the track beyond and pours straight into the doctor's "villa"… Of course, I'm in total panic myself, trying to find a tap somewhere, attempting to staunch the flow by placing stones over the pipe and seeking to divert the water from the doctor's property – all to no avail. The desperate doctor soon appears but has little to offer but curses and abuse.

Then, behind the wall, just at the point where "el siniestro" occurred, two figures appear: not Monchi himself, but his wife, Fátima, the one who runs the guest house and her son, a thick-set bruiser about 20 years old – Nino. My expectations are low – a torrent of bile to match the gusher in the garden is a given.

But no! Fátima has something positive to propose! She says that the water board just finished a job in the village, and I might just be lucky… She sends off Nino to look for them. Ten minutes later, two workmen in orange suits appear and set to work.

While they're at it, I retire indoors. I can't bear to watch and I'm wrestling with the conundrum it poses. For here I am, the sudden beneficiary of an act of extraordinary altruism on the part of our slippery neighbours, a family who've hitherto caused nothing but grief. Surely, I should seize the moment to cauterise the wound? Put an end to the puerile enmity at last? That's Marina's advice, anyway. Unlike me, she's an instinctive peacemaker. But how much simpler it was when the Monchis were the personification of evil! Now I'll need to be more nuanced. It'll be a challenge.

I'm still cogitating when there's a sharp rap on the front door, making me jump – it's the two orange suits. Good news, they tell me, they've fixed the leak, I shouldn't have any problems, "provided I put away that hoe, jajaja!"

Then there's a pause. Looking shifty, eyes on the ground, the *older of the two says:*

"Es que…"

That phrase, "the thing is that…" nearly always spells trouble. Sure enough:

"It was an unscheduled stop. Unpaid. We can't reclaim it, neither time nor materials…"

Of course, I should have foreseen that – hardly unreasonable, I suppose. And didn't Adolfo, one-time Presidente of the Junta Vecinal, deliver one of his maxims on the subject, years ago: "When did anyone round here ever do anything for free?"

Truth be told, when the geyser was in full flood a short while ago, I would gladly have mortgaged the children's future, anything almost, to plug it.

"So, what exactly do you want?"

The figure he cites sounds like a respectable win on the Christmas lottery; as a call-out fee, it'd easily trump many a white-collar superstar such as Perky. I splutter impotently – I don't have that kind of money on me.

"We're happy to wait. There's a cash machine in Tobillo," *he says, regaining confidence,* "by the ferretería… If not, we can always put it back as it was... if you're unhappy with the workmanship."

On the round trip I join up the dots. Not only did our leak bring a tidy windfall to the workmen. For sure, there will be a healthy tithe for the neighbours, too…

Well, at least that solves the Monchi quandary.

Such was our property drama of the season. But Aunt Macu also suffered a reverse with the old wine warehouse, which has been empty for months. She's now desperate to sell. Every time someone looks in earnest, they start to prevaricate about the subsidence, despite guarantees and studies showing the problem is soluble. This time, however, they found somebody willing to take it on at the full asking price. Rumour has it that it was made on behalf of the richest family in the vicinity, the Ruiz-

Toledos. We've long known about their interest in the bodega.

And the reaction? Despite the best efforts of Marina's aunt to persuade her cousins (as joint owners, they must all agree), they refused to budge. The price was too low after all, and the offer was rejected! Bear in mind it needs a fortune spent on the foundations alone... It probably means the whale will be rotting on its strand for decades. Meanwhile, who'll pay the debts and support those indigent family members?

Well, Jack, I'm relying on you to suggest a suitable route for our next walk. After last time, I should probably abstain…

Rico

7

Months after our joint meeting with Perky (the sabbatical's now a fast-receding memory), Mamí undergoes a heart operation. There are complications: at one point, her pulse ceases altogether, and Marina flies out in a hurry. I join her a fortnight later, by which time Mamí has staged a remarkable comeback and been released from hospital. I find her recovering at home, assisted by a luminous virgin in a box, on loan from the church, which presides from the dining table.

"I expect you found the experience changed your mother," I say to Marina as she takes me upstairs to visit the convalescent, "that kind of brush with mortality so often has that effect."

"Yes, you're right, it did change her."

She calls my bluff with that reply, however, because my remark was half in jest. For all her public piety, Mamí strikes me as far too worldly for the kind of serenity and detachment that supposedly derives from near-death experiences.

But Marina hasn't finished: "Yes, it changed her; but

not permanently. Only for about an afternoon, in fact. She returned to normal soon enough, buoyed by the compliments on her resilience and youthful appearance."

That's confirmed when we see her: "They refused to believe my age at the hospital," she repeats a dozen times. "And what do you think about my scar? Everyone was amazed it healed so quickly… they thought I must be 20 years younger. "*What skin you have!*" they told me."

Her ordeal also elicits sympathy – useful currency in the bid for attention from her stingy offspring, who can no longer spurn her pleas for lifts to the Medical Centre or other errands quite so readily.

But cheerfulness is now the exception. Already, before Sancho's marriage, Mamí's complaints about her "solitude" and her "abandonment" started to multiply. It counts for nothing that she lives right in the middle of town, next to the church, directly opposite her best friend Nunci, her sister Macu's new flat in the block next door and known to all in a broad radius: almost everyone over the age of about 20 has at least heard of *Gloriuca*.

Her latest beef is Rocío. The girl, in her view, is "*una zángana*" – an idle so-and-so. Recently, she discovered that her Sancho, as well as running a winery, often had to knock up his own *tortilla de patatas* of an evening. It dulls the sheen on what, unlike her sisters, Mamí can't help thinking a rather glittering alliance.

For her entire philosophy is rooted in the deal whereby girls stay at home to nurture, and boys go forth to earn a living, though she's willing to entertain a few specifically male tasks around the house, such as removing dead fauna, fetching firewood and addressing female-unfriendly jobs involving plumbing, electrics etc. All of this explains her annoyance at discovering that Rocío's failing to live up to her side of the historic bargain.

In any event, Mamí seems to have lost much of her vitality and our efforts to lift her mood are seldom successful. One such attempt is an outing to *El Urogallo Perdido*, a new restaurant in a fine old *casona* up the valley behind Bárcena. It takes a while before it dawns on us that this is the place Guillermo brought us to about 20 years ago. It was the time he tried to wrest the house in Valledal from us.

Unfortunately, Mamí's in a negative frame of mind. Nothing meets her dietary strictures and, anyway, she considers the menu pretentious. Her way of signalling disapproval is to ask for a plain *filete* with no salt, and a few leaves without dressing. She picks up her knife and fork as soon as she's served, ignoring everyone else, steering her food round the plate desultorily. Then she dismisses the waiter with a flip of the hand when he starts filling her wineglass. She spends much of the evening monitoring our intake: "You'd better watch out," she says, "the last thing we need in the family's another Chus... ... *¡Que Dios nos coja confesados!*[33] Who's driving, anyway?"

Clearly, we're wasting our time on these gestures. What Mamí needs is an occupation to distract her, though she rejects specific ideas, especially anything cultural or academic, which she holds in contempt. When Marina announced her own plans to take a fine arts degree, Mamí asked her what she was doing that for and added that her "brother was always the clever one, anyway". Then she asked what she was "going to do with it" once she'd finished? In her view, that kind of thing's no use to anyone, especially girls.

The suggestion that she try knitting or crocheting elicits an equally sharp retort: "And how am I supposed to do

---

[33] 'God help us!'

that with this finger?"

Another time, Marina tried to interest Mamí in the family tree that she herself had started to piece together. She thinks Mamí's links to the church might be helpful and she'd enjoy figuring out the puzzle. But Mamí's reaction was unequivocal: "If you think I want to spend the few years left to me visiting graveyards and scraping moss off tombstones, you're very wrong. Won't I be there myself soon enough for you anyway? Ugh! All those dead people... What's the use of it? What does it bring to anyone?"

Indeed, we might have predicted her reaction. Mamí's dismissive of almost anyone over 60, including her friends, many younger than herself. She wants to socialise with a younger set, hence there's no quarter for the deceased.

Once, I contributed an idea of my own: why not commit all that vanishing culinary know-how to paper? In her day, Mamí was celebrated for her *sopa de mejillones,* her *bacalao al pil-pil,* her *tarta de Santiago* and a host of other dishes. These would surely make an interesting time-capsule and an enviable resource. To this end, I buy a pretty notebook from a stall at the market and, to speed things along, suggest the completed item would be much appreciated for my next birthday. Her response is lukewarm and non-committal; and whether she's forgotten how to cook or simply lost interest, no such recipe book comes to light, either for my birthday or at any other time.

With so many rebuffs, I've started to jib at these initiatives. Instead, my preferred strategy for Mamí-management is via *piropos* – cheap flattery: "How wonderful you look in that dress!" "Have you had your hair done since I last saw you? You look younger than ever!" "What a great story! You're the life and soul of this village!" It's a win-win: Mamí glows in contentment; I buy indulgence for minimal outlay. I must concede, though, that the Law of Unintended Consequences occasionally intrudes, when Mamí responds with the odd *piropo* of her own... *"odd"* being the *mot juste*, given their often embarrassingly enthusiastic and even juvenile tenor ("Your wife looks good, but nothing compared with you!"; "Whenever I see you, I feel young again!" and such like).

But Marina deplores my cynicism. Besides, she has another idea: "How about learning to use a computer?" she suggests. "You could keep in touch with people – *living* people – so much more easily."

"I'm far too old to learn that at my time of life."

"Nonsense. Look at Nunci – she manages fine! She chats online to Maite and Lupita all the time! There's a course starting in September, right here in Bárcena. We'll put you down for it."

Marina feels the mention of Nunci should clinch it, because Mamí always revered her genteel neighbour. They probably even discussed Nunci's exploits in the field together. Whether she follows through or not is another matter. In any event, we bring an old desktop from Valledal for practice and put her name down for the course.

Meanwhile, Mamí's campaign to discredit the new management at *Bodegas Pinar* receives an unexpected boost. It's entirely fortuitous...

The three sisters have signed up for a coach trip for "The Third Age" organised by the parish. It starts with a tour of a city on the *meseta*; an opportunity to acquire a luminous saint or virgin from the cathedral shop; a lunch of *lechazo* (suckling lamb) or *cochinillo* (suckling pig) at a vast roadside restaurant dwarfed only by its coach park; and, if the mood's right, a sing-along to piped music on the way home.

It's when the three sisters are seated at lunch that a toothless fellow traveller approaches them.

"Gloriuca Pinar?" he asks, tentatively.

"Yes?" Mamí answers, trying to place him. He proffers an arthritic hand.

"It's Eugenio! Eugenio Pato," he says, then, seeing she still looks vacant: "You may remember me as 'Geno'. In Guinea! Cipri and you; Amparo and me. The fun we had! All those years! Remember the scramble when they threw us out?"

"Of course! Geno! *¡Qué ilusión! ¡Madre mía!* It must be over 30 years, I should think! Please come and join us! I don't think you met my sisters – Luz Divina – Ludi, and Inmaculada – Macu…. You're alone?"

"Yes, I'm afraid Amparo died three years ago. And Cipri?"

"Gone too, sadly, some time ago."

Geno retrieves his *tinto* from the other end of the table and squeezes into a seat next to Mamí.

After the expulsion from Guinea he gave up the timber business and settled in Pueblo de la Vega, where he owned a small grocery store until his wife died.

"Didn't your family own the *bodega* in Bárcena – the famous *Bodegas Pinar*?"

"Yes, that's right," Mamí responds and her sisters nod vigorously.

"Such a great business! But whatever happened? The wonderful old warehouse – shut down! And what a shame to lose the old team! I knew Sancho quite well when he was in charge in Pueblo… Your nephew, Gloriuca, I take it?"

"No, no, Sancho's my younger son… An afterthought… after Guinea… He ran the outpost in Pueblo for about three years."

205

"*¡Vaya chaval, tu hijo!*[34] Nothing too much trouble! But now? Ever since it changed hands it's gone downhill… *¡A la porra!*[35] Do they really know what they're doing these days? The *soleras* just aren't up to scratch," he says, wading in ever deeper — yet still, the sisters fail to stop him. "I had to go to the new place on the main road in person. What a dump! And the service? Abominable! When the girl finally deigned to sort out my *solera* she failed to fix it and I haven't seen the ghost of them since. It's near impossible to get a decent *blanco* in Bárcena at all! *Zero!*" He holds his hand at eye level, forming an emphatic "zero" between forefinger and thumb, shaking it three or four times.

"It's the new barrels," Macu intervenes, alluding to the transfer of the old on-site *soleras* at the time of the move. "They're struggling on that account. If the barrels are tainted, the wine is too, and it's really beyond their control. But it should settle down in due course. We do still own the business…"

"Oh, I'm sorry… I didn't realise…" Eugenio stutters, his *faux pas* beginning to dawn.

After that, not even the most oblique allusion to the episode echoes between the sisters. But there's a marked difference in mood among the three on the way home. Aunt Ludi and Macu sit glumly on one side by themselves and leave sister Gloriuca, now sitting next to Geno across the aisle, to sing along. At a suitable moment, holding her finger to her lips to signal the sensitive intelligence she's about to impart, she whispers to Geno that Sancho now runs the *Aurelio* winery in Tobillo. He gives her a discreet thumbs up.

And of course, Gloria shares the story with us as soon

---

[34] What a great chap your son is.
[35] To the dogs

as they arrive back in Bárcena. For a while, her former spirit and animation return.

8

Nowadays, on arriving for the first time, we usually bypass Bárcena in our haste to reach Valledal. It's partly to satisfy curiosity. What will the place look like with the latest addition to house or garden? Which the mooted aggressions will have materialised and with what collateral damage? And which will have been dropped, as has become more frequent these days?

Indeed, the current crisis has caused a lull in private projects, encouraging the builder-mayors of the region to expand road budgets to keep idle machinery busy. We're therefore hardly surprised when we turn down the minor road to Valledal at Christmas to find a battery of diggers and bulldozers carving up our very own *via sacra*.

We've often wondered when The Authorities would turn their attentions to it and asked ourselves how this anomaly escaped so long. Numerous twisty back routes round here have undergone intestinal surgery – contorsions bypassed, polyps removed, wounds stitched up – all in the name of *saneamiento* or "sanitation", as the euphemism has it.

At the turning to Valledal, there's a bold notice, red on white. Below the technicalities, the deed is sanctified by a vital signature: *Obra cofinanciada por la Unión Europea*: ever-generous Europe, it seems, is chipping in.

Below that, right at the bottom, the notice reads: *Presupuesto de Obra*: 8.674.355,07 €. (*Construction Budget: 8,674,355.07 Euros.*)

It's not the sum *per se* that's striking. It's hard to know if it's a lot or a little because it's unclear exactly what it covers and, in any case, what do we know about how much such things cost? Rather, it's the extraordinary precision of the budgeting, right down to the last seven cents, that's impressive. After all, seven cents would hardly stretch to a single kirby grip in Julito's now defunct haberdashery.

A short way beyond, on a patch of gravel by the roadside, the heavy machinery's drawn up. A large digger is waiting and an officious figure in a yellow jacket and helmet waves a stop sign at us, then signals to the digger to reverse into the road.

It takes a moment or two to recognise this official. Then we realise: it's none other than brother-in-law Chus. I wind down the window.

"*¡Hombre!* Chus! What are you doing here? Aren't you chopping timber in Eastern Europe?"

"*¡Coño! ¡Rico! ¡Marina!* No, no unfortunately that's over. All good things come to an end! Our licence was revoked – all the foreign permits cancelled. I've taken this job as a stopgap. But for the long term, I've got a great prospect – I'll tell you about it."

Then I ask him about that extraordinary budgeting.

"*Jajaja!* That's The Authorities playing games. Attention to detail! Accuracy equals honesty is the message. I don't suppose it includes the brown envelopes! But don't you worry, we're doing a great job down here. I agree it looks bare now but once we've put up the crash barriers, you'll see: lined in wood. Just the right *rústico* touch. You can guess who's behind it," he adds, "Oscar Ortega, of course. He's bored with Bárcena politics: too parochial. So it's back to construction for now. But don't be surprised if he runs for *Presidente* at the next regional elections."

Vandalistic though it is, there's no choice but to be philosophical about this kind of aggression. Life goes on; and it probably won't look too bad once the vegetation grows back.

In any event, as has become the rule since we moved in at Valledal, seasonal celebrations require our full attention. It's our duty these days to share the burden with Mamí. Sancho and Rocío will be tied into the Caudal festivities in Tobillo and won't be joining us. Though wounding to Mamí, it's more than offset by her elder son's return, especially as he's alone, leaving behind that "common whore" and the baby, her new grandson, about whom Mamí shows no curiosity whatsoever.

Her pleasure is marred, however, when she learns that there's no immediate job for Chus to return to. Yes, he's talking about a job in Mexico but it sounds like wishful thinking and he's probably grounded for the foreseeable future. To fund his habits, he sells the Toyota. The Bárcena flat goes too but, following the property crash, the proceeds barely cover the mortgage.

The alternative occupation he's talking about is mediated by a cousin, Quique, a fully qualified *ingeniero de caminos*. (In fact, he's Marina's one-time suitor, the one I supplanted, according to Mamí's simplified historiography.) This time, it is indeed in Mexico but it's no longer in forestry. Chus will be using his topographical skills to build roads. He just needs the contract and when that comes through, he'll be off. If he could but find a computer, he could…

Then he discovers that Mamí, of all people, has the very device he needs, up on a shelf in her dressing room. It's the one we lent her for practice. Against expectations, she has stuck with the course for several months and has managed to send Marina an email or two and even access her replies.

Marina catches Chus *in flagrante*, absconding from Mamí's dressing room with the screen and a bundle of cables under his arm.

"If I'm going to land this job, I'll need a computer!" he tells her, rudely shutting his bedroom door in her face.

Later, when he comes downstairs, he finds out about Mamí's computer course.

"¡*Tonterías!*"[36] is his view; "what does a housewife need that for? Don't tell me you're sending Mamí out to work?"

"That computer's ours, you know?" Marina says.

Chus doesn't respond, he just smiles inanely, as if it's not even worth discussing. Marina looks to Mamí for back-up. But nothing comes.

Judging by the sound effects from his room, the urgent need for a computer is mainly for video games. They cease when Marina complains. Maybe he's attached headphones. Whatever, the reality is that the computer has been sequestered, probably for good.

A few days later, a whoop of triumph loud enough to be heard downstairs comes from Chus's room. He rushes out to share the tidings and bask in adulation. The Mexican job is his!

Mamí doesn't even congratulate him. Instead, she proffers advice, accompanied by a wag of the crooked index-finger: "I know you, *hijo mío*… the first waitress you meet and *PUM!* That'll be another bun in the oven. Again! It's a certainty! You understand what I'm saying? Before you go, I insist you visit the clinic and have that little operation. It's a very simple procedure, apparently. All under local anaesthetic."

Over here, festivities are less formulaic than back home. Mamí, increasingly assisted by Marta, generally serves dressed crab (Papí's one-time *forte*), langoustines with alioli and suckling goat or lamb. At our return event, a large fish usually provides the centrepiece, preferably sea bream,

---

[36] Stupid idea

bass or turbot, depending on availability and price. It entails a trip to the fish market in the local capital as soon as it opens on Christmas Eve. It's one the more stressful moments of the year, often entailing a scuffle.

If we have visitors (Hamish this year) I take them along for support. Because the instant the market doors are flung wide and the pack bursts into the fish hall, a raw blood lust is unleashed, as a pack of rapacious matrons stampedes across the floor after the quarry. The immediate goal is to grab a ticket for a place in the queue; those arriving late or moving too slowly risk losing precious advantage, or even – horrible prospect – returning home empty-handed.

The fish counter, a huge zinc basin tilted towards the customers, measures about fifteen metres across by two fore to aft, sagging beneath the bounty of the ocean. Behind it, a dozen or more Amazons in white boots and overalls chop up the flesh and sluice the offal, blood and scales down a drain in the floor. When your number flashes up on the screen you have but an instant to register, claim attention and yell your order above the racket, a moment when it's easy to forget whether Christmas lunch goes by the name of *lubina, rodaballo* or *besugo*[37]... Once descaled, eviscerated and bagged up, they toss it onto the dangling scales, print a ticket, staple it to the bag and hand it over, whence you hurry to the line at the tills.

The party in Valledal this year, somewhat diminished, comprises the remaining regulars – Mamí, Aunt Macu, Chus, Marta and boyfriend (Chito, a recent replacement for a seemingly serviceable predecessor), Toni and the four of us – plus the monoglot Hamish, whom we banish to the far end of the table to be fielded by Clara and James. Last time, his frustration and boredom became palpable once

---

[37] Sea-bass, turbot or bream

he grasped that his respun Italian fell short for a Spanish *sobremesa*, an epic gossip round the table that's taxing even for Marina.

Aunt Macu hardly counts these days because her faculties have declined dramatically since she let go of the *bodega*. She's still the guest of honour: she still claims the head of the table, the only chair with arms and a cushion, and grumbles if we forget the coffee spoons, there's no nativity crib, or the wine is not from *Pinar*. She collects presents from everyone, but never reciprocates.

Allegedly, her silence comes down to poor hearing. She reserves her few interventions for censure, for instance about the Santa Rita golf course ("why can't they play '*a los bolos*'[38] like their ancestors?") or about Clara's plan to see a PG-rated film ("is she old enough for that sort of thing?"). Her sisters forced her to fit hearing aids, but she leaves them at home because she "likes being deaf". It sounds perverse, but in fact it's just a symptom of retreat from everyday slights, most troubling of which are the slurs against the new team at the *bodega*.

Eyesight, on the other hand, is another matter.

It might be expected that, now retired, Aunt Macu would be ready to scrap the puddle-scooper, the rusty SEAT Ritmo she's piloted round her one-way circuit for decades. But there's a new factor. Aunt Macu long since lost interest in the big house and garden in its dank corner of *la mies*, that untidy stretch of allotments, scrub and suburbia between Bárcena and the poplar-lined riverbank. The garden she laid out years ago has gone to seed and the house itself needs urgent attention. Besides, she's ill at ease alone at night, despite the dog, Hamlet, and the fact that her dutiful sister Ludi comes to keep her company

---

[38] Local bowls/*pétanque* hybrid

whenever she can.

Before the losses mounted at the *bodega*, Aunt Macu purchased a first-floor apartment in a new block between Mamí's house and the church. Her choice of one of the few sunless flats in the building raised eyebrows; but Macu bought it for the view, not just of the church square but of the church interior itself, at least on feast days, when the doors are left wide open. She thus secured a balcony seat at key events: processions, funerals, *fiestas* and the like. It's in this flat where she, and increasingly Aunt Ludi, her *de facto* chaperone, now spend much of their time. But that means the car's needed for trips back to the house to feed Hamlet and Betty the cat, who roam free in the neglected garden together as a team. This is fulfilled by tossing a few off-cuts over the wall – no need to venture inside the wilderness itself. But it does mean Aunt Macu must renew her license, which at her age entails an eye test.

To address the challenge, Aunt Macu weighs up various strategies. One is to learn the letters of the eye test by heart, at least the top four or five rows. That should suffice, they're unlikely to test on the very small letters as there's no need to read such small things on the roads, she reasons. When she's told they change the letters to prevent cheating, she's unfazed, because there's always the traditional approach, a small *propina* (tip) for the examiner. The latter strategy indeed bears fruit and Aunt Macu returns from the eye test waving the certificate and salving her conscience by saying she won't be driving more than one kilometre a day, at the outside.

"It's always the same route, so of course it won't be dangerous, not in the least," she declares, lucid for a few moments.

Just to emphasise how reasonable she's being, she claims to have told the same story to the examiner to ease his conscience as she handed over the notes.

It's over the *sobremesa* that the liquor comes out, much of it vintage whisky this year – courtesy of Hamish. Toni and James distribute the gifts, with Chus also exempt from gifting on grounds of poverty. This year, Mamí gives me a lemon-tree sapling. It's one of her better efforts – preferable to yet another pair of pyjamas, for certain.

Fortunately, Marina calls time after a few hours, allowing me to escape with Hamish for a post-prandial stroll. There's one track I've wanted to try for a while. If the map's right, there should be a bridge at the bottom. But it means passing Soco's house. Hamish pulls a face.

"Just so long as we don't get trapped by the lardy lady and her son Porco," he says, perhaps dreading another linguistic ordeal.

"That would be 'Puerco', anyway. But why not stick to 'Chato'? Less controversial."

Chato has exceeded his own high bar with this year's decorations. It's not just the usual props – tinsel trees, baubles, gnomes, cribs and flashing lights. He's added a model railway that somehow traces a circuit round the outside of the house, which could at any moment fall victim to local hazards – Monchi after a few drinks at the bar, or one of the skips barrelling through the chicane between Soco and the neighbours on its way down to a building site. For it's astonishing how much heavy traffic whistles down this narrow, twisty road with no issue beyond our hamlet, the *barrio bajo*, even on Christmas Day.

"The strange thing is," I remark to Hamish, contemplating Chato's display, "that Soco misses the signals. I mean, he's well into his twenties and there's no sign of a girlfriend. Meanwhile, she keeps up the banter, which he must find excruciating. He lives at home watching back numbers of the *Eurovision Song Contest* and expending his energies on pot plants and trinkets. Soco either doesn't notice or pretends not to. Such are the taboos round here, even now…"

Despite our fondness for Soco, it's not just Hamish who'd rather avoid her after the heavy lunch. Her hospitality is both mandatory and overwhelming. But she must have spied us as we passed, because before we're past the dwellings that replaced her old farm, her voice reaches us: "Aha! Where are you two off to? Not down to the river, I hope?"

I look round to see Soco's grinning visage, peering at us from the porch. She's singled out by the low sun and haloed by her son's artefacts. Soco finds the idea of any gratuitous walk irresistibly comic, especially as indulged by a couple of elderly *forasteros* like us two. Unlike last time she caught us, though, today is one of those balmy winter days when the wind blows from the south, drives away the clouds and the shadows fall jagged as shards. The high mountains with their snow mantle, so often blurred by the haze, come into focus, and the azure ocean sparkles, at once alluring and disingenuous.

"Thought you'd escape me that easily, did you?" Soco says with the mandatory finger-wag and a grin. "I'm expecting you for drinks! Seven-thirty… Marina and the family too, obviously… I've big news for you. And don't get into trouble down there… if that's where you're heading."

By now she's stepped onto the road and I can see that, despite the season, there's no change in uniform – the usual floral dress folded over her bosom, reaching to the knees and protected by a grubby little apron; below, *albarcas* – clogs – shield her bedroom slippers.

But today, there's a difference: for "lardy" the lady is no more. It's a shock, though Marina did warn me. Both of us

215

look at the new svelte edition of our friend with a blend of marvel and dismay: a miraculous transformation, no question, and an upgrade aesthetically; but her bulk afforded Soco presence and authority; now, by morphing from ocean-displacing Dreadnought to sleek Corvette in a single season, she's no longer quite so awe-inspiring.

Perhaps unsurprisingly, she's more boisterous than ever. After promising to join them later, we branch off the road down to the stream.

"Bariatric surgery, I gather," I tell Hamish as we make our way down the hill. "I should have told you."

The map scores a bullseye this time: the promised concrete bridge really does exist; but beyond are a pair of forbidding steel gates draped with barbed wire and daubed with warnings to trespassers. There's no obvious way round and in seconds, the black snouts of several hounds appear at the foot of the gates, where they race from side to side, sniffing, whining and snarling frenetically. From a safe distance, the shape of three or four large polytunnels can be made out through the gap between the gates.

This must be our local cannabis farm. I'd heard about it before, but never knew where it was, exactly. Apparently, the place has been raided several times by the police, but that never seems to disrupt it for long.

"Skin in the game, no doubt," Hamish says, learning fast. "I expect they come to shake it up once in a while – just to remind them who's in charge and make sure they get their cut."

"Success?" Soco asks with a grin when we arrive later on. "Were they polite? Not very? They do have a reputation, you know! I won't tell you who's involved, but suffice to say, he's a close relation of your favourite neighbour. Nice little operation they've got down there, though, eh?"

We're on the ground floor, measuring no more than a few square metres, which hosts a kitchen, staircase, dining table, sofa, television and three residents (though only one of them by now XXL). In addition, at this time of year, available surfaces are buried under a panoply of cross-cultural artifacts, including poinsettias, candles, cribs, angels, snowmen, Christmas trees, Santa Clauses and heaps of presents. Finally, Soco's culinary offerings balance on whatever flat surfaces are left. It's strictly standing room only – uncomfortable, but at least it keeps it brief. Apart from force-feeding (starting with Soco's speciality, *rabas* – battered squid rings) and plying us with *calimochos*, the main agenda is gifting.

But first, Soco has other business:

"So let me tell you my news: I won the lottery! €75,000! After tax!"

"That's amazing! Congratulations!" Marina says, "I'm so pleased... I can't think of anyone more deserving... Due reward for sheer perseverance, I mean..."

"And it wasn't just me," she says, "two of my brothers, too... But keep it to yourselves. If it gets out, Monchi'll be here like a shot. He's desperate right now."

She shares the quirk of fate that led up to the windfall. The story revolves round a bar, *El Viajante* in Tobillo, one that Soco tars as *"cutre"*, disgusting. It's a miserable den at the "wrong" end of the straight stretch through that village, next to the petrol station, its main appeal a *futbolín* table that attracts local youth.

With the reserve fuel light blinking, Miguelín insisted on filling up, despite his wife's pleas to head straight home – she'd "have an accident" if not, for the garage offers no facilities, not even for staff. Miguelín said she'd have to try her luck at *El Viajante*, the first visit since her teen years.

That's where she found her two brothers, Luis and Juanjo, on bar stools, clearly drunk.

When she emerged from the bathroom, she told them Miguelín was waiting, so she couldn't stop. But by way of atonement, she bought lottery tickets, one for each of them. As an afterthought, she added one for herself, too.

A few weeks later, these three tickets shared in the winning draw… it's the first time in living memory the jackpot landed not just in our province, but in our very own *comarca*.

"Miguelín's buying a *todo terreno* on the winnings. He's always wanted one…"

"A Mitsubishi *Pajero?*" I ask.

"*Jajaja,*" Soco laughs, dismissively, as I knew she would. I mean, what self-respecting branding guru christens a topflight 4x4 a "*W*nker*", which is how *Pajero* translates into English? Though, in their defence, I suppose it does encapsulate the typical *Pajero* driver, hot on your tail, lights flashing, forcing you to make way.

Following the lottery win, *El Viajante* suddenly became Tobillo's shrine: everyone has heard the story and wants a share of the magic that visited bounty on such an unlikely spot.

Then the gifting ritual begins. On that matter, maybe a truce is called for. One whole cupboard at home is dedicated to Christmases past, courtesy of Soco and family, embarrassingly generous, for the most part, but neglected. We struggle to find a use for a porcelain box containing a pop-up Santa Claus that tinkles *Jingle Bells* for five minutes. There's just too wide a gulf between our respective notions of what's useful or desirable. However, that cupboard stands at the ready in case of an impromptu visit, though we'd need a few minutes' warning to unpack it all. Luckily, the 200 or 300 metres that separate us mean that has yet to occur.

Soco's present to me usually takes the form of a bottle of liquor, *orujo* doctored with honey or spices, or some obscure brand of Scotch. This year, for example, I'm presented with a large flagon of 15-year-old "Glen McTweedy".

No, our Scottish visitor tells me on the way home, he hasn't heard of it either. That must be a make-up too.

Chapter VI: Heir Craft

1

"What upsets me most," says Aunt Macu in a flash of lucidity, "is that we've become a country of emigration once more."

The effect is electric, a rising from the dead. Nowadays, she spends weeks at a time in her own universe; but every so often a palimpsest of the old Aunt Macu reappears.

"What do you mean by that?" The question, in gravelly tones, comes from Tere, Julito's wife. We're standing in a group in *La Parientuca*, a bar in the village of San Onofrio de la Sierra. But Aunt Macu has already zoned out. She's reverted to muttering *hm-hm-hm* noises to herself.

The occasion is the send-off for the Pinar family, an annual fixture just before the so-called *Operación Retorno*, the day the nation sets off home after the holidays. As with its counterpart at the start, the *Operación Salida*, the exodus exacts a grim toll on the roads. It will be the mainstay of this evening's news, with key statistics delivered in jaunty tones along with a few blurry shots of mangled vehicles by the roadside.

This year, the plan for the party is different. For in recent years, a quiet revolution has occurred in Spanish attitudes to exercise and the outdoors, with hiking and so-called "*ronnin'* " (running) hot new fashions among the young and aspirational. In sympathy, a two-hour hike is mooted for those who wish, with a picnic of *bocadillos de chorizo* at the top of the *sierra* before returning for coffee at the bar with the aunts and other laggards.

When we arrive, we find the Blasco cousins huddled around Julito in a lively exchange. They fall silent when they see us, but not before I grasp their gist: there's a rumour that Iñaki Ybasta, the pushy Basque accountant snapped up by *Aurelio* weeks after his dismissal from *Pinar*, has now been fired by them too.

Sancho himself, the sinner, nowadays avoids family reunions of this type. The scope for an ugly scene is simply too great. But it means I can't ask him to confirm the rumour, one way or another.

Before the walkers leave, Mamí has an announcement to make.

"Just so we're all in the picture," she says, "don't expect to see Chito at these events in future! It's all over with him and Marta! No longer an item… As of this morning. That's right, isn't it, Marta?"

"But Mamí! Please!… Not in public! You promised…"

"Why not? You can't expect me to keep quiet… you know very well how pleased I am! That young man's going nowhere. I never liked the look of him anyway. That beard! He could at least comb it! And a cry-baby to boot… What kind of a man is that?"

"I was more upset than he was." Marta looks wobbly herself, about to break down at any moment.

"Nonsense! You did it because you had to. You did the right thing! But try hard and choose better next time. We've had enough of that kind of *jarcia!*"[39]

It's the right moment for those on the walk, including Marina, Marta and me, to make our exit. In addition, Paloma and Carlos, Beni and Lulu and most of the youngsters join us. Chus, Julito and Tere and various infants stay behind at the bar with the three aunts.

"In case you think we're shirking," Tere calls from the door as we set off, "we're making sure there's something to look forward to. This bar has a great reputation for

---

[39] Riff-raff

seafood!" Her promise puts a spring in our step.

"What Aunt Macu meant," Carlos says, resuming the emigration debate as we start the tramp up the zig-zag track through the beech woods, "is that thanks to *La Merkel*, there's nothing left for anyone here anymore. Just think about it… almost half of us, forced out – in exile!"

For Carlos and his acolytes, *La Merkel* has inflicted starvation on Spain. Her matronly figure, an improbable target for vitriol, prompts all the predictable tropes in the press – *La Merkel* in jackboots, *La Merkel* with toothbrush moustache, *La Merkel* piloting a dive-bomber, that kind of thing.

But Carlos is right that the diaspora has torn the Pinar clan asunder, with many of the cousins now living and working abroad. There's Puri in Latin America; Beni at his research institute; Domingo, now in China plus wife and baby Alfa; and recently Nacho, a brainy young programmer, in Belgium. On our side of the family, Marina lives abroad, and Sancho suffers *de facto* internal exile. Only Chus bucks the trend. The Mexican job has come to an end – there are no more roads following the latest financial meltdown. Once more, he has returned, empty-handed, to the pre-glamour world of Bárcena de la Mina.

I venture that perhaps Aunt Macu had the wider historical context in mind. For centuries, rural depopulation decanted peasants into the cities, then abroad, first Latin America, later Northern Europe. Briefly, that process went into reverse, in step with the years of Euro-triumphalism, while politicians crowed about Spain's resurgence as the *"Eighth Great Power"*. For ten years or more, immigrants poured in, transforming a once homogenous population into something more like its neighbours'. Then, just as quickly, that spark of optimism died. The young and ambitious began to emigrate, heading north once more, abandoning the debt-ridden Spanish economy.

A few hundred metres further up the steep climb, Paloma catches up with me, clearly keen to talk. I'm surprised but pleased: we've scarcely exchanged words in years. Since that awkward clash a few years back, a slight but uncomfortable chill settled over our formerly warm rapport.

But she catches me off guard with her jump straight into the fray.

"How's Sancho getting on at *Aurelio*?" she asks,

"He's very discreet – hardly says a thing. Feels he can't – he'd be in big trouble with Caudal if anything got out. Just imagine, in that position, feet in both camps. He treads extra carefully. For example, I didn't even know Iñaki just left: I found that out from you, just now!"

"Left? I heard they fired him. I wonder what's really going on?"

"As far as I can see, Sancho's busier than ever."

"Perhaps he really is," Paloma replies, "because we heard that Caudal's about to step down. We were wondering where that leaves Sancho. I mean, how will he cope without Iñaki or Caudal? Sancho's a good salesman, I grant you, but does he have any idea how to run a business?"

"Don't underestimate him… That's the mistake your aunt made."

By now, we're above the treeline on a grassy pasture or *braña*, and soon we've reached the crest, hot and puffed, but still able to admire the impressive panorama all round. To the North, the scribbled line of the coast runs more or less due east-west, separated from us by the coastal strip, increasingly given over to suburban blancmange. But it contrasts strikingly with the wild and rugged terrain stretching far into the haze on the South side.

Having bolted our *bocadillos*, we start the weary stumble back down the long path to the bottom.

An hour later, we rejoin the others in San Onofrio, where Tere reveals her treat for the intrepid hikers. It's a platter of *percebes* ('gooseneck barnacles'). These crustaceans, harvested under the cliffs where they grow several metres long, are a local delicacy. To eat the small, multi-headed hydra at the extremities, you wring each gooseneck one by one and, with luck, out pops the edible morsel. Sometimes, though, a jet of seawater shoots you straight in the eye; and that's exactly what happens to me.

"*¡Jajaja!*" Tere croaks, "Bullseye! Beginner's luck? Let me show you how to avoid that. You hold them this way. Watch how I do it!"

She picks up one of the diamond-shaped heads between finger and thumb. Holding it away from herself she twists it and the seawater squirts harmlessly onto the paper tablecloth. Then she nips off the pink flesh she has revealed. She savours it sybaritically… Nirvana… It's a small gesture, but effective in showcasing my philistinism in matters culinary.

"We certainly know how to eat over here, don't we?" she continues. "I sometimes wonder how you survive over there. Fish and chips? Those vile sauces? Baked beans for breakfast? *¡Madre mía!* I'll never forget! It was torture, our stay! We had to come home early for some proper food. Back to the best cuisine in the world."

I could claim that nobody else thinks Spanish cuisine is that great; how it's all about greasy food, a dearth of fresh vegetables, factory-made desserts, dusty, rock hard bread and tart wine. That heresy would be greeted with blank incomprehension, or, more likely, with righteous indignation…

Afterwards, I feel I should share the gossip with Sancho. We arrange to meet up at *El Politena* the next day.

It turns out relations between *Pinar* and *Aurelio* reached a nadir a couple of weeks back. He explains: "You see, we just won the Ortega account from *Pinar*. One of their best… As you know, the mayor never rests. Now he's opening high-end restaurants and that's what gave us our break. He needs grown-up wines for those places, *Rioja*, *Ribera del Duero*, *Bierzo* and so on. As it happens, that's the turn we took ourselves a while back. It's a lot more profitable than the bottom end, and it's still growing. I almost felt sorry for Julito… I saw him in Oscar's carpark the day he lost the account… Quite painful.

"But I'm sorry to say the rumour's true about Iñaki. He was fired, Paloma's quite right. It had nothing to do with the job itself, though. He's a capable man, I'll miss him. The trouble is, he took a shine to Caudal's cook; truly besotted, he was, quite out of control. What's more, she wasn't interested. She made a complaint. To cap it all, Iñaki claims to be happily married. Don Gonzalo's very traditional about these things and, as soon as he found out, he ordered Iñaki out, there and then… There'll be a backlash, for sure. Unfair dismissal suit, at the least. Remember what happened at *Pinar*? That's what Iñaki's like, a hustler and a streetfighter, which is great, so long as he's on your side."

2

According to Soco, contrary to the gloomy predictions of Carlos and his in-laws, sentiment is on the turn, in Valledal at the least. Once again, there are signs that speculative interest is creeping back. Her excitement is palpable next time we see her, even more than usual. She's eager to share her enthusiasm with us.

"What do you mean, you haven't seen what's going on in the *barrio alto*?" she asks, referring to the "upper village".

When we say we haven't had time for our usual round of inspections, Soco insists: "I thought it'd be the first thing anyone would notice! Hasn't your mother told you about it, Marina? It's the biggest mansion built in the village since – well – since I've been living here, certainly. And I'm told the owner's a real bigwig, a top honcho from one of the banks in Madrid... I hope you realise that, after Sotogrande, this is *the* top spot for the *Madrileños*.[40] It's where they all want to be."

I know Valledal's important to all of us, but I sense she's over-estimating its resonance, which as far as I know seldom even reaches Bárcena. But we're minded to temper our scepticism the day we encounter a uniformed Filipina, wheeling an infant in a *Silver Cross* pram down the hill, dodging the cowpats and risking the boy racers, Monchi's son Nino foremost among them in his canary yellow hatchback or, more recently, astride a quadbike.

According to Soco, the project up the hill is far from alone. Further down, the "ex" of a well-known but scandal-tarnished politician has put down roots. She's also building and, for Soco, that's highly significant because the field right next to the construction site belongs to her.

"My field's one of the best sites in the village. Mountain views one side, sea on the other. I reckon three or four *chalés* will fit on there, no trouble," Soco says, grinning. "In fact, I have a firm buyer, another *Madrileño*. It would all be done by now, but for one small problem: we were at the notary, all ready to sign, when the official noticed my

---

[40] Inhabitants of Madrid

carnet[41] was 12 years out of date!"

Fortunately, she sees the funny side; she obviously thinks her buyer won't renege while she sorts it out.

She's not offering a tour, because it's a bit further than the 20 metres or so to the parking lot, which pretty much defines her radius, even in her compact new shape. In any case, she wants to share the good news on her access and parking dispute, too. Angelita, her touchy neighbour, who refused to compromise, is leaving at last. Her expectations took decades to budge and, when at last she started dropping the price, it was never quite enough. Finally, after six or seven years, chasing down the price but always a bit behind the curve, she capitulated at a fraction of the original asking price.

"I won't be sorry to see her go," Soco continues, "especially if it means we can park the new car by the door… But let me tell you about Monchi's silos."

She's referring to our own neighbour who, several years ago, decided to turn some old silos into a dwelling. Nowadays, if successful, it's a far more lucrative use for them, especially as the farmers don't seem to bother with silos anymore. Instead, they leave compacted hay on the ground, seed it with a bit of dung, cover it up with a layer of thick black plastic and pin it down with old truck tyres; it transforms into a ready-made cesspit after a few damp months under the sun.

However, the right to convert agricultural buildings, however humble, into housing is something the council still makes a fuss about. To fox The Authorities, the silos were billed as a *lavandería*. Work started, but Monchi was caught out as soon as the silos emerged, not as the promised *lavandería*, but as an eccentrically shaped house, betraying

---

[41] Identity card

its origins as three conjoined concrete cylinders with a porch tacked on the back. At that point, the work stopped. Evidently, the council had intervened.

But with a little patience and well-calibrated incentives, such prohibitions are seldom final. Thus it proved with the silos. Mysteriously, council objections melted. Monchi applied the finishing touches, including tessellated slabs on the façade. The last we heard was that he had found a buyer, a lady called Esther from the south.

That's where Soco takes up the narrative: "Our friend Monchi sold in the end, but not without trouble – trouble for Esther, I mean. It was all agreed, deposit paid, when, suddenly, he tried to pull out. It seems he found someone willing to pay more – I expect all this new activity in the village had something to do with it. Esther refused to back out and the law was on her side… It took over a year to sort it out.

"But once she moved in, strange things started happening. At first, she blamed her memory when knives and forks appeared in the wrong drawers. Then the furniture began to shift – little by little, just a few centimetres out of true, apparently when she was out, or during the night. Either she was losing her mind, or the place was haunted or… Then it dawned on her. Of course, it must be Monchi. Who or what else could possibly account for it? Who else would be able to carry it out? She called the *Guardia Civil*.

"Monchi denied it and there was no proof. But at least the chilling events ceased once Esther changed the locks."

Soco's talkative today, even by her standards and has another story to share. It's about her experience with a recent Valledal arrival, Nicolette, a Dutch lady Soco resolved to dislike from the day she came, taking early exception to her "ridiculous" name.

Nicolette resides in the last house in the village where the tarmac yields to muddy conduits that feed out to the few meadows on the final tongue of land overlooking the beach, from which it is separated by a semicircle of impenetrable eucalyptus, the spot where our friend Charlie famously lost his bearings. (It's a cardinal rule round here: footpaths *never* join up… mistrust of neighbours, walkers, *Ecologistas*, "so-called pilgrims" and in this instance, "drug addicts" who might otherwise sneak into the village from the beach…) We still refer to that house as *La casa de la Larga*, though *La Larga* herself, *'The Tall One'*, a spectral apparition during our early years in Valledal, must have died years back. Clara and I, walking Aunt Macu's dog Hamlet, met Nicolette and fell into conversation with her on our way past and, in the interests of diversity, invited her round for a drink.

Nicolette, it turned out, was a refugee from two or three unfortunate marriages; but in the absence of any link with Valledal or its environs, her reasons for landing here remained obscure. Ostensibly, a photo of Villafranca from the sea prompted the move – no doubt one of those artful shots with a zoom lens showcasing the Ruiz-Toledos' *Casa de Indianos* on its promontory with a backdrop of snow-capped mountains. The rows of *pisos* fall just outside the frame. She was writing a novel; or was it memoirs? Whatever, she spurned our efforts to empathise with the agonies of the creative process. How could we possibly understand her suffering?

Soco tells us that a note from Nicolette appeared under her door one day asking to see her at five that afternoon. She didn't answer, but shortly before five took to watering the plants with which the exterior of her house is festooned.

"I didn't fancy letting her in," Soco tells us. "Nicolette came to complain about an attack on her cat. She's quite sure it was Midas' dog and she knows I was there the time it bit Pepita… Imagine what she asks… She wants me to *testify* against Midas, testify in court, if you please! I've known Midas all my life… I said I would never do any such a thing… Upset the richest farmer in the district? Madness!"

But I do sympathise with Nicolette's complaint. The passion for vicious mongrels blights the countryside; almost every dwelling harbours a frothing Cerberus ready to snap its anchorage at any moment. It's far from clear what these creatures are really for.

This is a subject to be avoided with Soco, so entrenched is it in her culture. In any case, she hasn't finished with Nicolette: "I'm not sure I ever told you about the time she and her friend bought some firewood; after a first trial, they complained that it *"burnt far too quickly"* and demanded a rebate. The seller couldn't believe his ears; in disbelief and indignation he threw a €50 note in Nicolette's face.

"Not long after, she asked me if by any chance I knew the odious cheat that sold her the firewood… and I told her: 'Yes, of course I know him: Juanjo, my brother!'"

3

Marina claims that, in her youth, there were just two desserts: *flan* (custard pudding); and *cuajada* (yoghurt). The repertoire had grown somewhat when I arrived, though a single cookbook was to be found in most kitchens. Entitled *Manual de Cocina*, it was published by the *Sección Femenina*, the women's arm of Franco's disbanded political movement, *El Movimiento*. Our copy formed part of our wedding trousseau, by which time it was already running into its 23rd edition.

The *Manual de Cocina* covered everything a dutiful housewife should aspire to in the kitchen. It left no space for frivolities, with half its pages dedicated to various types of offal – from testicles via trotters and tripe to teats. As a surprise, though, it made room for a roster of long-forgotten kitchen implements and, in an eccentric touch, a glossary of about 40 different terms for "to cook".

All that has changed: cookery has become a national obsession. But instead of homage to everything foreign, this time aspiration is bent on reviving *Spanish* cuisine. Standards have risen dramatically. Maybe Tere's claim to "the best cuisine in the world" wasn't so fanciful.

That's what I'm thinking as the four of us head for supper at one of the new restaurants springing up even in this offbeat province. This one, *La Mozuca del Mar*, is Villafranca's attempt at something chic, with a covered terrace overlooking an arm of the sea.

We arrive too early for the locals and, annoyingly, our table stands within earshot of the only other guests who, as luck would have it, are English… There's something instantly familiar about them and it's not confined to the language: it must be the posture; or the tendency to whisper apologetically.

In response, I propose a rigorous Spanish-only policy at our table in the hope of avoiding detection. Marina laughs off my misanthropy; in any case, I'm not fooling anyone, because before we've even ordered drinks, one of their party, a lady of about 65, settles the matter by rising from her chair and crossing the space between our tables. She looks at Marina and me quizzically.

"I swear we've met before, haven't we?" she asks, calmly conjuring up a Home Counties ambiance in just a few words.

"Are you sure?" I say, still wary. "Where do you think that was?"

Marina is less inhibited: "You do look familiar, but I'm

afraid I can't place you…"

"I'm Jane," says our new friend, holding her hand to Marina. "Pleasure… We live here, we have for years. You too?"

"Not exactly. But I'm originally from Bárcena," Marina responds. "We split our time between here and England."

"It'll come to me," Jane says. "Let's work it out while we have supper."

By the time we reach dessert, Marina's keen to try again – she's less inhibited than the rest of us and brushes off our efforts to restrain her. Now it's her turn to cross over to their table, where before long they're exchanging biographies. A few snippets of the conversation reach us, including the mention of Quintanilla del Río, where they now live. As it happens, the name is familiar to me, and I interject: "Quintanilla? Perhaps you know Benedict, then?"

At this point, the only man in their party of four, sitting with his back to our table, wheels round his broad frame to face me: "But I *am* Benedict…"

He immediately recognises me: "Good heavens! If it isn't my trusty teacher friend!" he says, repeating the remark he made last time almost verbatim, if I remember rightly…

"You're still in the same line too?" I ask.

"'*How boring!*' you're thinking… Don't be too obvious about it! Well, we've diversified. We run the exams these days – a bit more money in it. Anyhow, teaching languages is *never* boring. It changes all the time. Heard the latest addition to the Spanish language, for example? Any idea who "*los okupas*" are? No? It's a new coinage thanks to the protests. Means 'squatters', of course… written with a 'k' to signal subversion – of the spelling rules, you see."

Within minutes we've joined tables and are catching up

on a decades-long interval – here we are now, with grown-up families, Clara and James being of similar age to their two girls, Victoria and Bridget. I remind Benedict that last time we met, we shared a *blanco* or two at *El Politena.*

"Good heavens, whatever happened to the family *bodega*? We still have our *solera* from *Pinar* at home, but they seem incapable of servicing it properly. Cloudy and undrinkable! Ever since your brother stopped coming, Marina. We've more or less given up. Sacrilege in this company, I realise, but we'd move to *Aurelio* if we could. But I gather they don't do *soleras.*"

"No, you're right. But you probably don't realise my brother effectively runs *Vinos Aurelio* these days," Marina says. "He married the owner's daughter."

"I bet that went down well with your aunt! But good for your brother; good for *Aurelio* too, the perennial outsiders! What you won't know either is that Bridget's a bit of an expert in this field," he says, signalling one of his daughters. "You tell them, Bridget."

"Well, I suppose so, I work for a wine consultancy," she answers, coyly, "and I may take the MW exams in due course."

"Master of Wine, is that? The Gold Standard, right? Very impressive… What about you, Victoria?"

"I'm a historian. I've just got my PhD on the Spanish Navy in the Napoleonic era."

"Congratulations!"

Bridget, Victoria and our two pursue their own conversation while I remind Benedict that, on the occasion at *El Politena,* he introduced us to his friend Guillermo, who tried to gazump us when we bought the house in Valledal.

"Ah, Guillermo, he's not in a good place, poor fellow," Benedict says, perhaps hoping to atone for that original lapse. "He's sick and he's almost blind. And he lost a fortune on the Santa Rita project. He tried to flog his shares to me, can you believe… not that I was tempted. That big place he had up the valley – it's a hotel now… But you bought your house after all, I take it?"

"Yes, we did. And by the way, we tried *El Urogallo Perdido* for the first time quite recently. Not bad…"

"Oh is that what they've called it? Good name. You know where it comes from, I take it? A tribute to that black, turkey-like fowl indigenous to this region… Capercaillie's the translation, I believe: it's also native to Scotland. One of a few things that binds Spain and Great Britain."

"After Guillermo's intervention. we were ready to up sticks and leave him to it, but…"

"Aha. 'Up sticks'. You know the origin of that saying, right?"

According to him, "up sticks" has something to do with English archers at Agincourt advancing their barrage of protective stakes after repelling French cavalry charges… I'd forgotten Benedict's addiction to arcane facts and anecdotes. We might be addressing a plate of *alubias con morcilla* – beans with black pudding – and he'd expound on Pythagoras' dietary edicts on the humble pulse, arguing that the attendant flatulence connotes leakage of the soul; or he'll remark on some quirk of vernacular architecture, such as the fashion for sand-coloured mortar on traditional stonework – sacrilege, in his view.

…Which reminds me of this couple's enthusiasm for antiquities and curiosities generally. He inherited and restored a *casona* by the banks of the river in Quintanilla, halfway between Bárcena and Pueblo de la Vega. I can't recall whether we ever visited it, but in any case, Benedict intends to make sure we do so now: "You must come and see my latest project, my *hórreo*," he says.

"What's that?"

"Well if you haven't seen one in this country, you might know what I mean by 'staddlestones'."

"Can't say I do."

"Mushroom-shaped stones, or rather, flat stones perched on narrower uprights. They're often used as ornaments outside old houses in England. Once upon a time, they kept the grain from the rats; they couldn't climb round the mushroom caps into the barn on top... Well, *hórreos* are the Spanish equivalent. The difference is that here, the wooden superstructure, often survives, not just the staddlestones. I found one on a recent trip, and I bought it off the farmer. We've dismantled it and rebuilt it in the garden."

The *sobremesa* extends well into the evening, by which point even a few locals have arrived and we've made substantial inroads into *La Mozuca's orujo.*[42] Benedict doesn't show much more restraint than I do.

Within days, we've received an invitation to Quintanilla to inspect the *hórreo*, the "horror" as they now call it, having sunk a small fortune into it. The structure itself, behind the *casona*, is all but complete. It's an eccentric two-storey building in wood. But Benedict's special pride is how the whole thing is a pioneering version of flat-packed furniture, everything interlocking, dismantled and reconstructed without recourse to a single screw or nail.

What's remarkable, though, apart from the magnificent lunch they lay on, is that Benedict found somebody to execute the work to this standard, not just the *hórreo*. The *casona* itself and the numerous outbuildings dotted about the *finca* are all immaculately restored. Perhaps we could borrow his team and tackle the long delayed *socarrena* after all.

---

[42] Grape-based spirit similar to *Grappa*

4

Dear Jack

I often remember your remarks about the "picaresque" – alive and well in this country, in your view: that chicanery and disrespect for the rules; that tendency to make do, to sail close to the wind; that economy with the truth and the self-deception that goes with it; that fierce pride and obsession with appearances. The more I think about it, the more I realise how well it fits my in-laws.

Maybe the surname itself, Expósito, is a clue. I learned that it was a name given to foundlings. A destitute mother would "expose" her baby on the steps of the local convent in hope of its adoption, preferably by the nuns.

*It implies that Marina's father descended from a foundling, the missing father being, conveniently, a nobleman (*hidalgo*), according to family lore. (I gather that, impoverished though they were, over half the entire male population round here claimed to be titled* hidalgos *at one stage.)*

My father-in-law Cipriano was a lifelong chancer and vagrant, seeding numerous offspring along the way – we'll probably never know the full tally. His son Chus follows in his footsteps, a master at corner-cutting and the progenitor of a small dynasty.

But perhaps it's my mother-in-law Gloria who captures the picaresque spirit as well as either of them, assuming it takes female form. She's extrovert, she's inconsistent and volatile, and appearances invariably trump reality – though sadly, she's no longer quite what she used to be: exuberant has become cantankerous; mercurial has become irrational.

Only vanity remains fully intact, the reason for her constant battle to maintain a status she can ill afford.

Two of these strands – father-in-law's peccadilloes and mother-in-law's vanity – coincided over the summer. It was roughly like this:

Marina's brother Sancho received a call from the family lawyer, Perky. He wanted to discuss a private matter, but suggested Sancho bring his siblings.

"All of us?" Sancho asked, thinking of his brother Chus, just back from Mexico, the latest financial crisis having put an end to the roadbuilding job.

"Entirely up to you. There are a few family matters to discuss, but I'm getting nowhere with your mother. That's why I turned to you. And I realise your brother has his own issues…"

That's why, one hot day just after the fiestas, Marina, Sancho and I (Marta's at work up the valley) visit Perky in his dreary despacho *in downtown Pueblo de la Vega.*

"It's like this," Perky says, once ensconced behind his desk, elbows on the blotter, fingers interlocked, forming a neat bookrest for his chin, "You all know, I take it, about the Colombian boys, I suppose? Yes? Well, they've spent a small fortune looking for your father's legendary stash, but they found nothing to add to the original €55. That's what I warned them would happen, but they wouldn't listen. Anyway, it's an opportunity – for you, I mean – because they can't afford the costs they've incurred, the legal fees, the investigators and so on. By settling those, you should be able to buy them out of their share of the house, which they stand to inherit when Gloria's no longer with us… It would probably take only a few thousand euros now in return for

their share of the house when the time comes… By any reckoning, that must be a good deal. I asked your mother, but she refused point blank to discuss it."

"That's because she doesn't have the money to settle and wouldn't want to ask for help. Too embarrassing," Sancho said, "and even if she did have the money, she'd rather spend it at Zara and leave us to squabble over it when the time comes."

"I suppose I should ask how she gets by. She can't manage on that spouse's pension, surely?"

"You're right, especially as there are now three mouths to feed as well as the house to look after. And she does love shopping! There's never enough, even with her sister's subsidy… and we chip in too."

The family's financial woes – Mamí's in particular – are perennial topics among the three of us. Marina remembers how, as a child, they were under constant stress, especially towards the month end, when money was extra tight, and her father's paycheque was supposed to arrive from the secretariat in Madrid. Often, that didn't happen, triggering frantic calls to trace its whereabouts.

Little has changed since then, because Gloria still awaits a monthly cheque to supplement her pension, but these days, it comes from her sister, Aunt Macu. The subsidy is part atonement for Gloria's lost share of the bodega, *but with the decline in its fortunes, it's getting ever harder to extract* "el cheque" *from Aunt Macu. In fact, Aunt Macu has turned from benefactress into Scrooge.*

This began soon after leaving the bodega. *For instance, as Asun, the teller, confided, her bank queried an account she set up 20 years ago, since untouched: "What* should we do with this account?" Asun, asked her. "It's in the name of your niece's daughter, Clara. I'll send you details – it's over 500 in credit. But there's been no movement on the account since it opened. That was 25 years ago, if I'm not mistaken."

"I'll transfer the money back to my main account," Aunt Macu said.

"Oh, but I'm afraid we couldn't do that – it's not in your name, you see… the account belongs to Señorita Clara… Since she turned 18, there's not a lot we can do about that."

Thus Clara received an unexpected windfall. It was the nest egg Macu promised when she became her godmother. The plan was to make contributions every birthday, but that part never materialised.

When full-blown dementia set in a few years back, the problems with el cheque multiplied, exacerbated by Macu's refusal to set up a regular transfer. Often, she declines to sign, and there's no point asking nephew Julito at the bodega to help, despite his authority to do so. He's focused on the inheritance that he intends to protect at all costs. It leads to a month-end dance, Gloria attempting to isolate Aunt Macu in her flat, find the cheque book and persuade her to write out the cheque. It causes Mamí to make generous offers to "babysit" her sister Macu at that time of the month, allowing Aunt Ludi some remission. Usually, Julito's at the bodega during the week. Even then, locating the cheque book is no easy matter, let alone manoeuvring her sister into writing and signing the cheque in her now spidery hand.

On one occasion, while Gloria hunted for the elusive

chequebook, Aunt Macu opened the balcony doors and started crying "¡socorro! ¡socorro!" at the top of her voice. Gloria says her sister's "very strong" and resisted her efforts to pull her back inside, while passers-by, including two guardias, looked up from the square in bafflement. Luckily, Gloria succeeded in winching her sister indoors, forestalling further embarrassment.

But since then, matters took a more serious turn. While Gloria rummaged around in the bedroom, Macu, finding the key in the lock, escaped down the stairs onto the street, before Gloria noticed. In horror, she watched her sister dodging the traffic from the window.

What to do? Call for help and waste vital seconds? (Ludi was at the doctor's and who else is there?) Or search for her herself, at the risk of public outing, her abiding dread. But that, she realised, was what she had to do.

By the time she reached the street, there was no trace of Macu – no leads at church, at El Politena or any obvious emporia. Then it dawned on her: the place closest to her sister's heart, the bodega: that's where she'd find her. And indeed, rounding the corner of the square, a pitiful tableau greeted her: her sister, propped up against the door of the warehouse, the main entrance she herself had helped to board up. The notice she had pinned to it was still there, now held by a single drawing pin, flapping in the breeze. But Macu wasn't alone; there was someone crouched by her side, supporting her, and comforting her. Gloria's heart missed a beat as she recognised Cayetana Ruiz-Toledo: the very same Cayetana she had once coveted as a longshot for her Chus. Cayetana, who had sealed a brilliant match with a lofty pijo, the Marqués de Getafe; Cayetana, who

240

inhabits a proper palacio *in Madrid's achingly smart Barrio de Salamanca and who spends the summer at the family's elegant* Casa de Indianos *in Villafranca del Conde. The grotesque contrast! Just too humiliating!*

Cayetana and Mamí, with Aunt Macu slung between them, staggered to the Medical Centre.

*These events prompted us to establish a fund managed by Marta, our loss adjustor. Apart from covering the odd new boiler or mower, it's a buffer to cover cashflow shortfalls whenever "*el cheque*" fails to materialise on schedule.*

After Marina's expurgated version of these arrangements, Perky let out a long sigh.

"Well, there are things you could do: ever thought of a reverse mortgage, for example? Release some cash from the house? The only trouble is you'd need your mother's signature and I rather doubt she'd agree to it. Anyway, how about I craft a proposal to your half-brothers and see where we get to on that issue? Obviously, everything will go through their lawyers. Needless to say, we'll make sure they stop all harassment or publicity about the matter, now or in the future."

*Jack, I should apologise for bending the "*picaresque*" so far out of shape. But I do think it has something to do with the puzzling antics of my adopted family… and I know there are parallels with your own.*

See you soon, I hope,

Rico

5

Shortly after the meeting with Perky, the time comes to return the hospitality from Benedict and family. This time, Hamish is with us on one of his escapes and has surpassed even his own high standards by presenting me with a bottle of 25-year-old Armagnac bought at the airport.

"Don't drink it all at once," he says. "It's to mark your birthday, a bit of a milestone this year, if my arithmetic's right."

The prospect of hosting these three gastronomes for lunch gives rise to some anxiety in our household. Expectations will be high, and honour will be at stake. Benedict and Jane are as dedicated in this respect as Hamish, and they seem to have trained the next generation rather better than we have.

Apart from our obligations to Benedict and family, we're taking the opportunity of introducing them to Sancho, who's joining us with his wife, Rocío. The thought is that he and Bridget will have interests in common. Given their disillusion with *Pinar,* he can supply them with wine and might even fix their *solera.*

For the main course, we settle on *marmitako,* the Basque dish seasoned with almost as much anecdote, controversy and chauvinism as the humble *tortilla de patatas. Marmitako* is a recipe for *bonito,* "white tuna", the allegedly superior variety found off the north coast. Like many such things, there are as many rules as chefs but there's really a single immutable one, which is to turn off the heat as soon as the cubes of *bonito* are dropped into the pot. If not, the fish toughens and *marmitako* becomes near inedible. To this day, one garden party given by Benigno, Aunt Ludi's late husband, sticks in the memory. The highlight was to be Benigno's celebrated *marmitako.* Suffice to say, he omitted to turn off the gas, leaving the *bonito* to shrivel into gobs of dry gristle.

"Ah, *sorropotún!*" Benedict says once we're seated outside, contemplating the still bubbling *cazuela* in the middle of the table, "one of my favourites. Or have you submitted to the Basque term, '*marmitako*'? Of course, the Basques plunder everything, recipes included. Surely it would be 'cultural appropriation' if the roles were reversed? … It's like the French and '*mayonnaise*'. As you may know, it's properly called '*mahonesa*', meaning 'from Mahón' in Menorca – nothing whatsoever to do with France! About time there was redress for that blatant act of plagiarism!"

I knew Benedict could be relied upon to find something to say on most subjects. I dare say the flow of *tinto* has inspired him more than usual, because he has more to add on the subject of *marmitako*: "The fishermen, whether Basque or not, would take a single cooking pot, a *marmita*, with them on their expeditions, together with a supply of potatoes, peppers, paprika and anything else to hand. They boiled up the vegetables and finally dropped the *bonito* into the *marmita*. That's your etymological link with the breakfast staple, Marmite, by the way. In both cases, they refer to the vessel, not the contents… I assume you know Marmite was a German invention? Bit of a shock to discover the Huns got there first, isn't it?"

This blend of anecdote and banter continues, while Jane and Hamish share a mutual interest in antiquities. Hamish purports to make a living by trading old furniture and silver and Jane hopes he will assess their heirlooms before he leaves.

Later, Benedict raises the subject of the covered porch, a plan that has been taking tangible shape since he told me about his architect.

"About this *socarrena*, as you call it (I say "*socarreña*" – but

243

there we go, I realise there's debate about that…) Is it really going ahead? You must show us what's intended…"

In fact, it's a little more complicated than just a covered porch, as I explain on a short tour with Benedict, Jane and Hamish during an interlude before the *sobremesa*. But first, I fetch the *Diccionario de la Lengua Española*, the volumes published by the *Real Academia Española* (one of very few mementos from late Uncle Toño, Clara's christening present). I find the entry proving that *"socarrena"* is a *bona fide* Spanish word. In fact, the same dictionary has no entry at all for *"socarreña"* with a *"ñ"*. I'm just savouring this small victory, thinking how pleased Uncle Toño would have been in like circumstances. But I should have realised Benedict wouldn't be so easily vanquished.

"The trouble with the *Real Academia*," he says, "is that it's a prescriptive, top-down organisation. So Spanish! It records the language *as it would like it to be* rather than *how it actually is.* Compare that with the Anglo-Saxon tradition. We don't have a normative organisation like that at all. The language is free to evolve, unmanaged by any academy, and good dictionaries record it *as it is…* That's why English is so much more creative, flexible and democratic… Or put another way: "pragmatic". You see, we English are *empiricists.* Compare that with Spanish dogma – you can see why they had the Inquisition. We had Magna Carta."

Who ever imagined that a single squiggle, the *tilde* that transforms *"n"* into *"ñ"* – like the "n" in American "new" to British "new" – thereby earning its discrete entry in the dictionary, could bear the burden of global culture wars on its tiny hunchback? But such is Benedict's genius at extrapolating the general from the particular.

In any event, the proposed *socarrena* (I'm sticking to that, regardless) implies moving the garage into a new, separate building, converting the freed-up space into a sitting room, from which the *socarrena* will be accessed via two sets of French doors.

"I think you probably mean casement doors, don't you? That is, opening outwards; French doors open inwards," Benedict observes.

At this point, we reassemble round the table, on which I place Hamish's Armagnac. It's a costly error: Benedict discovers a special weakness for it.

But it serves another purpose, for Sancho and Bridget to explore their shared interest in wine; he offers to show her round the *Aurelio* winery so she can assess installations and the product.

After they've gone, I hold up my birthday present, squinting at Hamish's bottle of Armagnac against the light and giving it a shake by the neck: as I suspected, there can't be much more than half an inch left. I place the bottle on the table and spread my hands in dismay.

6

A few weeks later, Sancho calls to ask if I can meet him at the *Aurelio* plant. By itself, that's surprising, because, to date, *Aurelio* has been off-limits to all Sancho's relatives, a rule tacitly enforced on both sides. Even our interaction with Rocío is rationed. On the phone, Sancho's guarded about his motive. He sounds bothered: he wants my opinion on something – he'll take me through it when we meet later. Nor does he extend the invitation to his sister. That would be taking things too far; it could prove incendiary, whereas my semi-detachment gives me greater license and spares me some degree of scrutiny and opprobrium.

Apart from a first sight of *Aurelio* from the inside, the trip will provide an excuse to visit my favourite shop, the *ferretería* (hardware store), also located in Tobillo. Not unjustifiably, Marina attributes an obsession with gadgets and tools to me, a by-product of living on a near-permanent building site. But when I mention that steel tacks are among the items I need, she immediately thinks I am planning some crazy retaliation against Monchi and family – in her view, utter folly.

There are two schools of thought: appeasement or confrontation. Marina's technique is to disarm Monchi with cheery greetings and smiles; in my opinion, it cuts no ice whatever. It hardly worked up until now. Not that I had a nefarious purpose in mind for the tacks, whose destiny was merely to anchor a wayward rug.

If anything, the silhouette of Monchi's son, Nino, now resident in the top floor of that jerry-built dwelling right behind (the original *casus belli*), casts an even more baleful shadow across the village than his father used to. These days, Monchi himself is more likely to be seen tottering down the hill from the bar in the *barrio alto,* too far gone to cause much trouble. Yes, he still affects to greet me with a smile that's close to a grimace; but in terms of mischief, Monchi has bequeathed the honour to his son Nino.

Marina may have in mind the incident the other day, when Nino spotted me in the garden and stormed over to berate me about a couple of overhanging twigs: "What the f***'s all this *maleza* overhanging my land? Can't you see it's encroaching by at least a metre? Look: right here, over there, down at the bottom, all over the place! What are you going to do about it? I want it removed, right now!"

And after I let him rabbit on in this vein for a minute or two without response, he added: "Well? I'm not in the habit of denouncing anyone, but…"

It's just the latest of countless altercations and aggressions, often involving petty vandalism.

I won't deny that his quadbike's a tempting target. It's garaged in a lean-to belonging to our other neighbours, Gusti and Dolores, the elderly couple we haven't seen on site for about 20 years. Every so often, Nino takes the quad for a spin but even he tires of it once he's terrorised the vicinity for an hour or two. Most of the time it sits in the shed under a plastic cover, otherwise unprotected. However, I do realise the urge has to be tamed. There's no upside in it at all – that's what Marina impresses on me, anyway, and her instincts are usually right: "Nino's worse, much worse than Monchi. *El tío es borde, borde, borde*" she says, reaching for that favourite Spanish locution, "cumulative emphasis", as Jack calls it, to convey a superlative: *That bloke's properly twisted…* "All the more reason for caution", Marina adds.

Besides, I'm developing other, more subtle, stratagems should relations deteriorate further. Ideally, I would grow a dense hedge right the way along the wall that separates us from Monchi and his son. (It needs to be tall as well as wide, because a balcony projects from the upper storey of their dwelling for access from the external stairs. That's where Nino lives, and it offers a commanding view over our garden. He sometimes sits up there, plus girlfriend and baby, tracking our every move.) But repeated hedge seedlings have been systematically exterminated, a flagon of bleach evidently doing the honours in our absence. Somehow, though, by planting a single, tiny seedling of slow-growing *griselinia* each year, it has escaped notice, the result of which is that, after 20 years, at least one third of the frontier now boasts a three-metre-tall evergreen barrier, which, for some reason, Nino has spared from the poison vial. Meanwhile, it has eliminated most eye contact and hidden Nino's offensive hot hatchback.

Ironically, on my way to Tobillo, I see that very vehicle

looming in my rear-view mirror. As soon as he realises it's me, he tails me, close and persistent as a randy dog. It's happened before, so I know there are only two places before the old main road where he can pass, the first being a short straight stretch after the *barrio alto,* on the slope down to the floor of the winding river valley. If Marina were with me, she'd say *"no seas necio"* or something similar – "don't be an idiot". But I'm alone, and this provocation is more than I can stomach right now. Besides, downhill at least, I have a good chance of thwarting his designs and so it proves this time, the old Golf juddering with the effort but allowing me to brake just in time for the hairpin at the bottom. On the second straight, however, Nino flashes his lights and this time I can't avoid letting him race past, scowling at me and raising a middle finger. He just has time to slide out of the way of a campervan dawdling round the bend in the opposite direction, before vanishing into the wood ahead… My heart's a-thumping.

Tobillo, reached ten minutes later, unfurls along the old main road, the long, straight artery that once irrigated the town end to end. But recently, that vessel has become sclerotic, a victim of the new bypass, a present from Europe, all stilts, cuttings and tunnels, sweeping imperiously from the French border to Portugal almost without a break, ignoring trivial capillaries in and around places like Tobillo. Once a thriving hub, Tobillo has withered to near oblivion, despite hosting several not undistinguished landmarks, including the local *ayuntamiento* (town hall), the *ferretería*, a flashy *CEPSA* garage, *Vinos Aurelio* and a few imposing blocks of flats. In one of these, opposite *El Viajante*, the bar of lottery fame, Nino lodges his semi-estranged girlfriend and baby. Sure enough, the yellow vehicle's drawn up on the tarmac outside.

Such are the family politics that I feel exposed, parking

on the *Aurelio* forecourt and making my way inside. There I find Sancho up a ladder, peering into one of a score of stainless-steel vats that fill most of the space. When he sees me, he comes straight down, gives me the usual bear hug, escorts me past the bottling plant, pauses for me to admire the underground cellar and finally leads me up some stairs into his functional office at the back that he used to share with Iñaki before the latter's sudden departure. It turns out to be an unexpected oasis, catching a ray of sunshine through the window on one side, while overlooking a mature garden on the other.

"Thanks for coming at short notice, Rico," he says, showing me to a low sofa on one side. "I'm sure you're wondering why I asked. I'll get straight to the point. It's because last night, we had a break-in… I'm pretty sure they came through the small window in the lavatory."

"Oh no! What did they take?"

"Nothing much as far as I can tell. There's next to no cash on site these days and anyway, it's locked up in a safe. Apart from that, anything valuable needs a truck to move it – that's why we never bothered with an alarm. But I'm pretty sure my papers were tampered with. I just wanted to talk it through with somebody before tackling my father-in-law. It'll be tricky."

"Well, I expect we're thinking the same thing. It's pretty obvious who'd be interested in your papers, I should think. What about the wine?"

"That's what I was checking when you came. But so far, no sign of dirty tricks, I'm relieved to say. Though just a few adulterated bottles would be enough to ruin our reputation. We've decided to throw out everything loaded or ready for dispatch, just in case. We're testing samples from every vat. It's an expense, but we can't risk it… Just come over to the window – you can see where they got in…"

He takes me to the side overlooking the garden, which, on this side ends right at the wall of the *Aurelio* plant. Beyond a lawn and a few mature trees, there's an old *palacio*, which I never knew existed. There's a young woman in the garden, watering pot plants.

"That's Cristina," Sancho says. "She runs the *palacio*. You see that small window by the kink in the wall? That's where they came in, I'm pretty sure, though a bit of a squeeze. The window was off the latch this morning."

"So they would've come through the *palacio*?"

"Seems like they'd have to. Through the garden anyway."

The woman in the *palacio* garden has spotted us, she waves, then holds forefinger and thumb apart and aloft by way of requesting some of our time. Sancho gives the thumbs up before returning to the sofa.

"What about the *Guardia Civil*?" I ask. "You called them, I assume?"

"Yes, but I'm not holding my breath. They came round, but were making excuses. '*Es que*' this, '*es que*' that. I suppose they had a point: where's the proof?"

"Nothing incriminating from your papers, I take it?"

"No, not really; they moved stuff around. They would have photographed anything interesting, but it's mostly old. It's all on computer nowadays…" He pauses, then suddenly, "Hey, that's a thought!" he says, jumping up and rounding his desk, where he opens the middle drawer and rummages around for a while. "That *has* gone, I'm pretty sure!"

"What's gone?"

"A pen drive. One I prepared for Bridget…"

"Bridget? You're not suggesting…?"

"Of course not. I gave it to her for the project she's

helping me with. But that's why confidential information found its way onto a memory stick. It wasn't password protected or anything. Bridget brought it back a couple of days ago. Stupidly, I put it in my desk and forgot all about it."

"What exactly was on there?"

"Just about everything: accounts, minutes, customer details, suppliers, sensitive correspondence…"

"Blimey! But if you can't pin it on anyone, I don't see what can be done. In any case, you're assuming it'll be useful to somebody else. If you're thinking of our friends at the *polígono*, I doubt it. They wouldn't recognise something useful if it bit them in the rear!"

"Actually, it's only the correspondence I'm really concerned about. Listen to this."

Sancho swears me to secrecy; then he reveals that *Aurelio* received an approach from the Ruiz-Toledos. At this point, talks are still wide-ranging, but everything's on the table. Bridget's advising – advising *Aurelio*, that is. The Ruiz-Toledos have long had an interest in wine and, as Aunt Macu informed me, once wanted to buy into *Pinar* and later the *nave* itself. Both times, they were rebuffed. That's why Sancho's confident that something will come of the present initiative. But he's also anxious about the leak. Who knows what Julito might do with the information, should it come his way?

"It's really quite exciting. Obviously, the R-Ts have the means. Everything's going our way at the moment. But look: it's time we met Cristina…"

A few minutes later we're sitting with Cristina, sipping coffee, in the *galería* of the *palacio*.

"Last night," she says, "I was watering the geraniums before bed and I thought I was hallucinating. There was a young man in the garden! Bit of a shock… When I shouted, he bolted and scrambled over the wall into the road at the front. By the time I'd unlocked the gate, he was gone. I don't suppose you saw anything?"

"No, but we were broken into last night. I thought there must have been several people involved, but perhaps it was just one. He or they got through the lavatory window by the garden. Did you see who it was?"

"I couldn't swear to it. It was dark and he was wearing a hoodie. But I have a hunch. Something about the posture. It could well have been that troublemaker from the flats just along the road."

"Not the one that drives the canary yellow hatchback, by any chance?" I ask.

"Yes, that's what I'm thinking…"

Afterwards, I explain the history of our own troubled dealings with Nino, Monchi and family.

"Leave Nino to me," Sancho says after we've left Cristina. "By the way, my father-in-law's very much in favour of the R-T connection… But I'm not looking forward to telling him about the pen drive… It won't be pleasant. He'll throw a tantrum. Not for the first time. His temper's volcanic even on a good day. With luck, he'll get over it. He usually does…"

7

After the drama, the detox of a visit to the *Ferretería Palacio* offers welcome respite. It's a scruffy shop, a thrombosis on the arterial road owing to the assorted paraphernalia spilling over the pavement. But today, everything looks unusually tidy. Why the sudden clean-up?

This store's a veritable treasure trove for any tool buff, replete with old-fashioned gadgets and rural idiosyncrasies such as the local wooden clogs, *albarcas*, mounted on three little feet like a trivet, designed to raise the wearer above the mud. It's a place where even I receive a hearty greeting as a cherished customer and friend – despite the store's ownership by José and Remedios Palacio, parents of Chus's first wife, Conchi Palacio. It's also a place where screws, nails, tacks and other fixings are dispensed one by one, wrapped in slivers of brown paper and sealed with Scotch tape – just as cousin Julito used to do with the kirby grips at the haberdashers in Bárcena. It has yet to surrender to the imperative that merchandise must dangle from a prong, pre-packed in plastic, thereby justifying an exorbitant price tag as well as nourishing the nascent recycling industry in its bid to *"catch up with Europe."*

Imagine my disillusion, then…

Ownership recently devolved on the younger generation, Fernando, son of José and Remedios, being the lucky heir. (His sister Conchi never showed any interest; in any case, she's now a regular contributor to *Voz del Golfo*…) But Fernando's obviously signalling his drive and ambition, and his embrace of the new, because I find the store has been refurbished in my absence, making way for a new-style, self-service emporium. Gone are the eccentric handtools, scythes, hoes and barrows, replaced by diesel generators, petrol-driven strimmers and ride-on mowers; gone, too, are the wicker chairs and earthenware cooking vessels, albeit – a concession to national pride, perhaps – the pressure cooker has survived the cull. For rightly or wrongly, many Spaniards, Marina among them, insist that the pressure cooker is in fact a Spanish invention, comparable in significance to Edison's lightbulb or Karl Benz's internal combustion engine.

The old wooden *mostrador,* the counter, has made way for a checkout desk, staffed by a bored teenager on a swivel-stool. The old ethos has vanished, leaving customers to grope unaided along the aisles in search of the right article, now dangling from a prong. No more the guidance of a nice old lady – that is, Remedios, Chus's erstwhile mother-in-law – sparing no efforts to meet recondite requests from a cornucopia of fixings stowed in small wooden drawers behind the counter.

To underline just how modish they've become, each packet is labelled in the English language, the paradoxical principle evidently being: "*Why use a Spanish word when there's a perfectly decent English equivalent?*"

Arriving home, I share my experience with Marina, economising, however, on the encounter with Nino on the way to Tobillo. I tell her about the break-in at *Aurelio*. But she already knows: "Sancho just called. It seems the thief was Nino, as you thought. Sancho threatened to hand him to the *Guardia Civil* if he didn't own up. It seems that Julito put him up to it, just as expected."

"What's he doing about it?"

"Nothing just yet. Family politics are so tense he needs time to think it through. But he'll confront Julito at the right moment."

Then Marina idly takes one of the bags of tacks from me and peruses the label.

Then she reads out the blurb on the back:

Instructions for use:
    Use on soft materials only
    Use a hammer
    Hold tack at 90 degrees to hammer
    Mind your fingers!
      Made in China

"This really is the New Spain," she says, handing back the bag.

"Yes, health 'n' safety finally got here…"

But when Marina and I think about the subject of *Health 'n' Safety* a bit more, this tiny detail parallels various stealthy developments that have played out over quite a while.

We need look no further than Mamí herself, for example. Whatever happened to the haughty stoicism that once characterised her generation? A strong sense of entitlement has replaced it.

I'm not just thinking of her disdain for generic palliatives, along the lines of "*those pills are so cheap they'll be useless*", a refrain that's passed her lips quite a few times. Instead, it's the assumption that there must be a cure for whatever ailment, condition or discomfort life throws her way, and she has an inalienable right to it. It's Marta who suffers most of the fall-out, adding the role of rehab clinician to those of loss-adjustor and paymistress.

Over time, for example, the dependency on sleeping pills has increased noticeably and Marta complains that Mamí spends most of the day semi-comatose. Then she discovers that, since her mother expects to sleep like an infant from eleven at night to nine the next day, she's begun to take a second fix when she wakes at about six in the morning.

When Marta tells her this cannot continue, Mamí issues a fierce rebuff, tantamount to a curse: "You're a very bad daughter and your punishment will come directly from God. He will see to it that you never have children of your own."

Since Marta underwent a hysterectomy a few years ago, it's a cruel curse that, unlike some, is almost certain to be fulfilled.

On the next trip to the Medical Centre, Marta takes the doctor aside for a quiet word. His alarm is such that he halts Mamí's prescription forthwith, sending her home instead with a supply of *Relax Tea* to take before bed.

It's an experiment that delivers disappointing results, as an incandescent Mamí makes clear: "I'm changing doctor straight away! That one's an imbecile! Do you realise how many times I had to get up in the night? And I didn't sleep a wink in between. I'm going to the pharmacy right now – they *have* to give me the proper pills!"

By now, one way and another, all three sisters are drug-dependent: Mamí in order to sleep and to control arrhythmia and hypertension; Macu to fend off dementia; and Aunt Ludi to manage depression, a direct outcome of the babysitting duties with her sister. The result is that all three of them pass much of life in a fog… for which they have also been prescribed caffeine tablets to aid concentration and stay awake during the daytime.

Of late there has been a worrying development. Marina now suspects that Mamí's mental capacities are dwindling, though less radically than her sister's, for the time being. After consulting her siblings, it's agreed Marta should take Mamí for a dementia test. Marta stands in as examiner for a couple of dry runs – she knows a bit about the process from her Aunt Macu's experience.

The test itself takes place at the Medical Centre, where a nurse explains the rules: top marks is 30 points – clean bill of health, no cognitive issues at all; above 24 is a pass; below that, a fail.

Most of the questions will be factual, but before starting on those, she adds: "I'm going to give you three words to remember. I'll ask you to repeat them once we've finished. It's to test your short-term memory. Now, please don't forget them: the three words are as follows: '*peseta*'; '*España*'; and '*pueblo*'. Each word is worth one point."

The nurse starts on the 27 factual questions, including such things as Mamí's date of birth; the number of children she has; her postcode; her late husband's full name and so forth. In five minutes, the nurse has all but finished. Mamí has put in a pretty robust performance.

"So, we've now reached the final questions," the nurse says. "Can you repeat the three words I gave you at the beginning?"

"Three words? What three words? You didn't give me three words!" Mamí looks vainly at her daughter for succour, but none's on offer.

Unfortunately, this final lapse tips her onto the wrong side of the scale, with a score of 22. According to the nurse, it's not calamitous; in principle, she can still look after herself, but she needs to practice mental exercises, which she then explains, handing Mamí some books and a set of colouring pencils.

Mamí's indignant and, as so often, Marta bears the brunt. As they head home, Mamí complains bitterly: "Why didn't you tell me about that? You never said anything about "*three words*". That's a trick question! Had I known, I'd have learned them by heart. Now I failed, and it's *all your fault*! Don't you dare tell anyone. And don't think I'm going to do those stupid activities. They're insulting; insulting for a child, even."

As for the *Safety* half of the H&S duopoly: over the last few years the Spanish government has upstaged its peers by introducing the most draconian drink-driving laws in Europe. Everyone assumed it was just for show (like the ban on indoor smoking, which they sneaked in ahead of the pack, to burnish those European credentials); initially, there were few signs of changed attitudes. Against expectations, however, the rules were enforced with draconian alacrity, involving immediate bans for minimal blood-alcohol readings. Worse, the offenders' cars were to be impounded, at the risk of outright mutiny: for most Spaniards would far rather pay a ransom or even spend a few nights at The Authorities' pleasure than relinquish their precious *coche* to anyone, however briefly.

To launch the new policy, ambushes were laid at strategic nodes in the small hours on New Year's Day. The first year, this bagged an impressive haul. The following year, however, revellers tried various ruses and detours to avoid detection. Those with four-by-fours explored new off-road routes through the eucalyptus, but in time, the *Guardia Civil* foiled these, too. To widespread dismay, not even waving a couple of banknotes at the *guardias* has much effect these days, other than to land you in a cell for the night. Worse still, your vehicle will be impounded for a minimum of six months.

In our case, the new drink-driving rules have paid an unforeseen dividend. Every year, Mamí hosts a New Year's Eve celebration. It comprises dinner at home in Bárcena – more or less a carbon copy of Christmas Eve – all to the accompaniment of TV banter and culminating in a countdown to the twelve chimes that ring in the New Year from Madrid's *Puerta del Sol*. That's the point when good fortune for the coming year rides on your ability to swallow twelve yellowish, leathery, pipped grapes (sometimes freshly decanted from a tin) before the chimes cease. Invariably, by the twelfth gong we've managed no more than three or four grapes, by now masticated to a gritty, bitter pulp, which it's humanly impossible to swallow. It's a ritual that's fun for children, but by now has become a tired vestige of a bygone life-stage, leaving little more than forced *bonhomie*. To make matters worse, last year *Voz del Golfo* reported the untimely demise of one over-zealous reveller, whose twelfth grape took a wrong turn half-way down. However, in our family, it's still mandatory for all present, fiercely enforced, not just by Mamí, but by Marta too.

That's why we now insist on slipping away to Valledal well before the ordeal begins, emphasising the fact that, at 15 minutes to midnight the roads will be entirely deserted and the *guardias* themselves will still be toasting one another (I doubt they really do stick to Coca Cola and alcohol-free beer, whatever they may say). Straight after midnight, they'll be back in their hideouts, ready to spring their traps.

Even Mamí accepts it's a wise move. Not that we're unduly anxious about losing a licence (or the car)… but better not to tempt fate.

Chapter VII: Heir Splitting

1

Surprisingly, Chus's Spanish road-building job, the substitute for his Mexican adventure, materialises after all. To widespread disbelief, cousin Quique once more expends personal capital – his *enchufes* – on behalf of his relative, surpassing anything that might be expected even from the closest family ties.

"What exactly will you be doing?" Marina asks her brother when he broadcasts his latest triumph.

"Ever heard of '*vertebración del país*'?" he says. "I'll be in Galicia. We don't want another Catalonia – pressing for independence, I mean. Our job's to stop that. And there's another reason," Chus continues with a smirk, "which is just as important. It's a bonanza for everyone, especially politicians and contractors… Why d'you think we have so many empty roads and railways in this country? What are all those airports and museums really for? Of course, the main purpose is to cost a lot of money. Better still, Europe ponies up at least half."

None of this clarifies what his job will be day to day. Mamí assumes he'll be on the management team, sharing the bonanza; Marina that he'll be driving a digger. And once in the job, he shares little more about it. However, he comes home regularly, his first pay cheque earmarked for a car. It's an ageing Audi saloon; but he's proud of it and drives it, he boasts, "like Fangio".

"I've got the journey down to three hours. That's an average of over 100 an hour and don't get the idea it's *autovía* the whole way: far from it! That's what I'm there to fix!"

A vicarious glimpse of his living conditions comes one

Christmas. Now he has a salary, he's back to dispensing patronage and it's in that spirit that he offers to source this year's *lechazo*, the suckling lamb served at Mamí's at Christmas and again at New Year.

On Christmas Eve, following crab and prawn starters, two steaming trays of meat are ferried in from the kitchen, together with their sole accompaniment, a tart green salad to cut through the grease. Marta's in charge of cooking but Mamí, as hostess, serves at table, where a strict pecking order prevails. It starts with me, thanks to sex, age and enduring "outsider" status. In Mamí's hierarchy, that's a hat-trick. Chus comes next, then James and Toni; finally, the women, in no special order, share whatever scraps are left, in this case a few scrawny chops.

Not long into the meal, Mamí, unusually tactful in the circumstances, whispers scepticism to me about the lamb: "A bit tough, don't you think?"

I keep schtum, but she's right: it's not falling off the bone or melting in the mouth as it should. That's the whole point of *lechazo*.

But Chus overhears and rounds on his sister: "Marta! Don't tell me you've ruined it… Overcooked? Again?"

"I don't think so…" Mamí intervenes, defending Marta for once and wagging that crooked index finger at Chus. "Most likely this wasn't *lechazo* in the first place!"

There's an ominous pause. At times like this Chus resembles his late father, temporarily taciturn, damming up the resentment, then bursting forth: "What do you mean, not *lechazo*? Of course it's *lechazo*! It comes from the farm I live on. I saw the lambs with my own eyes, grazing in the field right outside my window, for God's sake! I selected it myself! I watched the farmer slit its throat, skin it, chop it up, bag up the offal and put the whole lot in the back of my car! You think I'm a dupe, or what?"

"I'm afraid that's *exactly* what I think… How can it be *lechazo* if the lambs were grazing? They're supposed to be milk-fed! Mother's milk only! *Vaya infeliz que eres, hijo mío, vaya infeliz!*[43] says Mamí, savouring a rare knock-out blow.

From that exchange, complemented by others from time to time, improvising a bit, no doubt, I build a mental image of Chus, lodged in dreary digs on a grubby little farm in the middle of nowhere. It doesn't sound like his ambiance at all – no women, no broadband, nothing much to recommend it save a pastoral setting with a few lambs gambolling by the window and a backdrop of wiry eucalyptus etched on a sullen sky. Luckily, he still enjoys novels of wartime derring-do; for without them, he would struggle to stay sane.

Chus has, however, fixed himself up with female company. She lives in the deep south, about as far away as could be, but allegedly, she's just as *despanpanante* as the previous incumbents. Chus never tells how they met – online, presumably – but whenever money allows, he takes the sleeper, first class, down south for a tryst. We imagine the dapper figure cut by *el señorito*, as he steps down from his first-class carriage, at his most urbane, and starts to divert his paramour with war stories drawn and embellished from his exploits around the globe.

But unfortunately, these trips cannot dispel the acedia that sinks back upon him on site; and that's when a familiar cycle starts.

With one or two notable lapses, Chus has foregone alcohol ever since his ejection from Gabon aeons ago. That's how he managed to last for several years without terminal incident – at least, not self-inflicted, since his last two jobs ended for reasons beyond his control. But now, a

---

[43] "How naïve you are, my son, how naïve!"

can of beer or two looks all too tempting to palliate the bleak and lonely evenings.

Mindful of the reaction last time he broke the pledge, he takes a six-pack back to the farm. Safety first, he reasons: any backlash will cause him to crash on the bed, where he'll wake up next morning, probably with a thick head, but otherwise ready for battle. In any case, this is a trial: he has no intention of risking more than a single can at this stage. In preparation, he eschews the crucial pill, the emetic triggered by alcohol.

The trial passes without mishap – no belated reaction from the drugs or anything unpleasant. Yes, he did experience a moment of sublime release as soon as the alcohol stole into his system, the more beguiling after prolonged abstinence; and yes, he would gladly have opened a second can, but resisted with steely resolve. The following day he wakes at the normal time and sets off to the site. What was the fuss about?

Chus only ever hinted, usually by accident or inference, at the steps leading from that cautious experiment to the debacle. What we know for certain is that he borrowed one of the small trucks for the drive to and from the farm, while the Audi took a break for repairs at a local garage. I also know that he befriended one of the wide boys on site. The chance of an evening jaunt to the local capital seduced them both. But on the return from an historic binge, Chus veered off the road into a ditch, where the front axle fractured against the lip of a concrete drain. They were unhurt, but from then on, events unfolded predictably: disappearance; discovery and detention by the police; confiscation of licence; dismissal from employment; return to base in Bárcena de la Mina; stinging maternal rebuke followed soon enough by rehabilitation; then unemployment.

By now, even Quique's flagging, running out of ideas as well as patience. In any case Chus, now in his mid-fifties, bears the scars of a lifetime of self-abuse, including "that virus", which, at one point, Mamí claimed he'd "shaken off". But even he himself feels the picaresque career must be drawing to a close.

Then he calls our bluff: "Remember our chat about computer consultancy?" he asks, one day while we're waiting for lunch in that dour and by now shabby sitting room at Mamí's house, with Chus comfortably ensconced in his late father's reclining armchair.

That would be hard to deny, since we ourselves floated the idea before his Spanish roads job surfaced. It's an unwelcome reminder, so soon after this latest disaster. At the time, we envisaged his working from a van and, in a moment of weakness, even suggested we might help him get it off the ground. It sounded plausible because, ever since he took Mamí's computer, the one originally on loan from us, Chus has seized every chance to lock himself away with it, having bullied Mamí into upgrading to an indispensable broadband subscription, one of the many outlays claiming a share of the siblings' subsidy.

It's better not to delve too deeply into what exactly he's up to. Obviously, there's piracy, since, for the first time, he gives Christmas presents, now that he can clone blockbusters on CD; but any question about what exactly he's seeking on "the dark web" (one of a few English phrases he tried out on me, accompanied by a conspiratorial grin) is best left unanswered.

But his skills are not limited to the web. The computer is ten years old, so he's turned his hand to repairs and upgrades, as a result of which he's learned the whole game from ground up. The times we've had an IT issue of our own, he's nearly always fixed it: for once, his boasts seem to be well grounded.

But it'll need seeding – a deposit on a lease (a shop, not a van), basic stock, and a float for a few months. Moreover, Chus's state subsidies will vanish as soon as he declares self-employment – a built-in disincentive to private enterprise, which The Authorities instinctively abhor, viewing it as an affront to their own patronage.

To share the pain, we decide to co-opt Sancho onto the scheme. If any family member can afford it, he's the one. His ailing father-in-law Gonzalo Caudal recently stepped back from management at *Aurelio*, leaving Sancho in charge. Judging by appearances, he's quite prosperous these days, graduating to the old man's former office, buried in dark furniture and surrounded by hunting trophies.

But Sancho has no intention of helping. He's at his most judgemental: "I'm not spending a single *duro* on that wastrel, it's out of the question… He's not a backable person – it's his personality, quite incapable of effort or focus, in my view. He's just looking for somebody else to sponge off. Even if it goes OK, he's bound to blow it on some drink-fuelled escapade or romantic entanglement. So you're on your own, I'm afraid! Don't expect anything back! But good luck!"

We might have expected that. Ever since the time he lifted his brother by the lapels and banged him against the panelling, the rift between them never healed.

Another snag is Chus's eyesight. The solution, Chus declares, is to recruit his son, because Toni's eyesight is so much better and, in any case, he needs an occupation. Hitherto, nothing worked out. Mamí persuaded her neighbour Nunci to approach the Ruiz-Toledos on his behalf, leading to a year-long apprenticeship at the textile factory that Toni dismissed before he even started.

However, he claims an interest in computers – years on Xbox have helped – and his father thinks this might hold a future for him, something for him to inherit when his own eyesight finally fails. That by itself is encouraging. Since when did Chus think so far ahead?

The final hurdle is Mamí's hostility. She thinks her son will be working from a van: "A *vendedor ambulante*?[44] Please, spare me that!"

"No, no of course not. I'm taking a proper *local*."

"Anyway, I think it's a bad idea. You, a shopkeeper? You were always an action man! Shooting and roasting your own bush meat in the mountains, that kind of thing. I can't see you sitting there all day long being polite to customers. The boredom! Whatever next? And I'm not even sure you know all that much about computers. At least you never get any films for me! That I do know!"

"Look, it's all arranged – the space is right across the street…"

"What do you mean? Not the place vacated by your friend Gabi, I hope?"

She's referring to Nunci's garage, rented by her son Paco's wife Gabi for her pet clinic. Recently, she returned the lease after splitting from her husband. Unexpectedly, in that quarrel, Chus lined up among her stoutest defenders. For Mamí, taking that unit is an absolute taboo. What if Chus defaults on the rent? Or damages the premises? Or uses them for lewd purposes? The last thing she wants is to sully her friendship with Nunci, however indirectly. Even Chus realises that retreat is called for; he finds another *local* for the venture 50 metres further off.

Once I've transferred an initial sum, the new venture starts trading. The firm is called *Computer Saviour*, an

---

[44] Door-to-door salesman

allusion in fashionable English to the boss, Chus: Jesús, our Saviour.

2

"You do realise you'll be the main protagonist at this event? No more sitting on the fence; no more semi-detachment this time!"

Marina's referring to my role at a fast-approaching ordeal that recently took centre stage; it's the final round of our son James's wedding celebrations. James's bride, "Sally" as she's known, is from China and custom demands ceremonies at both ends, not counting a preliminary event at a Chinese registry office. We've chosen to arrange ours in Spain.

It's always been a source of irritation to Marina that, while she's locked in perpetual combat with her mother, I escape almost unscathed. From the moment we met, Mamí slapped a "do not disturb" order on my forehead that guarantees special treatment. I'm generally off-limits when it comes to family strife. That won't be so easy at the wedding, which we plan to host at home, in Valledal.

That's the reason I'm spending a few days there, alone, to sort things out. The first task is to meet Jordi, the architect I inherited from Benedict. Once again, the place is a building site and, adding to nascent remorse, the caretaker, Lorena, is stomping about in the kitchen, banging pots and pans in annoyance at the piles of furniture and films of grit on every surface. Mercifully, she soon leaves, managing a perfunctory grunt by way of farewell.

I'm sitting in the middle of the building site, wondering how all this gets done in time when Jordi draws up in his Jeep.

"As you can see, they're rebuilding the pyramids, *jajaja,*" he says, jumping from the vehicle and pointing at the huge piles of dressed stone from various breakers' yards. "Have you met Alexandru yet?"

"You mean the builder?" I shake my head.

"Amazing fellow. You'll see what I mean. Built like a menhir! He shuffles these flagstones around like playing cards. Anyway, let's take a proper look."

The excavations for the *socarrena* by the house confirm that it rests on a slab of clay without foundations. It explains the damp. I anticipated rock, too, but there's no sign of that.

Up in the far corner of the garden is the site of the new garage, where a wedge-shaped bridgehead, flanked by enemy territory (Monchi/Nino on one side, Dolores, now widowed, on the other), debouches onto a short section of road frontage. That's where the planned opening onto the public highway will be, providing access to the garage. Jordi assumed that at least two 4x4s would need lodging and his initial plans for a pair of contiguous cubes of monstrous proportions caused a breach between us right at the outset. The revised version wasn't a lot better: "But why does it need to be so boxy?" I asked an increasingly grumpy Jordi. "I mean, couldn't it mirror the shape of that stretch of wall, like I suggested before? That should give it some character."

"I'll think about it… tricky, though. It'll be a very strange shape indeed."

In fact, it's him who's often "tricky", with a tendency to take umbrage at any whiff of insurrection. But once he's decided it was his idea all along, he relaxes. In this case, by echoing the two obtuse angles of the exterior wall, his drawings promise an eccentric pentagonal landmark slotting into that corner of the garden on three of five sides. It will be a one-storey structure in the local vernacular, stone-faced, with an overhanging conical roof decked with Roman tiles. The interior will be vaulted with five oak beams for the ribs, converging on a hanging post at the apex. Jordi is inordinately proud of it – "*chulo*" he reckons, an architectural landmark of regional significance. But today, all that seems a distant fantasy. The only visible progress on this drab winter evening is a pentagonal hunk of concrete awaiting a superstructure.

At the house itself, the former garage will be turned into a sitting-room, linked to the rest by a stone arch through the metre-thick wall separating the two halves. So far, there's just a rough hole in the masonry, propped up with scaffolding but affording a view of the stones, straw and mortar that normally come to light only when a *desconchado*, a suppurating blister of damp, bursts through the plaster and spits its gritty pus onto the floor. But Jordi intends to line the arch with stone, which he claims will lend it an air of solidity and *solera*. And confidence is reinforced by the massive flagstones, another of Jordi's finds, which looked like a pile of rubble when he told us to buy them.

"Question for you," he says, "where do you stand in the mortar debate? I recommend the beige type – gives such a lift to the whole house! Benedict had strong opinions about it and forced me to use that ugly grey mortar on his job. I'm fond of Benedict, but the man's so stubborn!"

I hadn't appreciated there was a "mortar debate" at all but, after agreeing to the beige variety and bidding him farewell, I realise I've had enough of the cold, damp bed and decide to migrate to a hotel in Villafranca for the rest of the stay. There's little of the famed charm in late January, and the only hotel open at this time of year is the cruise ship lookalike on the road out to Valledal. Luckily, it's only for two nights; then I head back to London, with some foreboding.

However, Marina joins me on the next trip. By now, the days are longer, the magnolia is in bloom, leaves are on the trees and the site looks a bit tidier, if far from finished. It's now easier to appreciate the transformation, reorientating the property southwards without spoiling the aesthetic and turning its back on all those well-wishers, Monchi, Nino, Tomás, Dolores *et al.* It should turn out well after all – even Marina must agree, though of course she insists it won't be done in time, nowhere near. She's almost certainly right.

She doesn't like the fireplace either, a cast-iron log-burner surrounded by solid stone – Jordi's design. In her view it's *"bruto"* – crude – and does perhaps bear the insignia of the local *Estilo Rústico*, owing something to the Celtic pre-history of our region; but according to Jordi, it fits in perfectly.

"Jordi is very proprietorial about it," I tell Marina, "Whatever you do, don't tell him you don't like it. He's not going to change it and it's no time to fall out with him… he could easily drop us with all this left to do."

First in the queue to inspect the project is Mamí. We draw up for an instant on the way down to the *barrio bajo*, whence the house can be seen from a distance, across the scoop of the valley.

"*¡Virgen María!* it looks like you're demolishing the place, not rebuilding it!" she remarks.

The verdict isn't much more favourable once we reach the house.

"So much old stuff! And it's not even ready. Think of all the things we could have done to the family house at a fraction of the cost… How much did you spend on this, exactly?"

Then we walk up to the new garage. I know she won't rate the architecture, so I'm hoping to distract her with the automatic gates. But when I press the buttons on the

270

remote, the gates chunter impotently but fail to swing open as intended. Then I notice that the horizontal bars that power the mechanism are bent out of shape. Marina and I exchange a glance. Nino? A safe guess. Almost as bad as the vandalism is Mamí's reaction, at once gloating and disapproving.

On the way back to Bárcena she adds: "I hope you'll ask Chito to help out. You know he's short of work."

"Chito?" Marina asks. "Is he back with Marta again? News to us! Anyway, I thought you didn't like him. Especially the beard."

"Who? Me? I never said any such thing… The beard's gone now, anyway. And he's so kind…"

"But he's a terrible workman… Last time he worked for us he spilled a whole pot of paint on the sitting-room rug."

"Well, at least he runs errands for me, which is more than some do."

The events of the afternoon have brought home that we must make other arrangements for the wedding. Not only the unfinished state of the house but the flare-up with the neighbours means that hosting at home is no longer an option. It's getting urgent, with only months before the date and no venue.

3

Jack:

Glad to hear that you're coming to the wedding after all. Let's hope it'll be worth the trip. At least there will be a few old friends to catch up with.

As you know, James is to wed a Chinese girl. She calls herself Sally, not her real name of course; it's her adopted, Western name. They all seem to have one. In fact, it'll be James's third wedding to the same bride after the registry office

271

in Sally's hometown, then a celebration over there a year later. We thought that was the end of it, until we found out we had to host a third, and guests would include Sally's parents. For better or worse, her father's a retired official of the Chinese Communist Party.

As it happens, it's not so much potential diplomatic incidents as our own family ructions that are causing stress at the moment. James is adamant that his uncle and godfather Sancho should be the third, Spanish, speaker alongside his father-in-law Mr Zhang and me on the podium. But we can't ignore the feud between Sancho and his cousins. What's more, we've ended up with a wedding venue right next to Sancho's office at his despised employer's. It overlooks the garden where the marquee will host the guests for lunch outside an old palacio. We've ended up there because we had to drop the plan to host it at home. In short, guerrilla war has erupted anew with the neighbours, and we can't rule out sabotage.

The latest trouble stems from an exit onto the road we opened behind the new garage. By opening that exit, we stole one parking space, sacrosanct, it seems, on grounds of precedent alone, though there are lots of alternatives. I know they resent it because they ignore the sign and protest whenever I ask them to move a car to let me out.

We were about to show off the automatic gates to my mother-in-law when I noticed the opening bars now drooped visibly in their middle reaches. My instinct was to grab the phone, ready to chide the architect for his fancy idea that didn't even work. Meanwhile, mother-in-law Gloria was relishing it all. Then we realised the damage must be vandalism.

Did I mention we set up brother-in-law Chus in his new repair business? It's mainly computers, but he turns his hand to anything technological. When we told him about it, Chus contrived a solution, albeit a rough-and-ready one, a chapuza, like most of his doings. It took the form of a motion-activated camera in camouflage, which his son Toni fixed up, hidden in the bushes and trained on the gates. Chus has a friend in the Guardia Civil *who patrolled menacingly outside the gates one morning, while Chus affixed a sign:* propiedad videovigilada 24h. *That didn't fool the neighbours either, because months afterwards, the same thing happened again.*

In theory, all we had to do was extract the film and find the footage with the culprit jumping on the crossbar, or however the damage was done. But the hedge had grown, and the camera had slipped on its moorings. The only images showed fronds of greenery waving in the wind – alas, no damning evidence whatever.

Perhaps a more subtle form of retaliation is called for.

The posada, *gallingly enough, boasts gushing reviews on the web. Maybe I could post an alternative take on it, something a bit more nuanced, thanks to long and intimate experience. It would have to be unattributed, of course, something along the lines of: 'Reasonable value for the unfussy but, oh dear, the hosts! Watch out and don't leave valuables around!'*

Or alternatively: "Posada passable, if basic; but beware the crazy son, a terror on his quadbike or at the wheel of his hot hatchback."

Or even: "Can we mean the same place as other reviewers? The proprietor's a well-known pilferer and flasher."

All it needs is a volunteer to stay the night and write the review…

That was my idea until Marina stepped in. She's a lot more cautious than me; she's sure they'd trace it. But one of her remarks really hit home: "You know what?" she said. "I'm getting worried about you. You're just like them! They've infected you! The same instincts, jealousies and rancour… you're becoming an embittered campesino[45] *yourself!" I took that to*

---

heart, and it prompted the search for an alternative venue.

It turned out we'd missed the best one of all. It's a palacio *in Tobillo, a village near Bárcena. Why didn't we think of it before? Probably because Tobillo bears a special stigma in the family, because that's where Sancho's rival winery, Vinos Aurelio is located. Indeed, as I say, it actually adjoins the palacio.*

However, unlike other venues, this one feels authentic – it's subtly restored, none of the pseudo-antique they call Estilo Rústico. *Best of all, the compound boasts a free-standing house with five bedrooms and a kitchen, perfect to corral the Chinese, who we plan to keep out of mischief with supplies of noodles and Moutai (Chairman Mao's favourite liquor, with a passing affinity to white spirit).*

That's what we've plumped for and that's where we'll expect you for the celebration.

I look forward to it…

Rico

4

"Have you seen the weather for Saturday? It's going to be *horrible, horrible, horrible…*"

That's Mamí's encouraging message, days before the wedding. Unfortunately, the weather app concurs.

"Nonsense," Marina says to her mother, brushing it off as best she can. "The forecasts are always wrong more than a day or two out."

"Don't worry," Mamí adds, "I'll light a candle at Mass this evening."

We're grateful for any support but, right now, it feels like autumn and we're sceptical. The coast is swathed in fog, and it doesn't promise well for any outdoor gathering.

The guest list runs to over 100 from half a dozen

countries. That alone proves a deterrent for one intended guest, our Valledal neighbour Soco, who takes Marina aside: "I hope you won't be offended if we don't come. But what would we talk about with all those people? Cows? Silage?"

"What about property prices? The Lottery? *El arrastre*?" Marina suggests, her last suggestion referring to the *fiesta* at this time of year, when a few diehards gather with their oxen for the log-dragging championships. Soco laughs but doesn't recant.

Meanwhile, Sally coaches me on my address (I plan a few words in Chinese at the outset) and we piece together a translation of her father's speech to circulate in advance.

The third speaker, completing the linguistic hat-trick, will be Sancho. He's James's choice and for him, it's non-negotiable. Of all his Spanish relatives, his godfather Sancho is by far his favourite, a close bond having formed at a young age on trips by truck up the valleys, wedged athwart the gearstick between Sancho and his co-pilot Chencho.

But it causes disquiet, albeit Sancho's in-laws, including Rocío and his daughter Alicia, are excluded from the guest list. For all his charm, Sancho can be erratic and occasionally vindictive; to minimise the scope for mishap, his appearance will remain secret until the very last moment. The choreography of the whole event is therefore not just about melding a disparate throng through inspired *placement*, with linguists at key nodes. Rather, it's about the need to neutralise Sancho. Since he and Julito assumed their current roles, the long rivalry between the two wineries has intensified, embodied in these two prickly and volatile characters.

Once Sancho has delivered his speech, we intend to whisk him off to the family photography session, then neutralise him at "top table" over lunch, where, aided by Janet, the interpreter, his social gifts can be deployed on the Chinese, while we keep him under close watch. If we fail, if he launches into one of his notorious rants, a public scene cannot be ruled out.

Two days before the event, Sally and James disappear to Madrid to pick up her relatives – parents, brother-in-law, niece and a mountain of suitcases. They plan to stop at a Chinese restaurant on the way back. Judging from the web, it sounds unappealing, an "all-you-can-eat" more than a restaurant; but James insists that it'll help the visitors settle in.

On the appointed day, encouraged by Mamí's candle, a milky sun makes an unscheduled debut. The guests mill around on the grass and gradually take their seats for the outdoor rites. Once assembled, the Master of Ceremonies signals to me to make my way to the lectern.

I'm ready to go; Mr Zhang's ready to go; but what's become of Sancho? We agreed he'd join us in front of the lectern at five minutes to twelve on the dot... There's no sign of him and he only needs to cross the short distance from the *Aurelio* plant right behind us. I have no choice but to march up to the lectern alone and launch into my speech.

Sancho's absence has thrown me off keel and that conspires with my non-existent command of Chinese. Despite the rehearsals, the looks of bafflement suggest I'm not connecting even with my intended audience. What's more, I keep remembering Sally's warnings about word traps for the unwary. Say "*Mua*" (or some such) with the wrong intonation and the meaning slips deviously from "mother" to "mother-f*cker".

That's why I gallop through it, probably snapping taboos like matchsticks along the way. Once I am finished,

I pitch for a reprieve with an off-stage "thank God that's over". It earns a polite titter. But my speech in English fares little better: where's the laughter that usually indulges the feeblest of wedding speeches? The audience stays stubbornly unmoved. I hurry to cut my losses and pass the baton to Sally's father as soon as decently possible.

To my ears, Mr Zhang's riposte sounds like a harangue at a party rally or a series of spine-chilling ejaculations at a martial arts contest. However, we later learn that it was in fact a poem written by Mr Zhang himself, a lament for his "little bird, flying the nest". There's no suggestion of that in the translation – not that anyone shows any surprise.

There's no sign of Sancho; we therefore drop the Spanish leg altogether and the ceremony concludes with music, a choir, an exchange of rings and kisses; then we split off for photos, while the younger generation swoops down on the snacks "like scavenging seagulls", as Cristina, our event organiser, later describes it. (She's the one I met with Sancho the day after the *Aurelio* break-in.)

Once the preliminaries are over, we take our seats in the marquee, and, when the liquor starts to flow, everyone relaxes a bit, ourselves included. Though James will be upset, Sancho's failure to appear is a blessing. Maybe, at the last moment, he grasped how incendiary it would be. Whatever, we can now devote ourselves to the rest of the proceedings in peace. Communicating with the Zhangs at one remove is a bit of a struggle, but we're coping all right. Only Mamí finds it impossible and takes flight from the top table, ceding her place to Clara and seeking refuge by her sisters in a corner of the marquee.

Halfway through, though, it's time for me to circulate. I need to mix with the other guests, and anyway, the toasts are starting to pall (each time I touch my glass, I find I've triggered a heartfelt "*gambe!*" from Mr Zhang, followed by clinking glasses all round and a mandatory slug of Moutai or whatever potion we're on by then).

There was a time when I expected our Chinese relations on the Blasco side of the family to play a useful role at this event, whether as interpreters or as company for the Zhangs, sharing a bit of common ground, I thought. Then I came to realise the risk of a diplomatic upset. I was thinking not just of Beni's wife Lulu, with her history of dissent and flight from the PRC. I also had Domingo's son, bolshy six-year-old Alfa in mind, who he brought over while his wife stayed home.

Now I can see that Alfa has split off from his paternal minder; he's strutting round the marquee in his miniature suit and bowtie as if he owned the place, dobbing out insults to anyone he doesn't fancy the look of. Domingo scurries after him a few paces behind, apologising for his son and looking harassed and outmanoeuvred.

This happens right by the table hosting much of the Blasco tribe, including Beni and Lulu, Julito and Tere, Paloma and Carlos. Jack and Chus are at the same table, opposite each other – two mavericks who, for self-preservation, have forged an alliance.

Carlos calls to me over the hubbub: "Aha! Our orator *extraordinaire*! Great speech, I must say!"

"Thank you… glad you liked it!"

"Well, not so much the content… I meant the delivery. You've come round to my way of thinking, at last. Bowing to the inevitable, right? *Lingua franca*, I mean. Not a word in Spanish, not a single one!"

"*¡Qué va!*[46] interjects Julito's wife Tere. "A Spanish wedding with no Spanish? From you, Rico? What a let-down! I had you down as a bulwark against the onslaught!

---

[46] "Nonsense"

How could you?"

"Sadly, our third speaker failed to show. Otherwise, of course you'd have had a speech in Spanish."

"Anyway," Carlos says, cutting me off, "we all want to hear your views on that topic of the moment, *El Brexit.*"

In fact, with my alleged *Euroescéptico* leanings, that's a discussion I want to avoid at all costs, knowing I'll be tarred a full-on Brexiteer, like it or not. Last time I erred into this terrain, it caused lasting grief with the cousins.

Fortunately, Jack has years of practice, as well as robust, Brexity, views and can be relied on to pursue the debate from the opposite side of the table. Here he is, in full flood: "The trouble with Spain, you see, is the absence of *civic society*. How could there be public spirit in a state that's gone bust a dozen times in the last couple of centuries alone? Of course, that's why nobody trusts the government! That's why everyone puts their faith in the EU instead! There's a huge hole to fill…"

I'm expecting Benedict, who is within earshot at the next table, to join in: it's just the kind of thing he would say – years of wrestling with Spanish bureaucracy have brought him to it. But he's in a huddle with fellow ruin-bibbers, including his wife Jane, Charlie and Priscilla, and Hamish, chatting about local architectural curiosities. He takes the moment to quiz me about the works at Valledal and about Jordi, asking me if we've found him as tricky as he does.

"I mean I had God's own job dissuading him from that sand-coloured mortar he insists on. A total anachronism!... I do like Jordi, but the man's *so* stubborn!"

At that moment, the sudden "*PING-PING-PING*" of a knife striking a glass puts paid to both discussions. I look round to see where it's coming from. It's James, signalling for us to return to our seats for dessert, during which he plans to say a few words himself.

Before he starts, the first spots of rain start to splosh heavily on the canvas, sending the staff scurrying round, dropping the side flaps of the marquee. Raising his voice above the thrumming on the tent, James acquits himself far better than I did, with his gentle teasing at Sally's expense. There's plenty of laughter this time, even at the standard gags… Naturally, the alcohol has worked its magic.

But suddenly, James senses a loss of concentration among the guests and it's not just the momentary abatement of the rain. Their eyes are no longer fixed on him but have turned towards a triangle at the side of the marquee where two flaps have been drawn aside.

There, against the light, shaking off the rainwater, is a figure in silhouette.

It's Sancho.

A hush falls across the tent. Even those who don't know the history realise something odd is afoot.

Sancho threads his way between the guests towards us. He's grinning. But he manages to look uneasy, too. When he reaches us, he whispers a few words to James, who nods and, with a gesture, invites him to take the floor, handing his godfather a drink as he does so.

Sancho clears his throat:

"Bride and Groom, Marina and Rico, Mr and Mrs Zhang, *señoras y señores*… what a pleasure, this is!" He takes a deep breath, then a swig from his glass.

"Instead of addressing you this morning as planned, I decided to wait until now. That way, you've had time to get to know each other, enjoy the hospitality and, I hope, enter the party spirit.

"And on that note, I should like to propose a toast to our wonderful hosts, Marina and Rico…"

Sancho reaches for a glass and soon the *"gambes"* ricochet round our table. At least the Chinese grasp that bit of the speech.

"I've been asking myself for a while what my role should be at this event. Then it came to me. Of course! My job is to give the bride advice about her new family! I'm as well placed as anyone, I think."

There's a short pause, while James moves a seat next to Sally to allow Janet to whisper a translation of Sancho's words.

"Sally? you've done well, I can assure you. Very well. I can't sing your husband's praises highly enough. They're obvious to everyone. He's a very solid and dependable *chaval* and I'm sure you know that already. I can vouch for him: his first job was with me in the truck, helping to take the wine to our customers all over the province.

"But this is an alliance between whole families. And in your case, Sally, there's a new country to discover as well. That's where I can help… help to shed some light, I mean.

"I've been trying to put my finger on what it is that ties the threads together? What do you need to know about the wider family and the culture of this country? Is it the tenuous hold on reality? The make-believe? The hazy border between fact and fiction? All facets of the same thing, I suppose, the quixotic spirit, which some claim is the quintessence of Spanish life… I don't disagree. It's not mere cliché. But let me give you a few examples, close to home.

"In pride of place: my dear mother, your grandmother-in-law, Sally. What an extraordinary person she is, and what brilliant company! She's Bárcena's celebrity, its entertainer and storyteller. *Everyone* knows Gloriuca… famous for her perpetual youth, her high spirits, her immaculate appearance, her sharp wit and her strong opinions. How much, I wonder, has she changed from the headstrong 20-year-old who eloped to Africa with the handsome Cipriano? Still an enigma of contradictions after so many years: outspoken but evasive; spontaneous but predictable; demanding but indulgent; pious but irreverent… Mother? You're unique, you're baffling, you're an oxymoron incarnate. You're wonderful. We all adore you!"

Mamí chooses to play along with the banter and her cackle resounds above all the others. Sancho resumes: "You notice I said the '*wider*' family… and I really did mean '*wider*'. Because you never know just *how* wide this family really is; it's an ever-expanding circle. New relatives keep popping up all the time! How many political relations, cousins, uncles, aunts and even siblings come with the territory? And where do they all come from? Because I'm not sure I know! Nor does anyone else! In the last few years, we met one from Romania, two from Colombia and surely, there are plenty more from Africa. Be prepared for new ones from Mexico or much closer to home, even. So be ready for surprises – happy ones, though!"

There's an audible intake of breath in the tent. Marina tries to catch Sancho's eye. He's overdoing it, really stirring things up, even by his standards. I can't see how Mamí's taking his latest remarks, but I've been watching Chus and I can see he's seething, with his fists clenched on the table, eyes locked fiercely, but impotently, on his brother.

"Whoever joins our ranks, I don't suppose it'll change one fixture in this family… Sally, if you don't already know, we're an argumentative clan. We come in all stripes, covering the spectrum, from hard left to extreme right, from anarchist to autocrat, from *Podemos* to *Vox*. You'll detect a fault line between the two sides of the family, that's us, the Expósito Pinars, and the other side, the Blasco Pinars… In a nutshell, you'll find the old school patriots on our side – we back Spain, warts and all; and you'll find the cosmopolitans on the other side: they'd like to dismember the country, along with its history, culture and language… It's the dichotomy of the Civil War, updated!

"That leaves the most important thing for you to grasp: the family's commercial pedigree. As you may know, *Bodegas Pinar's* the oldest business in the province, founded in 1846, with a long history at the centre of the town's affairs. As my Aunt Macu used to say, "We kept everyone going!" I'm well placed to tell you about that, too, because I worked there for years. All that time, I expected I'd stay for the rest of my life. My aunt always told me she was 'doing this' for me, so I thought the future was bright. But for years, nothing happened! I can't say I 'worked my way up from the bottom' exactly, because the bottom's where I stayed, or close to it, right to the very end, by when it was too late! Still rolling barrels 20 years on! But since I married, things changed. I'm now on the outside. Yes, I committed a mortal sin: I married the competition. Still selling wine; still in the same province; but what a change in perspective! Now I have a ringside seat, but no involvement in the family business. And what a sad story, not to say, tale of neglect, I've witnessed at the old firm…"

"Hey, steady on!" somebody heckles from the crowd and heads turn towards its author. It's Julito, of all people, someone who usually shuns the limelight. He jumps to his feet, indignant; Carlos, Paloma and Tere stand up too, in solidarity. After a short interval, Beni and wife Lulu do likewise.

"I think you stayed at the bottom for a reason!" Julito says.

"And what reason would that be? I think the contrast

with *Aurelio* speaks for itself. One of us all but bust; the other forging ahead, winning clients by the score."

"You're a disgrace to this family!" Paloma says.

"No, I don't think so. The disgrace is on your side! Your brother takes over the family firm and watches it slip towards the abyss. What does he do about it? We're still waiting! Yet even now, he manages to extract the last few *perras* to turn up to this event in a brand-new Range Rover!"

"Utter cheek! We won't take these insults a moment longer!"

But Sancho presses on: "…and you know what? I know for a fact they organised a burglary… a burglary at the *Aurelio* premises, if you please, seeking out our trade secrets. But of course, they have form… Cousin Domingo…"

"Slander! Libel!" Paloma shrieks.

"If that's what you believe, try taking me to court. But don't say I didn't warn you: they even botched a simple burglary! I have proof."

"*¡Mentira!*"[47] Julito responds. "That simply isn't true! Your so-called proof, whatever it is, cannot stand, as I can demonstrate beyond any doubt whatsoever!"

But nobody's listening by now. It's all Paloma can do to make herself heard above the commotion: "Mother? Aunt?"

She's hoping for Aunts Ludi and Macu to rise in unison and join an angry exodus. But all three sisters are sitting side by side in the corner. Not one of them stirs. They are either failing to compute or shrinking back from the chasm. In the last resort, the solidarity between them beats almost anything.

"Domingo?" she tries, scouring the tent. But in a

---

[47] "That's a lie!"

moment of farce, Domingo's once more chasing his disobedient son, who's staging a getaway through the same gap in the canvas from which Sancho appeared.

"Look over there!" Sancho says. "I see Cousin Domingo's pointing out the very window through which the thief entered our premises."

"… Chus?" Paloma adds in desperation, a very long shot, one that misses the target. Chus doesn't flinch.

"Don't worry," Sancho says, "I can see you don't have much support – no surprises there. In any case, I wouldn't want to give you the pleasure, Paloma. Nor do I want to break up the party… I'll leave you to enjoy it in peace… Sally, James: congratulations!"

Thereupon, having disgorged his bilious diatribe, Sancho strides back to the same opening and disappears into the drizzly afternoon. The Blasco cousins take their seats once more.

Minutes later, Domingo returns, holding Alfa by the scruff of the neck.

Slowly, tentatively, the hubbub returns, and the proceedings resume their course, including a band and dancing; but the 'party spirit' Sancho evoked has almost entirely evaporated.

5

The immediate post-mortems promise to be ugly. We feel abused by Sancho, grandstanding on the wedding platform like that and overshadowing the whole event with his shocking finale. True or false, the accusations against the cousins were mortifying and wholly inappropriate. And for James and Sally, the memory of their wedding day will be forever blighted by its jarring conclusion.

Luckily, though, we stand to gain some immediate distance, thanks to one last wedding duty. It's the short road trip we promised the Chinese through the north with Janet, during which we lodge in a *Parador*, a converted *palacio*, that even now wears the ponderous air of the Franco years. Afterwards, the newlyweds will accompany them on a whistlestop tour across Europe.

After meandering through the spartan landscape of northern Spain, albeit with our guest of honour in a sonorous sleep; after traipsing round several castles, monasteries and ruins, and after sampling *cochinillo* – suckling pig – at a famous restaurant *en route*, we arrive at the station to meet the train that will spirit the party away.

Before they go, through the offices of his daughter, I ask Mr Zhang what part of his visit he most enjoyed. The monasteries? The Parador? The *cochinillo*? The wedding itself? At first, he looks puzzled; then, his face lights up and he whispers something to his daughter. Before she relays the message, she looks at him quizzically, as if to confirm: "You're quite sure?" Then she turns to me.

The highlight, Sally says, was none of these; it wasn't the monasteries, nor the Parador, nor even the *cochinillo*. No: the highlight of his stay was the roadside eatery they stopped at on the route north, the day they arrived: the Chinese "all-you-can-eat", as it indeed turned out to be – even James admitted it was a "tacky joint".

I'm taken aback, disillusioned, indignant even. I might have guessed: "Philistines", "pearls before swine", "what's the point?" and so on. Then it dawns on me: I just witnessed a phenomenon I took to be quiescent, extinct even. It's the *Zhang sense of humour*. For the first time, the tectonic plates crease into a smile. I see the sparkle in his eye. Then we shake hands. It's a warm farewell.

Finally, we leave the Zhangs to Sally and James, watching them navigate the platform with their trolleys stacked with cases and other trophies. They wave cheerfully from the carriage window as the train slides from the platform, heading south for the string of blue mountains, the *cordillera*, between us and the capital.

That moment of release when the train slips from view is sweet but brief. For when did euphoria last more than a few instants? On our return, there's a new source of stress to supplant the wedding. It comes from Chus, pleading for "one final" cash injection to see him into profit at the shop. After two years, it's still not viable.

As we pace the short distance to *Computer Saviour*, we can't help feeling alienated from the compulsory jollity of the annual *fiestas*, now in full swing. It's a season when a clammy heat sets in, beaches and bars overflow, and children run amok into the small hours; the funfair sets up camp for a fortnight and the *churrerías*[48] ply a lucrative trade in fried, sugary batter, suffusing the town with odours from their bubbling cauldrons. It's the time when the *Virgen del Mar*, Bárcena's Patroness, totters through the streets at the front of the procession, while bands of young pipers in white and scarlet parade up and down the main avenue, and the old place reverberates to their nostalgic melodics.

Given our mood, we're almost relieved at the low-pressure system promising to arrive imminently, if the forecast's right. The locals may regret it, but are generally stoical, about such things. They belong to the territory; but they do take exception to inaccurate predictions that bring summer to a premature close, or scupper otherwise lucrative *puentes* (long weekends). Once, after a wrongly forecast washout killed one balmy spring *puente*, the regional government invited the offending weatherman and his family for Holy Week, all expenses paid, to set the record straight. That time the weather lived up to

---

[48] Stalls selling *churros*

expectations: it tipped down without remission. Alas, the weather forecasts remained as unhelpful as ever.

Whatever, we must brace ourselves for another confrontation. The shop faces a litany of problems, mostly stemming from ineptitude. Above all, for "the clever one" of the family, Chus wrestles with the most elementary bookkeeping.

"All we need is a record of cash in minus cash out," I repeat yet again, once we've joined him, perched on stools at the counter. "It's not what you *might* receive, let alone what you'd *like* to receive; it's what *actually comes in*: cash, cheques, transfers, no matter. And on the cost side, it's *everything* that's actually gone out, whatever the reason, no exceptions."

It sounds simple, but even these instructions meet immovable obstacles. And the shop should surely break even on minimal revenues. Rent for the unit is low, utilities a pittance – Chus uses a single electric bar for heating and there's water only for the flush and the coffee machine. Apart from a few dusty items in the window, there's very little stock; and Toni does most of the work. He's not on the payroll and there's no other staff apart from Chus himself, who takes an agreed monthly draw. So, what comes in and where does it go? But Chus can't – or won't – give a clear explanation.

Meanwhile, Marina already noticed how smart he looks these days, "*un brazo de mar*" – "an arm of the sea" – as she puts it, in that new suit he wore for the wedding, for instance. And he's still making occasional train trips to the south plus, no doubt, visits to the *Conde de Lugo*, Bárcena's premier house of ill-repute.

What's more, Chus is distracted by the book he's writing. *Stories of the Colonials in Equatorial Africa*, *Volume I*, is well advanced, and *Volume II* will follow soon after.

Whenever we pass the shop, there is Chus at the counter, hunched over his work. But in fact, it's *Masa Chus* at work, because he's not repairing cracked phone screens or updating software; he's reliving his African fantasies through his memoirs.

"I'm afraid Bárcena hates paying for repairs," he says. "I now realise just how skint everyone is and they haggle over everything. But I've plenty of good ideas how to turn it round! We're taking parcels, starting tomorrow. Also, I could do with more stock – everyone's interested in games, and we can sell them at a good price."

Since each parcel brings in a few cents and only about three arrive each day, it's no panacea. As for the extra stock, it's too late for that, I really must resist.

Nonetheless, I do release that "*one final*" subsidy. This always has been a charitable endeavour, I tell myself, in the hope of keeping Chus and Toni out of mischief, if hardly gainfully employed. All we need is an insolvency in the family; and I'm still hoping for a miraculous upturn, though it doesn't look very promising.

6

Next day, Marina receives a disagreeable email. She doesn't recognise the address, **jytbp@gmail.es**. Ever on the alert for scams, she opens it warily. It's odd that it should be copied to Chus and Marta, but that Sancho's name should be absent. Then she sees that it starts "My Dear Cousins" and bears the signature "Ever yours, Julito".

The email, couched in ceremonious prose, but making no attempt at concealing a boiling resentment, reads as follows:

'My Dear Cousins,

In first place, allow me to thank you, Cousins Marina and Rico, warmly on behalf of all of us Blasco Pinars for your hospitality. Please also convey our many congratulations to the charming and so evidently happy young couple.

But after what I can only term the shocking denouement to an otherwise delightful and convivial occasion, it won't surprise you that my siblings and I gathered to consider our position. Needless to say, we took gross exception to Cousin Sancho's grotesque, unprovoked and slanderous attack. It was a shameless ambush, which, as no doubt intended, caught us off-guard and ill-prepared to respond. I hardly need reiterate that neither Bodegas Pinar *nor any of us personally had any involvement whatsoever in any burglary at the Aurelio premises, as I shall prove beyond any doubt. But I'm quite sure there's no need to tell you that! Nor, by the way, do I own a "brand-new Range Rover": that was a vehicle I hired while my own car is at the garage.*

Against this background, there's one situation that really cannot be allowed to continue any longer. As I'm sure you know from your mother, Aunt Macu's condition continues to deteriorate. Belén's daily visits (four hours, mornings and evenings) are a great help, but these days, Aunt Macu requires help round the clock. My mother, who looks after her the rest of the time, can no longer cope, either physically or mentally. Aunt Macu's behaviour swings from complete apathy to violence, owing to her advanced Alzheimer's, with all the difficulties that entails for anyone caring for her, especially for my mother, aged 88.

Belén's salary alone absorbs most of Aunt Macu's pension and the bodega *cannot afford to contribute any more, especially not in the currently challenging environment.*

As you know, your mother continues to receive a significant monthly draw from the bodega. *I would remind you that, when Aunt Macu acquired shares from both our mothers, they received lump sums by way of compensation. Aunt Gloria therefore has no legal nor moral right to these payments, which have continued out of goodwill. Given the circumstances and mindful of your brother's evident ability to step in, we intend to discontinue these payments forthwith.*

As holder of a general authority and guardian of Aunt Macu, it's my legal obligation to ensure that she be properly looked after and, as a son, that my mother desist from a role that has become excessively burdensome to her.

Please let me know your thoughts.

Ever yours,
Julito

"Expensive remark of my brother's, that was, *Aurelio* 'forging ahead…'" Marina says. "Now there's another hole to fill… Sancho better help us sort something out. He can afford it if anyone can."

As soon as we draw up on the *Aurelio* forecourt to discuss Julito's mail, it's clear Marina's right: Sancho himself really is *forging ahead*. There's somebody to meet us, and we're ushered through the plant, up the stairs and this time, into the ample office formerly occupied by his father-in-law. There we find Sancho, looking plutocratic behind his imposing mahogany desk, walls adorned with boars' heads and stag antlers.

We're fully expecting Sancho to embark on a historic rant. Instead, he's almost indifferent to Julito's ultimatum. In his view, he owes nothing to his close relations. They've all let him down, Papí, Aunt Macu, Chus, Toni, cousins and, of course, Mamí.

"At last! Those losers will have to live within their means and won't be bailed out anymore. Chus and Toni can get proper jobs and rent a flat. And you should stop throwing good money after bad at that useless shop, Rico! Mamí can either live with her sisters next door or take up residence in the *asilo.*[49]"

"But we can't possibly kick her out of the house! Can you imagine the effect that would have? A death sentence. Anyway, how could we achieve it without her consent?"

"What do you propose instead, then?"

"What about Perky's idea, remortgaging the house? It seems sensible: all the heirs meet the cost in proportion."

"No, no, I don't like that idea, not at all. It won't solve anything. We can't keep the spongers afloat an instant longer. It's time Chus and Toni stood on their own feet! Mamí can sell the house if she needs money. I'll help bridge it for a few months, but otherwise you can count me out!"

It's ironic that the only two spared from Sancho's criticisms (Marta and Marina) are the ones most affected by them. They'll have to find the extra funds to bail out Mamí. For Marta especially, it'll make a big dent in her budget. No doubt we'll keep the shop afloat too, because even the fit and young struggle to find work, let alone the superannuated like Chus. In any case, the chances the house will be sold are, in practice, close to zero.

Days later, an unexpected visitor appears in Bárcena, unannounced, accompanied by two young men. It's Marga, Chus's daughter and Toni's sister, now grown-up, with her boyfriend plus a spare. It's her first time here since her solo visit as a child.

Marta calls to warn Marina: "It's difficult here right now. They caught Mamí at a bad moment – hair in rollers and drying her tan for the beach this afternoon. She just

---

[49] Old People's Home

292

didn't want the interruption and she's refusing to give them lunch… She won't even rouse Toni to welcome his sister – he hasn't seen her in more than ten years! They drove overnight from France…"

By the time we arrive in Bárcena, Chus has come from the shop, hugged his long-lost daughter and sealed a truce with his mother; the party has crossed the threshold and penetrated the inner sanctum, still a shrine to Magín's efforts in tropical hardwood and the family's African trophies, though many of the photos are now faded, lopsided, or both. The three visitors occupy the sofa, teasing Toni's cat, but Mamí has retreated upstairs for urgent ablutions. Meanwhile, Chus's pidgin French helps bridge the linguistic gap between the siblings and I'm obliged to resuscitate mine too. Marga has mellowed a bit since the last visit, the time I drove her to the airport. But she's still almost as abrupt.

The story runs as follows: sitting in a bar in Grenoble, conversation turned to Marga's phantom Spanish family. Neither of her companions believed her. They've long known about her African childhood; but the elusive Spaniard, the father she claims bolted under duress, has remained a shadow, as has Toni. It's not even that far away! Wasn't she imagining that visit so long ago?

"OK, so you don't believe me? Let's go right now and you'll see for yourselves!"

That's how the trip came about. It seems a long way to drive for a 24-hour stay. Even that dubious dive the *Conde de Lugo's* full tonight, so the best option is a motel outside Pueblo de la Vega. On Sunday morning they come for morning coffee, then they're gone.

Mamí hasn't quite finished with them, though.

"I hope that's the last time you do that to me!" she says to Chus. "I've told you before: *I'm too old for it*. Don't I have

293

burdens enough already? Looking after you and your son? No more nasty surprises! I absolutely refuse!"

Chus starts to interject, but she cuts him off: "Anyway, I'm afraid to say she's not nearly as pretty as her mother... Now where was I? Oh yes," she says, catching sight of the tanning lotion and bending a well-known proverb into service: "*¡Genio y figura hasta la sepultura!*"[50]

7

Nunci's house across the street is a near replica of Mamí's, but of more recent construction; indeed, Mamí claims Nunci's house was *inspired* by hers and modelled on it. However, there's one key difference: a few years back, the rear of Nunci's once detached house became affixed to a tall, broad, blank wall, the blind side of a new six-storey slab that now towers above the property. So oppressive is the effect that its real purpose might have been to drive Nunci and Curro to an early sale, allowing the developer to sew up the last available plot on the block. But curiously, they didn't seem to mind much; at least, they refrained from any action that might have prevented it. Nor did they decide to sell. Maybe their indifference owed something to the dramas that have played out in slow motion behind the lace curtains opposite: their minds were otherwise engaged.

It was only when Nunci mentioned it to her sister, married to a Ruiz-Toledo, that it was brought home to her just how damaging it was to her house and its value. Early inquiries showed that the land right up to the wall belonged to the developer; due process was followed, with council minutes showing that planning consent was properly sought, notification posted to neighbours and permission

---

[50] 'Spirit and bloom, right up to the tomb'

granted after a period for objections. If skulduggery of any kind was involved, it was expertly executed, with any tell-tale traces diligently expunged.

However, as soon as the Ruiz-Toledos registered interest, the developer took fright and proposed a compromise, which Nunci and her husband accepted. A small sum by way of compensation was paid and the developer agreed to soften the look of the wall. This was achieved by painting four dummy windows high up above Nunci's rooftop, complete with make-believe blinds lowered to different levels and fake glass winking in the sun. Perhaps it looks more homely than before, less stark, but as a result, Nunci's house is arguably now overlooked as well as overshadowed. All that's missing is a face at one of the "windows", keeping watch over the garden.

Whenever I see Curro, he transports me back to an era when *caballeros* of his ilk were a familiar sight on Bárcena's streets. They upheld the highest sartorial standards, with carefully groomed salt and pepper hair, clipped moustache, blazer with polished buttons, knotted cravat or tie held fast with a silver pin. This look was sometimes lent a sinister air by dark spectacles that signalled you were in the presence of a *Franquista*, an apologist for the old regime, biding his time until the collapse of *so-called democracy*. Hooked on his arm would often be a tweedy, stout but steely, blue-rinsed spouse half his size, likely a one-time member of the *Sección Femenina*. Thus it was with Curro and Nunci on their village outings, during which progress would be slow as they navigated their admirers: for both are among the most revered of Bárcena's scions.

Regular visits to Curro and Nunci have been mandatory ever since I set foot in Bárcena. Hence at Epiphany (presents at Christmas are a "Pagan custom", in their book) we bear gifts of smoked salmon, mince pies and brandy butter and share *Roscón de Reyes*, 'Three Kings Cake' around the table in their drawing room, surrounded by elongated figurines and other ornaments peering wonkily through frosted yellow glass.

On these occasions, Curro likes to collar me for proper discussions, man to man – he's dismissive of the women around him; they in turn humour him: tolerant, but gently mocking. Apart from the time we clashed over the despoliation of the coastline, when I was tarred as *both* elitist *and* lefty, we've enjoyed lively but friendly debate and I clinched a place in his affections by declaring that, while this corner of the country may claim to be *the most beautiful place on earth* as Aunt Macu used to say, the real *soul of Spain* lay on the sparse plateau of Old Castile where Curro comes from and which spiritually, he never left.

However, over the last decade, Curro has declined steadily. Even in good health, he was pugnacious and outspoken, but since his confinement to bed in an alcove off the sitting room, he's become obstreperous. A steady stream of imprecations in imperious but wavering tones flows from his bed to his harassed and devoted wife.

A further blow to their composure comes from their son Paco's separation. Paco's wife Gabi is also a vet, but unlike Paco and Curro, she belongs to the type tending to pets, not pigs. For many years she ran a clinic in Nunci's garage – in fact, in the unit that Chus considered taking after Gabi moved out. The absence of children may have catalysed the breakdown, but whatever the facts, the quarrel echoes across the street, Mamí being one of Paco's stoutest defenders while, uncharacteristically, Chus roots for the wife, his friend Gabi.

Then one day, at a small family get-together in Valledal, we're debating this very subject, including the proposed compromise that each party occupy their co-owned property in alternate years.

"Who came up with that idea? Ridiculous! Worst of all worlds!" Mamí says, "How's that going to work? Pack up the furniture every year? No use to either of them. Paco paid for it; Paco should keep it!"

"But he didn't – she earns as much as he does," Chus says. "And she's the one with the brains. If Paco won't agree to sell, what other option is there? What about charity? What about sharing?"

"Things you, in particular, know all about!"

There's no time for Chus's retort because a call comes in for him.

"… Sorry, I'll have to take this," he says, scowling and heading for the garden.

Ten minutes later, he returns.

"That was Gabi…" he says, chastened. "It's bad news, I'm afraid… Curro just died."

"*¡Ave María purísima!* My poor Nunci! Chus, you must take me home, take me now. Nunci needs me."

Before they leave, Mamí's grief yields to excitement about the funeral, which she shares even as she's climbing into the Audi.

"They do things well, the Azoríns… It'll be a proper funeral, you'll see – First Class, at least three priests, half a dozen *monaguillos*,[51] body laid out in church, candles all round… But one of you will have to take me to Zara. I need a proper black dress for this. And I need to do something about my hair. When did I last have my hair coloured? *¡Madre mía!*"

Marina for one thinks her mother looks better without the caramel hue so highly prized among Bárcena ladies of her demographic.

---

[51] Choirboys

Hence two days later, I find myself accompanying Mamí and Marina to yet another Bárcena funeral or memorial service. It's a growing tally, cars at a *corrida*, so to speak: Uncle Toño, Benigno, José Angel, Papí, Poncho and now Curro. All men, I reflect. The women are generally immortal, or the next best thing to it.

The tearful relatives, less Gabi, file into the reserved pews. Apart from the extraordinary turnout, standing room only, and the pomp of a First Class funeral, it's no less baffling than other such occasions, with its puzzling stand-sit-kneel routines and half-dirge, half-hearted responses. When it comes to the goodwill handshake, I offer a hand to the woman behind. She looks straight through me. Lamely, I'm forced to withdraw.

Emerging into daylight I see Aunt Macu watching the proceedings from her eyrie opposite as we struggle against the multitude to offer our condolences to the family.

"Please thank Sancho for the amazing flowers," Lupita tells me when at last I reach her in the porch.

I pass on the message to Mamí, who's unimpressed: "What a waste! Of all the things Sancho could have spent the money on!"

The sudden death of so illustrious a Bárcena dignitary would normally warrant a front-page tribute in the local press. But these days *Voz del Golfo* is replete with speculations around a sex and corruption scandal ensnaring King-Emeritus Juan Carlos I. Despite his abdication in favour of his son a few years ago, the rumours refuse to abate. Indeed, the once lionised "Saviour of Democracy", the man who triumphed almost single-handed in the *coup* of 23-F, may yet be forced into exile.

Half submerged by the commotion, Curro earns a single paragraph next to the *esquela:*

'Bárcena loses a Favourite Son

Curtains finally drew on the long and distinguished career of Don Francisco ("Curro") Azorín, the eminent veterinary surgeon and sometime town counsellor. Many years have passed since Bárcena hosted such obsequies, with a congregation measured in thousands...'

Chapter VIII: Heir of Repose

1

Alongside that brief homily to Curro Azorín in *Voz del Golfo*, I notice a discreet report about a sinister bat-virus apparently stalking some city in central China. But it's only once we're back in Blighty, confronted by images of overcrowded hospitals and gasping patients, that its gravity starts to impinge on us. In particular, they bring home the threat to the three elderly sisters in Bárcena de la Mina.

But ironically, all three of them avoid infection; instead, it's Marina's brother Chus who succumbs. Before long, he's confined to bed at home; he's short of breath, but apparently stable, giving no great cause for concern. Meanwhile, Toni minds the shop, a matter of weeks since it reopened for business following mandatory closure during the pandemic.

Then, one afternoon, my phone beeps manically. I have no time to catch up until I'm on the bus home.

Here's what I read. It's on the family *WhatsApp*:

> Marina: *I just had a call from Sancho… Chus died! R, where on earth are you?*
> James: *Uncle Chus? Jesus Christ!*
> Clara: *What?*
> Marina: *God knows where your father is, he's just not picking up! Never there when you need him!*
> James: *When's the funeral? Should I go?*
> Marina*: No, no, it's too late for that… I'm already on my way. You can't imagine how hard it's been getting a flight! He'll be cremated tomorrow, at 4 p.m.*
> Clara: *So soon? Do we know why it happened?*

Marina: *Yes, Covid, for sure… or related complications. BTW, Titi already arrived. Marga + BF are on their way.*
Clara: *That's good for Toni.*
Marina: *If you say so. Here's the* esquela*:*

Mr
Jesús "Chus" Expósito Pinar
Died Bárcena de la Mina, 4 October 2021 aged 61 years
Having received the Holy Sacraments and the Apostolic Blessing
R.I.P.
His mother, M^a. Gloria Pinar de Expósito; wife, Nefertiti Lemaître; children, Antonio and Marga; siblings, Marina, Sancho and Marta; siblings-in-law, aunts, nephews and nieces, cousins and other family
Offer a prayer for his soul and join the funeral for his eternal rest, which will take place tomorrow, Tuesday 5 October at five in the afternoon at the Parish Church of Bárcena de la Mina.

When I explore my phone, I find numerous missed calls, messages, texts, emails…

I call Marina, who's already at the airport, a little testy, but otherwise calm. She adds: "No need for you to come anyway. You did all you could while he was alive. I expect you can guess that we're paying for the *esquela*. Probably the funeral too."

"Is everyone OK? Mamí? How's she taken it?"

"Hasn't sunk in yet, I think – in shock. Just worried about the funeral and annoyed Titi's on the *esquela*. I reminded her they're still husband and wife… or were until this morning. And Mamí thinks it should be in the national press. Look, I'm sorry, we're boarding, I'll call you when I get there…"

That bit about last rites sounds implausible, whatever the *esquela* claims. As far as I know, the last time Chus visited a church was for Curro's funeral, and I don't recall his tackling the wafers and *tinto* on that occasion. In any case, from memory, Chus was standing outside, smoking and chatting, while it was us who focused on the matters of moment: grieving, worshipping and praying for Curro's speedy passage to the Pearly Gates.

I take it "Other family" includes the Romanian arm as well as a catch-all to cover unofficial offspring wherever there may be, in Africa or elsewhere.

The other surprise is the choice of *"Pinar de Expósito"* for Mamí's surname – literally, 'Pinar *belonging to* Expósito'. To my knowledge, she has never used that before. Just a decorous touch, apt for so grave an announcement?

Once Marina's landed and heading for Bárcena, she calls back with more details.

"Yes, it was Covid of course. Years of heavy smoking can't have helped. And those other complications, I assume… It was Toni who discovered him. There was nothing the ambulancemen could do."

"I'm so sorry," I say.

That sounds like hypocrisy on my part, but it isn't entirely, because, despite the shop, we struck up a good rapport with Chus. For all the recurrent disasters, we were fond of him and we'll miss him and his rants – our bespoke muzak, as it were.

But Marina drops the pieties, as is her wont: *"Nos vino dios a ver,"*[52] she says.

"What's that supposed to mean?"

"That it's the best thing that could possibly have happened."

_____

[52] "God visited us"

Slowly, her meaning seeps in: 61 years old; next to nothing to his name but a 23-year-old Audi with dodgy brakes; charity-dependent for survival at the loss-making shop; failing eyesight; HIV positive (albeit "*shaken off*"); scattering of semi-estranged or unofficial offspring in who knows how many jurisdictions… It's an impressive legacy. Not forgetting the magnificent work… what should it be called? "Memoir"? Perhaps "faction" or plain "fiction" would be more fitting. Probably a mélange of all three.

Marta's rehabilitated boyfriend Chito, who accompanied the ambulance with Chus's corpse, claims he persuaded them to "drop the postmortem" on the grounds Chus's son Toni had no idea about his father's HIV. It would be such a shock. But are The Authorities quite so malleable? Admittedly, Chito's in a class of his own when it comes to grinding almost anyone into submission.

By the time Marina arrives in Bárcena, the formalities are over, and she joins her mother and Toni in the private room at the morgue. That's where Chus is laid out – kitted out in that smart suit and a tie for the first time since James's wedding.

She finds her mother's worries over the funeral to be obsessive.

"It'll be a humiliation! It'll be a pauper's funeral. Third Class! Third, because there's no Fourth! No body, no choristers, no candles, no heating, just one priest… Everyone will know just how poor I am… How will I live it down? *¡Ay! ¡Dios mío! No tengo años para esto.*"[53]

Then another thought occurs: "It wouldn't be much to give him a proper send-off, would it? Between the three of you?"

By the time I speak to Mamí over the phone later that

---

[53] I'm too old for this

303

evening, her lament is becoming more rehearsed: "I'm too old for this… Goodness me, how old I am! Mothers shouldn't bury their sons! My Chus was too good to me… *a saint* to his old mother! Now who'll find films for me? Who'll bring me *¡Hola!* every week? Who'll mend the dishwasher? Who'll raise the blinds in the morning? This has destroyed me! But you wouldn't understand, neither you nor Marina; not Marta nor Sancho… you, the young and carefree: so distant! So selfish!"

After a pause, she adds: "I'm relying on you to give Chus a proper funeral!"

Marina tells me the situation at home is tense. Mamí views Titi's presence as an insult and isn't above broadcasting her views, loud enough to be overheard: "She's a common whore, that's what she is! Cheated him. Of course she did. Did we ever hear from her? In 25 years? Did she ever call Toño on his birthday? No, no, not once! Too busy with her minister, mothering his brood of… And she's been with all these other men…"

"And Chus, as we know, was pure as mountain air."

"It's different for him, as you very well know. Also, it's written all over her, the minx: she's here to claim her share!"

"Share of what would that be?" Marina says. But there are too many ideas crammed into Mamí's last few sentences, all familiar dead-ends and it's clear Mamí will ignore it anyway. In any case, further discussion is curtailed, because Titi comes downstairs with her suitcase, ready to quit, having heard everything; Marta intercepts from the kitchen; but Titi pushes past.

"For your information," she says to Mamí in her heavily accented Spanish, as she crosses the sitting room, heading for the exit, "your son had two more children in Gabon. They asked to meet their father. When I told Chus, you

304

know what he say? He say: 'Tell them I'm dead'. Well, that was too soon, but it was almost true… The first time! The one time my 'usband nearly tell the truth… by mistake!"

The irony of her claim is clear to all those present. For Titi, never divorced from Chus, by now boasts at least four further offspring in addition to Toni and Marga, of whom two count the Gabonese minister as father while the others are of uncertain lineage.

Then she leaves the house. But Marta follows and before long, returns with Titi and Toni, who was tidying up in the shop. He's clutching the two new iPads we funded weeks before his father's demise.

2

Wednesday's a "bloody fiesta" as Marina tells me by WhatsApp and, as she returns on Thursday, she has only Tuesday morning to devote to Chus's affairs. Top priority is therefore a visit to the *gestoría* over the road. It's a small outfit dedicated to the kind of paperwork anathema to many Spaniards, their late client exemplary among them. Allegedly, the *gestoría* helped Chus with the accounts, although to my knowledge they never produced anything tangible – perhaps they experienced the same roadblocks with Chus as we did. Marina joins Marta and Toni to take stock.

Thanks to our warm relations with Asun, the bank teller (before the pandemic, we brought her a rhubarb plant for her kitchen garden – a luxuriant one metre tall by this summer, she told us), we were able to extract Chus's statements, so we know for sure that his account stood at €64 to credit at the moment of death, a 16% improvement on his father's tally at the same life-stage. But it's only on speaking to Pepe at the *gestoría* ("The Syndic" as he's known – he was once a union official at the Ruiz-Toledos' textile factory) that the debts are revealed – several thousand euros due to suppliers (stock etc.), arrears on the lease, utilities and so forth. Taking those into account, the estate's deep under water.

We've debated at length whether Toni's capable of taking on the shop. Marta's against (she never rated her nephew much higher than she did her brother himself); however, having sunk several thousand euros into it, I'm still hoping to salvage something from the wreckage, even at the cost of more funding. Marina is unsure. As soon as the idea's tabled, Pepe leans back on his chair and sucks through his teeth to signal scepticism, especially as Toni's wearing a hoodie, looking more like a budding drug dealer than an entrepreneur.

But Toni more or less rules it out himself, claiming to be stunned by the losses. According to him, he "*did all the work*", was told "*we're doing well*" and now he knows the truth, he's rowing back from the idea of inheriting the shop.

"I need to know how much I'll have at the end of the month," he says. "Otherwise, how will I run the car?"

"Don't imagine you can drive your father's car," says Pepe. He's jumping to conclusions, but his instinct serves him well. "As soon as the owner dies, the insurance lapses. You'd be uninsured – a criminal offence, you realise – unless explicitly authorised by the insurer…"

Apart from that, we wonder just how useful the car really would be, because once Toni's secured the parking space right outside Mamí's front gate, he's loath to move it, for fear of losing the coveted spot. He's unlikely to risk that for excursions to the Medical Centre, all of 100 metres away.

"Anyway," Pepe adds, "there may be some good news in all this." He swivels round to retrieve an envelope from his in-tray, from which he extracts a bundle of papers. "…because a new pension law was passed just recently. It's not impossible your brother's heirs might qualify for a pension… But I'll need to write to The Authorities to confirm the position."

As we know, few things in Spain ever happen without appeal to *Las Autoridades*. In light of Chus's chequered career, all but three years of which were spent abroad, a pension sounds improbable. But there's no harm in trying.

Pepe agrees to prepare the accounts of the shop and explore the pension rights. Once Toni has left them, Marta can't resist crowing over her foresight: "I told you it could never work. Can't you see Toni hasn't a clue? Anyway, he has mental issues… He needs a psychiatrist, not a business to run. Look at the patches all over his scalp! There's something badly wrong with him. I'll fix him up with a few sessions. Perhaps we can club together to fund it. I'll ask Sancho."

Marina peels off towards the *quiosco* to buy the local paper; then she returns to Mamí's, where the belligerents appear to have suspended hostilities, because Titi's now seated in Papí's *trono*, the reclining armchair. Surprisingly, Mamí's in the sitting room too. Further, it transpires Marga and her boyfriend have just arrived from France – they're planning to stay with Titi in Chus's room.

Marta tells them about the meeting at the *gestoría*. Titi gets the gist of it because she suddenly becomes agitated: "What happened to the money from the flat?"

"There was nothing left once we repaid the mortgage," Marta says.

"And nothing, *pas un sou*, from the 'ouse in Gabon, either!" Titi adds.

"What house?"

This is news to everyone. Titi says she and Chus bought

a beach house together facing the ocean on the Cape, just outside Libreville. When she appeared at the *Prison Centrale* in Libreville all those years ago, she had to post bail for Chus. Of course, Titi had no large sum to her name; she could raise bail only by pledging the beach house and moving in with the "Minister" along with her young family. Thereupon, the Minister applied himself to the task of founding a dynasty, courtesy of his *despanpanante* new mistress.

There's much to digest from her short speech, which provides yet more evidence of Chus's reflex obfuscation. According to him, the whole affair was simply an aberration, high jinks, driven by drink that he would never have touched had he found the drugs that afternoon in Libreville.

And the charges? They weren't mentioned before either. Titi elaborates: on the rampage in the small hours with Seb, Chus also had a pot of black paint, with which he daubed seditious slogans on the perimeter walls of several houses in the compound, including insults about the President and the Minister for Security.

"You see, he did that before," says Titi. "He already spent two nights in jail for the same thing."

3

After lunch, Marina settles down with her copy of *Voz del Golfo*.

The item that grabs her attention fills the centre spread, a half-page article, somewhere between a book review and an obituary – or perhaps a hagiography in the style of *¡Hola!* magazine. But it's not a local canonisation, nor even a tribute to some worthy from *Las Autoridades*; it's about Marina's brother, Jesús "Chus" Expósito.

What's more, the author is Conchi Palacio – yes,

Conchi, Chus's first wife, the flighty daughter of Tobillo hardware store owners José and Remedios; the same Conchi who bolted from Guinea almost as soon as she arrived and has scarcely been sighted since, though her articles have appeared in the papers from time to time.

Here's what Marina reads, in growing disbelief, as the prose turns an ever more lurid shade of purple:

Jesús "Chus" Expósito

It is with greatest regret that we report the tragic death of Don Jesús Expósito, author of an extraordinary memoir, Stories of the Colonials in Equatorial Africa. *By the strangest of coincidences, this, the first volume of a planned trilogy, was published on the very day of his death. Conchi Palacio, our reviewer, offers her take on his extraordinary career:*

> *"Once upon a time we were close, but we lost contact until just a few weeks ago, when I heard about Chus Expósito's book and made contact for an interview with* Voz del Golfo.
>
> *Chus's life was remarkable. Born in Guinea in colonial times, he was raised with other children, black as well as white, whose parents worked for the company founded by his grandfather – specialists in tropical timber, coffee and cocoa.*
>
> *After Macías' seizure of power, he came back to Spain, only to return later, working in Gabon and Guinea with some of the world's largest timber groups, where his well-known talents as organiser, businessman and topographer were highly valued – not forgetting, of course, his extraordinary gift with people, his sagacity and good sense, his sensitivity and intelligence, that helped him avoid missteps and earn the respect of the 'big fish'. We were able to corroborate all of this because so many others from Bárcena went to work in Guinea*

in the same plantations and Chus, "Masa Chus", was a legend.

In the 80s, he would come to Bárcena where he'd enchant and amaze his many friends with his stories; because, above all, Chus was a great raconteur. Moreover, as the soul of generosity, they always enjoyed his extraordinary hospitality. He earned well, and he spent his money as fast as it came in.

He told me that, at one class reunion, he began telling anecdotes and his friends insisted he commit them to paper, offering help on the editorial and promotional sides. Thanks to an instinctive sense of order and unusual linguistic talent – using synonyms and the natural cadences of the Spanish language, for example – he started writing about what he had never managed to tear from his heart: his Africa.

The product was an extraordinary volume of reminiscences – exciting, entertaining, engaging and droll – yes, very droll. He was totally absorbed by the work and no sooner was the first volume finished than he embarked on the second. Bárcena was too small for him, there was nothing left for him to explore, nothing to discover, nothing exotic. He was bored and the writing allowed him to relive the excitement of his life's work.

Chus was taken ill with Covid a few weeks ago. Yesterday morning, his son went to check on him in his room… Picture the horror!

He left us shocked and bereaved… a bereavement that really hurt.

But very soon, we started to sense his presence close by, so close we caught ourselves smiling.

We were sure that he left us because he was ready to do so.

And for sure, he returned to Africa, his beloved Africa.

From a hammock suspended in the porch of an old but luxurious house, Chus watches the largest, reddest and lowest sun in the world sink into the ocean. He hears the sound of the river close by, and, far off, the trumpeting of an elephant. That odour of damp, mixed with tropical wood that so many evoke, lingers in the air; his eyes are half-closed and he holds a bottle of beer in his hand. A gentle drowsiness takes over and a copy of The Lord of the Rings, *his favourite, slips from his chest onto the floor… A pretty mulata sits on the steps, waiting patiently for him to resurface…'*

Marina tries to reconcile Conchi's piece with her own experience. They can't both be right! "Talents as a businessman"? "Sagacity and good sense"? Almost the only overlap is the allusion to his spendthrift tendencies and the understatement of his wandering eye. By now, though, Sancho and Marta have also seen it and before long Mamí, Toni and Titi too.

"Conchi! Fancy that! I knew she had a heart of gold," Mamí says, exultant, tears welling up. "She still loves him! Loves him after so many years! Nobody can resist my Chus!"

Best of all is his meriting half a page in *Voz del Golfo* compared with Curro's token entry a few months back. She'll be able to look Nunci in the eye.

"We need this for the service! Marta? You're in charge of copies… Marina, you can pin the original in the porch… Ask Don Pedro for the key to the cabinet."

From impending disaster, the funeral now promises a resounding triumph for Mamí. On top of "that wonderful article" Don Pedro decides to reward her for her loyalty and dedication: the candles she's lit, the catechism she's taught to generations of Bárcena's young, the epistles she's read at Mass, the services she's attended doggedly over so many decades. There will be three priests at Chus's funeral, one swinging incense in a thurible; the heating will be switched on; there will be *monaguillos*, choristers, to sing the responses; the coffin will be brought into the nave in stately procession and will rest on a makeshift catafalque in the sanctuary in front of the candle-bedecked altar throughout the service; Don Pedro will lead the final obsequies at the crematorium outside town. There can be no doubt in anybody's mind: it will be a *First Class Funeral*.

The tears of grief – the ladies at the fruitshop, Asun the bank teller, the girls at the print shop – the article from *Voz* and the candles in his honour at the *Politena* raise Mamí to a pitch of euphoria unknown for ages; and Marina admits to sharing it. This is more *fiesta* than mourning.

When the time comes, the crowds exceed even Curro's funeral, despite the murky afternoon. Even Sancho overcomes the enmity with his late brother and makes an appearance at the back of the church. Remarkably, he's accompanied not only by Rocío and his young daughter Alicia; that shiny pate in the same pew can only belong to Caudal himself: it's a nice gesture from the sick old man.

Aunt Macu is also to be seen following the event, wrapped in a mink coat, from her balcony opposite the porch. Strange that the *Vinos Aurelio* truck parked in full view on the other side of the square seems not to trouble her these days. She probably hasn't even realised that, just beyond, the sloping warehouse, the historic home of *Bodegas Pinar E Hijos*, has finally fallen to the wrecker's ball.

4

A few months later, the stars finally align for my own

return. The year's winter celebrations, unusually muted so soon after Chus's funeral, pass without drama. But just before the last hurrah of the season, Epiphany, Mamí tells us we're wanted by Pepe, *The Syndic*, at our earliest convenience. Marta invites us for lunch so we can drop in at the *gestoría* on the way.

"I take it you've decided about the shop?" Pepe asks, once we've made ourselves comfortable in his small first floor office.

My philanthropic fantasy to set up Toni in a profitable enterprise has dissipated in the weeks since the funeral. Apart from his own scepticism, the psychiatrist told Marta that Toni couldn't run much more than a bath. He's also failed miserably at the few tasks – digging and pruning – we asked him to perform since summer, in return for a generous *propina*.

"I don't think it's likely," I respond, "and whatever we do, we need to shut the shop itself, it's a permanent haemorrhage – if he wants to carry on, he can do it from home, or from the back of a van."

"OK, understood… We'll need to speak to the landlord. But I have other news for you," Pepe says, "*good* news, this time, I'm happy to say. Marina, your sister-in-law should be delighted. Thanks to the recent change, she's eligible for a pension… and not *any* pension, I have to say, but a very handsome pension indeed. I had to double check the figure with The Authorities. I couldn't believe it, it's so extraordinary. €1,500 per month, with annual rises for inflation! I confess I expected a quarter of that sum at the outside. I'm told it's the largest pension of its type ever awarded in the province."

"How did that happen?" Marina asks in disbelief.

"Your brother may have spent everything, but for a time – must have been when he was in Romania or Mexico

– he had a really good salary, and the pension's based on his *highest earnings in any single year* out of the last ten…"

"Incredible!"

"Yes, and his daughter Marga gets one too. Much smaller, of course."

"And Toni?"

"No, I'm afraid not – he no longer qualifies as a dependant: over 25."

We return to Mamí's but decide not to break the news in public – Marga and her boyfriend have joined Titi and Marta. We feel we should inform Titi first and we'll have to work out how to tell Toni that he's the only one carved out from the state's largesse: it seems iniquitous, as he's the only Spanish resident out of the three of them. Besides, we want to understand the dynamic now that, despite Mamí's repeated insults, Titi moved in with her. She is planning to apply for Spanish citizenship, which requires long periods of residence as well as an exam covering the language and a section on Spanish Practices generally. Once that's in the bag, she's talking about a job. Unexpectedly, we learn that she already has a qualification as a forklift truck driver.

After breaking the news in private to a stunned Titi (she'll help Toni with the car to make amends), we return to Mamí, discovering she has developed a quite different lament about this "common whore" from last time.

"She just told me she has to go back to France…" Mamí complains. "What shall I do without her? She cooks the lunch, she makes Toño's bed, she cleans better than any cleaner, better than Luisa, even… And who'll raise the blinds in the mornings? If only she'd lose a bit of weight, she'd be a real treasure! I shall miss her so much!"

"But isn't she planning to come back?" Marina asks.

"That's what she says, but I don't believe her, not for one moment!"

"Well, I think maybe you should... She wants her Spanish passport and to qualify for it, she must live in Spain most of the time and take the exams. What's more, she'll have to be here to collect her pension!"

"Pension? What pension?"

"The pension we just heard about from the *gestoría*," Marina says, "1,500 euros a month, every month, until she dies."

"*¡Ave María Purísima!*" Mamí says, swooning onto the sofa.

5

This time, we have an excuse for dodging Mamí's *sobremesa*. We're supposed to meet Sancho at *Casa Polín*, Papí's erstwhile haunt. Sancho says he has news for us before we head north.

Casa Polín is a dark little dive in the village of Ontaneda, just outside Bárcena, that has been all but swallowed up by the outgrowth of its larger neighbour. But Sancho prefers it, not just because it's the client that *Vinos Aurelio* famously snatched from under Aunt Macu's nose and retains to this day. It's also because, out here, the chance of unwanted encounters is slim.

"I don't suppose you've heard about Titi's pension," Marina starts, once we're supplied with *cortados*. She takes him through the morning's events, to Sancho's growing disbelief.

"If true, that's amazing..."

"Of course it's true! You don't expect a serious character like *The Syndic* to make it up, do you? One of the few reliable people round here!"

"Well, it seems so unlikely. But wait till you hear my news..."

He keeps us on tenterhooks by taking a call – evidently

315

Caudal, asking him to run an errand while in Bárcena.

"I don't need to tell you how bad things are at *Bodegas Pinar*," he says, picking up the thread as soon as he hangs up. "The town's missing a front tooth now they've knocked down the old *bodega*, don't you think? But we could have a solution for what's left of it…"

"Really? What's that?"

"We're going to buy them out!"

"What do you mean, '*buy them out*'?"

"Remember when you came to see me about the burglary? Perhaps you've forgotten, Rico, but the Ruiz-Toledos once approached Aunt Macu about a stake in *Pinar*."

"Of course I haven't. It was the time she told me how lucky I was to have ensnared Marina."

"Aunt Macu claims it fell through because they didn't value our *soleras*. I dare say that was part of it, but if you ask me, we were just too greedy… like the time we tried to sell the building and turned down a really good offer from them. Now it's worth next to nothing. This time, the Ruiz-Toledos tried *Aurelio* instead."

"Sounds good news for you, Sancho. But what's it got to do with *Pinar*?"

"It's a long story, but the Ruiz-Toledos are joining forces with *Aurelio* to buy what's left of *Bodegas Pinar*. It's not worth much anymore, except for the client list and the name – just about. It won't fetch very much. Even cousins Adelina and Chábeli realise that; and nowadays, Julito signs for Aunt Macu… So it's almost a done deal. The cost? We're taking on their debt and the owners get some pocket money plus a small stake. What's more, we're dressing it up as a merger. The name will change to *Vinos Aurelio-Pinar*. Speaking selfishly, that'll make my own position so much easier!"

"What about Julito?"

"I think it's a relief to him, especially the merger. He's found a way out for the *bodega* and for himself and he'll pocket a tidy sum. His heart wasn't in it from the start. Aside from that, he's had some luck. That old rogue Ortega's taking a run at the regional elections this autumn. He needs a team and Julito's found a place on the campaign."

"Extraordinary! Why hire Julito, of all people?"

"Don't forget that their paths often crossed over property matters. What's more, you remember Julito used to write speeches? He was good at it and made quite a lot of money… Then he decided to become a small-town tradesman…"

There is a short pause.

"By the way," Sancho continues, "I have a confession to make about Julito…"

"Really? What's that?"

"The burglary… I was quite wrong about it: neither Julito nor *Pinar* were involved. Julito came to see me about it after the wedding. You two had already gone home, as I recall."

"How come? If it wasn't them, who *was* behind it then?" I ask.

"Iñaki Ybasta! He had a grievance, you remember – he was fired by Don Gonzalo for harassing the cook. Days before James's wedding, Julito received a request to meet Iñaki. Julito was wary, so he recorded their whole exchange on his iPhone. That was when Iñaki attempted to sell him the memory stick."

"But I thought Nino confessed right up front that he was working for *Pinar*?"

"That's what I told Julito. He pointed out, of course, Iñaki must have put Nino up to that – pinning the

317

burglary on *Pinar* was a key part of Iñaki's cover."

"How was it resolved?" Marina asks.

"Ironically, that was the origin of the current deal. As soon as we started talking, it became clear that the merger would solve many issues for both sides – not least, freeing Julito from his burden. We already had interest from the Ruiz-Toledos, so money wasn't the issue. But I had to eat humble pie with the cousins for my wrongful accusations… As for Iñaki, we settled out of court."

"And Nino?"

"Once we had his confession on tape, we let him sweat."

Buoyed though we are by Sancho's story, we're annoyed to be so far out of the loop, especially as we, the hosts, and the young couple suffered injury almost as severe as Julito himself. But Sancho pre-empts any complaint:

"I realise I owe you both an apology, too… It's well overdue… the pandemic, one thing and another. I know my outburst at the wedding was unforgivable, even if it had been correct."

"You're right. We were pretty upset about it. You could have told us a long time ago! But don't worry," Marina says, "we got over it… more or less. Life goes on."

"Maybe there's a small consolation in this, Marina: as part of the deal with the Ruiz-Toledos, we're keeping Abuela's old *casona*. If we'd waited a week longer that would have gone too – demolished, I mean – just like the *nave* next door. We're turning the upper floors into a flat, where I'll be moving with Rocío and Alicia."

"You should get Jordi to do it. He'll do it properly," Marina says, without much conviction. Sancho seldom takes advice.

"Perhaps… he's pricey, though, I'm sure… Downstairs, in the old cellar, we're going to open an *enoteca*. And we plan to reinstate the *solera* business, on a very small scale. Just a few barrels at the back of the cellar to start with, to see how it goes. It'll give us something different from everyone else. James can help me fix your friend Benedict's *solera* next time he's here if he's up for it and Sally allows."

6

We leave Bárcena because we have other business in Valledal: our friend Soco has invited us for an eve of Epiphany drink with the family.

For the short drive to Valledal we could save a few minutes by borrowing a segment of the Euro-highway that slices through the eucalyptus on its busy progress westward. But we prefer the leisurely trip along the old main road, by now nearly redundant, that takes us through Tobillo and past other landmarks, or "signs", as the children might once have said.

The route starts at the junction in the centre of Bárcena, just by the hole in the ground over which the *bodega's* sloping profile once presided.

Over the years, the junction has morphed into a roundabout, adorned with a few struggling bushes, bits of antique farm equipment half-embedded in the grass and, we now see, a brand-new work of sculpture: it represents a Celtic warrior from the region's obscure past. Although in a modern idiom, cobbled together from bits of wood and scrap metal, it shares something with that other local favourite, *estilo rústico*, the much-loved style with debts to the pre-modern.

For our province, like so much else round here, is itself largely a fabrication. It was never a polity in its own right, with pretensions to statehood; it never enjoyed region-wide *fueros*[54] or *Cortes*[55] and, pre-1492, was invariably subsumed within one or other of the adjacent statelets. Hence on its recent elevation to autonomy, The Authorities had to delve deep to find "stories" around which to craft and foster a sense of identity and cohesion. Lacking anything recent, inspiration came from the Palaeolithic caves that riddle the local hills, as well as from legends of fierce warriors resistant to occupation, Roman and Moorish. In a way, this figure on the roundabout, just as much as *estilo rústico*, pays homage to this pre-history.

It's a stretch, of course, this linkage with the distant past, but, for all the accelerating change – the erosion of rural life, the obsession with things foreign, the building booms and busts – it's remarkable how little the local DNA seems to change, at least judging by the last 40 years. So perhaps The Authorities have a point.

What, for example, could be more atavistic than the handwritten notice in bright blue paint we catch sight of as we drive up the hill from the wooded valley towards the *barrio alto*? In fact, we stop and reverse to take a closer look (it's on one of those straight stretches where Nino tests the paces of his canary yellow vehicle…):

> *'PARA EL HIJO DE*
> *LA GRAN PUTA*
> *ROBAMANILLAS'*
>
> *TO THE SON OF*
> *THE GREAT WHORE*
> *LATCH-THIEF*

---

[54] Exemptions and departures from central government writ
[55] Parliament

Neither of us is much the wiser, puzzling over what a "latch-thief" might be.

When we join Soco later, she explains: "I know exactly what you're referring to. Miguelín's cousin put that there. Some *hijo de la gran puta* stole part of his electric fence and several of his cows escaped... He's been searching for them ever since. God knows where they are by now... chopped up into *filetes*, most likely."

"Surely there's an obvious culprit?" Marina asks. "These things invariably come home to roost with our old friend..."

"You mean Monchi, I imagine? I don't think so, not this time. You see, last weekend, before the cows escaped, Monchi really distinguished himself at the bar. On his way home, he must have been far gone because he strayed off the camber halfway home and slipped right down the slope into one of those prickly thickets opposite the plot I'm trying to sell... As you know, the drop's very steep along there. He was lucky! Could easily have been there all night! Ironically, he was rescued by a group of the very "pilgrims" he hates so much. A group of them, heading along the *Camino* in the dark, heard his pitiful moans from the undergrowth. They had to call an ambulance. They simply couldn't prise him out of the thorns, let alone drag him back up to the road. I gather from Fátima he's still recovering, unable to get out of bed."

"In that case it's got to be Nino. He's taken over in that department," Marina says.

"Sorry to disappoint there, too," Soco responds. "It can't have been him either, for a very good reason: Nino's in jail! I don't think he'll be causing much trouble even when they let him out because his driving licence has been confiscated and his car impounded. He and his mates from the cannabis farm ran into the *Guardia Civil* during the *fiestas.* Of course, all three of them were in possession of illegal substances and high as kites…"

It's now the time for gifts, and Soco has once again outdone herself in generosity. We're presented with an octagonal box containing four huge, Santa-themed, platters; tins of dusty sweets for the young; and a bottle of *Triple Seco*, "Triple Dry" – so syrupy a spoon would almost stand up in it unsupported.

Luckily, we're prepared, Marina having brought a deckchair for Soco's allotment. I, too, have a small offering, for once: it's a painting in my very own hand. Its subject is the chapel at Santa Rita, complete with contorted tree, calloused toes clutching the pediment, withered arms gesticulating at the heavens.

"Oof!" Soco says, "I do like it… Didn't know you were an artist, though: you kept that to yourself! But when did you paint it? Not that recently, I reckon. You do know the tree lost a whole branch in the gales this autumn, I suppose? It doesn't look so good anymore, so this'll be a great souvenir. It's not quite dead, I think, but it must be touch and go… Speaking of Santa Rita: remember the famous project? Looks like it'll be revived, after all – different promoters this time, though, and slightly changed plan. They found a loophole. Half the site falls outside the *Parque Natural*, you see…"

What will they throw at us next? But in such struggles, we long since capitulated – not indifference, but weary resignation… It is what it is, and nothing we say or do will change anything one iota.

It's a ridiculously warm evening, as so often at this time of year, *viento sur*, – "*vaya tiempo de sur*", [56] as we keep hearing. That's why Soco suggests we try out the deckchair

---

[56] South Wind – "amazing South Wind"

in the kitchen garden before dark. That's quite an honour: to date, only Marina has been admitted to this hallowed ground. When Miguelín abandoned dairy farming, he retained this patch as a pressure valve from their cramped abode and that's where he now spends most of his waking hours, tending vegetables and fruit trees.

Access isn't easy; it involves squeezing between the side of the house and the neighbour's wall along a narrow, stony passage. But unexpectedly, it widens out into a large kitchen garden, lush and orderly even at this season. It's angled towards the *barrio bajo,* the whole of which is spread out in front of us, our own house closest, just across the *valledal,* the little valley, from which the village takes its name. It's the first time I've seen our needy project from this revealing angle, as if through a wide-angled lens.

"Now you see how I keep tabs on the village," Soco says, "including you! Not only can I see what goes on from up here, but I can often hear it too!"

That's one thing we do know for certain. The *valledal* that separates Soco's house from our own is shaped like a classical theatre and, when the wind is in the right quarter, a sneeze and even a hiccough can be heard clearly across the intervening 100 metres or so.

But right now, no voices can be heard; the soothing harmonics of the countryside, the strimmers, diggers, mixers, leaf-blowers, drills and quadbikes, have retired to bed for the night. The only sounds reaching us in the penumbra are the gentle jangle of cowbells and the low grumble of the surf beyond.

CODA

Over four decades I had generated many jottings, diaries and posts, many of them focused on Spanish Practices and the world that shaped them. Now that The Authorities, British and Spanish, had decided to lock us up for months at a stretch, what better fix for my Valledal cravings than to spin the threads into a narrative? But I kept it to myself, at least until I could see where it was heading. It took a couple of years' work before I was ready to submit my scribblings to Marina's harsh scrutiny: it's one of the ways she takes after her mother.

Marina's a voracious reader – she has been ever since her youth, escaping the boredom of the *casona*. It's humbling, in fact, because there's scarcely a classic she hasn't read, English or Spanish, often several times over. It's therefore with trepidation that I come clean about my efforts and submit the typescript to this plain-speaking arbiter.

It takes her a worryingly long time to wade through it, during which she remains tight-lipped – no apparent reaction at all, as far as I can tell. Then, after almost a month of slow progress, she unexpectedly skewers the last few chapters in one sitting.

And her judgement, as she turns the last page? It's characteristically unsparing: "I hope you realise you're just as bad as everybody else in the book! Don't get the idea this is an accurate account of anything... How would you know, as an outsider, anyway? Embarrassing! But you better tell me what you plan to do with it."

It's her last challenge, especially, that wrong-foots me, because I really have no idea what I "plan to do with it". I have few illusions about the publishing world. I'm just the sort of writer *nobody* wants these days: the entire gamut of deplorable attributes in a single package, I fear. It follows that my narrative hardly presses a single fashionable button.

With no clear answer to the book's destiny, I home in on Marina's allegation about my supposed distortions. Not that I'm surprised by her remark. Most of what I say is wrong, on principle. It's something she shares with so many of her compatriots: woe betide any outsider with the temerity to pass judgement on Spanish ways, as I learnt to my cost on several occasions set forth in these pages. But paradoxically, quite unlike most of her family, Marina's also a stickler for dead accuracy, often taking me to task for embellishing anything for effect, however trivial. ("No, we didn't tell them *'a hundred times'*. More like three or four!" "Hardly *'an eternity'*! No more than half a minute at the outside!")

"Doesn't it take an outsider to see things for what they really are?"

"What they really are? You're joking, I assume? Though I grant you, it's pretty obvious who's who – that's the worst of it. What am I supposed to say when it gets out?"

It's a giveaway: "What am I supposed to say when it gets out?" Perhaps what she really means is that it's "too close for comfort". Indeed, therein lies the conundrum around the book's fate. Release it on Amazon and the relatives will be fluttering round it in a jiffy. It'll be as clear as daylight who's who and what's what, with worrying ramifications for family peace and harmony...

OK, I freely admit to taking a few liberties, including names and places, to shield identities. But it's a bit more fundamental than that. For who wants the details every time a character goes to the lavatory, for example? Did I dwell in painstaking detail on Soco's visit to the bathroom at *El Viajante*? Obviously not! So, *of course* there's selection, simplification, emphasis, omission, **conflation** and rearrangement... And, dare I say, the odd flash of supposition and imagination, too – 'poetic truth' in the words of a long-deceased schoolmaster of mine: 'That which is historically false may be poetically true. Discuss.' Such minor deviations from fact are intrinsic to the writer's craft, which is to seek the essence of truth by disentangling the knotted strands of existence.

It's true that such excursions into the twilight between fact and fiction have led to a state of mind I can only describe as 'Spanish', in honour of Spaniards' sometimes casual relationship with reality. I now catch myself referring to people by their fictional names and even to snatches of dialogue that are the product of my intuition.

And, in this oblique fashion, by taking up residence in that murky marchland between fact and fiction, prose and poetry, I feel that I myself should by now qualify for an honorary diploma from that virtual seat of cultural studies: *The School of Spanish Practices*.

Appendix – Pinar Family Tree

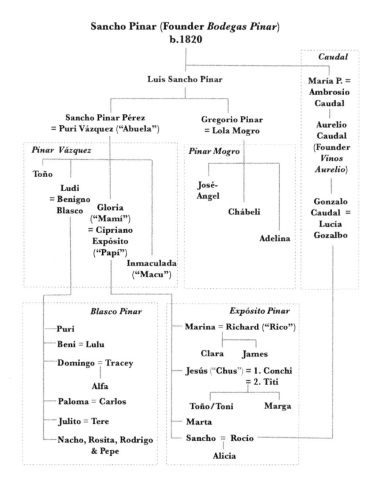

Sancho Pinar (Founder *Bodegas Pinar*)
b.1820

Caudal

Luis Sancho Pinar

María P. =
Ambrosio
Caudal

Sancho Pinar Pérez
= Puri Vázquez ("Abuela")

Gregorio Pinar
= Lola Mogro

Aurelio
Caudal
(Founder
*Vinos
Aurelio*)

Pinar Vázquez

Pinar Mogro

Toño

José-
Angel

Ludi
= Benigno
Blasco

Gloria
("Mamí")
= Cipriano
Ex14pósito
("Papí")

Chábeli

Gonzalo
Caudal =
Lucía
Gozalbo

Adelina

Inmaculada
("Macu")

Blasco Pinar

Expósito Pinar

Puri

Marina = Richard ("Rico")

Beni = Lulu

Clara   James

Domingo = Tracey

Jesús ("Chus") = 1. Conchi
= 2. Titi

Alfa

Paloma = Carlos

Toño/Toni   Marga

Julito = Tere

Marta

Nacho, Rosita, Rodrigo
& Pepe

Sancho = Rocío

Alicia

About the Author

Richard Townsend is a linguist and historian by training who ended up as a self-employed adviser to private companies on their financial and other affairs. This is his first novel.

He is married with two adult children and two small granddaughters. He lives with his Spanish wife in London and Northern Spain.

Printed in Great Britain
by Amazon

21381338R00195